THE
BEST OF
JOHN BELLAIRS

THE
BEST OF
JOHN BELLAIRS

The House with a
Clock in Its Walls

The Figure
in the Shadows

The Letter, the Witch,
and the Ring

BARNES
&NOBLE
B O O K S
NEW YORK

THE HOUSE WITH A CLOCK IN ITS WALLS

JOHN BELLAIRS
pictures by Edward Gorey

For Priscilla, who lets me be myself

CHAPTER ONE

Lewis Barnavelt fidgeted and wiped his sweaty palms on the seat of the bus that was roaring toward New Zebedee. The year was 1948, and it was a warm, windy summer evening. Outside, that is. Lewis could see the moonlit trees tossing gently beyond his window, which was sealed shut like all the windows on the bus.

He looked down at his purple corduroy trousers, the kind that go *whip-whip* when you walk. He put his hand up and rubbed it across his hair, which was parted in the middle and slicked down with Wildroot Cream Oil. His hand was greasy now, so he wiped it on the seat again. His lips were moving, and he was saying a prayer. It was one of his altar-boy prayers:

Quia tu es Deus fortitudo mea; quare me repulisti, et quare tristis incedo, dum affligit me inimicus?

For Thou O God art my strength; why have you cast me off, and why do I go sorrowful, while the enemy afflicts me?

He tried to remember more prayers, but the only one he could come up with was another question:

Quare tristis es anima mea, et quare conturbas me?

Why art thou sorrowful O my soul, and why do you trouble me?

It seemed to Lewis that all he could think of these days were questions: Where am I going? Who will I meet? Will I like them? What will happen to me?

Lewis Barnavelt was ten years old. Until recently he had lived with his parents in a small town near Milwaukee. But his father and mother had been killed suddenly one night in an auto accident, and now Lewis was on his way to New Zebedee, the county seat of Capharnaum County in the state of Michigan. He was going to live with his Uncle Jonathan, whom he had never met in his life. Of course, Lewis had heard a few things about Uncle Jonathan, like that he smoked and drank and played poker. These were not such bad things in a Catholic family, but Lewis had two maiden aunts who were Baptists, and they had warned him about Jonathan. He hoped that the warnings would turn out to be unnecessary.

As the bus rounded a curve, Lewis looked at his reflection in the window next to his seat. He saw a moony fat face with shiny cheeks. The lips on the face were moving. Lewis was saying the altar-boy prayers again, this time with the wish that they might make Uncle Jonathan like him. *Judica me Deus . . .* Judge me O God . . . no, don't judge me, help me to live a happy life.

It was five minutes to nine when the bus pulled up in front of Heemsoth's Rexall Drug Store in the town of New Zebedee. Lewis got up, wiped his hands on his trousers, and tugged at the enormous cardboard suitcase that hung out over the edge of the metal rack. Lewis's father had bought the suitcase in London at the end of World War II. It was covered with ripped and faded Cunard Line stickers. Lewis pulled hard, and the suitcase lurched down onto his head. He staggered back across the aisle with the suitcase held perilously in the air; then he sat down suddenly, and the suitcase landed in his lap with a *whump*.

"Oh, come on! Don't kill yourself before I have a chance to meet you!"

There in the aisle stood a man with a bushy red beard that was streaked in several places with white. His Big Mac khaki trousers were bulged out in front by his pot belly, and he was wearing a gold-buttoned red vest over a blue work shirt. Lewis noticed that the vest had four pockets; there were pipe cleaners sticking out of the top two, and a chain of paper clips was strung between the lower pair. One end of the chain was hooked to the winding knob of a gold watch.

Jonathan van Olden Barnavelt took his steaming pipe out of his mouth and held out his hand.

"Hi, Lewis. I'm your Uncle Jonathan. I recognized you from a picture your father once sent me. Welcome to New Zebedee."

Lewis shook hands, and noticed that the back of Jonathan's hand was covered with a springy mat of red hair. The coat of hair ran right up his sleeve and disappeared. Lewis wondered if he had red hair all over his body.

Jonathan hefted the suitcase and started down the steps of the bus.

"Good Lord, what a monster! It ought to have wheels on the bottom. Unh! Did you pack some of the bricks from your house?"

Lewis looked so sad at the mention of his house that Jonathan decided to change the subject. He cleared his throat and said, "Well, now! As I was saying, welcome to Capharnaum County and beautiful, historic New Zebedee. Population six thousand, not counting . . ."

A bell overhead began to strike the hour.

Jonathan stopped talking. He froze on the spot. He dropped the suitcase, and his arms hung limp at his sides. Lewis, frightened, looked up at him. Jonathan's eyes were glazed.

The bell continued to toll. Lewis looked up. The sound was coming from a tall brick steeple across the street. The arches of the belfry made a howling mouth and two gaping eyes; below the mouth was a large, glowing clock face with iron numerals.

Clang. Another stroke. It was a deep-throated iron bell, and its sound made Lewis feel hopeless and helpless. Bells like that always did. But what was wrong with Uncle Jonathan?

The tolling stopped. Jonathan broke out of his trance. He shook his head convulsively, and with a jerky motion raised his hand to his face. He was sweating profusely now. He mopped his forehead and his streaming cheeks.

"Hmh . . . hah! Hrumph! Ooh! Sorry, Lewis, I . . . I just remembered that I had . . . that I had left a kettle boiling on the stove. I always phase out like that when I remember something I've forgotten, or vicy versy. Bottom of the pot's probably ruined by now. C'mon. Let's get moving."

Lewis looked hard at his uncle, but he said nothing. Together, the two of them started to walk.

They left the brightly lit Main Street, and before long they were trotting briskly down a long, tree-lined avenue called Mansion Street. The overhanging boughs made Mansion Street into a long rustling tunnel. Pools of lamplight stretched off into the distance. As they walked, Jonathan asked Lewis how his schoolwork was coming, and whether he knew what George Kell's batting average was this year. He told him that he would have to become a Tiger fan now that he lived in Michigan. Jonathan did not complain any more about the suitcase, but he did stop frequently to set it down and flex his reddened hand.

It seemed to Lewis that Jonathan talked more loudly in the darkness between the streetlights, though why he did this Lewis couldn't say. Grownups were not supposed to be afraid of the dark, and anyway this was not a dark, lonely street. There were lights on in most of the houses, and Lewis could hear people laughing and talking and slamming doors. His uncle was certainly a strange person, but he was strange in a likable way.

At the corner of Mansion and High, Jonathan stopped. He set down the suitcase in front of a mailbox that said: FOR DEPOSIT OF MAIL ONLY.

"I live at the top of the hill," said Jonathan, pointing up.

High Street was well named. Up they went, leaning forward and plodding slowly. Lewis asked Jonathan several times if he could carry the suitcase, but each time Jonathan said, no, thanks, he could manage it. Lewis began to be sorry that he had packed all those books and lead soldiers.

When they got to the top of the hill, Jonathan set down the suitcase. He took out a red bandanna handkerchief and mopped his face with it.

"Well, there it is, Lewis. Barnavelt's Folly. What do you think of it?"

Lewis looked.

He saw a three-story stone mansion with a tall turret on the front. The whole house was lit up, downstairs, upstairs, and upper upstairs. There was even a light in the little oval window that was set, like an eye, in the bank of shingles at the top of the turret. In the front yard grew a large chestnut tree. Its leaves rustled in the warm summer breeze.

Jonathan was standing at parade rest, his hands behind him, his legs wide apart. Again he said, "What do you think of it, Lewis? Eh?"

"I love it, Uncle Jonathan! I've always wanted to live in a mansion, and this is sure some mansion!"

Lewis walked up to the frilly fence and touched one of the iron pompons that ran in a row along the top. He stared at the sign that spelled out "100" in red glass reflectors.

"Is it real, Uncle Jonathan? The house, I mean."

Jonathan glanced at him strangely. "Yes . . . yes . . . yes, of course it is. It's real. Let's go inside."

Jonathan lifted the loop of shoestring that held the gate shut. The gate squeaked open, and Lewis started up the walk. Jonathan followed close behind, lugging the suitcase. Up the front steps they went. The front hall was dark but there was a light at the far end of it. Jonathan set down the suitcase and put his arm around Lewis.

"Come on. Let's go in. Don't be bashful. It's your house now."

Lewis walked down the long hall. It seemed to take forever. At the other end he emerged into a room full of yellow light. There were pictures in heavy gilt frames on the walls; there was a mantelpiece covered with a wild assortment of junk; there was a big round table in the middle of the room, and over in the corner was a gray-haired woman in a baggy purple dress. She was standing with her ear to the wall, listening.

Lewis stopped and stared. He felt embarrassed. It was as if he had walked in on someone who was doing something he shouldn't be doing. He thought that he and Jonathan had made a good deal of noise coming in, but it was very apparent that the lady, whoever she was, had been surprised when he entered the room. Surprised and embarrassed, like himself.

Now she straightened up, smoothed her dress, and said cheerfully, "Hi there. I'm Mrs. Zimmermann. I live next door."

Lewis found himself staring into one of the wrinkliest faces he had ever seen. But the eyes were friendly, and all the wrinkles were drawn up into smile lines. He shook hands.

"This is Lewis, Florence," said Jonathan. "You remember Charlie writing about him. The bus was on time for a change. They must have gotten the driver drunk. Hey! Have you been stealing any of my coins?"

Jonathan walked over to the table. Now Lewis noticed that the red checkered tablecloth was covered with heaps and stacks of coins. All kinds of coins, most of them foreign. Doughnut-shaped Arabian coins with Boy Scout knots all over them; a heap of dark-brown copper coins, all of which were stamped with the picture of a bald man who wore a handlebar moustache. There were big heavy English pennies that showed Queen Victoria in various states of chinniness, and there were tiny silver coins no thicker than your fingernail. There was an egg-shaped Mexican silver dollar and a genuine Roman coin, covered with green rust. But most of all, in shiny golden stacks, were brass coins with *Bon Pour Un Franc* printed on them. Lewis liked the phrase, and since he didn't know any French, it got twisted around in his mind till it came out *Bon Sour One Frank*.

"No, I have not been stealing any of your precious Brasher doubloons," said Mrs. Zimmermann in an irritated voice. "I was just straightening up the stacks. Okay, Brush Mush?"

"Straightening up the stacks. I've heard *that* one before, Hag Face. But it doesn't matter, because we're going to have to divvy up the coins three ways. You play poker, don't you, Lewis?"

"Yes, but my dad won't . . ." He stopped. Jonathan saw tears in his eyes. Lewis choked down a sob and went on, "My . . . my dad wouldn't have let me play for money."

"Oh, we don't play for money," said Mrs. Zimmermann, laughing. "If we did, this house and everything in it would belong to me."

"Poop, it would," said Jonathan, shuffling the cards and puffing clouds of smoke from his pipe. "Poop, it would. Get 'em all divided up, Frumpy? No? Well, when you're ready it's going to be dealer's choice, and I'm the first dealer. No ladies' games, like Spit-out-the-Window or Johnny's Nightshirt. Straight five-card draw. Nothing wild." He puffed some more and was about to deal the first hand when he stopped and looked at Mrs. Zimmermann with a mischievous smile.

"Oh, by the way," he said, "you might bring Lewis a glass of iced tea, and get me a refill. No sugar. And bring out another plate of chocolate-chip cookies."

Mrs. Zimmermann stood up and clasped her hands subserviently in front of her. "How would you like your cookies, sir? Stuffed down your throat one by one, or crumbled up and sifted into your shirt collar?"

Jonathan stuck out his tongue at her. "Ignore her, Lewis. She thinks she's smart because she's got more college degrees than I have."

"I would be smarter than you in any case, Weird Beard. Excuse me, folks. I'll be back in a minute." She turned and walked to the kitchen.

Jonathan dealt a practice hand while she was gone. When Lewis picked his cards up, he noticed that they were old and worn. Most of the corners were missing.

But on each faded blue back was a round golden seal with an Aladdin's lamp in the middle. Above and below the seal were the words:

CAPHARNAUM COUNTY

MAGICIANS SOCIETY

Mrs. Zimmermann returned with the cookies and iced tea, and the game began in earnest. Jonathan gathered up the cards and cut them together with a very professional *zzzzzit!* He shuffled and started to deal. Lewis sipped his iced tea and felt very comfortable, very at home.

They played until midnight, by which time Lewis had red and black spots in front of his eyes. Pipe smoke hung in layers over the table and rose in a column from the shade of the floor lamp. It made the lamp seem magic, like the one on the playing cards. And there was something else magic about the game. Lewis won. He won a lot. Usually he had rotten luck, but in this game he got straight flushes, royal flushes, four of a kind. Not all of the time, but enough to keep winning steadily.

Maybe it was because Jonathan was such a lousy poker player. What Mrs. Zimmermann had said was certainly true. Whenever Jonathan had a good hand, he snortled and chortled and blew smoke out of both corners of his mouth. When he had a bad hand, he sulked and chewed his pipestem impatiently. Mrs. Zimmermann was a crafty player who could bluff you under the table with a pair of deuces, but that night she just wasn't getting the cards. Maybe that's why Lewis was winning. Maybe. But he had his doubts.

For one thing, he could have sworn that once or twice when he was reaching out to turn over a card that had been dealt to him, the card had changed. It had changed —just like that—while he was picking it up. This never happened when Lewis was dealing, but it did happen when Jonathan or Mrs. Zimmermann was dealing. And more than once he had been about to throw in a hand when, after a second look, he discovered that the hand was a good one. It was odd.

The mantel clock cleared its throat with a *whirr* and started to chime midnight.

Lewis shot a quick glance at Uncle Jonathan, who was sitting there perfectly composed, puffing his pipe. Or was he composed? He seemed to be listening for something.

The other clocks all over the house joined in. Lewis sat entranced, listening to high-pitched dings, tinny whangs, melodious electric doorbell sounds, cuckoos from cuckoo clocks, and deep sinister Chinese gongs roaring *bwaoww! bwaoww!* These and many other clock sounds echoed through the house. Now and then during this concert Lewis looked at Jonathan. Jonathan did not look back. He was staring at the wall, and his eyes had that glazed look again. Mrs. Zimmermann sat through the whole thing with her eyes fixed on the tablecloth.

/ 15 /

The last clock to strike was the grandfather clock in the study. It made a noise like a steamer trunk full of tin plates falling slowly and solemnly down a flight of stairs. When it stopped striking, Jonathan looked up.

"Hm. Yes. Where were we? Well, Lewis, it's midnight, isn't it? Game's over. Time for bed."

Jonathan cleared the table briskly. He gathered up the playing cards, stacked them, and put a rubber band around them. Snap! Then he reached under the table and came up with a red tin candy box with a picture of the New Zebedee County Courthouse on the lid. He scraped the clattering coins into the box, snapped the lid shut, pushed back his chair, rapped out his pipe into a saucer, and folded his hands in his lap.

"Well! And what do you think of 100 High Street, Lewis?"

"I think it's wonderful, Uncle Jonathan. I like the house, and I like the town, and I like you two an awful lot."

Lewis wasn't lying. In spite of Jonathan's strange behavior and the eavesdropping habits of Mrs. Zimmermann, he had had a very good time during his first evening in New Zebedee. In fact, for most of the evening, he had had a great deal of trouble keeping himself from jumping up and down in his seat. He had been told that it was a bad thing to do in company.

Jonathan took Lewis's suitcase upstairs, and Lewis got his first look at his new room. There was a tall black bed with battlements at the top of the headboard and foot-board. In the corner was a black mirror that matched the bed, and near it was a black marble fireplace with a coffin-like black clock on its mantelpiece. Up against one wall was a tall glazed bookcase full of old books, and on top of the bookcase was a vase with cattails in it. In the mid-dle of the floor was a large hooked rug. The pattern re-minded Lewis of a map of the United States—a map of the U.S. done by a crazy person. Many children might have been put off by the dark woodwork of the old room, but Lewis loved it. He imagined that this was the sort of room Sherlock Holmes would have slept in.

Lewis got into his pajamas, put on his bathrobe and slippers, and shuffled down the hall to the bathroom. When he got back, he found that Jonathan had just finished building a fire in his fireplace.

Jonathan got up and brushed twigs off his vest. "Well, Lewis, there you are! Need anything else?"

"Gee, no, I guess not, Uncle Jonathan. This is a great room. I've always wanted a room with a fireplace in it."

Jonathan smiled. He went over to the bedside table and turned on the reading lamp. "Read as long as you like tonight, Lewis. Remember, school doesn't start for another three weeks."

"I don't know if I'll read much after all the poker playing," said Lewis, yawning. "But thanks anyway. Good night, Uncle Jonathan."

"Good night, Lewis."

Jonathan started to close the door, but he stopped. "Oh, by the way, Lewis. I hope all these clocks don't keep you awake. They're kind of noisy, but . . . well, I like them. Good night." He closed the door.

Lewis stood there with a puzzled frown on his face. There was something going on in this house that he couldn't quite get hold of. He thought of Jonathan standing paralyzed while the clock in the church steeple tolled; he thought of Mrs. Zimmermann listening at the wall. It was strange.

Oh, well, he thought, shrugging his shoulders, people are funny sometimes. Lewis climbed into bed and turned off the light. A few minutes later he turned it back on. He realized that he was still tense, excited, and wide awake.

He climbed out of bed and walked over to the shaky-looking bamboo bookcase that stood by the closet door. What a lot of old dusty books! He pulled one out and wiped the dust off with his sleeve. The faded gilt letters on the black buckram spine said:

John L. Stoddard's Lectures

VOL. IX
Scotland England London

Lewis opened the book and flipped through the slick glossy pages. He held the book up to his nose. It smelled like Old Spice talcum powder. Books that smelled that way were usually fun to read. He threw the book onto his bed and went to his suitcase. After rummaging about for a while, he came up with a long, narrow box of chocolate-covered mints. He loved to eat candy while he read, and lots of his favorite books at home had brown smudges on the corners of the pages.

A few minutes later Lewis was sitting up in bed with his pillows propped behind him. He was reading about how the Scotch nobles had murdered poor Rizzio right in front of Mary, Queen of Scots. Stoddard compared Rizzio to a purple-velvet plum spurting plum juice in all directions. The nobles dragged the poor man, kicking and screaming, into the hallway, where they stabbed him some more. Fifty-six times, said Stoddard, though he didn't say who counted the stabs. Lewis flipped the page and bit into a peppermint patty. Now Stoddard was talking about the permanence of bloodstains and wondering whether or not the stain on the hall floor in Holyrood really was Rizzio's blood or not. Lewis began to yawn. He turned off the light and went to sleep.

But he was awakened—quite suddenly—a little while later. He had been dreaming that he was being chased by the Queen of Spades. Now he sat up, wide awake. He was scared, and he didn't know why.

Creak, creak. Someone was tiptoeing down the hall.

Lewis sat still and listened. Now the sound was outside his door. Now it was going away down the hall. *Creak, creak, creak.*

Lewis slid out of bed. As slowly and carefully as he could, he tiptoed to the door. He opened it, just as slowly and carefully. He didn't open it far. Just a crack. He looked out.

The hall was dark, except for a glimmering gray window down at the far end. But Lewis could hear someone moving. And now he saw the faint, pale circle of a flashlight beam moving over the wallpaper. Frightened, Lewis pulled the door shut and then opened it just a crack. The flashlight beam had stopped. Now the figure with the flashlight brought his fist down on the wall—hard. Lewis heard little clots of plaster falling down into the space between the walls. The figure pounded again, and again. Lewis stared and opened the door wider.

Now the shadowy intruder stepped back, and Lewis saw a bulky shadow against the hall window. A bulky, bearded shadow with a pipe in its mouth. Jonathan!

Lewis closed the door as softly as he could and leaned against it, shaking. He hoped Jonathan hadn't seen him. A horrible thought came into his mind. Was Jonathan crazy?

Lewis went to the wing chair by the fire and sat down. He watched the black honeycombs as they crumbled into deep red wells. *What if Jonathan were crazy?* His parents had always warned him against crazy people, the type that lured you into their cars and offered you candy with glue in it. Or was it glue? He couldn't remember. But Jonathan didn't really seem like *that* kind of person. Or the kind that sneaked into your room at night and stabbed you to death. Lewis sighed. He would just have to wait and see what happened.

He went back to bed and had a dream in which he and Jonathan were running round and round the block that had the church on it: the church with the monster-faced steeple. All the houses on the block were lit up, but they couldn't go into any of them to hide. Something tall and dark and shapeless was following them. Finally they stopped in front of the church, and the tower began to sway as if it were made of rubber. The howling face got closer and closer . . . and then the dream changed. Lewis was sitting in a room full of glittering coins. He let them run clinking through his fingers until morning came.

CHAPTER TWO

Lewis woke up the next day with confused memories of the previous night running around in his head. In general, his impression was a happy one, despite the dark things that lurked in the corners of the picture.

He got dressed, went downstairs, and found Jonathan and Mrs. Zimmermann at breakfast. It seemed that Mrs. Zimmermann always came over to cook Jonathan's breakfast because Jonathan was such a terrible cook. Well, that was fine with Lewis. He sat down to pancakes and sausages, and before long he was figuring out how best to use the three weeks of freedom that were left before school began.

Lewis soon found out that three weeks was not nearly

enough time for exploring the town of New Zebedee and the house at 100 High Street. In three weeks he barely got started.

To begin with, the town was marvelous. It was the sort of place he had always wanted to live in. Lewis's old hometown in Wisconsin looked as if it had been built yesterday; all the houses were the same size, and the main street was just a row of bars and gas stations. New Zebedee was different. It was full of tall, elaborately decorated old houses. Even the ordinary white-frame houses had things that made them seem different—a stained-glass window or a bouquet of iron flowers on top of a cupola. And so many of the houses seemed to be hiding secrets.

Jonathan took Lewis for some walks around the town, but more often he just let Lewis find out things for himself. Sometimes Lewis just walked up and down Main Street and stared at the high, elaborate, false fronts of the stores. One of the stores had an abandoned opera house in its upper stories. Jonathan said that the old scenery was still up there, leaning against cases of Mounds bars and five-cent writing tablets. At one end of Main Street was the Civil War Monument, a fantastic stone object shaped like an artist's easel. Each of the joints and corners of the easel had a soldier or sailor standing on it, threatening the rebel army with a musket or a sword or a cannon swabber or a harpoon. The flat part of the easel was covered with the names of Capharnaum County residents who had died in the Civil War. There was a small stone arch near the monument, and it was called the Civil War Monument Annex, because it contained the names that the carvers hadn't been able to get on the big monument. Jonathan's grandfather had fought in the war with the Fifth Michigan Fire Zouave Lancers, and Jonathan was full of stories about the old man's exploits.

As for the house at 100 High Street, it was every bit as wonderful as the town, besides being strange and more than a little bit scary. There were lots of rooms to explore: third-best upstairs front parlors and second-best back bedrooms; linen closets and playrooms and just plain rooms. Some of these were empty and full of dust, but there were others that were crammed with antique furniture. There were marble-topped tables galore, and upholstered chairs on squeaky casters, and doilies pinned to the backs of the chairs, and stuffed partridges under glass bell jars. Each room had its own fireplace made of marble that looked—depending on the room—like blue cheese or fudge-ripple ice cream or green hand soap or milk chocolate.

One afternoon Lewis was walking down the back staircase in the south wing of the mansion, when he came to a stained-glass window on a landing. There were quite a few stained-glass windows in the house. Lewis found them on back staircases like this one, or in unused bathrooms or at the ends of hallways. Sometimes he even found them set in the ceiling. He had seen this one before, or rather, he had seen another window where this one was now. That was why he stopped and stared.

He remembered the other window very well. It had been a big oval window that showed a red tomato sun setting into a blue sea the color of old medicine bottles. The oval frame was still there, but in it Lewis found a window that showed a man fleeing from a forest. The forest was plum colored, and the grass under the man's feet was bright green. The sky in the picture was a squirming, oily, brownish-red. It reminded Lewis of furniture polish.

What had happened to the other window? Did Jonathan go around changing them during the night? It was pretty strange.

Another thing that was strange was the coat rack in the front hall. At first Lewis had thought that it was just an ordinary coat rack. It stood about six feet high, and it had a little round mirror on the front. There were pegs for coats and hats, and there was a little wooden compartment in the front for rubbers. It looked very ordinary. But one day when Lewis was hanging up his raincoat, he looked at the mirror and saw a Mayan step pyramid in a steaming green jungle. He knew that the pyramid was Mayan because he had a picture of it among his Viewmaster slides. Only this scene was not fake three dimensional, the way the slides were. It looked as if you could reach through the mirror and touch the vines. As

Lewis watched, a brilliant red bird with a long tail flew from one tree to another. Waves of heat made the pyramid ripple. Lewis blinked and stared again. He was looking at the reflection of the rainy gray window behind him.

Lewis thought a lot about the stained-glass windows and the coat rack. Were they magic? He believed in magic, even though he had been taught not to. His father had spent one whole afternoon explaining to Lewis that ghosts were caused by X rays bouncing off distant planets. But Lewis was a stubborn boy, and besides, hadn't he seen the Aladdin's lamp on the back of Jonathan's playing cards, and the words *Capharnaum County Magicians Society?* He was convinced that magic was at the bottom of this mystery.

Lewis was also convinced that he would have to solve another mystery before he could tackle the problem of the coat rack and the stained-glass windows. He would have to find out why Jonathan prowled the house every night with a flashlight in his hand.

Lewis had discovered that the strange incident on his first night in New Zebedee was part of a regular pattern. Every night after twelve, Jonathan was out there searching. What he was searching for, Lewis couldn't say.

Again and again, as on that first night, he had heard the floor boards creak outside his door. Again and again he had heard Jonathan tiptoeing stealthily down the hall, entering rooms, closing doors. He heard him overhead on

/ 27 /

the third floor, where Jonathan hardly ever went during the day. Then he would be back downstairs, poking around, stumbling into furniture. Maybe he was scared of burglars. Maybe so, but then why did he pound on the wall? Burglars seldom got into walls.

Lewis had to find out what was going on. And so, one night a little after twelve, Lewis lowered himself silently from his bed to the cold floor boards. As stealthily as he could, he tiptoed across the room, but the warped boards complained under his feet. By the time he got to the door, he was thoroughly shaken. He wiped his hands on his robe several times and turned the knob. He took a deep breath, let it out, and stepped out into the dark hallway.

Lewis clamped his hand over his mouth. He had stepped on the protruding head of a nail. It didn't really hurt much, but Lewis was scared of tetanus. When his panic had died down, he took another step. He began to edge his way down the hall.

But Lewis was no better at stealthy creeping than you might think and, by the time he had bumped his head against a heavy, gilt picture frame for about the third time, Jonathan called to him from one of the distant rooms.

"Oh, for heaven's sake, Lewis! Stop playing Sherlock Holmes! You make a better Dr. Watson. Come on and join me. I'm in the bedroom with the green fireplace."

Lewis was glad that his red face didn't shine in the dark. Well, at least Jonathan wasn't mad.

Lewis picked his way down the hall until he found an open door. There was Jonathan, standing in the dark with a flashlight in his hand. He was playing the light over the mantel clock, a boxy black affair with gold handles on the sides, like a coffin.

"Evening, Lewis. Or morning, as the case may be. Would you care to join me on my rounds?"

Jonathan's voice sounded tight and nervous. Lewis hesitated a moment and then he plunged in. "Uncle Jonathan, what are you doing?"

"Stopping the clocks. During the day it's nice to have clocks ticking all over the house, but at night it keeps me awake. You know how it is, Lewis, with faucets and . . . and the like."

Still chattering nervously, Jonathan turned the clock around, reached into the back of it, and halted the stubby pendulum. Then he motioned for Lewis to follow him and, waving the flashlight a little too cheerfully, walked on to the next room. Lewis followed, but he was puzzled. "Uncle Jonathan, why don't you turn the room lights on?"

His uncle was silent for a minute. Then he said, in that same nervous voice, "Oh, well, you know how it is, Lewis. If I were to go from one room to another snapping lights on and off, what would the neighbors think? And what about the electric bill? Do you know that you get billed for an hour's worth of electricity every time you snap the lights on and off?"

This explanation did not sound convincing to Lewis. In the first place, Uncle Jonathan had never before given any sign that he cared what the neighbors thought about anything he did. If he wanted to sit in the glider under the chestnut tree and play a saxophone at 3 A.M. he was likely to do just that. In the second place, Jonathan had more than once left the floor lamp in his study burning all night. He was a careless man, and not the sort who worried about big electric bills. It was true that Lewis had only known his uncle for three weeks, but he felt that he already had a pretty good idea of what Jonathan was like.

On the other hand, he couldn't very well say, "Uncle Jonathan, you're lying through your teeth!" so he silently followed his uncle to the next room, the second-best upstairs bathroom. It had a fireplace too—a white tile one —and there was a small, white plastic clock buzzing on the mantel. Jonathan unplugged it without saying anything and went on to the next room, where he stopped a cherrywood clock with a pendulum that used three columns of mercury as a weight. And then on to the next room.

The last clock to be silenced was the grandfather clock in the study. Jonathan's study had a very high ceiling, and all the walls were lined with books. There was a fat, slouchy, brown-leather easy chair that hissed when you sat down in it and, of course, there was a fireplace, and there was still a fire burning in it. Over in a corner by the sliding doors that opened into the dining room stood the tall gloomy clock. The brass disk on the pendulum flashed dimly in the light of the dying fire. Jonathan reached inside and grabbed the long black rod. The clock stopped.

Now that their strange tour was over, Jonathan lapsed into silence. He seemed to be thinking. He walked over to the fireplace, stirred up the fire, and put on another log. He threw himself down into the leather chair and waved his arm at the green easy chair on the other side of the fireplace.

"Have a seat, Lewis. I'd like to have a talk with you."

Lewis wondered if he was going to get bawled out for sneaking up on his uncle. It didn't seem likely. Jonathan looked and sounded friendly, though his voice was still a little edgy. Lewis sat down and watched as Jonathan lit up his hookah. Lewis always liked to watch him do this. The hookah was shaped like a Spanish galleon, and the crow's nest on the mainmast was the bowl. The body of the ship was full of water for cooling the smoke, and up on the bow stood the tiny ceramic figure of a boatswain with his pipe to his lips. A long hose was plugged into the ship's stern, and there was a black rubber mouthpiece on the end. When you blew into the hose, the burning tobacco in the crow's nest sent up a long column of smoke, and the boatswain went *fweee!* on his little pipe. Sometimes, when Jonathan made a mistake and filled the boat too full of water, the boatswain went *blp!* and blew bubbles.

When Jonathan had the pipe going good, he drew in a big mouthful of smoke, let it out slowly, and said, "Lewis, I think it would be better for you to be scared than it would be for you to think of your uncle as a crabby old lunatic."

"I don't think you're crabby," said Lewis.

Jonathan laughed. "But you *do* think I'm off my rocker. Well, after tonight I wouldn't blame you."

Lewis blushed. "No, Uncle Jonathan! I never meant that! You know I don't think . . ."

Jonathan smiled. "Yes, of course, I know. But all the same, I think it would be better if you knew something about this clock business. I can't tell you all about it because I don't know all about it. In fact, there are times when I think I don't know much about it at all. But I'll tell you what I know."

He crossed his legs, sat back, and puffed some more at his pipe. Lewis sat forward in the big green chair. He kept clasping and unclasping his hands and he stared hard at Jonathan. After a brief dramatic pause and a particularly long drag at the galleon-hookah, Jonathan began.

"I haven't lived in this house always, Lewis. In fact, I only moved here five years ago. I used to live down on Spruce Street, near the waterworks. But when the old owner died, and the place was put up for sale cheap, and it meant a chance to live next door to my best friend, Mrs. Zimmermann—"

"Who was the old owner?" asked Lewis, interrupting.

"I was going to get around to that. His name was Isaac Izard. Initials I.I., like a Roman numeral II. You'll find his double *I* carved or painted or stamped on all sorts of things all over this house: the wainscoting, the floorboards, the insides of cupboards, the fuse box, the mantelpieces—everywhere. You'll even find a Roman numeral II worked into the tracery on the wallpaper in the upstairs front hallway." Jonathan paused for a second and looked thoughtful. "Have to get that paper replaced some day . . . oh, well, back to what I was saying. Old Isaac Izard—his name is odd, isn't it? Mrs. Zimmermann thinks that it comes from *izzard*, which in some parts of England is the word for *zed*, which is the word the English use to identify the letter Z. I go along with Mrs. Zimmermann's theory because I can't think of a better one. And besides, she is a Z-lady, so she should know. But, as I was saying, and I will get around to saying something *sometime*, Lewis . . ." He puffed on his pipe some more and wriggled around in the chair to get comfortable. "As I was saying, old Isaac was a warlock."

"What's that?"

Uncle Jonathan looked very serious. "It's the word for a male witch."

Lewis shuddered. Then, out of nowhere, a strange

thought came to him. "Are you one too?" he asked in a tiny, frightened voice.

Jonathan looked at him with a strange smile. "Would it scare you if I said I was?"

"No. I like you an awful lot and you can be a warlock if you want to be one, I guess. You wouldn't be a bad one, I know."

"That depends on how you mean 'bad,'" said Jonathan, chuckling. "If you mean that I wouldn't be an evil one, you're right. If you mean that I wouldn't be too bad at wizarding . . . well, I don't know. I'm pretty much of a parlor magician, though I have a few tricks that go beyond rabbits and playing cards."

"Like stained-glass windows and coat racks?" said Lewis, grinning.

"Yes. Exactly like those. And just to make you *perfectly* secure, let me inform you that Mrs. Zimmermann is also a wizard, though in her case the term should be witch."

"Couldn't you find a better name?" asked Lewis timidly.

"Well, she prefers 'maga' or 'enchantrix,' but I can't use such words without breaking up, so she's old witch Florence to me. She's really a much more serious wizard than I am. Got her D.Mag.A.—that's *Doctor Magicorum Artium*—from the University of Göttingen in Germany in 1922. I just have an A.B. from Michigan Agricultural College."

"What in?" asked Lewis, as if he were interviewing Jonathan for a job. Actually he was interested in Jonathan's college work. Both of Lewis's parents had gone to college, and they always talked a lot about their college work.

"What in?" said Jonathan, blushing. "What in? Why, Agricultural Science. Animal Husbandry and all that. I was going to be a farmer till my grandpa died and left me a pile of money. But back to Isaac Izard. You're still interested, aren't you?"

"Oh, yes! Of course! Please tell me. I want to know."

"Isaac, as I say, was a wizard. He fooled around with black magic, the worst kind of thing a wizard can do. I can't tell you about anything bad that I absolutely know he did—for sure—but if one wizard can judge another, I'd say he was an evil one. A very evil one. Mrs. Zimmermann thinks so too. She lived next door to him for years, remember. You'll have to ask her about him yourself, of course, but there were many evenings when she and I would stand in her back yard and look up and see old Isaac's evil face in the window of the cupola on top of the house. He'd be holding an oil lamp and just staring out at the night. Mrs. Zimmermann claims that he would sit for hours in the cupola during the day. He seemed to be taking notes."

"Gee, that *is* weird. What was he taking notes for?"

"Lord only knows, Lewis. But I'm sure it wasn't anything good. At any rate, to get on with my story. . . . It must be getting pretty late by now, but without the clocks I have no idea what time it is. Where was I? Oh, yes. Old Isaac died during a wild thunderstorm, one of the worst in the history of Capharnaum County. You can look it up in the New Zebedee *Chronicle* if you want to: roofs blown off barns, trees uprooted, and a bolt of lightning melted the iron doors on the tomb Isaac is buried in now. I'll have to show you that tomb some day. Ugly old dump—one of those little stone houses for the respectable dead. There are several of them up in our cemetery, some of them really fancy. This one was built by Isaac's family in the 1850's, but it was never used till they put his wife in there. She died before he did."

"What was she like?"

"Pretty strange, as you'd have to be to choose Isaac Izard for a husband. I don't remember anything about her but her eyeglasses."

Lewis stared. "Her eyeglasses?"

"Yes. I passed her once on the street and she turned and looked at me. It might have been the way the sun caught her spectacles, but I remember two freezing circles of gray light burning into me. I turned away and closed my eyes, but those two cold spots stayed there. I had nightmares for a week after that."

"How did she die?" Lewis imagined Mrs. Izard falling from a cliff during a hurricane, or flinging herself from the cupola of the house.

"How? Quietly and mysteriously. No funeral. Some

strange-looking people from out of town came and helped Isaac bury her. After that, he went into seclusion. Further seclusion, that is. He and she had always been hermits, but after her death he really shut himself up. Built a big high board fence between this house and Mrs. Zimmermann's. I had it torn down as soon as I moved in." He smiled contentedly. Lewis felt that his Uncle Jonathan was happy living at 100 High Street, despite the fact that old Isaac Izard had made the place his castle.

"Is that all there is to the story?" asked Lewis cautiously.

"Oh, my, no. We're just getting to the good part. Look, here I am selfishly puffing away at this boat, and you have nothing. Let's go out to the kitchen and get a couple of glasses of milk and some chocolate-chip cookies. Okay?"

"Sure!" said Lewis, who liked chocolate-chip cookies even more than he liked Welch's Fudge Bars.

In a few minutes they were back in the study, sitting by the quietly crackling fire and munching cookies. Suddenly a book fell out of the bookcase. *Flop.* Two more fell out. *Flop. Flop.* Lewis stared at the black gap in the row of books. A long, withered, bony hand appeared. It seemed to be groping for something.

Lewis sat rigid with terror, but Jonathan merely smiled. "A little to your left, my dear. That's it. Now you've got it."

A latch clicked and a large section of the built-in bookcase swung outwards. More books fell to the floor. And there stood Mrs. Zimmermann, with a strand of cobweb hanging from her left eyeglass. Her sleeve was covered with whitish dust.

"Fine way to build a secret panel," she grumbled. "With the latch on the room side instead of on the passage side."

"It adds to the mystery, Doll Face. As you might have guessed, Lewis, this house has a secret passageway. You enter it through the china cupboard in the kitchen. Come on in, Florence. I was just going to tell Lewis about the clock in the walls."

Mrs. Zimmermann gave him a look as if to say, "Do you think that's a wise thing to do?" But she shrugged and helped herself to the cookies and milk.

"Good cookies," she said, munching. "Very good."

"She always says that because she makes them," explained Jonathan, helping himself to two more. "And now that everyone's mouth is stuffed, including mine, I guess I'll go on. Where were we? Oh, yes. Well, I had no sooner moved in here than I felt that something was wrong. The house had a kind of listening stillness. And then I heard it."

"Heard what?" This was Lewis, who had worked himself to the edge of his chair. He had even stopped eating his cookie.

"The clock. You know how you can be in a room with

a clock ticking, and you won't notice it for a long time. Then, when things are very, very quiet and you aren't thinking about anything in particular—there it is!"

Lewis jumped up and looked around wildly. "Where?"

Jonathan laughed. "No, no, no. I didn't mean to frighten you like that. I mean I heard it for the first time in this room. It was ticking away in the walls. You can go over to that wall and listen for it, if you like."

Lewis got up and walked over to the book-lined wall. He put his ear to a row of black leather volumes and listened. His eyes opened wide.

"It *is* there, Uncle Jonathan! It is!" He was excited by the discovery, but then his face changed. He looked afraid. "What is it for, Uncle Jonathan? What does it do?"

"I haven't the faintest idea," said Jonathan, "though I know that I want to blot it out. That's why I have all these stupid clocks. I didn't used to be so fond of incessant ticking and sudden, loud, hell raising every hour on the hour. But I prefer my clocks to his."

Jonathan's face had turned grim. He shook his head, smiled a little half-hearted smile, and went on. "You may be wondering why I don't just tear down the wall and rip out the clock. Well, it wouldn't do any good. It sounds like it's behind every wall: up in the attic, down in the cellar, in the closets and storerooms and parlors. And sometimes it seems to be slowing down. I keep hoping it will stop. But then it picks up and keeps going.

I don't know what to do." There was a note of real despair in his voice. For a minute Lewis thought his uncle would cry. Then Mrs. Zimmermann broke in.

"I'll tell you one thing you ought *not* to do, Jonathan Barnavelt. You oughtn't to frighten Lewis with something you don't know anything about. After all, the ticking may be some leftover magic from the old coot's experiments. Or death-watch beetles. Or an illusion of some kind, like in houses that have whispering galleries. I get a funny kind of hum in my head now and then. It goes *dooooo* for a while and then it goes away."

Jonathan looked irritated. "Oh, Florence, there's no need to kid around. You don't think it's something harmless and neither do I. I wouldn't have told Lewis just to frighten him. But I thought it would be better for him to know about the clock than to think that his uncle was getting ready for the loony bin. You see, he caught me making my nightly rounds."

"Well," said Mrs. Zimmermann, "I don't know about the loony bin, but Uncle Jonathan had better be getting ready for beddy-by if he's going to take us on a picnic tomorrow." She reached into the folds of her dress and pulled out a silver watch on a long chain. She popped the lid open and announced that it was three A.M.

Jonathan looked up with surprise. "It is? Good grief, I had no idea——"

"Please, Uncle Jonathan," said Lewis, interrupting. "Can you tell me one thing more?"

"Sure, Lewis. What is it?"

Lewis looked fidgety and embarrassed. "Well . . . if the clocks are supposed to drown out the noise of the clock in the walls, why do you stop them at night?"

Jonathan sighed. "I don't stop them every night. Some nights I just walk around checking all the rooms. It makes me feel secure, somehow. I can't explain it. But some nights, like this one, I get the urge to stop all the blasted everlasting ticking. I get the feeling that if I were to make the house quiet—perfectly quiet—then maybe I could hear the real clock, the magic one, ticking behind one particular wall, or in some cubbyhole. But it never works, and I always feel half crazy for trying."

Lewis still looked puzzled. "If it's a magic clock," he said slowly, "then wouldn't it be invisible? I mean, wouldn't it be something you couldn't actually put your hands on?"

Jonathan shook his head. "Not really, Lewis. Most magic is accomplished with solid everyday objects. Objects that have had spells said over them. One witch I knew tried to obliterate her enemy by leaving a photo of him under the running water of her gutterspout. Her reasoning was that he would die when the face on the picture was wiped out. It's a common method. No, Lewis. This is a clock as real as grandpa over there. Only it's enchanted. But what it is enchanted to do I don't for the life of me know."

"Well, *I* know something, Weird Beard," said Mrs.

Zimmermann, dangling her watch like a pendulum before Jonathan's eyes, "I know that if we don't catch just a little, teeny bit of shut-eye, we're all going to be wearing our crabby caps in the morning. Lewis, off to bed. Jonathan, same with you. I'll rinse the cookie plates and put away the milk."

Later, up in his room, Lewis stood in the middle of the floor staring at a patch of flowered wallpaper near the fireplace. He walked quickly over to the wall and put his ear to it. Yes, the ticking was here too. He walked across the room and listened to another wall. More of the same.

Lewis walked back to the center of the room and then, abruptly, he began to pace. He paced in quick strides with his hands behind his back, the way he had seen his father do when he was upset. He paced and tried to think logically. But logic wasn't much help where the clock in the walls was concerned, so at last Lewis gave it up. He jumped into bed and went to sleep.

CHAPTER THREE

On the first Monday after Labor Day, Lewis started going to school in New Zebedee and, before long, he had forgotten all about the mysterious clock in the walls. He had troubles enough of his own.

They weren't new troubles. They were the troubles that a fat boy who can't play baseball carries around with him from place to place. Lewis had always been overweight. He couldn't remember a time when he hadn't been. All his life—all ten years of it—he had been listening to children who chanted:

> Fatty, fatty, two by four
> Can't get through the kitchen door.

Sometimes he wanted to beat up the kids who made fun of him, but he couldn't box and he wasn't very strong. That was another problem. But the worst problem of all was the baseball problem. Lewis still spun all the way around when he swung at a ball, and he threw his bat. At first he tried to excuse himself by saying, "Watch out, I'm gonna throw the bat!" But the other kids said, "Look, you throw the bat and we're gonna beat you up. You hang onto it when you swing or you can't play."

That is what they said when they let him play, which was not very often. Most of the time when he lined up to be chosen he was the last one left, and the captain of the side that was supposed to take him usually said, "Why do we hafta take *him?* He can't field, he can't hit, he can't pitch. He can't even run. Come on, we'll play one man short."

What they said about Lewis was true. Sometimes a new boy or a kind boy would get to be captain, and he would choose Lewis for his team. But when Lewis came to bat, he usually struck out. If he hit the ball, it popped up and the pitcher caught it. Or he might ground out to first base. When his team was out in the field, the boys made Lewis play right field, because not many balls got hit out that way. But when one did, Lewis always dropped it, unless it hit him on the head. He would stagger back and forth as he tried to keep track of the ball that hung there, high over his head, but he always got dizzy and covered his face with his glove and screamed "No! No!" as the ball came down. After a while even the kind boys turned him down.

One afternoon, when the usual routine had been gone through, and Lewis had run off the field sobbing because they would not let him play, he found himself standing at home plate on a baseball diamond that wasn't being used that day. At his feet was a bat, a thick old club with a split handle that had been wrapped up with black friction tape. There was a softball nearby, or what was left of one: a black, sticky, egg-shaped lump covered with string. Lewis picked up the ball and bat. He threw the ball into the air and swung at it. He missed. He picked the ball up and tried again. Again he missed. He was about to try for the third time when someone said, "You're doin' it all wrong."

Lewis turned and saw a skinny boy about his own age squatting next to the bicycle rack. There was a big fluff of brick-red hair on top of the boy's head, and his right arm was in a sling. The boy was Tarby.

Everybody in the school knew who Tarby was. Even Lewis knew, and he had only been in New Zebedee for a couple of months. Probably everyone in New Zebedee and most of the people in Capharnaum County knew who Tarby was. At least, that was the impression that Lewis got. Tarby was the most popular boy in the school. He was a daredevil, the kind of boy who rode his bicycle through bonfires and hung by his knees from the limbs of trees. All the girls liked him, and he was the big home-run hitter in the softball games. He got chosen first so often that most of the time the boys made him a captain, just to avoid all the fighting over who got to have Tarby on their team. But here he was with his arm in a sling, watching Lewis as he tried to hit the ball.

"I said, you're doing it all wrong. You're supposed to keep your feet planted flat. Then you swing from the hips. Here. Let me show you."

Tarby scrambled to his feet and walked over to where Lewis was standing. He grabbed the bat and hefted it in one hand, choking up on it a bit.

"Okay," he said, "get out there and pitch. Just lob it up here."

Lewis had never seen anyone trying to hit a ball with the bat held in only one hand. He was afraid that Tarby would miss and get mad and go home. With a nervous grin on his face, Lewis lobbed the ball toward the plate. Tarby swung and the bat connected. *Clack!* It struck the ball with that rickety hollow sound that split bats have. The ball shot on a line toward center field. It would have been a clean single.

"See? And that's just with one arm. You ought to be able to do that well with two. C'mon. I'll pitch."

Lewis walked in from the pitcher's mound and took the bat from Tarby's hand.

"I didn't know your arm was broken," said Lewis shyly. "How'd you do it?"

"Fell out of a tree. I was hanging by my knees. Upside down, like in the monkey house. It's okay. It'll heal up."

Tarby walked out to the mound. Lewis pounded his bat on the plate and waved it the way he had seen George Kell do in Briggs Stadium in Detroit. But when Tarby threw the ball, Lewis missed as usual.

Every day for the next two weeks Tarby met Lewis after school, and they practiced batting. Slowly, gradually, Lewis's swing got better. He even managed to hit a few line drives. But something even more important was happening. Lewis and Tarby were getting to be friends. Tarby liked Lewis's jokes, and Lewis found out that Tarby hated some of the kids that he hated. Lewis liked Tarby's imitation of Mrs. Fondrighter, a mean teacher at school. Mrs. Fondrighter always called her husband "Jerrold," which was a funny thing to do. Tarby made a loop in the end of a green twig and pretended it was an eyeglass on a stick. Then he would stare through the loop at Lewis and say, in a high voice, "How *deah* you say such things to me, Jer-*rold!*"

Then Lewis and Tarby would sit around planning how they were going to take care of Carol Kay Laberdeen, a snotty girl in the sixth grade who got away with murder because her father was on the school board. It was usually dark by the time Lewis and Tarby said goodby to each other by the mailbox at the bottom of High Street.

One afternoon early in October, Lewis and Tarby

were out at the athletic field playing flies and grounders. Lewis had gotten good enough so that he could hit Tarby some pretty long fly balls. Tarby's arm was still in a cast, but he picked off the line drives and caught the pop flies as easily as if he had had two hands.

Lewis was out in the field. It was getting dark, and he was having trouble seeing the ball, and besides he was a little bored. He stood there thinking, or "doping off" as Tarby called it.

He wanted to do something nice for Tarby. Something nice that would really impress him and make him a stronger friend than ever. Maybe he could get Uncle Jonathan to do a magic trick for Tarby. Sure, that would do it. Lewis hesitated a minute, remembering Jonathan saying that he was only a "parlor magician." The kind that pulled rabbits out of hats and told you what card you were holding in your hand. But then he *had* said that he knew a few tricks that went beyond that. . . .

Lewis thought some more. Oh, well, Jonathan could probably do it. Anyone who could make windows change their pictures could do what Lewis had in mind. And anyway, Lewis thought that he remembered hearing Jonathan say that he had done such a thing once.

"Hey, Lewis! I hit the ball out to you about six hours ago. Did you go to sleep?"

Lewis looked up. "Huh? Oh, gee, I'm sorry, Tarby. Say, how would you like to see my uncle eclipse the moon?"

Tarby stared at him. "What did you say?"

"I said . . . oh, c'mon, Tarby, let's go home. It's too dark to see the ball. C'mon and I'll tell you all about my Uncle Jonathan. He's a real wizard."

The two boys walked back under the streetlights, playing catch as they went. Lewis tried to explain about Uncle Jonathan's magic powers, but he could see that Tarby was not convinced.

"Boy, I'll *bet* your uncle can eclipse the moon. I'll just *bet* he can. He prob'ly sits up in his room drinking beer, and then he goes out in back and stares up at the moon, and boy does it go rround . . . and . . . rraounnd." Tarby staggered out into the street and rolled his eyes.

Lewis felt like hitting him, but he knew that Tarby could beat him up, so he just said, "You wanta see him do it?"

"Yeah," said Tarby in a sneery voice. "I wanta see him do it."

"Okay," said Lewis. "I'll ask him tonight. When he's ready to do it, I'll let you know."

"Gee, I hope I won't have to wait too long," said Tarby sarcastically. "I really do want to see Old Lard Guts eclipse the moo-hoo-hoo, moo-hoo-ha . . . ."

"Stop it. Stop making fun of my uncle." Lewis's face was red, and he was almost crying.

"Make me," said Tarby.

"I can't, and you know it," said Lewis.

Tarby went on moo-hooing until they reached the

khaki-colored mailbox at the foot of High Street. This time when they split up to go home, Lewis didn't say goodby to Tarby. He didn't even wave. But by the time he was inside the gate at 100 High Street, Lewis had gotten over his mad—more or less—and so he went straight inside to see his uncle. He found Jonathan laying out a game of solitaire on the dining-room table. It was a complicated game called "Napoleon at St. Helena," and the layout covered most of the ivory-colored oilcloth pad. Jonathan looked up and smiled as Lewis walked into the room.

"Hi, Lewis! How's baseball these days?"

"Getting better, I guess. Tarby helps me a lot. Say, Uncle Jonathan, do you suppose we could do something nice for Tarby? He really is a good friend of mine."

"Sure, Lewis. We'll invite him to dinner. Is that what you mean?"

Lewis blushed and fidgeted. "Uh . . . well, yeah . . . kind of. Do you think that maybe after dinner we could . . . uh, that is, *you* could . . . eclipse the moon for him?"

Jonathan stared at him. "Did I tell you I could do *that?*"

"Yes. Remember, one night when you were bragging . . . er, talking to Mrs. Zimmermann about whether earth magic was stronger than moon magic? You said that a moon wizard could eclipse the moon any time he felt like it, and that you were a moon wizard."

Jonathan smiled and shook his head. "Did I say that? My, my, how I do run on. Let me see, I do seem to recall eclipsing the moon one night in 1932. That was during a picnic out at Wilder Creek Park. I remember the date, April 30, which is Walpurgis Night. That's the night when witches and warlocks all over the world get together for whoop-te-doos. Ours was just a convention of the Capharnaum County Magicians Society, but some of them are real wizards. At any rate, to get back to what I was saying . . ."

"Never mind," said Lewis, turning away with a pouty look on his face. "I'll tell Tarby that you can't do it."

"Oh, Lewis!" cried Jonathan, throwing the pack of cards down on the table. "You are the most easily discouraged boy I ever met. If I did it once, I can do it again. It's just that it's not a normal occurrence. And everything has to be just right. In the heavens, that is."

"Oh."

"Yes, oh. Now, as soon as I have won this silly game from myself, you and I will go to the library and consult the almanac. So be quiet for a minute."

Lewis fidgeted and clasped and unclasped his hands and stared at the light fixture until Jonathan finished his game. Then the two of them went to the library, slid back the panelled doors, and entered the marvelous room that smelled of damp paper, wood smoke, and Turko-man's Terror, Jonathan's personal tobacco blend. Jona-

than moved the stepladder to the part of the wall that
contained his magic books, climbed up, and pulled down
a thick dusty volume labelled:

HARDESTY'S
Universal Omnium Gatherum

*Perpetual Calendar, Date Book,
Almanac, and Book of Days*

He flipped to the section on eclipses, did some rapid
mental calculations, and said, "You're in luck, Lewis.
1948 is a good year for lunar eclipses. The planets will
be favorable next Friday. Invite Tarby to dinner for
that night. I'll be ready."

Friday night came around, and Lewis brought Tarby
home for dinner. There was nothing especially magic
about the meal, except that the cider jug on the table
burped a lot, and that might have been because the cider
was getting hard. After the dishes were cleared away,
Jonathan asked Lewis and Tarby to help Mrs. Zimmermann carry some kitchen chairs out into the back yard.
Then he walked out into the front hall and consulted
his cane rack, a blue Willoware vase full of walking sticks
of all sizes and shapes. Some had ivory or bone handles,
some were tough, crooked old pieces of hickory or
maplewood, and some had thin springy swords concealed
inside. But only one cane was magic.

It was a long black rod of some very hard wood. At one end was a ferrule of polished brass, and at the other was a glass globe the size of a baseball. It seemed to be snowing inside the globe. Through the swirling little flakes you could see, now and then, an odd little miniature castle. The globe burned with an icy gray light. Jonathan picked up the cane, hefted it, and walked back toward the kitchen with it tucked under his arm.

Out in the back yard, the audience was ready. Mrs. Zimmermann, Lewis, and Tarby sat in straight chairs facing the birdbath. It was a chilly, clear October night. All the stars were out, and a large full moon was rising over the four elm trees at the far end of Jonathan's yard. The screen door slammed, and everyone looked up. The magician had arrived.

Without saying a word, Jonathan went around to the north side of the house. An old mossy rain barrel stood there against the sandstone wall. Jonathan looked into the barrel, breathed three times on the dark water, and with his left forefinger cut the faintly shimmering surface into four quarters. Then he leaned low over the mouth of the barrel and began whispering in a strange language. The three spectators had not left their chairs—Jonathan had told them to stay where they were—but they craned their necks around a good deal trying to figure out what the wizard was doing.

The whispering, weirdly magnified by the mouth of

the barrel, went on for some time. Lewis twisted way around in his chair, but all he could see was the dark shape of Uncle Jonathan and the faintly glowing gray globe of the magic cane. Finally Jonathan returned. In one hand he held the cane, and in the other he had a saucepan full of rain water.

"Is your uncle going to wash his hair?" whispered Tarby.

"Oh, be quiet!" hissed Lewis. "He knows what he's doing. Just you watch."

Tarby, Lewis, and Mrs. Zimmermann watched anxiously as Jonathan poured the saucepan into the birdbath. Then he went back to the rain barrel for more. *Dip. Splash.* He came back with another panful. He emptied it. And he went back for a third.

The third panful seemed to be enough. Jonathan set down the empty pan and picked up his cane, which had been leaning against the birdbath. The glass ball glowed and sent out a ray of dusty gray light. The ray rested on the surface of the water in the birdbath. Jonathan made signs over the water with the cane and started muttering again.

"Come on and look," he said, motioning to the three spectators. They got up and walked over to the birdbath. The water in the flat, shallow concrete pan had started to heave and pitch, like ocean water in a storm. Lewis was surprised to see tiny whitecaps forming. Then long rollers began to crash silently into the rim, sending pin-point flecks of foam out onto the grass. Jonathan watched for a while along with the rest. Then, suddenly, he raised the cane and cried, "Peace! Peace to the waters of the earth! Show unto us the round disk of the moon, even as she now appeareth in the heavens above!"

The water calmed down. Soon it was a flat pool again, and floating on the still black surface was the cold reflection of the full moon. Now Jonathan did something very unlikely. As the others watched, he bent over and pulled a small boulder out of the pile of rocks at the base of the birdbath. Then, lifting it high in the air, he shouted, "Stand back!" and dropped the rock. *Splash!* Water slopped everywhere, and Lewis did not get out of the way soon enough to keep from getting some on his shoes.

When the water had calmed down again, Jonathan picked up the rock and looked into the pool. There, wobbly and creased with ripples, was the moon's reflection.

"Still there?" said Jonathan, grinning. "Well, we'll just see about that!"

He reached down into the water and picked up the reflection. It might have been a trick, but the cold, icy-gray disk he held up looked like the reflection that had floated in the pool a moment before. And sure enough, when Lewis looked into the water, all he saw now was a shiny blackness.

/ 55 /

Jonathan held up the reflection and turned it back and forth as if it were a dinner plate. The disk burned cold and bitter, and sparkled like freshly fallen snow. It hurt Lewis's eyes to stare at it for very long. Now Jonathan snapped his wrist and sent the disk flying across the yard. It sailed clear across to the dark thicket in front of the four elm trees. Then Jonathan, cane in hand, ran off after the disk. It was a long yard and, even in the moonlight, the boys and Mrs. Zimmermann could not see what he was doing down there.

Suddenly the air was filled with the inane glockling and blockling of bamboo wind chimes. There was a set of them hanging from one of the elm trees, and Jonathan had given it a good hard yank. Now he came dancing back up the yard, dueling with shadows and saying things like, "Ha! Have at you in your bladder for a blaggardly slacker! Hoo! Hunh! And the third in his bosom!"

He stopped in front of the birdbath and held the ball of the cane up under his chin so that his face looked like an actor's face when it is lit from below by footlights. Slowly he raised his right hand and pointed at the sky. "Look!" he cried.

All three of the spectators looked up. At first they saw nothing strange. Then, slowly, a black, tarry, drippy shadow oozed down over the face of the surprised moon. In no time at all the moon was dark, completely dark, blacked out, without even the faint brownish umbra that marks its place during an ordinary eclipse.

And now Uncle Jonathan's back yard came to life. It was full of strange sights and sounds. The grass glowed a phosphorescent green, and red worms wriggled through the tall blades with a hushing sound. Strange insects dropped down out of the overhanging boughs of the willow tree and started to dance on the picnic table. They waltzed and wiggled in a shaking blue light, and the music they danced to, faint though it was, sounded to Lewis like "Rugbug," the famous fox trot composed by Maxine Hollister. This was one of the tunes that Jonathan's parlor organ played.

Uncle Jonathan walked over to the tulip bed, put his ear to the ground, and listened. He motioned for the others to join him. Lewis put his ear to the damp earth, and he heard strange things. He heard the noise that earthworms make as they slowly inch along, breaking hard black clods with their blunt heads. He heard the secret inwound conversations of bulbs and roots, and the breathing of flowers. And Lewis knew strange things, without knowing how he came to know them. He knew that there was a cat named Texaco buried in the patch of ground he knelt on. Its delicate ivory skeleton was falling slowly to pieces down there, and its dank fur was shrivelled and matted and rotten. The boy who had buried the cat had buried a sand pail full of shells near it. Lewis did not know the name of the boy, or how long ago he had buried the cat and the pail, but he could see the red and blue pail clearly. Blotches of brown rust were eating up the bright designs, and the shells were covered with green mold.

After a long while, Lewis sat up and looked around. Tarby was kneeling near him, his ear to the ground and his eyes wide with wonder. But where was Uncle Jonathan? Where, for that matter, was Mrs. Zimmermann? At the far end of the yard, in the shadow of the four elm trees, Lewis thought he saw them moving around. He tapped Tarby on the shoulder, pointed, and the two boys silently got up and went to join the magicians.

When they found them, Jonathan was arguing with Mrs. Zimmermann, who argued right back, though her ear was pressed flat to the ground.

"I say it's the old storm sewer system," she muttered. "It was lost track of in 1868 because the charts got thrown out with the wastepaper."

"Well, you can think what you like, Frizzy Wig," said Jonathan as he knelt down for another listen. "*I* say it's an underground stream. Capharnaum County is full of them, and it would account for the fact that Sin-and-Flesh Creek is much bigger when it leaves New Zebedee than it is when it enters it."

"You're full of beans, Fatso," said Mrs. Zimmermann, whose ear was still pressed to the ground. "I think I know the sound of water rushing through a brick tunnel. It's all vaulty and hollow."

"Like your head?"

Lewis and Tarby pressed their ears to the ground, but

all they could hear was a sound like the one you hear when you press your ear against an inner tube that you are floating on in a lake. Lewis felt very excited. He wanted to be all over the garden at once, touching things and smelling them and listening. The magic in the back yard lasted for over an hour. Then the phosphorescence changed to plain old ordinary moonlight, and the moon floated high overhead, free from enchantments.

As they walked back into the house, Lewis asked his uncle if the police department didn't get mad when he eclipsed the moon. Jonathan chuckled and put his arm around Lewis.

"No," he said, "strangely enough they don't. I've never been quite sure why, but maybe it's because the eclipse is only visible in this yard."

"You mean it's not real?"

"Of course, it's real. You saw it, didn't you? But one of the troubles with human beings is that they can only see out of their own eyes. If I could be two people, I'd station the other me across town to see if the eclipse was operating over there."

"Why don't you ask Mrs. Zimmermann to go watch?"

"Because she'd be crabby. She always wants to be in on things. Don't you, Pruny?"

"Yes, I do. And right now I'd like to be in on some chocolate-chip cookies. Why don't you all come over to my place?"

And that is what they did. Lewis was happy to have a chance to show off Mrs. Zimmermann's house to Tarby. It was not a mansion, by any means. Just a little two-story bungalow with a screened-in front porch. But it was full of strange things, most of them purple. Mrs. Zimmermann had a thing about the color purple. Her rugs, her wallpaper, her staircase runner, her toilet paper, and her bath soap were all purple. So was the large surrealistic painting of a dragon that hung in her living room. It had been done for her specially by the French painter Odilon Redon.

As they munched their cookies and drank their milk and walked around looking at the purple things in Mrs. Zimmermann's house, Lewis noticed that Tarby wasn't saying much. When it came time for him to go, Tarby shook Jonathan's hand while staring at the carpet, and he mumbled, "Thanks for the cookies" to Mrs. Zimmermann in such a low voice that he couldn't be understood. Lewis saw Tarby to the front gate. He knew this was odd behavior for Tarby, who was usually loud and sassy-acting, even in front of grownups.

"Thanks for the magic show," said Tarby, shaking Lewis's hand and looking very serious. "It was kind of scary, but it was fun. I take back all the things I said about your uncle, I guess. Well, see you around." And with that, Tarby went trudging down the hill.

Lewis stared after him with a worried frown on his

face. He hoped that Tarby had had a good time. Most people do not like to be proven wrong, even when they enjoy themselves in the process. Tarby was a popular boy, and he was used to being right about everything. He had turned out to be wrong about Jonathan's magic powers. Now what would he do? Lewis didn't want to lose his only friend.

CHAPTER FOUR

It was the last week of October, and Tarby's arm had almost healed. Lewis saw less and less of him now. He still waited for him on the baseball diamond out behind the school, and sometimes Tarby showed up, and sometimes he didn't.

Of course, Tarby couldn't be expected to be very interested in flies and grounders at this time of year. The football season was getting underway. Lewis had seen Tarby playing football with the other boys after school. Needless to say, Tarby was always the quarterback. He threw long passes and made end runs and pulled off tricky plays, like the "Statue of Liberty."

Lewis had thought of trying to join the football game,

but he remembered what had happened back in Wisconsin. Whenever anyone charged over the line at him, he fell to the ground and covered his head with his hands. He couldn't catch passes and, if he tried to kick the ball, he usually wound up bunting it with his knee. Maybe if he got really good at baseball, he could get Tarby to teach him football next year.

But he wasn't going to learn much about baseball without Tarby. Of course, these days he wasn't learning much even with Tarby's help. On those rare occasions when Tarby showed up to play ball with Lewis, he seemed to want to get the game over with in a hurry. Lewis knew that he was losing Tarby, but so far he hadn't figured out how in the world he was going to hang on to him.

One Saturday afternoon when the two of them were poking around in the cemetery, Lewis had an idea. New Zebedee's beautiful old cemetery was on a high hill just outside of town. It was full of elaborate gravestones that showed weeping women leaning on urns and cupids extinguishing torches. There were pillars made to look as if they had been broken, and there were pillars with hands on top, pointing up. There were little tombstones made in the shape of lambs, and these were over the graves of children. Some of the lambs had been there so long that they were worn into grimy white blobs that reminded Lewis of soap.

On this particular day, Lewis and Tarby had been

inspecting a lot where all the gravestones were carved to look like wood. Each grave was marked by a little granite log, complete with bark and rings and knotholes. The curb around the lot matched the tombstones, and in the center of everything rose a broken tree of stone. The top was jagged, as if lightning had struck it, and a stone woodpecker was whetting his beak on the realistically carved bark. Lewis and Tarby had been playing in this petrified forest for a while, but now they were getting tired. The sun, red as the tomato sun in Jonathan's stained-glass window, was setting between two crooked pine trees. Lewis shivered and zipped up his jacket.

"Let's go back to my house," he said. "Mrs. Zimmermann can make us some cocoa, and I'll show you some *real* petrified wood. My uncle got it in a forest out west that was actually turned to stone."

Tarby looked bored, and he also looked mean. "Who wants to go back to your old uncle's house? It's a pretty crazy place, if you ask me. And how come old Mrs. Zimmermann is over there all the time? Is she in *luuvv* with him?" Tarby threw his arms around the stone tree and started kissing it with loud smacks. Lewis felt like crying, but somehow he managed to keep down the tears.

"I . . . I bet you think all my uncle can do is eclipse the moon," said Lewis. It sounded silly, but he couldn't think of anything else to say.

Tarby looked interested, in a bored sort of way. "Well," he said, "what else can he do?"

Lewis did not know why he said what he said next. It just came to him.

"My uncle can raise the dead."

Tarby did a somersault over one of the log-shaped markers. "Oh, sure he can," he snorted. "Look, your uncle is a fake. That night when he made it look like the moon had gone out and all that other stuff was happening, he just had us *hypnotized*. My dad told me that was prob'ly what happened."

Lewis stared at him. "You said you'd never tell anyone about what we did that night. Remember? I made you promise."

Tarby looked away. "Oh, yeah, I guess I did promise. Sorry."

Both of them sat quietly for a long while. There was nothing left of the sun but a faint red afterglow. A night wind had sprung up, and it stirred the long grass on the graves. Finally Lewis got up and spoke. His voice came from way down in his throat.

"What if I were to raise a dead person by myself?"

Tarby looked at him. He giggled. "Boy, that would be some fun. I can see you runnin' down Main Street in the middle of the night with a ghost after you." Tarby got up and waved his arms. "*Woo-oooo!*" he wailed. "I am the ghost of miss-terr-reee! *Woo-oooo!*"

Lewis's face was getting red. "Wanta see me do it?"

"Yeah," said Tarby. "I do. When are you gonna do it?"

"I'll let you know," said Lewis, although he didn't have the faintest idea of what he was going to do, or when he was going to do it, or how he was going to do it. All he knew was that he had to try, if he was going to hang on to his only friend in New Zebedee.

During that week before Halloween, Lewis spent a lot of time in his uncle's study. Normally it was okay for Lewis to browse in the library, but if Jonathan had known what books Lewis was looking at now, he would have stopped him. Lewis knew this, so he always waited till Jonathan was out visiting, or raking leaves, or tying up corn shocks in the garden. When he was sure he would not be disturbed, Lewis would slide back the paneled walnut doors, tiptoe into the study, and roll the stepladder down to the section of the library wall that contained Jonathan's magic books. Jonathan had forbidden Lewis to look through these books without his permission, so Lewis felt very bad about what he was doing. He felt bad about the whole business. But he went ahead anyway.

He looked through all the strange old volumes, with their pentacles and pentagrams, their anagrams and talismans and abracadabras and long incantations printed in Old English lettering. But he spent most of his time with a big black leather volume entitled *Necromancy*. Necromancy is the branch of magic that deals with the raising of the dead. The frontispiece of the book was an engraving that showed Dr. John Dee, personal astrologer to Queen Elizabeth I of England, as he and his assistant,

Michael Kelly, raised the spirit of a dead woman in an English churchyard at midnight. The two men were standing inside a chalk circle drawn on the ground. The border of the circle was covered with strange symbols and words. Just outside the charmed circle hovered a figure in a long nightgown. On her head she wore an odd ruffly bonnet, the kind they once buried women in. Lewis kept turning back to the illustration because it frightened him. But he read the rest of the book. He read it all, and he memorized some of the charms. He even copied one of the pentagrams and the spell that went with it onto a piece of notepaper and put it in his pocket.

Halloween was a windy dark day. Lewis sat in the window of his bedroom and watched the wind strip the trees of the few ragged brown leaves that remained. He felt sad and scared. He was sad because he had disobeyed his uncle, who was always kind to him. And he felt scared because he had promised Tarby that he would meet him in the graveyard at twelve o'clock on Halloween night, so that the two of them could raise up the spirit of a dead person. Or try to. Lewis didn't think it would work, and he was kind of hoping that it wouldn't.

They had the grave all picked out. It was a mausoleum stuck into the side of the hill the graveyard was built on. Lewis didn't know anything about who was buried in the tomb. Neither did Tarby. There wasn't even a name on the door. But whatever the name was, it probably started with *O*, because there was an *O* in the triangle over the heavy old stone arch. It was a funny kind of *O*, and it looked like this:

At dinner that night, Lewis did not say much. This was odd because he usually talked his head off about everything under the sun, especially those things he didn't know anything about. Jonathan asked him if he was all right, and Lewis said that of course he was all right, anybody could see that. Jonathan and Mrs. Zimmermann exchanged worried glances and stared at him again, but Lewis went on eating with his head down. At the end of the meal, he pushed his chair back and announced that he was not going trick-or-treating, because he was too old for it.

"Does that mean that you're not coming over to my place for cider and doughnuts?" asked Mrs. Zimmermann. "Because if it does, I'll show up at midnight at the foot of your bed in my role of Grinning Griselda, the resuscitated cadaver. It's a horrible thing to see."

Lewis looked up. There was a wild look on his face, but he managed to force his mouth into a smile.

"No, Mrs. Zimmermann," he said. "I wouldn't miss one of your cider-and-doughnut parties. Not for the world.

But right now I've got to go up to my room and finish one of John L. Stoddard's books. I've gotten to the exciting part." Whereupon he jumped up, excused himself, and ran upstairs.

Jonathan looked at Mrs. Zimmermann. "I have a feeling," he said, "that something is up."

"Hooray for your lightning-quick mind," said Mrs. Zimmermann. "Yes, something is up, and *I* have a feeling that we won't know what it is till it's over with."

"Maybe not," said Jonathan as he lit his pipe. "But I can't believe that Lewis is mixed up in anything bad. And I'm certainly not going to grill him like a mean stepfather. Still, I'd like to know what he's up to."

"So would I," said Mrs. Zimmermann thoughtfully. "Do you suppose it has anything to do with Tarby? The boy's arm is healing, and he'll probably be going back to play with the other boys soon. That leaves Lewis out."

Jonathan scratched his chin. "Yes, maybe that's it," he said. "I'll have to have a talk with him. Oh, by the way, have you noticed that the clock is louder now?" He was trying to sound nonchalant, but Mrs. Zimmermann could read the look in his eyes.

"Yes," she said, trying hard to smile. "I've heard it too. And maybe if we ignore it, it'll just die down. It has before, you know. One thing for sure: you're not going to do any good by barging around the house with a crowbar, prying open the wainscot and peering between floorboards."

"I suppose not," said Jonathan, sighing. "Though I might come across the blasted thing by sheer persistence. On the other hand, that would mean wrecking the house, and I'm not quite ready to do that. Not until I have some clearer idea that the clock is something that can do us harm. And so far, I'm just guessing. I'm even guessing when I say it's a real, physical clock, and not just some illusion left here by old Isaac Izard to drive people mad."

"It's best not to think about the thing," said Mrs. Zimmermann. "Not until you have to, at any rate. You can't prepare for all the disasters that might occur in this frightening world of ours. If the devil appears or if we find that the End of the World is at hand, we'll do something."

"Mm-hmmm. We'll hide in the cellar. Come on. Let's wash the dishes."

Lewis came down from his room at ten o'clock and went next door to have cider and doughnuts. He found Jonathan and Mrs. Zimmermann waiting for him in the dining room. There was a big round oak table at one end of the long room, and it was covered with a clean checkered tablecloth. On the table stood a gallon jug of cider and a plate of powdered doughnuts, or "fried cakes," as Mrs. Zimmermann called them. At the other end of the room, a violet fire crackled in the fireplace. Purple shadows rushed back and forth over the hearthrug and, over the mantelpiece, the purple dragon in the painting seemed to writhe and squirm. He looked very fierce indeed.

"Evening, Lewis," said Jonathan. "Pull up a chair and dig in."

After Lewis had eaten two or three doughnuts and downed four big glasses of cider, Jonathan announced that tonight's entertainment would be Historical Illusions, or Famous Scenes From the Past. He asked Lewis what past scene he would most like to see.

Lewis answered immediately. "I want to see the defeat of the Spanish Armada. Not the battle scenes, because I've read all about them in John L. Stoddard. But he doesn't tell what happened when they had to sail all the way around England and Scotland to get home. I want to see that part."

"Very well," said Jonathan. "Let's go over and sit by the fire."

They got up and walked over to the fireplace, where three big comfortable chairs waited for them. When they were all settled, Jonathan pointed his pipe at the two electric candles over the mantelpiece. Slowly the power began to drain from them. They flickered and went out. Then the bulbs in the chandelier over the table began to do the same thing. It was like watching the house lights dim in a theater. Lewis felt something tickling his nostrils and his tongue. It was the smell and taste of salt. Grainy blowing mists filled the room, and Lewis found himself standing on a grassy headland. Jonathan was on his left, and Mrs. Zimmermann was on his right. Before them a cold gray sea tumbled and tossed.

"Where are we?" asked Lewis.

"We are standing on John O'Groats," said Jonathan. "It is the northernmost point in Scotland. The year is 1588, and out there is the Armada, or what is left of it. You'll need the telescope to see them."

"Telescope?" said Lewis, and then he realized that they were standing on a little stone platform behind a curving waist-high wall. It was the kind of wall you find on scenic lookout points in state parks. And mounted on the wall was a small pay telescope with a set of instructions under glass. Lewis bent over and peered at the little card, which said:

SEE THE ARMADA
Last chance this year
Deposit five shillings, if you please.

Jonathan fumbled in his vest and dug out two large silver coins. He handed them to Lewis. They were half crowns, and each one was worth two and a half shillings in old-fashioned British money. Lewis slid the coins into the slot. There was a whirring sound. He put his eye to the telescope and looked.

At first all he saw was a milky blur but, after he had fiddled with the adjusting wheel a bit, Lewis could see several big galleons ploughing sluggishly through the waves. Their sails were ripped and torn, and their tattered rigging flew about crazily in the wind. The long rows of gunports were closed tight against the battering sea, and

/ 73 /

Lewis could see patches on the sides of three or four ships. One lumbering hulk had a cable passed around its middle, presumably to hold it together.

As Lewis watched, the ships wallowed on. Now he could see their tall ornamented sterns. Saints and bishops and dragons supported gilded window frames or clung to scrolled corners. Lewis noticed that several statues had arms or hands or heads missing. One scowling bishop was wearing his miter at a rakish tilt.

Lewis turned the telescope. Now he was looking at a strange little man. The man was pacing the quarterdeck of the biggest, richest-looking, but most badly damaged ship of all. He wore a black cape that barely reached to his knees, and he was shivering. His whiskers were long and weepy, and he looked very worried.

"Who is the man on the biggest ship?" asked Lewis.

"That," said Jonathan, "is the Duke of Medina-Sidonia. He is the Captain General of the 'Ocean Sea,' which means that he is the commander of the Armada. The whole, shot-riddled, sinking mess. I'll bet he wishes he were at home right now."

Lewis felt sorry for the poor Duke. When he was reading John L. Stoddard in bed the night before, he had wished that he could be there in the Narrow Seas, commanding a stout English galleon. He would have emptied broadside after broadside into the Duke's flagship, until she sank. But now he wanted to help the man, if he could.

While Lewis stood thinking, Jonathan tapped him on the shoulder and pointed to something Lewis had not seen before. There, mounted on the wall, stood a cannon. A brass twenty-four pounder with a wooden, step-sided carriage and ropes running from rings in the base of the carriage to rings in the wall. The ropes were to keep the gun from rolling down the hill after it fired.

"Come on, Lewis," said Jonathan, smiling. "Let's have a shot at the Armada. Isn't this what you've always wanted to do? It's all loaded and ready to fire. Come on!"

Lewis looked as if he were going to be sick. Tears came to his eyes. "Oh, no, Uncle Jonathan! I couldn't! The poor Duke and his men. Can't we do something for them?"

Jonathan stared at Lewis and rubbed his chin. "You know," he said slowly, "for a boy who loves to play at sieges and war, you are remarkably peaceable. When confronted with the real thing, that is. Fortunately for you, however, this isn't the real thing. It's an illusion, as I may have said before. We're really still in Mrs. Zimmermann's dining room with the table at one end and the purple fire at the other. If you go feel that rock there, it will feel remarkably like an armchair. The Duke and his ships out there are less real than smoke and mist, and so is that cannon. Go on. Have a shot."

Lewis brightened up now. This would be fun. A soldier appeared out of nowhere, dressed in the red costume of an English Beefeater. He handed Lewis a smoldering wick on a long rod. Lewis applied it to the touchhole of the cannon. *Boom!* The cannon jerked back against its ropes. Bitter smoke drifted past. Jonathan, who was fighting with Mrs. Zimmermann for the use of the pay telescope, said, "I think that—oh, g'wan, Florence, find your own peephole—I think . . . yes, you have brought down his fore-topgallant spritsail."

Lewis felt pleased, though he didn't know what a fore-topgallant spritsail was. The soldier reloaded, and Lewis fired again. This time he knocked a wooden bishop off the heavily ornamented poop deck. He fired several more times, and then Jonathan gestured, and another Beefeater came running up the hill carrying a wooden bucket full of sizzling, red-hot cannon balls, or "hot potatoes," as the Elizabethan sailors used to call them.

The two soldiers loaded the cannon. First they poured in a kegful of powder. Then they stuffed in wet wadding to keep the cannon ball from setting off the powder. Then came the cannon ball itself. It hissed and steamed when it touched the wadding. Lewis applied the linstock again, and the gun leaped backwards. He watched the cannon ball as it whizzed toward the Duke's galleon. It looked to him like a tiny insane harvest moon. When the ball hit, the ship burst into flames. The weepy-bearded Duke sailed up toward heaven, playing a harp and sitting on a powdered doughnut. And now Lewis, Jonathan, and Mrs. Zimmermann were back in the dining room by the fire.

"Well!" said Jonathan, rubbing his hands. "And what would you like to see next?"

Lewis thought a bit. He was so excited and happy that he had almost forgotten about what he had to do later that night. "I'd like to see the Battle of Waterloo," he said.

Jonathan waved his pipe and the lights went out again. Now they were standing on a muddy hillside in Belgium. The year was 1815. It was raining, a steady smoking drizzle that half hid the high hill opposite the one they were standing on. In the valley below were little red squares. As they watched, blue arrows crashed into these squares, dented them, turned them into parallelograms, trapezoids, and rhombuses, but did not break them. Little puffs of smoke sprang out on the opposite hillside. They reminded Lewis of mushrooms. Behind him he saw geysers of dirt and chipped rock fly up.

"Napoleon's artillery," said Jonathan calmly. More mushrooms sprang up on their hillside as Wellington answered with his own cannons. Rockets exploded overhead, green and blue and sizzling white, and, of course, lovely purple. Flags rose in the valley, dipped, rose, and fell again. Lewis, Jonathan, and Mrs. Zimmermann watched the whole thing from behind a low wall that looked a great deal like the wall on John O'Groats.

After what seemed like a long time, Lewis became aware of a figure standing off to their right. A tall skinny man in a cocked hat and a black cutaway coat.

Lewis recognized him immediately. It was Wellington. He looked exactly the way he did in John Clark Ridpath's *History of the World*.

Wellington scanned the horizon with his telescope. Then he sadly clicked the telescope shut and took out his watch. The watch, which resembled the one Mrs. Zimmermann wore on a chain, dinged eight times. Wellington rolled his eyes toward the sky, put his hand on his heart, and said gravely, "Oh, that Blücher or night would come!"

"Why did he say that, Uncle Jonathan?" asked Lewis. He had looked at all the illustrations in Ridpath's book, but he had never read the account of the battle.

"Blücher is a Prussian general who is coming to aid Wellington," said Jonathan. "Napoleon has sent Grouchy off to keep Blücher busy."

Lewis giggled. "Why is he called Grouchy?"

"Because that's his name," said Mrs. Zimmermann. "Only it's pronounced Groo-*shee* because it's a French name. Fat Ears here knows that, but he's trying to be funny. Well, Jonathan, do you think Wellington will win this time?"

"Dunno, Florence. Wait and see."

Since it was Jonathan's illusion and not the real battle, and since he was feeling silly that evening, he decided to let Napoleon win for a change. Night fell with a clunk like a book falling out of a bookcase, but Blücher did not come. The blue arrows sliced into the red squares, split them up, tore them to pieces. Now the blue arrows turned into an army marching up the hill, an army of tall men wearing bearskin hats that made them even taller. They had long black moustaches and carried muskets with bayonets on the end. They were coming for Wellington, who now looked very red-faced and crabby. He tore off his hat and stomped on it. He threw his watch on the ground and stomped on it too.

"Ooh-*waah!*" he screamed. "Greenwich Mean Time! Very mean time! I want to go home *now!*"

Whereupon the scene changed, and Lewis and Uncle Jonathan and Mrs. Zimmermann were back in the dark shadowy dining room by the warm fire. The purple china clock on the mantel whanged tinnily eleven times. The whole show had taken only an hour.

Jonathan got up, stretched, yawned, and suggested that they all go to bed. Lewis thanked Mrs. Zimmermann for the wonderful party and went home with Jonathan. He went upstairs to bed, but he did not sleep.

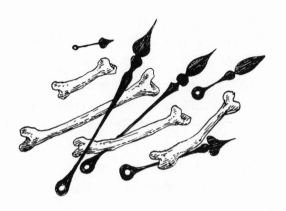

CHAPTER FIVE

As the luminous hands of his new Westclox bedside clock crept around toward midnight, Lewis lay, fully dressed, under his covers. The room was dark. His heart was pounding, and he kept saying over and over to himself, "I wish I didn't have to do it. I wish I didn't have to do it."

He felt in his pants' pocket for the piece of paper with the magic circle copied on it. There was a fat piece of yellow chalk in his other pocket. What if Uncle Jonathan came to his room to see if he were all right? He'd just have to pull the covers up to his chin and pretend that he was asleep. *Tick-tick-tick-tick.* Lewis wished that it was next week, and that he had never made his stupid promise to Tarby. He closed his eyes and stared at the patterns that formed on the insides of his eyelids.

Minutes passed. Suddenly Lewis sat up. He threw back the covers and stared at the clock. It was five minutes after twelve! He had promised to meet Tarby in the cemetery at midnight, and now he was going to be late! What could he do? Tarby wouldn't wait for him. He would go home, and tomorrow he would tell all his friends how Lewis had chickened out.

Lewis rubbed his face and tried to think. The cemetery stood atop a long ridge that rose just on the other side of Wilder Creek Park. You had to walk half a mile beyond the city limits to get to the road that ran up the ridge. There was a short cut, of course, but Lewis hadn't intended to take it. Now he had no choice.

Slowly, carefully, Lewis eased himself down onto the floor. He knelt down and groped under the bed for his flashlight. It was a long, old-fashioned flashlight with a fluted handle and a big round lamp on the end. The metal felt cold and slimy in his hand. He went to the closet and put on his heavy jacket. It would be cold up on Cemetery Hill.

Lewis opened the bedroom door. The hall was dark, as usual, and from the next room he could hear Uncle Jonathan snoring. Lewis felt awful. It was like being sick to your stomach. He wished with all his heart that he could run into Jonathan's room, wake him up, and tell him all about the adventure he was going on, and why he had to go through with it. But he didn't do any of these things. Instead, he tiptoed across the hall and opened the door that led to the back stairs.

It didn't take long for Lewis to get to the other side of town. When he had reached the CITY LIMITS sign, he poked around by the side of the road until he found a little wooden staircase that ran down the gravel bank to Wilder Creek Park. The creek was fairly shallow at this point, so Lewis waded across. The water was freezing on his ankles. When he got to the other side he looked up. His hands felt sweaty, and he almost turned around and went home.

He was looking at Cemetery Hill. It was a high, flat-topped ridge cut across in two places by a narrow dirt road. It wasn't a hard hill to climb: New Zebedee children went up and down it every day during the summer. But to Lewis, who was scared of heights, it might as well have been Mount Everest.

Lewis looked up at the dark hill, and he swallowed a couple of times. Maybe if he took the long way around . . . no, he was already late, and Tarby might get bored and go home. The last thing Lewis wanted was to be in the cemetery alone at this time of night. He got a tight grip on his flashlight and started to climb.

At the first landing, Lewis stopped. He was breathing hard, and the front of his jacket was soaked through.

There were black smudges on the knees of his trousers, and there was a twig in his shoe. Two more stages. Lewis gritted his teeth and went on.

At the top of the hill, he dropped to his knees and crossed himself several times. The sweat was running down his face, and he could feel his heart thumping. Well, he had done it. It was no great triumph because Tarby had probably scaled the ridge in a tenth of the time it had taken him. But at least he had done it.

Lewis looked around. He was standing at the edge of a long avenue lined with willow trees. The bare strings of the willows swayed in the wind, and Lewis shivered. He felt very cold and very alone. At the far end of the avenue, the gray gate of the cemetery glimmered. Lewis started to walk toward it.

The cemetery gate was a heavy arch of stone covered with elaborate carving. On the lintel were inscribed these words:

THE TRUMPET SHALL SOUND

AND

THE DEAD SHALL BE RAISED

Lewis pushed open the squeaky iron gate and walked quickly past the rows of white headstones. The mausoleum was on the other side of Cemetery Hill, the side that looked out across the deep valley beyond the town. A little narrow path led down to the stone platform in front of the tomb door. Where was Tarby?

/ *84* /

As Lewis looked around, someone said, "Boo!" Lewis almost fainted. It was Tarby, of course, hiding in the shadow of the stone arch on the front of the mausoleum.

"Hi! You sure took long enough," said Tarby. "Where were you?"

"It was hard work climbing," said Lewis, staring sadly down at his wet and dirty trousers.

"It's always hard climbing for fatsoes," said Tarby. "Whyncha lose some weight?"

"Come on, let's do what we're supposed to be doing," said Lewis. He felt depressed.

The cracked and mossy stone slab that lay at the doorstep of the tomb was in the shadow of the hillside now. Everything around it lay in bright moonlight. Lewis turned on the flashlight and played the pale beam over the ugly iron doors. A heavy chain held the doors together, and it was fastened by a large, heart-shaped padlock. Lewis flashed the beam up. There was the strange-looking O on the cornice. The wind had died down. Everything was quiet. Lewis handed the flashlight to Tarby and knelt down. Out came the scrap of paper and the chalk. He drew a big circle and then a smaller one within it, like this:

As Tarby held the flashlight steady, Lewis filled in the border of the magic circle with symbols from the piece of paper. When he had chalked in the last strange sign, there was still a blank space in the border. Lewis had read in Jonathan's book that you were supposed to fill in the space with the name of the dead person. But he didn't know the name.

"Well," said Tarby, "I don't see any dead people."

"It's not finished," said Lewis. "We've got to put in the name."

Tarby looked disgusted. "You mean you don't know it?"

"No, I don't," sighed Lewis. "Maybe if we sit here for a minute or two it will come to us."

They knelt silently at the door of the tomb. A sudden gust of wind rattled the dead leaves on an oak tree that grew nearby. Minutes passed. Lewis's mind was completely blank. Then, for some reason, he picked up the chalk.

"Hold the flashlight down here," he said.

Slowly, carefully, he spelled out a name. The funny thing was that he was not thinking of a name at all. It was as if someone else was guiding his hand. With one last down-stroke of the chalk he completed the word: *Selenna*. It was a strangè name. Lewis had never known anyone called Selenna. He didn't even know how to pronounce the name. But there it was.

He stood up with the creased paper in his hand. Now

he started to chant in a high-pitched nervous voice: *Aba bēbē bachabē* . . .

He stopped. Tarby, who was crouched beside him, grabbed his arm and squeezed it hard. From deep within the tomb came a sound. *Boom!* A deep hollow sound. The iron doors jolted, as if they had been struck a blow from inside. The chain rattled, and there was a *clunk* on the pavement. The padlock had fallen off. And now, as the boys knelt, terrified, two small spots of freezing gray light appeared. They hovered and danced before the doors of the tomb, which now stood ajar. And something black—blacker than the night, blacker than ink spilled into water—was oozing from the space between the doors.

Tarby shook Lewis and squeezed his arm harder. "Run!" he shouted.

They tumbled over the bank and started to scramble down the hillside. Part of the way Lewis slid on his belly, with roots scratching at his face. He clawed at the wet slippery grass, but he could not get a handhold. Then he was tumbling over and over, and then he was sliding on his back. Rocks scraped his shoulder blades and bumped the back of his head. And then he was sitting on the dirt road, thoroughly shaken and sick and scared.

The moon drifted out from behind a thin veil of clouds and stared down at Lewis as if it were scared too. Tarby was sprawled near him in a weedy ditch. He got up quickly and stared back up the hillside. Now he was tugging at Lewis's arm. "Come on! We've got to get out

of here! It might come after us! Oh, come on! Please come on!"

Lewis was dazed and shaken, but he got up and followed Tarby over the next stage of the hillside, and the next one. They waded across the stream and were soon on the gravel road that led back to New Zebedee.

As they walked along, Lewis kept stopping and shuddering. Tarby told him to quit it.

"I can't help it," said Lewis in a sick voice. "Did you see it? It was awful!"

"I don't know what I saw," said Tarby sullenly. "Maybe it was the moonlight or something."

Lewis stared at him. Was Tarby kidding, or was he trying to deny to himself that he had seen what he really had seen? Lewis didn't know, and he didn't care. All he knew was that he was terribly frightened.

Lewis sneaked back into the house a little before three A.M. He tiptoed up the back stairs, checked to make sure that his uncle was asleep—he was—and quietly opened the door of his own room. Just as quietly, he shut it behind him. Then he slowly began to strip off his wet and dirty clothes, which he wadded up and threw into a dark corner of his closet. Where was his flashlight? Tarby must have taken it. He would get it back from him later. As for the clothes, he could get them cleaned without Jonathan knowing about it.

Lewis went to bed. He tried to sleep, but all he could see when he closed his eyes were those two burning circles of light. Finally he did drift off, but he had a strange dream. Clock hands and skeleton bones were chasing him around and around a high stone tomb. Lewis awoke with a start and, for a moment, it seemed that his room, and the whole house, was filled with a loud ticking noise.

CHAPTER SIX

The next morning, when Lewis came down to breakfast, Uncle Jonathan was reading an article on the front page of the New Zebedee *Chronicle*. Curious, Lewis leaned over his shoulder and this is what he read:

TOMB DESECRATED BY VANDALS

Answers Sought to Senseless Act

Last night vandals broke into the Old Izard mausoleum in Oakridge Cemetery. The doors of the tomb were found standing ajar, with the padlock lying shattered on the pavement. This incident has sadly marred what was

otherwise a Halloween remarkably free from
incidents of vandalism and wanton destruc-
tiveness. What these human ghouls hoped to
attain lies mercifully beyond conjecture, but
it may be hoped . . .

"Morning, Lewis," said Jonathan, without looking up.
"Did you sleep well?"

Lewis turned pale. Did Jonathan know?

Mrs. Zimmermann was sitting across the table, munching her Cheerios. "Does it say whether they disturbed the
coffins?" she asked.

"No, it doesn't," said Jonathan. "The caretaker probably just shoved the doors shut and fastened them with a
new padlock. I don't blame him. I wouldn't want to look
inside old Isaac Izard's tomb."

Lewis sat down. There were too many things whirling
around in his head, and he was trying to get them
straightened out.

"I . . . I was up in the cemetery with Tarby a couple
of times, Uncle Jonathan," he said cautiously, "but I
didn't see any tomb with 'Izard' on it."

"Oh, well, he didn't want his name on the tomb. When
he had it fixed up for his wife's body, he brought in a
stonecutter who chiseled off the family name and carved
an omega."

"An omega?" said Lewis. "What's that?"

"It's the last letter of the Greek alphabet, and it's used
a lot by wizards. It looks like an *O*, except that it's open

at the bottom. It is the sign of the Last Judgment—the End of the World."

Lewis sat there staring at the little *O*'s floating in his bowl. He forced himself to eat a few of them.

"How come he wanted something like that on his tomb?" asked Lewis. He was trying to conceal the tremble in his voice.

"Lord knows, Lewis," said Jonathan. "Say, you're not scared about this tomb-breaking business, are you? Old Isaac Izard's dead and gone. He's not going to bother us."

Lewis looked at Jonathan. Then he looked at Mrs. Zimmermann. He knew, as well as he knew anything, that they couldn't wait for him to go off to school so they could discuss the matter alone. So he finished his breakfast, mumbled goodby to them both, grabbed up his books, and left.

Jonathan and Mrs. Zimmermann did indeed want to discuss the break-in alone. Any tampering with the tomb of two powerful wizards like Isaac and Selenna Izard was a matter for serious discussion, and they didn't want to frighten Lewis with their talk. But they had no idea of what Lewis had done. Jonathan was not in the habit of peering in at the sleeping form of his nephew during the night, so he had no idea that Lewis had been out of the house. Of course, he and Mrs. Zimmermann had been concerned for some time about Lewis's strange behavior. But they did not connect it with what had happened on Halloween night.

After their discussion—which came to no conclusions at all, except that there was dirty work afoot—Jonathan and Mrs. Zimmermann decided that it would be nice to take Lewis on an evening ride around Capharnaum County. They knew he loved to ride, and since they hadn't taken him out in some time, they thought that maybe an excursion would shake some of the gloom out of his system.

But when Lewis came home from school that day, he was depressed and worried. He had been thinking about the tomb business all day long. So, when Jonathan pushed back his chair after dinner and asked Lewis if he'd like to go for a nice long ride, Lewis merely shrugged his shoulders and said, "Yeah, I guess I'd like to go" in a dying-cat sort of voice.

Jonathan stared at Lewis for a minute, but he said nothing. He merely got up and went to get his car keys. Soon all three of them—Jonathan, Mrs. Zimmermann, and Lewis—were crammed into the front seat of Jonathan's 1935 Muggins Simoon, a big black car with running boards and a windshield that could be cranked open. The car, spewing clouds of bluish smoke, backed down the rutted driveway and into the street.

They drove for hours, as the afterglow of sunset stayed and stayed, and the hollows filled with purple mist. They drove past barns with big blue signs on their sides that said: CHEW MAIL POUCH. They drove past green John Deere tractors parked in deep muddy ruts. Up

hill and down hill they drove, over bumpy railroad cross-
ings with X-shaped signs that said: RAIL-SING CROS-ROAD
if you read them the wrong way, through little towns
that were no more than a church, a food store with a gas
pump outside, and a flagpole on a triangle of green grass
where the roads met. By the time it got dark, they were
miles from New Zebedee.

They were on their way home when—for no reason
that Lewis could see—Jonathan stopped the car. He
turned off the motor and sat there staring at the row of
green dashboard lights.

"What's wrong, Uncle Jonathan?" asked Lewis.

"I keep imagining that I hear a car somewhere," said
Jonathan. "Do you hear it, Florence?"

"Yes, I do," said Mrs. Zimmermann, giving him a puzzled look. "But what's so odd about that? They do let
people drive these roads at night, you know."

"Do they?" said Jonathan in a strange voice. He
opened the car door and stepped out onto the gravel.
"Stay here," he said to them. He walked up the road a
little ways and stood there, listening. Even with the car
door open, Lewis could hear nothing but the wind in
the roadside trees and the clattering of a tin sign on a
barbed-wire fence. The car was parked near the top of a
high hill, and now Lewis could see headlights rising out
of a gully and then dipping into the next one.

Jonathan came running back to the car. He slammed
the door and started the motor. With a squealing of tires,

he turned the car around and headed back the way they had come.

Lewis was frightened. "What's wrong, Uncle Jonathan?" he asked.

"Ask me later, Lewis. Florence, what's the best way—other way—back to New Zebedee?"

"Take the next side road to your right. That's Twelve Mile Road, and it runs into the Wilder Creek Road. And step on it. They're gaining."

Many times, when he had been out riding with his father and mother, Lewis had pretended that they were being followed by some car or other. It was a good game to pass the time on long dull evening rides, and he remembered how he had always felt disappointed when the mystery car turned away into a side street or a driveway. But tonight the game was for real.

Around sharp curves they went, lurching dangerously far over and squealing the tires. Up hills, down hills, then seventy or eighty miles an hour on the straightaway, which was never straight for long on these winding country roads. Lewis had never seen Jonathan drive so fast, or so recklessly. But no matter how fast he drove, the two cold circles of light still burned in his rear-view mirror.

Both Mrs. Zimmermann and Uncle Jonathan seemed to know who or what was in the car behind them—or at least they seemed to know that it was someone that had the power to do them harm. But they said as little as possible, except to confer now and then about directions. So Lewis just sat there, trying to feel comforted by the green dashboard lights and the warm breath of the heater on his knees. Of course, he also felt comforted by the two wizards, whose warm friendly bodies pressed against his in the furry darkness. But he knew that they were scared, and this made him twice as scared.

What was after them? Why didn't Uncle Jonathan or Mrs. Zimmermann just wave an arm and turn the evil car into a wad of smoldering tinfoil? Lewis stared up at the reflected headlights, and he thought of what he had seen in the cemetery, and of what Uncle Jonathan had told him about Mrs. Izard's eyeglasses. He was beginning to have a theory about how all these things fitted together.

The car raced on, spitting stones from under its tires. Down into hollows bordered by dark skeletal trees, up over high hills, on and on while the setting moon seemed to race to keep up with them. They covered a large part of Capharnaum County that night, because the way around was a long way. After what seemed like hours of driving, they came to a place where three roads met. As the car screeched around the turn, Lewis saw—for a few seconds—a Civil War cannon white with frost, a wooden church with smeary stained-glass windows, and a general store with a dark glimmering window that said: SALADA.

"We're on the Wilder Creek Road now, Lewis," said

Mrs. Zimmermann as she put her arm around him. "It won't be long now. Don't be afraid."

The car raced on. Dead roadside stalks bent in its hot wind, and overhanging branches whipped along the metal roof. The burning white holes danced in the mirror as before, and it looked like they were getting closer. They had never, since the start of the chase, been more than two or three car lengths away.

Jonathan shoved the accelerator to the floor. The needle moved up to eighty, which was dangerous, to say the least, on these roads. But the greater danger was behind, so Jonathan took the big roundhouse curves as well as he could, and the tires screeched, and the fenders almost touched the crumbling asphalt at the side of the road. This was blacktop, and you could go faster on it than you could on loose gravel.

At last they came to the top of a high hill and, there below them, glimmering peacefully in the starlight—the moon had gone down some time ago—was Wilder Creek. There was the bridge, a maze of crisscrossing black girders. Down the hill they barrelled, faster and faster. The car behind followed, just as fast. They were almost to the bridge when the lights in the rear-view mirror did something headlights had never done before. They grew and brightened till the reflection was a blinding bar of white light. Lewis clapped his hands to his eyes. Had he been struck blind? Had Jonathan been blinded too? Would the car crash, or . . .

Suddenly Lewis heard the rolling clatter of the bridge boards under the car. He took his hands away from his face. He could see. Jonathan was smiling and putting on the brakes. Mrs. Zimmermann heaved a deep sigh of relief. They were across the bridge.

As Jonathan opened the door to get out, Lewis twisted around in his seat and saw that the other car had stopped just before it got to the bridge. Its headlights were dark now, except for two smoldering yellow pinpoints. Lewis could not tell if there was anyone in the car, because the windshield was covered by a blank silvery sheen.

Jonathan stood there, his hands on his hips, watching. He did not seem to be afraid of the other car now. Slowly the mysterious car turned around and drove away. When Jonathan got back to the Muggins Simoon he was chuckling.

"It's all over, Lewis. Relax. Witches and other evil things can't cross running water. It's an old rule, but it still applies."

"You might throw in the fact," said Mrs. Zimmermann in her most pedantic tone, "that Elihu Clabbernong built that iron bridge in 1892. He was supposed to be doing it for the county, but he was really trying to make sure that the ghost of his dead uncle, Jedediah, didn't cross the stream to get him. Now Elihu was a part-time warlock, and what he put into the iron of the bridge . . ."

"Oh, good heavens!" cried Jonathan, covering his ears.

"Are you going to go through the whole history of Capharnaum County at four A.M.?"

"Is it *that* late?" asked Lewis.

"That late or later," said Jonathan wearily. "It's been quite a ride."

They drove on toward New Zebedee. On the way they stopped at an all-night diner and had a large breakfast of waffles, eggs, American fries, sausage, coffee, and milk. Then they sat around for a long time talking about the narrow escape they had just had. Lewis asked a lot of questions, but he didn't get many answers.

When they got back to New Zebedee, it was dawn. Dawn of an overcast November day. The town and its hills appeared to be swimming in a gray grainy murk. When Jonathan pulled up in front of his house he said, "There's something wrong, Florence. Stay in the car with Lewis."

"Oh, dear!" she cried, wrinkling up her mouth. "What more can happen?"

Jonathan swung back the iron gate and marched up the walk. From where he was sitting, Lewis could see that the front door was open. This could easily be explained, since people in New Zebedee never locked their doors, and sometimes the latches didn't hold when they closed them. Jonathan disappeared into the house, and he didn't come back for ten full minutes. When he did reappear, he looked worried.

"Come on, Florence," he said, opening the door on her side. "It's safe to go in, I think. But the house has been broken into."

Lewis burst into tears. "They didn't steal your water-pipe, did they? Or the Bon-Sour coins?"

Jonathan smiled weakly. "No, Lewis, I'm afraid it's not as simple as all that. Someone was looking for something, and I think they found it. Come on in."

Lewis expected to find the house in wild disorder, with chairs and lamps smashed and things all scattered around. But when he got to the front hall, he found everything in order. At least, that's the way it looked. Jonathan tapped him on the shoulder and pointed toward the ceiling. "Look up there," he said.

Lewis gasped. The brass cup that covered the place where the ceiling fixture met the ceiling had been pried loose. It dangled halfway down the chain.

"It's like that all over the house," said Jonathan. "Every wall sconce and ceiling light has had its cup jimmied loose. A few chairs were overturned and a couple of vases were broken, just to make it look like this was an ordinary break-in. But we ought not to be fooled. Whoever it was had a general idea of where to look. Come here."

Jonathan led Lewis and Mrs. Zimmermann into the front parlor, a more or less unused room full of fussy little red-velvet chairs and settees. On the wall over the parlor organ was a brass light fixture like all the others in the house: a tarnished cup-shaped thing fitted to the wall, and a crooked little brass tube sticking out of it. On the end of the tube was a socket and a bulb with a frilly pink shade.

"I thought you said the cup was loose," said Lewis.

"It was. It is," said Jonathan. "In this case Whosis tried to fit it back just the way it was, which was kind of stupid, seeing as how all the other cups in the house are at half mast. Some of them are slid all the way down to the socket. But I think Whosis was trying, in a clumsy way, to keep me from looking too closely at this one."

Jonathan pulled over a chair and stood up on it. He slid the cup out and peered inside. Then he got down and went to the cellarway for a flashlight. When he got back, Mrs. Zimmermann and Lewis had taken turns looking into the cup. They both were puzzled. What they saw inside the dusty bowl was a greenish rust blot. It reminded Lewis of the stuff in the cracks and crevices of the copper Roman coins they played poker with. It was the mark of something that had lain concealed inside the old brass cup for a long, long time. The mark looked like this:

"It looks like a clock key," said Lewis in a weak, throaty voice.

"Yes, it does," said Jonathan. He played the light around inside the cup and squinted hard.

"Uncle Jonathan, what does all this mean?" Lewis sounded as if he were about to burst into tears.

"I wish I knew," said Jonathan. "I really wish I knew."

CHAPTER SEVEN

It rained a lot in New Zebedee that November. Cold rain fell steadily through each night and left the sidewalk a glaze of ice in the morning. Lewis sat in his window seat and watched the rain peck at the chipped slates of the front porch roof. He felt sick inside. It was an empty, black feeling in the pit of his stomach. He was eaten up with guilt and remorse because he knew what he had done—or thought he knew, at any rate. He had let Mrs. Izard out of her tomb, and now she had stolen the key. The key that wound up the magic clock ticking in the walls of Jonathan's house, ticking away morning, noon, and night; sometimes loud, sometimes soft, but always there.

What was going to happen? How could anyone stop her? Had she used the key? What would happen if she did? Lewis had no answers for any of these questions.

It might have helped if he had been able to talk the whole matter over with Jonathan, but then he would have had to admit what he had done. And Lewis was afraid to do that. It was not that Uncle Jonathan was such a hard man to talk to. He was easier to talk to than most people Lewis knew, easier by far than Lewis's own father had ever been. Then, why was Lewis afraid?

Well, he was afraid because he was afraid. Maybe it was because his mother had once threatened to send him to the Detention Home when he was bad. The Detention Home was a big white house on the outskirts of the town that Lewis and his parents had lived in. It stood on a high hill and had bars and chicken wire over the windows. Bad boys and girls were sent there—at least, that's what everyone said. Lewis had never known anyone who had actually gotten sent there. Of course, Lewis's mother would never have sent him there for being bad. Not really. But Lewis didn't know that, and now when Lewis thought of telling his uncle about Halloween night, he thought of the Detention Home, and he was afraid. It wasn't a reasonable fear, considering the kind of man Jonathan was. But Lewis had not known him for very long, and anyway, people are not always so reasonable.

And there was another thing that added to Lewis's despair. He had lost Tarby. He had lost him in spite of all his sneaking and planning—or maybe he had lost him because of it. It was one thing to say that you could raise the dead, but when you did it—well, ordinary people have never cared much for the company of wizards. Tarby was afraid of Lewis now, or else he was enjoying himself with the other boys, the boys who could hit home runs and catch fly balls. Whichever way it was, Lewis had not seen Tarby since Halloween night.

The month wore on, the rain kept falling, and nothing mysterious or evil happened. Until one day—the third of December it was—when the Hanchetts moved out.

The Hanchetts lived across the street from Uncle Jonathan in a boxy, dark-brown house with tiny windows, the kind of windows that have little diamond-shaped panes and swing out instead of sliding up and down. The Hanchetts were a friendly, middle-aged couple, and they liked Jonathan and Mrs. Zimmermann a lot, but one morning they were gone. A couple of days after their disappearance a truck came and a couple of movers in gray uniforms packed all the Hanchetts' furniture into it, and drove off. A real-estate man came around and hung a big red and white sign on their front door. The sign said:

HI THERE!

I'M FOR SALE

Call Bishop Barlow Realtors

Phone: 865

Bishop Barlow was not a real bishop. Bishop was just his first name. Lewis knew the man: he was a fat loud-mouth who wore sunglasses all the time, even on rainy days. He smoked cheap smelly cigars and wore sports coats that looked like awnings.

Jonathan seemed really upset at the departure of the Hanchetts. He phoned their son, who was a lawyer in Osee Five Hills, and he found out that the Hanchetts were living with him. The frightened couple would not talk to Jonathan over the phone, and they seemed to blame him for whatever had made them leave. The son did not seem to know much about the matter. He muttered something about ghosts and "messing around with magic" and hung up.

One day Lewis was walking home from school when he saw a small moving van pull up in front of the empty Hanchett house. The big black letters on the side of the van said: TERMINUS MOVERS INC. Lewis was about to cross the street to watch the men unload the truck when he realized, with a shock, that he knew the driver. It was Hammerhandle.

All the children in New Zebedee knew Hammerhandle and, if they were smart, they were afraid of him. He was a mean old hobo who lived in a tar-paper shack down by the railroad tracks, and he had a reputation for being able to foretell the future. Lewis had stood once on the outskirts of a crowd of kids gathered about the door of Hammerhandle's shack on a hot summer day. He remembered seeing Hammerhandle seated in the doorway on a broken kitchen chair. He was telling stories about the World's Last Night, which, if you believed him, was not far off. Behind Hammerhandle, in the disorder and darkness of the old shack, stood ranks of smooth yellow poles: ax handles, hoe handles, hammer handles. He made them and sold them. That was how he got his name.

Lewis stood there wondering what he was doing driving a moving van. Hammerhandle slammed the door on the driver's side and walked across the street. He looked around him quickly and then grabbed Lewis by the collar. His bristly face was close to Lewis's now, and his breath smelled of whiskey and tobacco.

"What the hell you starin' at, kid?"

"N-nothing. I-I just like to watch people moving in." It was getting dark, and Lewis wondered if anyone could see him. If he yelled, would Jonathan or Mrs. Zimmermann come?

Hammerhandle let go of Lewis's collar. "Look, kid," he said in his harsh scraping voice, "you just keep yer nose on your side of the fence, okay? An' that goes f'ya fat uncle too. Just don't bother me, okay?" He glared at Lewis, turned, and went back to the truck.

Lewis stood there trembling for a few moments. He was sweating all over. Then he turned and ran in through the open gate, up the walk, and into the house.

"Uncle Jonathan! Uncle Jonathan!" he shouted. He

yanked open the doors of the study and looked. No Jonathan. He shouted into the front parlor and into the kitchen and up the stairwell. At last Uncle Jonathan appeared at the top of the stairs. He was wearing his bathrobe, which was made in the shape of the robes professors wear at graduation ceremonies, black with red stripes on the sleeves. In one hand he held a dripping, long-handled scrub brush. In the other, he held the book he had been reading in the tub.

"Yes, Lewis? What is it?" He sounded cross at first, but when he saw the state that Lewis was in, he dropped the book and the brush and clumped down the stairs to throw his arms around the boy. It was a damp embrace, but it felt good to Lewis.

"Lewis, my boy!" said Jonathan, kneeling in front of him. "What in the name of heaven is wrong? You look awful!"

Lewis, stuttering and breaking down several times, told Jonathan what had happened. When he was through, he watched Jonathan's expression change. There was a hard, angry look on his face now, but his anger was not directed at Lewis. He stood up, knotted his bathrobe tighter about him, and stalked to the front door. For a minute Lewis thought that Jonathan was going out to challenge Hammerhandle right then and there. But he merely opened the front door and stared across at the Hanchett house. The workmen were just hitching up the tail gate and getting ready to drive off. Apparently there hadn't been much to unload.

With folded arms Jonathan watched the truck drive away. "I might have known he'd be in on it," he said bitterly. Lewis stared up at his uncle. He didn't have the faintest idea of what was going on, and for some reason he was afraid to ask what Jonathan meant.

That evening at supper, Lewis asked Jonathan why Hammerhandle had acted so mean. Jonathan threw down his fork and said angrily, "Because he's mean, that's why! Do you have to have explanations? Just stay away from him and you'll be all right. And stay away . . . stay away . . . oh, I don't know what I mean!" He got up and stomped out of the room. Lewis heard the study doors slam.

Mrs. Zimmermann reached across the table and laid her hand gently on Lewis's. "Don't worry, Lewis," she said. "He's not angry at you. But he does have a lot on his mind these days, and he hasn't been getting much sleep. Come on over to my house and we'll have a game of chess."

"Okay." Lewis was grateful for the suggestion.

They played chess till ten o'clock at night and, since Lewis won most of the games, he was in a happy mood when he went home. Upstairs he saw a line of light under the door of Jonathan's bedroom. He decided not to disturb him. When he had gotten ready for bed, Lewis

went to his window seat, sat down, and pulled back the heavy curtain.

It was a bright, cold, starry night. The water tower at the top of the hill glimmered in the moonlight, and the roofs of the houses were dark pointed shadows. There were lights on in the houses that stood on either side of the Hanchett house and, in one window, Lewis saw the gray aquarium-glow of one of those new television sets. Jonathan hadn't gotten one yet. The Hanchett house seemed to lie in deep shadow, except for faint patches of moonlight on the roof. By the light of a street lamp, Lewis could see that there was a car parked in the driveway.

He was about to close the curtain and go to bed when the porch light of the Hanchett house came on. The two frosted panes of the front door glowed yellow. Then one of the panels of the door moved inward. Someone stepped out onto the front stoop. Lewis watched as who-ever-it-was stood there, just stood there, taking in the frosty air of the December night. He thought he caught the faint glitter of spectacles, but he couldn't be sure at this distance.

After a little while, the dark figure went inside and pushed the door shut. The hall light went out. Lewis sat there for a while thinking, then he lowered the curtain and went to bed.

CHAPTER EIGHT

The next day Jonathan was helping Lewis rummage in the front hall closet for his ice skates. Lewis had weak ankles, and he was terrified of falling down on the ice, but he had decided to try to learn to skate. If he got good enough he might be able to worm his way back into Tarby's favor. He had never seen Tarby ice skate, but he was sure that the team's greatest home-run hitter was also the champion ice skater of New Zebedee. He probably could sign his name across the ice of Durgy's Pond.

So Lewis and Jonathan threw warped badminton rackets, raccoon coats, galoshes, and picnic baskets into the hall. Finally Jonathan came up with what looked like a short aluminum ski for a midget. It was a beginner's skate, with two little ridges for runners.

"This it?"

"That's one of them. Thanks a lot, Uncle Jonathan. Now all we need is the other."

As they went on searching Lewis said, in what he thought was a casual way, "Who's living in the old Hanchett house?"

Jonathan stood up suddenly in the closet and banged his head on a shelf. When he had stopped rubbing his head and wincing, he looked down at Lewis and said, rather sharply, "Why do you want to know?"

"I just wanted to know," said Lewis shyly. Once again, he wondered what his uncle was angry about.

Jonathan stepped out of the closet with the other skate. He dropped it into a pile of clothes.

"So you just wanted to know, eh? Well, Lewis, there are some things it would be better for you *not* to know. So if you'll take my advice, you'll just stop poking around where you're not wanted. There's your other skate and . . . and good day. I have work to do in the study, and I've already wasted enough time answering your foolish questions."

Jonathan got up abruptly and stalked off to the study. He had slid back the doors with a loud clatter when he paused and went back to the closet, where Lewis was still kneeling with tears in his eyes.

"Please forgive me, Lewis," said Jonathan in a tired

voice. "I've been feeling really rotten lately. Too many cigars, I guess. As for the house across the street, I hear that it's been rented to an old lady named Mrs. O'Meagher. She acts kind of crabby—or so I'm told. I really haven't met her, and . . . and I just didn't want anything bad to happen to you." Jonathan smiled nervously and patted Lewis on the shoulder. Then he got up and walked to the door of the study. Again he stopped.

"Don't go over there," he said quickly, and then he stepped inside and slammed the double doors, hard.

Lewis felt crisscrossing lines of mystery and fear and tension hemming him in on all sides. He had never seen his uncle acting like this. And he wondered, more than ever, about the new neighbor across the street.

One night during the week before Christmas, after a heavy snow had fallen, Lewis was awakened by the sound of the doorbell ringing. *Brr-rr-rring! Brr-rr-rring!* It was not an electric bell, but an old, tired mechanical bell set in the middle of the front door. Someone was turning the flat metal key, grinding the stiff old chimes around. *Brr-rr-rring!*

Lewis sat up and looked at his bedside clock. The two luminous hands were straight up. Midnight! Who could it be at this hour? Maybe Uncle Jonathan would go down and answer it. Lewis felt cold just thinking of the drafty front hall. He bundled his quilt about him and shivered.

The bell rang again. It sounded like a whiny person

insisting on some stupid point in an argument. No sound from Jonathan's room. No waking-up sounds, that is. Lewis could hear his uncle's loud, steady snoring even though there was a thick wall between their rooms. Jonathan could sleep through an artillery bombardment.

Lewis got up. He threw back the covers, slipped on his bathrobe, and found his slippers. Quietly, he padded down the hall and then down the dark staircase. At the entrance to the front hall he stopped. There was a street-light burning just outside the front gate, and it threw a bent black shadow against the pleated curtain on the front door. Lewis stood still and watched the shadow. It didn't move. Slowly he began to walk forward. When he reached the door, he closed his fingers around the cold knob and turned it. The door rattled open, and a freezing wind blew in over his bare ankles. There stood his Aunt Mattie, who was dead.

Lewis stepped back as the old woman, her head cocked to one side as it always had been, tottered across the floor toward him. A shaking blue light filled the air around her, and Lewis, his eyes wide open in this nightmare, saw Aunt Mattie as she had been the last time he had seen her alive. Her dress was black and wrinkled, she wore heavy shoes with thick heels, and she tapped her bunchy, black umbrella as she went. Lewis even thought he smelled kerosene—her house, her furniture, and her cloth-ing had always reeked of it. The white fungus blotch that was her face shook and glowed as she said, in a horribly familiar voice, "Well, Lewis? Aren't you glad to see me?"

Lewis fainted. When he awoke, he was lying on his back in the cold hallway. The shaking blue light was gone. So was Aunt Mattie, though the front door was open. Skitters of snow blew in over the worn threshold, and the street lamp burned quiet and cold across the street. Had it all been a sleepwalker's dream?

Lewis didn't think so. He had never been a sleepwalker before. He stood there thinking for a minute, and then, for some reason, he shuffled out onto the front porch and started to pick his way down the snow-covered steps. His feet were so cold that they stung, but he kept going until he was halfway down the walk. Then he turned and looked at the house. He gasped. There were strange lights playing over the blank windows and the rough sandstone walls. They wouldn't have been strange lights at midday in the summer, but on a December night they were eerie. For they were leaf-lights, the shifting circles and crescents cast by sunlight falling through leaves.

Lewis stood and stared for several minutes. Then the lights faded, and he was alone in the dark, snow-covered yard. The chestnut tree dropped a light dusting of snow on his head, shaking him out of his trance. His feet were numb and tingling, and he felt, for the first time, the cold wind whipping through his thin pajamas and his half-open cotton bathrobe. Shuddering, Lewis stumbled back up the walk.

When he got to his room, he sat down on the edge of his bed. He knew he wasn't going back to sleep. There were the makings of a fire in his fireplace, and he knew where the cocoa was kept. A few minutes later Lewis was sitting by a warm, cheerful fire that cast cozy shadows over the black marble of his own personal fireplace. He sipped steaming cocoa from a heavy earthenware mug and tried to think pleasant thoughts. None came to him. After an hour of sitting and sipping and brooding, he plugged in the floor lamp, got John L. Stoddard's second lecture on China out of the bookcase, and sat reading by the fire until dawn.

The next morning at breakfast, Lewis saw that Jonathan was red-eyed and nervous acting. Had his sleep been disturbed too? Jonathan had not discussed the break-in or the car chase or the Izard tomb with Lewis, and Lewis was not about to bring up any of these subjects. But he knew that something was bothering Jonathan, and he also knew that, ever since the night of the break-in, Jonathan and Mrs. Zimmermann had been holding midnight conferences. He had heard their voices coming up through the hot-air register, although he had never been able to make out what was being said. He had thought a couple of times of hiding in the secret passageway, but he was afraid of getting caught. A passage that is entered through a china cupboard full of rattling dishes is not as secret as one might wish. And if some secret spring lock snapped shut on him, he would need to scream his way out, and then there would have to be explanations.

Lewis almost wished that something like that would happen, because he was sick of his secret. He was sick of it because it kept him away from Jonathan and Mrs. Zimmermann. He always felt that they were watching him, waiting for him to break down and tell them everything. How much did they know?

Christmas at 100 High Street was both good and bad that year. There was a big tree in the study and the glass balls on it were magic. Sometimes they reflected the room, and sometimes they showed you ancient ruins on unknown planets. Jonathan gave Lewis several magic toys, including a large pink Easter egg—or Christmas egg, if you wish—that was covered with sparkly stuff and what looked like icing, although it couldn't be eaten. When Lewis looked into the egg, he could see any battle in history. Not the battle as it really was, but as he wanted it to be. Though he didn't know it, the egg, like the balls on the tree, was capable of showing him scenes on other planets. But it was not until he was a grown-up man, working as an astronomer at Mount Palomar, that he was able to discover that property of the magic egg.

Jonathan did a lot of other things that Christmas. He put candles in all the windows of the house—electric candles, not real ones, since he liked the electric kind better—and he put strong lamps behind the stained-glass windows, so that they threw marvelous patterns of red and blue and gold and purple on the dark, sparkling snow outside. He invented the Fuse Box Dwarf, a little man who popped out at you from behind the paint cans in the cellarway and screamed, "Dreeb! Dreeb! I am the Fuse Box Dwarf!" Lewis was not scared by the little man, and he felt that those who scream, "Dreeb!" are more to be pitied than censured.

Needless to say, Jonathan put on a very good show with the coat rack mirror, though it had the habit of showing the ruins at Chichen-Itza over and over again. Somehow the mirror managed to pick up radio station WGN on its bevelled edges, so that when Lewis went out the door in the morning, he heard the Dow-Jones averages and livestock reports.

Lewis tried to enjoy himself that Christmas, but it was hard. He kept thinking that Jonathan's magic show was meant to cover up what was happening to the house. What was happening was hard to figure out, but it was strange and terrifying. After the night when Lewis saw— or dreamt he saw—Aunt Mattie, the house seemed stranger than it ever had. Sometimes the air in certain rooms seemed to shimmer as if the house was going to disappear in the next second. Sometimes the stained-glass windows showed dark and terrifying scenes, and sometimes Lewis saw in the corners of rooms those awful sights that nervous people always imagine are lurking just outside the borders of their eyesight. Walking from room to room, even in broad daylight, Lewis forgot what day it was, what he was after, and at times almost forgot who he was. At night he had dreams of wandering through the house back in the 1890's, when everything was varnished and new. Once or twice Lewis woke from such dreams to see lights flickering on his bedroom wall. They were not leaf-lights this time, but rags and patches of orange light, the kind that you see in the corners of an old house at sunset.

These strange things didn't go on all the time, of course; just now and then over the long cold winter of '48–'49. When spring came, Lewis was surprised to see that the hedge in front of the Hanchett house was wildly overgrown. It was a spiraea hedge, and had always had bristly little pink-and-white blossoms. This spring there were no blossoms on the hedge; it had turned into a dark, thorny thicket that completely hid the first floor windows and sent long waving tendrils up to scrape at the zinc gutter troughs. Burdocks and ailanthus trees had grown up overnight near the house; their branches screened the second-story windows.

Lewis still had not seen much of the new neighbor. Once, from a distance, he had caught a glimpse of a dark, huddled figure rattling a key in the front door. And from his window seat, he had seen her passing to and fro on the second floor. But, aside from that, the old woman had kept out of sight. Lewis had figured it would be like that.

She did have visitors though: one visitor. That was

Hammerhandle. Lewis had seen him coming away from Mrs. O'Meagher's back door late one night. And twice, on his way to the movies in the evening, Lewis had literally bumped into Hammerhandle, who was huddling along High Street toward the Hanchett house, his shabby overcoat buttoned up to the neck. Both times Hammerhandle had been carrying packages, odd little bundles wrapped in brown paper and twine. And both times they had collided because Hammerhandle kept looking behind him.

The second time they met this way, Hammerhandle grabbed Lewis by the collar, the way he had before. He pressed his unshaven muzzle to Lewis's ear and growled, "You little snip! You're lookin' to have your throat cut, aren't you?"

Lewis pulled away from him, but he didn't run. He faced Hammerhandle down.

"Get out of here, you rotten old bum. If you ever try to do anything to me, my uncle will fix you."

Hammerhandle laughed, though it sounded more like he was having a choking fit. "Your uncle!" he said, sneering. "Your uncle will get his sooner than he thinks! The End of the World is at hand. Don't you read your Bible like a good boy? There have been signs, and there will be more. Prepare!" And with that, he stumbled on up the hill, clutching his parcel tightly.

The day after this strange meeting was cold and rainy, and Lewis stayed indoors. Jonathan was over at Mrs.

Zimmermann's helping her bottle some prune brandy, so Lewis was alone. He decided to go poke around in the back rooms up on the third floor. The third-floor rooms were generally unused, and Jonathan had shut the heat off in them to save money. But Lewis had found interesting things up there, like boxes full of chessmen and china doorknobs and wall cupboards that you could actually climb up inside of.

Lewis wandered down the drafty hall, opening and closing doors. None of the rooms seemed worth exploring today. But wait. Sure! The room with the parlor organ. He could go play it; that would be fun.

One of the disused parlors on the third floor had a dusty old parlor organ in it. It was one of the few pieces of furniture that was left from the time Isaac Izard had lived in the house. Of course, there was the parlor organ downstairs—the good one—but it was a player organ, and often refused to let Lewis play what he wanted to play. This one up here was wheezy, and in the winter its voice was only a whisper. But you could sometimes get good tunes out of it if you pumped hard.

Lewis opened the door.

The parlor organ was a bulky shadow against one wall. Lewis found the light switch, and the light came on. He wiped some dust off the seat and sat down. What would he play? "Chopsticks," probably, or "From a Wigwam." His repertoire wasn't very large. Lewis pumped the worn treadles, and he heard a hissing and puffing that came from deep inside the machine. He touched the keys, but all he got was a gaspy tubercular sound. Darn.

He sat back and thought. Over the keys was a row of black organ stops with labels that said things like *Vox Humana*, *Salicet*, and *Flute*. Lewis knew that these stops were supposed to change the sound of the organ in various ways, but he had never pulled any of them out. Well, now was the time. He grabbed one of the black tubes and tugged gently. It wouldn't budge. He wiggled the stop and pulled harder. The whole thing came out in his hand.

Lewis sat there staring stupidly at the piece of wood. At first he felt bad about breaking the organ, but then he looked more closely at the stop. The end that had been in the organ was blunt, smooth, and painted black. There was no sign that it had ever been hooked up to anything.

What a cheesy outfit, Lewis thought. I wonder if they're all like that. Let's see. He pulled at another. *Pop!* He pulled them all out. *Pop! Pop! Pop! Pop! Pop! Pop!*

Lewis laughed. He rolled the black tubes back and forth over the keyboard. But then he stopped and thought. He had read a story once where a car had had a dummy dashboard that came out so you could hide things behind it. What if this organ . . . ?

He got up and went downstairs. He went all the way down to the cellarway, where Jonathan kept his tools. He opened the toolbox and took out a screwdriver, a hammer, and a rusty butter knife that Jonathan kept there for prying things open. Then he went back upstairs as fast as he could.

Now Lewis was sitting at the organ again. He scanned the long wooden panel; seven round black holes stared back at him. There were four screws holding the panel to the organ case, and they came out easily. Lewis stuck his fingers into two of the holes and pulled. The panel was stuck. He thought a bit, then he picked up the butter knife and slid it into a crack. *Skreek!* A little eddy of dust rose and tickled his nostrils. He moved the knife along to the right a bit and pried again. *Skreek!* The panel flopped out onto the keyboard. Ah! Now we would see what was what.

Lewis bent over and put his head close to the hole. He could smell a lot of dust, but he couldn't see a thing in there. Darn it, he had forgotten to bring a flashlight! He reached in and felt around. His arm went in all the way up to the armpit. He groped some more. What was this? Paper? He heard a dry crackling sound. Maybe it was money. He grabbed hold of the bundle and drew it out. His heart sank. It was just an old pile of papers.

Lewis sat there staring at them in disgust. So this was the secret treasure of Izard's castle! Some treasure! Well, there might be something interesting in them, like secret formulas. He flipped through the papers. Hmm . . . hmmm. . . . He flipped some more. The light in the room was very weak, and the old paper had turned practically the same shade as the copper-colored ink Isaac Izard had used. He figured the writing must be Isaac Izard's, since the first sheet said:

CLOUD FORMATIONS

AND

OTHER PHENOMENA

Observed from this Window

by

ISAAC IZARD

Hadn't Mrs. Zimmermann said that she had seen old Isaac taking notes on the sky? There were dates here and entries after them. Lewis read a few entries, and his eyes opened wider. He leafed some more.

A spatter of rain hit the window. Lewis jumped. Outside he could see thick masses of blue clouds piled up in the west. Through them ran a jagged red streak. It looked to Lewis like a hungry mouth. As he watched, the mouth opened and a ray of blood-red light shot into the room. It lit up the page he was holding. On the page were scrawled these words:

Doomsday not come yet! I'll draw it nearer by a perspective, or make a CLOCK *that shall set all the world on fire upon an instant.*

Lewis felt very frightened. He gathered the papers together and started to get up. As he did so, he heard a noise. A very faint noise. Something was fluttering around down inside the organ case.

Lewis stumbled backward, knocking over the bench. The papers slid out of his hand and scattered over the floor. What should he do? Run for his life or save the papers? He gritted his teeth and knelt down. As he gathered up the sheets, he said to himself over and over again, "*Quia tu es Deus fortitudo mea . . . quia tu es Deus fortitudo mea.*"

Now he had all the papers again. He was about to dash for the door when he saw something come floating up out of the darkness inside the organ. A moth. A moth with silver-gray wings. They shone like leaves in the moonlight.

Lewis ran to the door. He rattled the knob but he couldn't get it open. Now he could feel the moth in his hair. Lewis went rigid. His face flushed. He was not scared any more. He was angry. Very angry.

He swatted at the moth and crushed it. Lewis felt a horrible runny stickiness in his hair, and all the fear came rushing back. He wiped his hand frantically on his trouser leg. Now Lewis was out in the hall, running and shouting, "Uncle Jonathan! Mrs. Zimmermann! Come quick! Oh, please come quick, I've found something! Uncle Jonathan!"

A little while later Jonathan, Lewis, and Mrs. Zimmermann were sitting around Mrs. Zimmermann's kitchen table drinking cocoa. The dusty papers lay in a heap on

the table. Jonathan put down his mug and said, "No, Lewis. I tell you again. They're nothing to worry about. Old Isaac was crazy—crazy as a coot. This stuff has nothing to do with that ticking noise in the walls. Or if it does, it can't help us any. It can only frighten us."

"I'd say that was why Isaac left those papers there, wouldn't you, Jonathan? To frighten us to death, I mean."

This was Mrs. Zimmermann speaking. She was standing at the stove with her back to Lewis, and she was making a great show of stirring the cocoa.

"Sure. I'd say that was it, Florence," said Jonathan, nodding. "One last trick for the road and that sort of thing."

Lewis looked from one to the other. He knew they were covering up. But what could he say? One thing would lead to another, and before long he would have to tell about Halloween night. When you are hiding something, you get the feeling that every other secret is connected to your secret. Lewis couldn't challenge anyone for fear of being exposed himself.

Late that same night, Lewis lay awake in his bed listening to Jonathan and Mrs. Zimmermann talking. They were in the study below and, as usual, their voices drifted up the hot-air register. And, as usual, he couldn't quite make out what they were saying. He got out of bed and crawled over to the wooden grating in the floor. A warm breath of heat softly beat at his face. He listened. Even now, he just couldn't hear well enough. There was only one thing to do. He had to use the secret passageway.

Lewis put on his bathrobe and tiptoed down the back stairs. The kitchen was dark. Good. Slowly, carefully, he removed all the china from the shelves of the china cupboard. Then he tripped the hidden spring, and the cupboard swung outward. He walked softly in.

This time Lewis remembered to bring a flashlight. Not that he needed it much. He didn't have far to go, and light shone through many chinks into the cobwebbed passage. Before long he was standing behind the book-cases that lined the wall of Jonathan's study. He peered through a crack in the boards, and there, beyond the books, were Jonathan and Mrs. Zimmermann. Mrs. Zim-mermann had just conjured up a match out of thin air, and she was lighting a long twisted cigar with it. She blew smoke out of both corners of her mouth.

"Well, now we know," she said.

"Yes, now we know." Jonathan's voice came from his leather armchair, where he sat slumped. All that Lewis could see of him was one blue-sleeved arm and a set of hairy knuckles grasping the chair arm.

"The question is," Jonathan went on, "can we do any-thing about it?"

Mrs. Zimmermann began to pace. Cigar smoke trailed off behind her. She scraped the large purple stone of her ring along the whole length of a bookshelf. "Do?" she said. "Do? We fight them. What else?"

Jonathan gave a hoarse laugh. It made Lewis feel very uncomfortable.

"Easier said than done, Florence. They're both stronger than we are, you know. We only fiddle around with magic; they gave their lives to it. As for her, she may have quite literally given her life for it."

"But why would they want to do what they're doing?" said Mrs. Zimmermann, folding her arms and puffing angrily at her cigar. "Why? This beautiful world. End it. Why?"

Jonathan thought a minute. "Well, Florence, I can't really see into the workings of a mind like Isaac Izard's, but I'd say the answer was scientific curiosity. Think of all that's been written about the Last Day: graves opening, bodies rising up fresh and new. Some think there will be a whole new earth, much better than the present one. Wouldn't you like to see it? And another thing occurs to me. Isaac and Selenna Izard didn't enjoy this world very much. Why shouldn't they try for the next one?"

Jonathan puffed on his hookah. There was silence for several minutes.

"And the clock," said Mrs. Zimmermann. "I have to hand it to you. You were dead right. There *is* a real, literal clock in these walls. He calls it a 'device,' but it has to be a clock. He wasn't kind enough to tell us where it is, of course, though it seems to me that he tells practically everything else. He even gives hints about where he hid the key. Not that that matters now." She broke her cigar in two and threw it into the fireplace.

"But there's one thing I'd like to know," she said, turning suddenly to Jonathan. "Why did he need a clock to bring about the End of the World?"

Lewis gasped and put his hand over his mouth. Then it *was* going to be the end of the world, after all!

"Because he lost the moment," Jonathan answered. "The moment he had been seeking all those years. It was quite a search that old Isaac made. That's why he has all those crazy notes about mackerel skies and Last-Judgment skies and clouds that look like chariots and trumpets and masks of doom. That was what he was after. A mask of doom. A sky that would be right for his incantations. Sky magic is old stuff, as you know. The Romans used to——"

"Yes, yes!" cut in Mrs. Zimmermann impatiently. "I know all about sky and bird divination. Who's got the D.Mag.A. around here, anyhow? All right. So the right sky comes along for old Droopy Drawers. Fine. Dandy. So why doesn't he just wave his wand and turn us all into mullygrubs?"

"Because by the time he had made sure it was the right kind of sky, the sky had changed. It doesn't take long for clouds to move and change their patterns, you know.

Or maybe he lacked the heart to do it. It sounds silly, but I keep hoping that was what held him off."

"Him? Lack the heart? Isaac Izard? He was a hard man, Jonathan. He'd have pulled out his mother's teeth one by one, if he had to have them for some devil magic."

Jonathan sighed. "Maybe you're right. I don't know. The important thing is that he did miss his opportunity. That's why he had to build the clock. To bring the time back. The exact time when everything was right and in its place. That's what he means when he talks about 'a device to redeem the time.' Redeem, indeed! He wanted to destroy us all!'"

Mrs. Zimmermann was pacing again. "All right," she said. "All right. So he built the clock. Why didn't he just wind it up?"

"He couldn't. Not all the way, at any rate. Didn't you read that passage?" Jonathan got up and went to the library table, where the papers were lying. He picked them up and leafed until he found the page he wanted.

"Ah. Here it is: 'But when the device was completed, I found that I lacked the skill to wind it all the way up. I have tried, but I must conclude that one with greater power than I possess will be needed for the final adjustment. Curse the day she left me! Curse the day she went away! *She* might have done it!' "

Jonathan looked up. "In that last sentence the word 'she' is underlined four times. 'She,' of course, is our friend across the street."

Lewis closed his eyes. Mrs. O'Meagher really was Mrs. Izard then! He had guessed it, of course, but he hadn't been sure. Mrs. Izard! And he had let her out. He felt like the stupidest, most foolish person in the whole world.

"Ah, yes," said Mrs. Zimmermann, smiling wryly. "Well, we shall see in the end who is stronger. But tell me one thing more, oh, sage, since it seems that you have been cast in the role of explicator and annotator of the testament of Isaac Izard."

"Yes? What would you like to know, Florence?"

"Well, he claims that the clock isn't wound all the way up. But it has been making a ticking sound for years now. A magic ticking that seems to be coming from behind every wall of this house. It's hard for me to believe that the clock is just whiling the time away until old Auntie Izard arrives with her key. *What is the clock doing?*"

Jonathan shrugged. "Search me, Florence. Maybe it's trying to drag the house back into the past without the aid of that 'final adjustment.' Maybe he fixed it so the ticking sound would scare away anyone who might be foolish enough to come and live in this house. Isaac didn't want his clock found by accident and destroyed, after all. I don't know why the clock is ticking, Florence. But I do know this. When Mrs. Izard or whoever is over there puts that key in the slot of that clock and finishes the job that Isaac started, then—at that moment—Isaac

/ *135* /

Izard will return. You and I and Lewis will be ghosts or something worse, and he will be standing in the turret with power in his right hand. And the End of the World will come to pass."

Lewis clamped both hands over his mouth. He fell to his knees, shuddering and sobbing. For a moment he was on the verge of shouting, "Here I am! Come and get me!" so they could come and take him away and put him in the Detention Home for life. But he didn't shout. He clamped his hands more tightly over his mouth and cried in muffled bursts that shook his whole body. He cried for a long time, and when he was through, he sat staring listlessly at the dark wall of the passageway.

Mrs. Zimmermann and Jonathan left the room. The fire burned low, but still Lewis sat there. His mouth was full of the taste of ammonia, and his eyes burned. He took his handkerchief out of the pocket of his bathrobe and blew his nose. Where was the flashlight? Ah. Here it was. He clicked it on.

Lewis got up slowly and started to pick his way toward the entrance. Even though he was walking upright, he felt as if he were slinking. Now he was running his hand over the splintery back of the china cupboard. He tripped the spring, and the cupboard swung silently outward. Lewis half expected to see Mrs. Zimmermann and Jonathan sitting there with their arms folded, waiting for him. But the kitchen was dark and empty.

Lewis went up to his room. He felt as if he had stayed awake three nights in a row. Without even stopping to take off his bathrobe, he threw himself onto the rumpled bed. Darkness filled his brain, and he fell into a dead dreamless sleep.

CHAPTER NINE

The next day was Saturday, and Lewis woke up in a state of panic. He was like a pressure cooker with the lid clamped on tight and the steam hole clogged up with chewing gum. Thoughts kept bubbling and seething to the surface of his mind, but none of them seemed to make sense. What was he going to do? What *could* he do?

Lewis sat up and looked around the room. Two long panes of sunlight lay on the splintered and paint-stained floor. Over by the fireplace stood a tall mirror with battlements on top that matched the ones on Lewis's bed. Before the mirror lay a beautiful hooked rug. Jonathan claimed that Mrs. Zimmermann's great-grandmother had made it. The pattern of the rug was "Autumn Leaves."

Scallop-edged leaves, bright gold and deep blood-red, with some green ones thrown in for contrast. The rug seemed to float before the mirror, and the leaves swam in the pool of bright sunlight. It was an illusion, of course. This was no magic carpet. But Lewis liked to stand on it in the morning while he was dressing. It made him feel that he was free of the earth, if only for a little while.

He stood on it now as he pulled on his pants and tucked in his shirt. The shimmer of leaves lifted him off the floor. Things seemed clearer now. He had to get hold of Tarby. Tarby would know what to do. It was true that he had been avoiding Lewis, but they weren't exactly enemies. And anyway, Tarby was in this thing as deep as he was. He had held the flashlight while Lewis drew the magic pentacle and chalked in the name, Selenna. That must be Mrs. Izard's first name, Lewis thought. She must have put it in my head. Then, behind those iron doors, she was never really dead. . . .

Lewis bit his lip to cut off this line of thought. He went downstairs, ate breakfast alone, and hurried out the door. Tarby, with his nine brothers and sisters, lived in a huge frame house halfway across town. Lewis had never been invited there and he did not even know the first names of Tarby's mother and father, let alone the names of any of the nine brothers and sisters. He knew that Mr. Corrigan—that was Tarby's last name—ran a hardware store. And that was about all Lewis knew.

It was a bright, windy April day, and the sky was full

of little white clouds that kept tearing apart and merging into each other. Birds were flying about and the lawns were showing that first livid wet green. When Lewis got to the Corrigan house he found a bunch of small children playing in the front yard, which was all chewed up and full of mud holes. One of the younger ones, who looked a lot like Tarby, was hanging by his knees from one of the limbs of a dead tree that had red taillight reflectors nailed all over it. Other kids were making mud castles, beating each other over the head with sand shovels, trying to ride broken tricycles, or just sitting around screaming at the top of their lungs. Lewis picked his way past the toy trucks and inner tubes that littered the front walk. He pushed the doorbell and waited.

After a while a fat, tired-looking woman came to the door. She had a baby in her arms, and it was batting her on the shoulder with a bottle that it held by the nipple.

"Yes?" She sounded crabby, and no wonder.

"Uh . . . Mrs. Corrigan? I wonder if you could tell me where Tarby is."

"Tarby? Gee, I wonder if he's in the house. I'll see."

She threw back her head and bellowed, "Taaar-beeee!" No answer, though it would have been hard to hear one over the racket.

"No, I guess not," she said. She smiled a tired, kind smile. "He's probably out playing ball with the other kids."

Lewis thanked her and was about to turn away when she said, "Say! Aren't you that Barnavelt boy?"

Lewis said that he was.

She gave him a pleading look. "Please don't tell Tarby any more stories about ghosts and graveyards. He had nightmares for a week after last Halloween. It was nice of your uncle to invite him over for a cider-and-doughnut party, and let him stay the night and all, but those stories . . . well, you know how sensitive he is."

Lewis managed to keep a straight face. "Mm . . . sure . . . okay, Mrs. Corrigan, I won't tell him any more ghost stories. See you."

As he picked his way back down the walk, tripping on toys and dodging one or two mud balls that were thrown his way, Lewis had a hard time keeping from laughing right out loud. So that was Tarby's version of last Halloween night! Well, well. And where had Tarby spent the night? Shuddering under the back porch? Sleeping in a tree? And a whole week of nightmares! Of course, he hadn't been scared. It was just the moonlight. Lewis's inner laughter turned into a wry grin.

Lewis stopped at a hitching block to tie his shoelace. Now what was he going to do? Well, there were only two regular baseball diamonds in New Zebedee. The one out behind the school, and the one at the athletic field. He decided to go to the one behind the school.

When he got there, he found Tarby playing ball with

a lot of other kids. He was pitching, and various boys were shouting, "Come on, Tar-babee! Strike him out!" and, "Give 'em the old knuckleball!" or, if they happened to be on the other side, "Yaah! Pitcher's got a rubber arm!"

Tarby wound up with a windmill motion, balked several times—this was allowed, because it was softball, not baseball—and when he had the batter making nervous little half-swings, he fired the ball up to the plate. The batter swung so hard that he fell down.

"Strrrike three! Yerrr—out!" yelled the boy who was the umpire.

Lewis, standing on the sidelines, cupped his hands to his mouth and shouted, "Hey, Tarby! Can I talk to you?"

"Not now, Fatty. I'm in the middle of a game."

Tears filled Lewis's eyes. Tarby had never called him "fatty" before. At least he couldn't remember him doing it. Lewis choked back the tears and stood waiting patiently while Tarby mowed down the next batter with three blazing fastballs. That was the third out, so Tarby's team came in from the field. Carelessly, Tarby threw his glove on the ground and said, "Hi, Lewis. C'n I do f'ya?"

"My Uncle Jonathan's in some awful trouble. We're all in awful trouble. You know that night when we went up to the cemetery?"

To Lewis's complete surprise, Tarby grabbed him

by the collar and yanked him forward till their faces were about two inches apart.

"Look. If they ever find out that you were up there that night, you tell them that you were there by yourself. If you don't, you'll have two broken arms and maybe a broken head."

Lewis tried to shake himself free of Tarby's grip, but he couldn't. He felt blood rushing into his face as he shouted, "Tarby, this is worse than Halloween stuff! This is ghosts and witches and devils and . . . *let go of me, you candle-head!*"

Tarby let go of Lewis. He stared at him with his mouth open. "Candle-head" was just a name someone had called someone in a comic book Lewis was reading. It didn't mean anything.

Tarby's lips drew together. "What did you call me?"

Several of the other boys started to shout, "Fight! Fight!" though they really didn't expect much of one. It was only Lewis, after all.

Lewis stood there red-faced and frightened.

"I . . . I don't know what I called you."

"Well, remember next time." Tarby raised his fist and brought it down hard on Lewis's shoulder. It really hurt.

"C'mon, Tarby," shouted a tall boy named Carl Holabaugh. "Don't waste your time with Tubbo. You lead off this inning, and we're six runs behind. Get up there and slug it."

Tarby turned back to the game, and Lewis stumbled

off down the street, rubbing his shoulder. He was crying.

With the tears still welling uncontrollably into his eyes, Lewis started to walk. He walked all over town, past rows of houses that stared at him blankly. They had no advice to give him. He walked down Main Street, and stared for a while at the Civil War Monument. But the stone soldiers with their upraised bayonets and cannon swabbers did not have anything to say to him, either. He walked to the other end of Main Street and stared at the fountain that spumed a crystal willow tree from within a circle of marble columns. At night the fountain was lit up and it turned from red to orange and from orange to yellow and from yellow to blue and from blue to green and back to red again. But right now it was clear. Lewis wished his mind were clear too, but it wasn't.

He walked around the fountain three or four times, and then he crossed the street and started to walk up U.S. 9, which took up where Main Street left off, and led out of town. When he got to the square, tin CITY LIMITS sign, he just walked off into some tall grass and sat there, watching the ants crawl and listening to the cars as they whooshed past. His eyes were dry now. He was through crying. It occurred to him that he had been doing a lot of crying lately. That wasn't going to solve anything. Thinking might help, though he wasn't sure it would. He sat and thought, and tried to make up his mind what to do.

It was late in the afternoon when Lewis got up. He almost fell over because his left leg had gone to sleep. After he had stomped around in the weeds for a while to get the circulation going again, he set out for home. His mind was made up. All he could hear in his head was the old church hymn that ran:

> Once to every man and nation
> Comes the moment to decide
> In the strife of truth with falsehood
> For the good or evil side.

He imagined that he was leading a cavalry charge. If he had had one of Jonathan's canes with him, he would have swung it like a sword. Now and then he stopped and felt goose-pimple shivers run in waves through his body. He felt very proud and brave, and very frightened too. It is a hard thing to describe.

That night, long after everyone had gone to sleep, Lewis crawled out of bed and tiptoed down the front stairs. The house was quiet, very quiet, because it was one of those nights when Jonathan had stopped all the clocks —all but the one he couldn't stop. Out in the front hall the mirror on the coat rack was talking to itself amid little bursts of static. Now and then its edges flickered faintly. Maybe it was trying to warn Lewis. If it was, he ignored the warning. His mind was made up. He had started this whole horrible business, and now he was going to try to end it.

His hand rested on the cool lip of the Willoware umbrella stand. He groped among the canes, rattling them a good deal. Ah, here it was. His hand closed on the black wooden rod and—what was this? Lewis pulled his fingers away with a sucked-in gasp. Touching the magic cane was like touching a living human arm. Life pulsed through it. Lewis stood there staring at the cane. Its globe was now faintly lit. In the gray light he saw snow swirling, and there, shadowy but real, was the strange little castle. The magic light cast a pale shaking blotch on the wallpaper. Could he use it, this thing of power? It occurred to him that Jonathan was being very modest when he called himself a parlor magician.

Lewis set his teeth and reached out with a hand that still tingled from the shock it had received. He grasped the rod firmly. He drew it out. The globe sizzled and crackled, and turned from gray to rosy pink and then back to gray again. Now he opened the front door. A wet fresh-smelling breeze blew in and banged the door gently against the wall. The leaves of the chestnut tree drifted and sighed, and white blossoms came sailing down. He looked across the street. Despite the overgrown hedge, he could see that there were lights on in the Hanchett house. Muttering a prayer, he started down the steps.

In the middle of the street he almost turned and ran, but something kept him going. Once he had crossed to the other side it seemed easier to go on. It was like running downhill with the wind pushing you. The hedge parted at the brick walk that led up to the front stoop. Lewis walked in under the overhanging branches. Now he was at the bottom of the steps.

The Hanchett house had an old-fashioned double door of black wood with two frosted panes set in it. The panes had always reminded Lewis of the Ten Commandments, and now he thought: *Thou shalt not enter.* But one door panel stood ajar. Was he expected? His heart was pounding, but he went up.

He stopped just inside the door, under the hall lamp. The corridor was empty. Empty and bare. There wasn't a stick of furniture in it, no chairs or chests or little tables. No umbrellas propped against walls. On the pale, rose-colored wallpaper Lewis saw dark squares. The squares were the color the paper had been when it was new. The Hanchetts had hung pictures in these spaces, but now the pictures were gone. Mrs. O'Meagher had not put up any of her own.

Lewis walked quietly to the wide arch that opened into the living room. No one there. Some furniture, but not much. A few weak-looking little chairs with bow legs and an uncomfortable-looking couch. One low coffee table with two postage-stamp-sized china ash trays. One blow from Jonathan's flat-bottomed pipe would have smashed either one to smithereens. Lewis went from chair to chair, touching polished arms and smooth upholstered backs. He half expected the furniture to pop, like soap bubbles, when he touched it. But everything was solid. The floor was so highly polished that you could see your reflection in it. Over on one wall was a brick fireplace. It was painted bright pink all over, even on its inside walls. There were no soot stains. Apparently the old witch didn't like fires. Two birch logs were balanced neatly on the shiny brass andirons.

On the mantelpiece Lewis saw something that surprised him: an ornament. It was one of those whirligigs with tin cutout angels. You lit the candles in the middle, and the heat made the angels go around. These angels were blowing trumpets. Lewis reached up and touched the little wheel. *Squeee.* It spun tipsily. The sound startled him so much that he whirled around, holding the magic cane up for protection. No one was there.

He looked in the kitchen. A couple of little plaster plaques on the wall and an electric clock. A red formica counter and a tubular steel chair, also upholstered in cherry red. In the corner there was an icebox. He opened it and found one bottle of Coke. Or was it Coke? He turned the bottle over in his hands. It was gritty on the outside. Covered with dirt. Like it had been buried. And the liquid inside—it was lighter than Coke. Sort of a brownish red. Lewis put the bottle back. He shut the icebox door. The house seemed to be filled with a hum-ming noise, and he knew that it was his blood in his ears. Gripping the magic cane with a trembling, sweaty hand, he went to inspect the other rooms.

He checked out the whole first floor, but he found

nothing—nothing but more half-furnished rooms. A chair here, a table there. What lamps there were, were unplugged, but a bare ceiling fixture burned in each room. Now Lewis was at the bottom of the brightly lit staircase. He paused for a moment and then, suddenly, he pounded the cane on the floor and shouted, "I have come to defeat you, Mrs. Izard! Show yourself! Are you afraid of me? You ought to be! I know who you are and what you want to do. I challenge you to a duel by the ancient rules of magic!"

Lewis had expected his challenge to sound grand and majestic, to ring high and clear like a blast on a silver trumpet. Instead, it fell flat. It died away in the heavy stillness of the house. Lewis felt foolish. His cheeks burned. And he began to get worried.

Lewis did not know a blessed thing about "the ancient rules of magic." He had come over here with Jonathan's magic stick in his hand, hoping that the stick would do his work for him. Now he was doubtful. What if the cane wouldn't work for anyone but its master? What if Mrs. Izard's magic was stronger than Jonathan's?

Lewis looked at the burning globe, and he looked up the staircase. He felt like turning around and running home as fast as he could. But then how would he save Mrs. Zimmermann and Jonathan and the world, and make up for what he had done?

The house was very silent. Lewis took a deep breath and started to climb the staircase.

Halfway up the stairs, on the broad landing, Lewis stopped to look at a picture. It was the only picture he had seen in the house. There, in a heavy oval black frame, was a photo of an unpleasant-looking old man. He was sitting or standing—you couldn't tell which—against a wall covered with intricately patterned wallpaper. Lewis looked at the picture for a long time. He took in all the details: the two or three strands of hair combed over the almost-bald head, the deep-set eyes that seemed to be staring right at him, the hawkish nose. He looked at the man's clothing. He was wearing an old-fashioned, stiff cardboard collar with folded-back points. And his left hand rested on the ball of what must be a cane. There appeared to be some writing on the cane, but Lewis couldn't read it.

Lewis stood there wondering who the old man was. Could it be . . . ? He snatched the picture down and looked on the back. No label. Quickly he turned it over and stared at the picture again. Something was familiar. Of course! The wallpaper! It was the wallpaper in the upstairs front hallway. Roman numeral II's hooked to-gether with curlicues. Lewis knew now that he was star-ing at a picture of Isaac Izard.

Then it was all true. This woman was his wife, come back from the grave to . . . to do what? Lewis felt his heart pounding. He was more scared than he had ever been in his life. He didn't want to fight Mrs. Izard any more. He just wanted to get out. He looked frantically up the stairs toward the dark doorway of the bedroom. No one was coming. He started down the stairs, but Mrs. Izard was in the way.

She stood there smiling. In her hand was an ivory-handled cane. "Well, young man, what is it? What makes you think you can roam around other people's houses at night? What do you want?"

Lewis was afraid he might faint, but he didn't. Instead, he felt himself stiffen. He raised the cane. "I don't know what you want to do to us, Mrs. Izard," he said, "but you're not going to do it. My uncle's magic is stronger than yours."

She laughed a harsh, nasty laugh. "Do you mean that toy cane? He probably got it at the Capharnaum County Fair. Don't be foolish, child."

All through the house the cane had burned with a steady gray light. Now, as Mrs. Izard spoke, the globe began to go dark. Lewis looked down and saw that he was staring at something that looked very much like a burned-out light bulb.

"And now," said Mrs. Izard, stepping forward, "and now, my fine young friend, you will see what it is to bother nice old ladies who just want to be left alone."

She snatched the cane from his numb hand and threw it clattering down the stairs. Now she was bending over him, and the light reflected from her spectacles hurt his eyes. Her voice was angry now, and she talked faster.

"Do you have any idea what it is like to be buried

deep in the earth, dark stone all around, no one to hear you or see you, your only company a dead man? *Do you?*"

"Stop right there, Mrs. Izard. You're not dealing with children now."

There at the bottom of the stairs stood Mrs. Zimmermann. Her face was lit by invisible footlights, and she wore a floor-length purple cape. In the folds, instead of shadows, were deep wells of orange fire. In one hand she held a tall black pole with a clear glass globe on top. Inside the globe a magenta star burned. It grew in brightness when she spoke and dwindled when she was silent.

Mrs. Izard turned around. She faced Mrs. Zimmermann calmly. "So it's you," she said. "Well, my power has not reached its height, but I am still strong enough to deal with you. *Aroint ye!*"

She pointed the ivory cane at Mrs. Zimmermann. Nothing happened. She stopped smiling and dropped her cane.

Now it was Mrs. Zimmermann's turn. She pounded the butt of her staff once on the floor, and the staircase was lit with a flash of ultraviolet lightning. With an awful scraping cry that no human ever made, Mrs. Izard rushed past Lewis and up the stairs. Mrs. Zimmermann started up after her.

"Run back home, Lewis!" she shouted as she dashed past him. "You're a brave boy, but you're no match for that thing. *Run*, I tell you!"

Lewis bounded down the stairs, taking them two at a time. He was terrified, but he was very happy too. As he ran down the front steps of the house he heard strange exploding sounds and sharp cries. Branches grabbed at him as he ran along the well-swept brick walk. One of them actually wrapped itself around his left leg and started to pull. With a scream and a frantic thrashing motion, Lewis tore loose and plunged across the street. He threw open the gate and ran *whump!* into something hard and yet soft. Jonathan.

Lewis broke down. He began to weep hysterically with his face pressed into Jonathan's blue work shirt. Jonathan wrapped his arms around Lewis and held him tight. Though Lewis could not see it, Jonathan was staring over his head at the Hanchett house, and there was a grim smile on his face. A purple flash lit up one of the upstairs windows. Now a cold, blue-white pinpoint was kindled in the adjoining window, as if someone had just lit a strange kind of match. The blue light spread till it filled the window. It spread to the other window and ate up the fading purple light. Now there was a dull powerful explosion like an aerial bomb at a fireworks display. It hurt Jonathan's ears. As he watched, both upstairs windows turned a brilliant purple. The chimney of the house toppled, and its bricks slid down the roof. The overgrown hedge thrashed and swayed as if it had been caught in a hurricane. Several diamond-shaped pieces of glass fell out of their frames and tinkled on the walk below. Then the house was silent and dark.

Lewis had stopped crying, and now he turned around to look. A full minute passed. Then the front door scraped open and Mrs. Zimmermann appeared. She walked calmly down the steps and down the brick walk and out into the street, humming as she went. The orange fires in the creases of her robe had gone out, and so had the magic footlights. In one hand she held an old umbrella. The handle of the umbrella was a crystal knob, and a tiny seed of violet fire still burned in it. In her other hand Mrs. Zimmermann held Jonathan's cane; its globe was still dark.

"Hi, Florence," said Jonathan, as if he were meeting her on the street on a Sunday afternoon. "How did it go?"

"Well enough," she said, handing him his cane. "Here's your magic wand. It's had quite a shock, but I think it'll recover. As for Mrs. Izard, I just don't know. I may have destroyed her, or I may have just put her out of action for a while. In any case, let's take the time that has been given to us and *find that clock!*"

CHAPTER TEN

When the three of them got back to the house, they had a shock. The ticking was very loud now, louder than it had ever been. It was like standing inside the works of Big Ben.

Jonathan turned pale. "It looks," he said, "as if things are drawing to some conclusion. Mrs. Izard may not be as dead as we could wish."

Mrs. Zimmermann began to pace back and forth. She rubbed the purple stone of her ring against her chin. "She may be, or she may not be. Either way, having her out of the way is no guarantee that the bomb won't blow up in our faces," she said. "But let's assume the worst. Let's assume that she's still in the game. All right." She took a deep breath and let it out. "It has been my theory, ever since yesterday, that the old hag is just waiting for the proper *time* to use that wretched key. The proper action at the proper time to achieve the proper effect. That would be like her. And like her old husband too. His magic is logical. It proceeds from A to B to C in nice, neat steps. As logical and neat as the movement of a hand around the face of a clock."

"Then there's no point in our being logical, is there?" said Jonathan. He was smiling very strangely and clicking the paper clips on his watch chain. This was always a sign that he was thinking.

"What do you mean?" said Lewis and Mrs. Zimmermann at the same time.

"I mean," he said patiently, "that we're no good at that sort of game. Our game is wild swoops, sudden inexplicable discoveries, cloudy thinking. Knights' jumps instead of files of rooks plowing across the board. So we'd better play our way if we expect to win."

Mrs. Zimmermann folded her arms and looked grumpy. "I see," she said. "It sounds very reasonable. If you're in a chess game, draw to an inside straight. If you're playing tennis, try to hit a home run. Very intelligent."

Jonathan seemed unruffled. "Why not?" he said. "It all seems clear enough to me. Lewis, what I want you to do is this. Get a pencil and paper, and dream up the silliest set of instructions you can think of."

Lewis looked puzzled. "Instructions for what?"

"For a ceremony. A ritual. A magic show for getting the clock out of its hiding place. Make it as goofy as you can."

Lewis felt very excited and happy. "Okay," he said. "If that's what you want, here we go!"

He ran to the sideboard and dug out a yellow Ticonderoga NO. 2 pencil and a five-cent pad of writing paper. Then he ran into the study and slammed the doors. Jonathan and Mrs. Zimmermann paced nervously outside, and the gigantic ticking continued.

Fifteen minutes later Lewis slid back the doors of the study. He handed Jonathan a blue-lined sheet of paper with writing on both sides. The first line that Jonathan read made him throw back his head and laugh loudly. He mumbled rapidly through the rest of the list, chuckling all the while. Mrs. Zimmermann kept trying to read it over his shoulder, but finally she lost her temper and snatched it out of his hand. She laughed even harder than Jonathan had. She snortled and cackled and giggled. Finally, she handed the paper back to Jonathan.

"Okay," she said. "So be it. First we put lighted candles in all the windows. Real candles, that is."

"Yes," said Jonathan, wrinkling up his nose. "I see Lewis has the poor taste to prefer real candles. Ah, well . . . let's get going. There are several boxes of candle ends in the sideboard."

Jonathan took the first floor, Mrs. Zimmermann took

the second floor, and Lewis took the third floor and the stained-glass windows, wherever they might be. Before long, the whole house was lit up for Christmas in April.

Lewis paused outside the door of the room that had Isaac Izard's organ in it. He looked into the shoe box that had been full of candle stubs. Only one left. Should he put it in there? No, there was a better place.

With a fat red candle in his hand, Lewis climbed the dusty spiral staircase that led to the cupola room. He shoved open the narrow door. The room was dark except for streaks of moonlight on the floor. Lewis moved over to the window. He knelt down and leaned forward into the deep embrasure.

The oval window gave him a bird's-eye view of the Hanchett house. Or would have, if he had been able to see it. Brilliant moonlight bathed the hill, but the Hanchett house lay in a mass of shadow. Only the dark point of its roof could be seen.

Lewis stared, fascinated. Then, suddenly, he began to hear the ticking, faint but audible, that filled even this room in the house at 100 High Street. He shook his head, got out his matches, and quickly lit the candle.

When he got back downstairs, he found that his second instruction was being obeyed. Mrs. Zimmermann was playing "Chopsticks" on the organ in the front parlor. When she got up and went back to the dining room, the organ kept on playing "Chopsticks," since it was a player organ, and she had set it on "Infinite Replay." The silly monotonous music almost drowned out the steady ticking—almost, but not quite.

Jonathan came bouncing in from the back bedrooms. His face was red, and he was breathing hard. "Okay," he said. "What's next?"

Mrs. Zimmermann picked up the paper and read in a solemn voice. "We are to play a game of Bon-Sour-One-Frank until the Ace of Nitwits appears."

As unlikely as it may seem, Jonathan knew what Bon-Sour-One-Frank was. It was Lewis's name for poker. The three of them had played a lot of poker since that first August evening, and Lewis had named the game for the inscription he thought he saw on the shiny brass one-franc pieces. When you called someone, you had to shout, "Bon Sour One Frank!" very loudly.

But Jonathan was puzzled about one detail. He turned to Lewis with a quizzical look on his face. "And what, may I ask, is the Ace of Nitwits?"

"I don't know. It just came to me. I guess we'll know when we find it."

Out came the red box of coins. Out came the blue and gold cards. Jonathan lit his pipe and unbuttoned his vest till it was only held together by the chain of paper clips. He got his dusty old gray fedora out of the closet and parked it on the back of his head. This, he explained, was the proper poker-playing costume.

Jonathan shuffled and dealt. Shekels and guilders, ducats and florins, drachmas and didrachmas clattered over the table. At first the hands were ordinary. Pair of eights, nothing, kings and tens. Then people started getting six of a kind and cards with square-root signs and question marks all over them. Jonathan and Mrs. Zimmermann were not pulling any tricks. The strange cards appeared all by themselves. On they played, while the giant clock ticked and the organ played "Chopsticks" and the candles threw fruit and flower patterns or plain yellow splotches onto the gray moonlit grass outside.

It was after a half hour of playing that Lewis picked up a card and found that he was staring at the Ace of Nitwits. There it was. Instead of clubs or hearts, it had ears of corn and green peppers all over it. In the center was a dopey-looking man in a flat black hat called a mortarboard, the kind of hat that college professors wear to graduations. Ice cream was heaped up on the hat, and the professor was tasting it with his index finger.

Lewis showed the card around.

"Why so it is!" cried Jonathan. "The Ace of Nitwits! I'd recognize it anywhere. Now just what does *that* mean, Lewis?"

"It means you have to wear it stuck to your forehead with a piece of bubble gum. Here." Lewis took out the piece he had been chewing and handed it to Uncle Jonathan.

"Thanks awfully," said Jonathan. He squashed the card against his forehead. "Now what?"

"You get all done up and come down with the eight ball, like it says in the instructions."

"Hm. Yes. Righty-ho, and all that sort of thing. See you, folks."

Jonathan went upstairs. He stayed up there a long time, so long that the parlor organ broke into "Stars and Stripes Forever" out of pure boredom. Mrs. Zimmermann sat tapping her fingers on the table, while Lewis did what he always did when he was nervously waiting for somebody. He slapped the sides of his chair, rocked back and forth, and wiggled his right leg.

"Well, here I am!"

Mrs. Zimmermann and Lewis looked up. There at the head of the stairs stood Jonathan. He was wearing a cape made from a crazy quilt, and on his head was a flowered toaster cover Mrs. Zimmermann had made. The Ace of Nitwits was still glued to his forehead, and he bore in his hands a small, round, black object. As he started down the stairs, the organ played "Pomp and Circumstance," but it soon got tired of that and switched to radio commercials:

> Call for Cuticura
> It's fragrant, and pura
> It's mildly medicated too
> It's grand for you and yoo-hooo!

Clark's Super One Hundred Gasoline
Thousands say it's best!
The largest-selling, independent gasoline
In the Middle West!

Super Suds, Super Suds
Lots more suds from Super Su-u-uds
Richer longer lasting too
They're the ones with Super Doo-oo-oooo.

To this solemn accompaniment, Jonathan advanced to the dining-room table and set down the black ball. It was one of those fortune-telling eight-balls, the kind you buy in dime stores. The ball was full of fluid, and when you shook it, ghostly white cards came floating up to the little window. There were only three of them: YES, NO, and MAYBE.

"Now what?" asked Jonathan.

"Ask it," said Lewis.

"Ask it what?" Jonathan looked blank.

"The circumference of the moon, you bearded booby!" screamed Mrs. Zimmermann. "Where I left my hat after the Chicago World's Fair! Now *think* a minute, Jonathan. What would you *want* to ask it?"

"Where the clock is?" asked Jonathan in a small voice.

A burst of rather mechanical applause came from the front room. It was the organ, smarting off as usual. Jonathan stuck his tongue out at it over his shoulder. Then he turned back to the table where the eight-ball lay.

Carefully, reverently, he picked it up. He held it like a microphone and talked into it.

"Where is the clock?"

The dark window stayed dark. Jonathan shook the ball till the liquid inside it foamed. *"Where is the clock?"* he shouted, and he repeated this question in Greek, Latin, French, German, and Middle-Kingdom Egyptian. Still no answer.

"Your French is terrible," said Mrs. Zimmermann, grabbing the ball out of his hand. "Here . . . let me try."

Holding the ball under a corner of her cloak as if she were protecting it from rain, Mrs. Zimmermann jabbered at it in Bengali, Finno-Ugric, Basque, Old High Norse, and Geez. She used all the commands for unlocking the secrets of specular stones that are favored by Regiomontanus, Albertus Magnus, and Count Cagliostro. Still nothing.

"Can I try?" asked Lewis. His voice was timid and weak.

Mrs. Zimmermann looked down at him. Perspiration was pouring along all the wrinkles of her face. Her eyes looked wild. "What did you say?"

"I wonder if I might try. I know I'm not a wizard or anything, but it *is* my ball. I bought it in Chicago and . . ."

"Of course!" cried Mrs. Zimmermann, pounding the table with her fist. "Of *course!* What fools we are! Like any magic object, it only responds to its owner. Here. But hurry!" She shoved the ball into his hands.

The ticking of the clock got softer, but it was faster now.

Lewis held the magic toy up before his face. His voice was calm and quiet. "Please tell us where the clock is," he whispered.

There was motion inside the ball. YES drifted out of the void like a ghostly newspaper in a black wind. It passed by. So did NO and MAYBE. Finally, after several tense minutes, a card appeared bearing the words: COAL PIT.

"It says coal pit." Lewis's voice was dull and lifeless now. He hung his head.

"May I see the ball?" said Jonathan softly. Lewis handed it to him.

Jonathan held the ball up to the light. He wrinkled his forehead, and the Ace of Nitwits fluttered away to the floor. "Yes, it certainly says 'coal pit.' Coal pit? *Coal pit?* What the devil does it mean by saying *that?*" Jonathan glowered at the shiny little ball. He was beginning to think it might be nice to dash the wretched thing against the mantelpiece.

Suddenly the ball hiccuped. Jonathan glanced quickly down at it, and saw that the little window was filled with bubbles.

"Oh, good grief! Look at this, Florence. Now it thinks it's a Bendix washer. Shall we get out the ouija board?"

"Wait a minute," said Mrs. Zimmermann. "It looks like the bubbles are starting to break up."

Lewis, Jonathan, and Mrs. Zimmermann watched breathlessly as the little bubbles popped, one by one. Pop, pop, pop. It seemed to take forever. Meanwhile, the clock ticked.

At last the window was clear. Now the sign said: COAL BIN.

"Oh, great!" said Jonathan. "Just great! Now it says coal *bin!* That's a big improvement."

"Don't you have a coal bin?" asked Mrs. Zimmermann.

Jonathan gave her an irritated look. "Of course not, Florence! You ought to know that. Remember, I switched to oil when I bought this . . . oh! *Oh!*" Jonathan clapped his hands over his mouth. "Oh! I think I see! Come on, everybody. We're going to the basement."

Lewis and Mrs. Zimmermann followed Jonathan to the kitchen. He opened the cellar door, and jumped back as if he had been hit in the face. The ticking down there was thunderous.

Jonathan looked at Mrs. Zimmermann. His face was haggard, and his eyes were wide with fear. "Got your umbrella, Florence? Good. Then down we go."

Over in a black sooty corner of the basement was the old coal bin. Two of its walls were formed by gray slats nailed to worm-eaten wooden pillars. The other two walls were whitewashed stone, and up against one of these lay a high rampart of coal. It had been there when Jonathan moved in, and he had always meant to have it hauled away.

"I certainly get the idiot prize," he said quietly. Jonathan took a long backswing and started shoveling. Lewis and Mrs. Zimmermann helped with their hands. Before long they had cleared all the coal away from the wall.

"Doesn't *look* like there's any secret panel," said Jonathan, feeling around for springs and hidden levers. "But then, if it looked that way, it wouldn't be secret, would it? Hmm . . . no . . . nothing. I'm afraid we'll have to use the pick. Stand back, everybody."

Lewis and Mrs. Zimmermann got well away from the wall, and Jonathan started swinging. By now the ticking was hurried and staccato, and the blows of the pick were like heavy beats in the rhythm. Every stroke sent whitish-gray chips flying in all directions. But it was an easier job than anyone would have thought. The wall began to shake and crumble at Jonathan's first stroke, and the whole solid-looking mass was soon lying in pieces on the hard dirt floor of the cellar. For it had not been a real wall, but merely a plaster mock-up. What lay behind was a weathered, old wooden door with a black china knob. There was a lock plate, but there was no keyhole.

Jonathan leaned his pick up against a pillar and stepped back.

"Don't dawdle!" said Mrs. Zimmermann nervously. "Get that door open! I have a feeling that we are on the very edge of disaster."

Jonathan stood there rubbing his chin. Exasperated, Mrs. Zimmermann grabbed his arm and started to shake it. "Hurry, Jonathan! What on earth are you waiting for?"

"I'm trying to think of door-opening spells. Know any?"

"Why not pull at it?" said Lewis. "It may not be locked."

Jonathan was about to say that he had never heard of anything so stupid in all his life. But he never got a chance to say this. The door opened all by itself.

Jonathan, Mrs. Zimmermann, and Lewis stared. They were looking down a long corridor—more like a mine shaft it was, really, with square wooden arches diminishing into the dark distance. Something vague and gray was moving at the far end of the tunnel. It seemed to be getting closer.

"Look!" cried Lewis.

He was not pointing at the gray shape. He was pointing at something that was sitting on the floor of the tunnel, right there at their feet.

A clock. A plain, old, Waterbury eight-day clock.

Its pendulum oscillated madly behind a little glass door, and it was making a sound like a Geiger counter gone crazy.

"I'm so glad you've done my work for me," said a voice behind them. Jonathan and Mrs. Zimmermann spun around and froze. Really froze. They could not move their hands or feet or heads. They couldn't even wiggle their ears. They were completely paralyzed, though they could still see and hear.

There stood Mrs. Izard. Or Mrs. O'Meagher, or whatever name you choose. She was wearing a black-velvet cloak with an ivory brooch at her neck. The brooch bore a raised Greek omega. In her right hand was a plain black rod, and in her left she carried what looked like a severed hand with a lighted candle growing out of its back. Concentric rings of yellow light spread outward from the hand, and through them Jonathan and Mrs. Zimmermann could see Mrs. Izard's glasses, which looked like tablets of gray slate.

"I do hope you haven't tired yourselves, my dears," said the old woman in a nasty, sneering voice. "I do hope you haven't. But if you have, it's all been in a good cause. I couldn't have done anything without you. Not a thing. Because, you see, since I was set free, I've been able to pass through walls and doors, but these poor old hands of mine just haven't been able to wield tools. I even had to get Mr. Hammerhandle to find this for me."

She let go of her wand—it stood up by itself—and reached deep into the folds of her cloak. What she brought out was a greenish copper key. She held it up and turned it around. "Pretty, isn't it? I told him where to look, but he had to do the work. He's really been very good at following directions, and he made it quite easy for me to set up light housekeeping across the street. But, alas, that is all over and done with. You played right into my hands as I thought you would. Did you *really* think you had defeated me, you foolish old biddy? You merely hastened the Day of Judgment. And it is at hand. My Lord and master is coming to meet us. And when he arrives it will be a very different world. *Very* different, I assure you. Let me see . . . you two will change first, I think." She pointed at Jonathan and then at Mrs. Zimmermann. "Yes, that's the way it will be. You two first, so Sonny here can watch. You'll want to watch, won't you, Lewis?"

Lewis stood with his back to Mrs. Izard. He was as still as a clothes-store dummy.

"Turn around, Lewis," said Mrs. Izard, in that nasty-sweet voice she had used from the beginning. "Don't you want to kiss your old Auntie Izard?"

He didn't move.

"Come now, Lewis. I command you. Don't be foolish. It'll just make things worse for you in the end. Turn around, I say!"

Lewis's body grew tense, and then he rushed forward into the tunnel. He picked up the clock, which had just begun to make that whirring sound clocks make when they are going to strike the hour.

"Stop, boy!" shouted Mrs. Izard. "Stop, you filthy fat

pig! I'll turn you into something that your own mother wouldn't—don't you dare! Don't . . . ."

Lewis threw the clock down. There was a sproinging of uncoiled springs and a clatter of cogs and a splintering of wood and a tinkle of broken glass. He reached down into the wreckage and ripped the pendulum free of the works, which were still buzzing furiously. At that moment, a figure which stood only a few yards from Lewis, the figure of an elderly man in a rotting black Sunday suit, vanished. Then there was an awful shriek, a loud, inhuman sound like a siren at the top of its wail. It filled the air and seemed to turn it red. Lewis covered his ears, but the sound was inside his head and in the marrow of his bones. And then it was gone.

He turned around. There stood Jonathan, smiling and trying to blink away the tears in his eyes. There stood Mrs. Zimmermann, smiling even more broadly. And behind them, on the cellar floor, under a swaying bare bulb, lay a crumpled pile of black cloth. A yellow skull was staring up out of it, staring up in gap-jawed amazement. A few wisps of gray hair clung to the crevices in the smooth dome, and over the empty eyeholes a pair of rimless glasses was perched. The glasses were shattered.

CHAPTER ELEVEN

Three days after the destruction of Mrs. Izard and her magic clock, Jonathan, Mrs. Zimmermann, and Lewis were sitting around a bonfire in the driveway of the house at 100 High Street. It was a chilly night, and the stars were cold overhead, but the fire burned a warm, bright orange. Mrs. Zimmermann had a steaming earthenware pot of cocoa by her side. She kept it close to the fire so it would stay warm. Jonathan and Lewis stared at the fire and sipped cocoa from their mugs. It tasted very good.

There was a pile of Isaac Izard's dusty papers in Jonathan's lap. Every now and then he would pick one up and throw it into the fire. Lewis watched each sheet as the fire licked at its corners, then blackened it, then wadded it into a fluffy ball of ashes.

After a while Lewis said, "Uncle Jonathan?"

"Yes, Lewis?"

"Was Mrs. Izard really trying to make the world end?"

"As far as I can tell, she was," said Jonathan. "And she would have done it, too, if you hadn't fixed her clock for her. But tell me, Lewis. Why didn't you turn around when we did?"

Lewis smiled broadly. "I looked at the glass door on the clock and I saw the reflection of what Mrs. Izard was holding, and I knew it was a Hand of Glory. John L. Stoddard tells you all about Hands of Glory."

"I'm glad he does," said Mrs. Zimmermann. "One look at that hand and you'd have been as numb as we were. But still, it took a great deal of courage for you to rush in and smash the clock. After all, you didn't know what would happen to you when you did that."

Lewis was silent. He had always thought that courage had something to do with riding your bicycle through bonfires and hanging by your knees from the limbs of trees.

Mrs. Zimmermann picked up a plate of chocolate-chip cookies and passed them around. Jonathan took two and Lewis took several. There was another silence while everyone munched and sipped for a while. Jonathan threw more papers into the fire.

Lewis squirmed around and stared at the dark house across the street.

"Do you think Mrs. Izard could ever . . . come back?" he said in a faltering voice.

"No," said Jonathan, shaking his head gravely. "No, Lewis, I think that when you smashed the clock in the walls, you destroyed any power she might have in this world. Just to be on the safe side, though, I put what was left of her back in the mausoleum and locked the doors with a nice shiny new lock. A lock that has had spells said over it. That ought to hold her for a while."

"What about the Hanchetts?" said Lewis. "I mean, are they going to come back to live in their house?"

Jonathan paused for a minute before speaking. He clicked the paper clips on his watch chain. "I think they are," he said at last. "But certain rites will have to be performed before they return. When an unclean spirit inhabits a house, it leaves behind a bad aura."

"Speaking of bad auras and unclean spirits," said Mrs. Zimmermann, "do you have any idea of what happened to Hammerhandle?"

Jonathan's face grew grim for an instant. He had made a few guesses about Hammerhandle's fate, but he had kept them to himself. For one thing, he knew that the blood of a hanged man went into the making of a Hand of Glory.

"No idea at all," said Jonathan, shaking his head. "He seems to have vanished from the face of the earth."

Suddenly Lewis began to squirm and scrunch around in his seat again. He was on the brink of saying something.

"Uncle . . . Jonathan?" Lewis's voice was dry and throaty.

"Yes, Lewis? What is it?"

"I . . . I let Mrs. Izard out of her tomb."

Jonathan smiled calmly. "Yes," he said. "I knew you did."

Lewis's mouth dropped open. "How did you know?"

"You left your flashlight up at the cemetery. I found it in a pile of leaves when I went up to put Mrs. Izard back in her tomb."

"Are you going to send me to the Detention Home?" asked Lewis in a tiny, frightened voice.

"Am I going to *what?*" said Jonathan, staring at him in disbelief. "Lewis, what kind of ogre do you think I am?

"And besides," Jonathan added with a sudden smile, "why should I punish you for doing what I tried to do myself when I was a boy? Like you, I was interested in magic at an early age. It runs in our family, I guess. I was trying to impress a girl. You wanted to keep Tarby for a friend. Isn't that right?"

Lewis nodded sadly.

"By the way, Lewis," said Mrs. Zimmermann. "How are things between you and Tarby these days?"

"Not so good," said Lewis. "I don't think Tarby and

I were meant to be friends. We're not the same type. But it doesn't matter."

"Doesn't matter?" said Jonathan. "Well, it certainly *does* matter! If he's such a stuck-up little . . ." He stopped because he saw that Lewis was smiling smugly.

Jonathan wrinkled up his eyebrows so that they looked like two mating auburn caterpillars. "Lewis Barnavelt!" he roared. "Are you hiding something from me?"

Lewis was trying very hard to keep from giggling. "Oh, nothing much, Uncle Jonathan," he said. "Except that I have a new friend."

"*Whaaat?* You *dooo?*" said Jonathan and Mrs. Zimmermann in unison.

"Yes. Her name is Rose Rita Pottinger, and she lives down on Mansion Street. She knows the names of all the different kinds of cannon. Want to hear them? Saker, minion, falconet, demi-culverin . . ."

"Aaaaah!" screamed Jonathan. He threw two fistfuls of paper into the fire. "That's all I need. An expert in Elizabethan ordnance. Promise me one thing, Lewis."

"What's that?"

"If you and tiny Rosie decide to start a cannon foundry in our basement, let Mrs. Zimmermann and me know so we can go visit my relatives in Osee Five Hills. Okay?"

Lewis giggled. "Sure, Uncle Jonathan. I'll let you know."

Jonathan waved his pipe at the bonfire. The leaves stirred uneasily, and then they gathered into a large black ball. The bonfire turned into a jack-o'-lantern. Now the three of them took turns pitching chestnuts into the eyes, nose, and mouth of the ferocious lantern. *Pop! Pop! Pop!* The chestnuts went off in a ripping string, like a fusillade of musket fire.

Jonathan, Lewis, and Mrs. Zimmermann sat around the fire talking until the scowling orange face fell in with an airy *whoosh*. Then they got up, stretched, and went wearily off to bed.

About the Author

This is John Bellairs' first book for young readers, and much of the material in it is drawn from things that happened or that he wished would happen when he was growing up in Marshall, Michigan. Mr. Bellairs has written several adult books, among them *The Pedant and the Shuffly* and *The Face in the Frost*. He lives in Haverhill, Massachusetts, with his wife Priscilla, their son Frank, a grandfather clock, and a piece of the elm tree under which George Washington took command of the American Army.

About the Artist

Edward Gorey is the well-known illustrator of many books, including *The Shrinking of Treehorn* and *Sam and Emma*, both selected for the 1972 Children's Book Showcase, and *Red Riding Hood*. He lives in New York City.

THE FIGURE
IN THE SHADOWS

Sequel to
THE HOUSE WITH
A CLOCK IN ITS WALLS

JOHN BELLAIRS
drawings by Mercer Mayer

For Don Wilcox, David Walters,

and Jonathan Grandine

Friends who have been friends indeed

*The Figure
in the Shadows*

CHAPTER ONE

Lewis Barnavelt stood at the edge of the playground, watching the big boys fight.

It was a real battle. Tom Lutz and Dave Shellenberger were two of the big wheels that ran Lewis's school. Usually they beat up on everybody else; now they were slugging it out with each other. In a funny way, it reminded Lewis of the battles of gods and heroes that he had read about in the Classics Comics version of the *Iliad*.

"Here, see how you like that, huh?" Tom threw a handful of gravel in Dave's face. Dave charged Tom, and now the two of them were rolling over and over on the ground, kicking and clawing and screaming dirty words. Lewis saw that the fight might be coming his way, so he backed into the shadowy alley that ran between the school and the Episcopal church next door.

Normally, Lewis wouldn't have been caught within miles of a fight like this one. Lewis was fat and moon-faced. In his brown sweater and baggy corduroy trousers, he looked like a balloon ascension. At least, that's what his mean Aunt Mattie had said about him once, and the phrase "balloon ascension" had gotten stuck in Lewis's mind. His hands were soft and padded, and wouldn't develop calluses, even when he rubbed them with sandpaper. When he flexed his muscles, nothing happened. He was scared of fights, and he was scared of getting beat up.

Then what was he doing standing there watching two of the toughest kids in school slug it out? Well, the back door of the school opened onto the playground, and Rose Rita had told Lewis to meet her by the back door, and when she said something, she meant it. Rose Rita Pottinger was Lewis's best friend, and she was being kept after school for sassing Miss Haggerty, their sixth-grade teacher—Rose Rita was a year older than Lewis, but she was in the same grade, which was nice.

Lewis paced up and down in the dark alley. What was taking her so long? He was getting more and more nervous, with the fight going on nearby. What if they got tired of fighting with each other and decided to beat up on him?

"Hi, Lewis!"

Lewis jumped. Then he turned around. There was Rose Rita.

She was a good head taller than he was, and she wore glasses. Her hair was long and dark and stringy. On her head she wore a black plush beanie with an ivory stud. The beanie was covered with cartoon-character buttons, the kind you used to get in Kellogg's cereal boxes. Rose Rita wore the beanie all the time.

"Hi," said Lewis. "Did you have to do a lot of stuff?"

Rose Rita shrugged. "Oh, not much. Come on, let's get going. I want to go home first and get out of these dumb clothes."

This was typical of Rose Rita. She wore a skirt and blouse to school because she had to, but the minute she was out of school, she ran home and put on blue jeans and a sweatshirt. Rose Rita was a tomboy. She liked to do things that usually only boys wanted to do, like fishing and climbing trees and playing baseball. Lewis wasn't very good at any of these things, but he enjoyed being with Rose Rita, and she enjoyed being with him. It was September now, and they had been friends since April.

They were on their way down the alley when Rose Rita noticed the paper bag that Lewis was carrying in his left hand.

"What's in there?" she asked.

"My Sherlock Holmes hat."

"Oh." Rose Rita knew about Lewis's Sherlock Holmes hat. Lewis's uncle had given it to him as a Fourth of July present. But she still was curious. "How come you've got it in a sack?"

"I want to wear it on Main Street, but I want to make sure there won't be any kids around when I put it on."

Rose Rita stared at him. "You mean you're just gonna whip it out and put it on and then stuff it back in your bag again?"

"Yeah," said Lewis. He felt embarrassed.

Rose Rita looked more puzzled than ever. "Well, if you're so scared," she said, "why do you want to wear it on Main Street at all? There's likely to be lots of people there to stare at you."

"I know," said Lewis, stubbornly. "But I don't care if a lot of grownups see my hat. I just don't want some smart-aleck kid to steal it from me."

Rose Rita smiled sympathetically. She knew that Lewis was always being pestered by bullies. "Okay, okay," she said. "It's your hat. Come on."

They walked on down the alley and over a block to Main Street. The town that Rose Rita and Lewis lived in was a small town, and the main street was only three blocks long. On it were drug stores and ten cent stores and clothing stores and restaurants and bars. They had gotten as far as Kresge's Ten Cent Store when Lewis stopped and looked hastily around.

"Do you think it'd be okay now, Rose Rita? I don't see any kids around." He started to fumble with the top of the bag.

Rose Rita got angry. "Oh, come *on*, Lewis! This is just idiotic! Look, I have to go in here and buy some pencils and paper and stuff. Then I have to go home and change. I'll meet you at your uncle's house. Okay?"

She was gone before he could answer. Lewis felt a little mad at her, and he also felt foolish. He looked around once more. No mean kids coming. Good. He took out the hat and put it on.

It was really a very fine hat. It was green plaid with stiff visors in front and in back, and ear flaps that were tied up over the top of the hat. When Lewis put it on he felt brave and clever, like Sherlock Holmes tracking down an evildoer in the London fog. Lewis looked around again. He decided that he would wear the hat for the full three blocks, right down to the G.A.R. Hall. Nobody could do anything to him in that short a space.

Lewis walked along with his head down, watching the sidewalk as it went by. A couple of grownups turned and stared at him as he passed. He saw them out of the corner of his eye, but he tried not to notice them. It was funny how he felt two different ways about the hat: on the one hand, he was proud to be wearing it. But he felt embarrassed too. He would be glad when he got to the G.A.R. Hall.

Lewis had just passed Heemsoth's Drug Store when he heard a nasty sarcastic voice say, "Gee, I wish *I* had a hat like that!"

Lewis stopped dead in his tracks. It was Woody Mingo.

Lewis was scared to death of Woody, and he figured that even Dave Shellenberger and Tom Lutz would think twice before they took him on. It wasn't that he was big and strong. He was just a little wiry guy. But he was tough, and he carried a jacknife in his pocket. There were stories that he had actually threatened kids with it.

Lewis backed away. A chilly breath blew through his body. "Come on, Woody," he said. "I never did anything to you. Leave me alone."

Woody snickered. "Lemme see your hat," he said, holding out his hand.

"Promise to give it back?"

"Oh sure. I promise."

Lewis's heart sank. He knew what that tone of voice meant. He would never see his hat again. Lewis looked around to see if there were any grownups nearby who might help him. Nope. Not a one. This end of Main Street was as empty as it was on Sunday morning.

"Come on. Lemme see the hat." Woody sounded impatient. Lewis's eyes filled with tears. Should he run? If he did, he wouldn't get very far. Like most fat kids, Lewis couldn't run very fast. He ran out of breath in a hurry, and he got pains in his side. Woody would catch him and take the hat and pound on his shoulders till he was sore. Sadly, Lewis lifted the hat off his head. He handed it to Woody.

With that same nasty smile, Woody turned the hat over in his hands. He put it on and adjusted the brim.

"Gee, now I look just like Sherlock Holmes in the movies. Well, so long, fatso. Thanks for the hat." Woody turned and sauntered away.

Lewis stood there and watched him go. He felt sick. Tears were running down his face, and his clenched fists were trembling.

"You gimme my hat back!" Lewis yelled. "I'll tell the police on you and they'll throw you in jail for a hundred years!"

Woody never answered. He just walked slowly away, swaggering. He knew Lewis couldn't do a thing to him.

Lewis stumbled blindly down the street. He was crying hard. When he wiped his eyes and looked around, he found that he was in East End Park, a tiny park at the eastern end of Main Street. There were a few benches in the park, and a flower garden surrounded by a little iron fence. Lewis sat down on one of the benches and wiped his eyes. Then he cried some more. How come he hadn't been born strong like other kids? Why did everybody have to pick on him? It wasn't fair.

Lewis sat there on the bench for a fairly long time. Suddenly he sat up straight. He dug into his pocket and pulled out his watch. It was late! He was supposed to meet Rose Rita back at his house, because she had been invited over for dinner. Of course, she had to go home first and change her clothes. But Rose Rita was pretty speedy. She was probably sitting on his front porch right now. Lewis jumped up and started walking quickly toward home.

By the time he got to 100 High Street, where he lived, Lewis was out of breath. There, sure enough, was Rose Rita, sitting next to his uncle on the green striped glider. They were blowing bubbles.

Lewis watched as his Uncle Jonathan blew into the carved meerschaum pipe he was holding. A bubble began to form. It grew and grew until it was about the size of a grapefruit. Then it broke away from the pipe and drifted slowly across the yard toward Lewis. The bubble halted about three inches from his face and began to revolve slowly. In its curved surface Lewis saw reflected Rose Rita, the chestnut tree in the front yard, himself, the tall stone mansion where he lived, and the laughing red-bearded face of his Uncle Jonathan.

Lewis liked his Uncle Jonathan a lot. He had been living with him for a little over a year now. Before that, Lewis had lived in Milwaukee with his parents. But one night, both his father and his mother were killed in a car accident. So in the summer of 1948 Lewis had come to live with his Uncle Jonathan in the town of New Zebedee, Michigan.

The bubble popped, and Lewis felt something on his face. He put up his hand and wiped some of it away. It was shaving lather. Purple shaving lather.

Rose Rita and Jonathan laughed. This was one of Jonathan's magic tricks. He was able to do magic tricks because he was a wizard, a real live wizard with mysterious powers. Rose Rita had found out about Jonathan's wizardry at about the same time that she got to be friends with Lewis. But it didn't faze her a bit. She had taken it all in her stride. Once or twice Lewis had heard her tell Jonathan to his face that she would like him even if he wasn't a wizard.

As Lewis stood there giggling at the shaving-lather trick, he heard a familiar voice say, "Lewis! You look beautiful!"

Lewis looked up. It was Mrs. Zimmermann. She was standing in the doorway of the house, drying a dish with a lavender-colored towel. Mrs. Zimmermann lived next door, but she was practically a member of the Barnavelt family. She was a strange person. For one thing, she was crazy about the color purple. She liked anything that was purple, from the violets of early spring to maroon-colored Pontiacs. And she was a witch. Not a cruel witch with a black hat and a broom and an evil laugh, but a friendly, likable, next-door-neighbor witch. She didn't show off her magic powers as often as Jonathan did, but Lewis knew that she was a more powerful magician than his uncle was.

Lewis wiped more shaving lather off his face. "It doesn't look beautiful at all, Mrs. Zimmermann!" he yelled. "You just think it does because you like everything to be purple!"

Mrs. Zimmermann chuckled. "Well, maybe so. But it's nice all the same. Come on in and wash it off. Dinner's ready."

Lewis was just sitting down at the table when he remembered that he was supposed to be unhappy.

"Gee, I forgot all about my hat," he said.

Rose Rita looked at him. "Yeah, that's right. What happened to your hat? Did you wear it for a whole block, or what?"

Lewis stared at the tablecloth. "Woody Mingo took it."

Rose Rita stopped smiling. "I'm sorry, Lewis," she said, and she really meant it.

Jonathan heaved a deep sigh and laid down his knife and fork. "I told you not to wear it on the street, Lewis. The hat was just for playing with around the house. You know what kids are like."

"Yeah, I know," said Lewis, sadly. He stuffed some mashed potatoes into his mouth and chewed them moodily.

"It was a rotten thing to do," said Rose Rita, angrily. "Maybe if I had stayed with you it might not've happened."

Somehow this made Lewis feel worse. Boys were supposed to protect girls, and not the other way around.

"I can take care of myself," he mumbled.

The meal proceeded for several minutes in total silence. Everyone stared at his plate and munched silently. Gloom lay over the table like a mantle of fog.

Jonathan sat there staring at the tablecloth like everyone else. But, unlike them, he was thinking. He was racking his brains, trying to dream up something that would cheer them all up. Suddenly he brought his fist down on the table. Plates rattled, and the lid jumped off the sugar bowl. Everyone looked up.

"What on earth is the matter with you?" said Mrs. Zimmermann. "Did you see an ant, or what?"

"Nothing's the matter," said Jonathan, grinning. Now that he had everyone's attention, he folded his hands and stared off into space. "Lewis?" he said.

"Yes, Uncle Jonathan?"

Jonathan continued to stare into space, but his grin got wider. "How would you like to see what's inside Grampa Barnavelt's trunk?"

CHAPTER TWO

Lewis's mouth dropped open. Grampa Barnavelt's trunk was a big heavy chest that stood locked at the foot of Jonathan's bed. Jonathan claimed that he hadn't opened it in over twenty years, and Lewis was always pestering him for a chance to peek into it. Now he was going to have that chance. He felt like jumping up and down in his seat, and he could tell that Rose Rita was excited too.

"Oh boy, Uncle Jonathan!" Lewis cried. "Oh boy, that'd be just great!"

"I think so too!" said Rose Rita.

"So do I," added Mrs. Zimmermann. "Seeing as how I'm a nosy old lady who likes surprises."

"You certainly are, Frizzy Wig," said Jonathan.

"Nosy, that is. Now tell me, folks. Would you like your ice cream and cookies now, or after we open the chest? All those in favor of opening the chest now, raise their hands."

Lewis and Rose Rita started to raise their hands, but then they remembered that the cookies were Mrs. Zimmermann's. Maybe her feelings would be hurt if they voted to postpone dessert. They pulled their hands down.

Mrs. Zimmermann glared at the two of them and raised her hand. "May I speak, teacher?" she said in a whiny little voice.

"Sure. Go ahead," said Jonathan, grinning.

"If you don't go up and help me bring that chest down *right now*, I'll turn you into a wastebasket full of pencil shavings. Understand?"

"Aye, aye!" said Jonathan, saluting. He and Mrs. Zimmermann got up and went to get the trunk.

Lewis and Rose Rita wandered into the study. They stood around leafing through books and drawing pictures in the dust on the library table. Before long they heard doors slamming and a lot of banging and one loud shout (from Jonathan) followed by some muffled swearing. At last the trunk arrived. Jonathan was holding his end of it with one hand and sucking at the knuckles of his other hand, which he had skinned while trying to take the trunk around a narrow corner.

"Well, here we are!" said Mrs. Zimmermann. She set

her end of the trunk down and mopped her face with a purple handkerchief. "What did your grampa store in here, Jonathan? Cannon balls?"

"Just about," said Jonathan. "Now as soon as I can find the key . . . hmm, I wonder where it is?" Jonathan scratched his bushy red beard and stared at the ceiling.

"Oh, don't tell me you've lost it!" said Mrs. Zimmermann in exasperation.

"No, I haven't lost it. I just don't remember where it is. Half a minute." Jonathan left the room, and they heard him going back upstairs.

"I hope it isn't lost," said Lewis, who could get gloomy at a moment's notice if things weren't working out just right.

"Don't worry," said Mrs. Zimmermann. "If worse comes to worst your uncle will shoot the lock off with Grampa Barnavelt's Civil War pistol—unless of course it's locked in the trunk with everything else."

While Jonathan was upstairs hunting for the key, Lewis and Rose Rita had a chance to examine the outside of the old trunk. It had a humped lid, which made it look like a pirate chest, but it was really a steamer trunk, a kind of suitcase that people used to take with them on ocean voyages a long time ago. The trunk was made of wood, but it was covered with alligator leather. Three big strips of hammered copper had been nailed across the lid for decoration. They had turned bright green with age. The lockplate was made of copper too, and it was shaped like a baby's face. The baby's mouth was the keyhole.

After what seemed like a very long time, Jonathan returned. In his hand he held a small iron key with a cardboard tag dangling from it.

"Where was it?" asked Mrs. Zimmermann. She was trying hard to suppress a giggle.

"Where?" snapped Jonathan. "Where? Exactly where you'd expect it to be. At the bottom of a vase full of Indian head pennies." He knelt down and stuck the key in the lock. Lewis, Rose Rita, and Mrs. Zimmermann gathered behind him. The lock was stiff and rusty, so it took Jonathan several tries, but at last the key turned. Carefully, he lifted the shaky old lid.

The first thing that Lewis and Rose Rita noticed when the trunk was opened was the inside of the lid. It was covered with faded pink wallpaper, and somebody long ago—maybe a child—had pasted pictures on the paper. The pictures looked as if they had been cut from a very old-fashioned magazine. Lewis and Rose Rita looked inside the trunk. Under a thick gritty layer of dust were a number of parcels done up in newspaper and string. One was long and curved and thin. Another was flat and square. Some were just big and bulky. The newspaper was old and yellow, and some of the parcels were coming undone because the string was rotting.

Jonathan reached in and started handing parcels around.

"Here you are. One for you, Lewis, and one for you, Rose Rita, and even one for you, Pruny. And one for little me."

"Hah," said Mrs. Zimmermann, as she tugged at a piece of string. "I'll bet you saved the best one for yourself."

Lewis had the long curved parcel. When he had ripped the paper off one end, he saw the tarnished brass hilt of a sword. "Oh boy!" he said. "A real sword!" He ripped the rest of the paper off and started swinging the sword around. Fortunately, it was still in its sheath.

"Have at thee for a foul faytour!" he shouted, lunging at Rose Rita with the sword.

"Hey, Sir Ector, watch it, will you?" said Jonathan. Lewis stopped and looked sheepish. Then everybody, including Lewis, laughed.

"You might have known what would happen when you put a sword in the hands of an eleven-year-old boy," said Mrs. Zimmermann. "Here, let me see it."

Lewis handed the sword to Mrs. Zimmermann. Tugging gently, she eased it halfway out of its scabbard. The tarnished blade flashed dimly in the lamplight.

"Whose sword was it?" asked Lewis.

"Grampa Barnavelt's," said Jonathan. "It's a cavalry saber—you can tell because it's curved and quite heavy. Put it back in the sheath, Florence. Knives make me nervous."

Lewis knew a little bit about Grampa Barnavelt. He had seen his name on the Civil War Memorial, and Jonathan had told him a few stories about the old man, but these stories had merely whetted Lewis's appetite.

"Grampa Barnavelt was a lancer, wasn't he?" asked Lewis.

"That's right," said Jonathan. "Rose Rita, open your package."

Rose Rita was holding a soft little parcel. When she had popped the string and ripped off the paper, she found that she was holding a pile of old clothes. On top was a blue shirt that had been folded up so long it wouldn't come unfolded. Under that was a pair of baggy red pantaloons and a flattened red felt cap with FIFTH MICHIGAN FIRE ZOUAVE LANCERS embroidered on it in gold thread.

"What are the Fifth Michigan . . . whatever they are?" asked Rose Rita.

"Idiots," snapped Mrs. Zimmermann. "Idiots they were, the whole bunch of them."

"That's true," said Jonathan, stroking his beard. "But that is probably not the answer Rose Rita wanted. In the first place . . . well, let's let Lewis answer this. He's read about lancers."

"Lancers are cavalry soldiers with long spears," Lewis explained. "They used the spears to run the enemy soldiers through."

"If they got close enough," said Jonathan. "You see, Rose Rita, lancers were sort of a holdover from the

Middle Ages, when knights used to knock each other off horses with spears. But in the Civil War, lancers had to charge against soldiers who had muskets and rifles and cannons."

"That sounds kind of dumb," said Rose Rita. "How come they wanted to do that?"

"Well, I'm not quite sure," said Jonathan, "but I think they had some idea that those long spears and flapping pennants and bright-colored uniforms would throw terror into the foot soldiers of the enemy."

"Did they?" asked Lewis.

Jonathan looked confused. "Did they what?"

"Strike terror into the enemy."

"Oh. Well, yes, sometimes they did. But more often than not the soldiers with muskets and rifles cut the lancers to pieces. That is what happened at the Battle of Spotsylvania Court House. The Fifth Michigan charged, and it got wiped out. Only Grampa Barnavelt and a man named Walter Finzer came back alive. And they survived because they never got into the battle."

Lewis's face fell. He had imagined his great-grandfather slashing and lancing and thrusting his way right through the enemy lines. "How come he didn't get into the battle?" he asked.

"Go ahead, Jonathan. Tell them," said Mrs. Zimmermann, grinning. She had heard the story a thousand times, but it still tickled her.

"Well, it's like this," said Jonathan. He coughed, folded his arms, and settled back into his storytelling pose. "Your great-grampa, Lewis, was not one of the bravest men in the world. I think he joined the Michigan Lancers because he thought their uniforms were pretty. But the closer he came to an actual fight, the more scared he got. The Battle of Spotsylvania was going to be his first taste of real combat. Well now. On the night before the battle, Grampa was playing poker by the campfire with some other members of the company, and he found that he was holding a very good hand. I think it was a full house or four of a kind or something like that. Anyway, before long, only Grampa and Walter Finzer were left in the game. Walter was a New Zebedee boy too, and he had joined up at about the same time as Grampa. Well, Walter raised Grampa and Grampa raised Walter, and before long the two of them had thrown every cent they had, and their swords and pistols, into the pot. But when Grampa took off his gold signet ring and tossed it in, Walter didn't have anything to answer it with. Walter tried to borrow money from some of the other men, but they all thought Walter was a deadbeat, and they wouldn't lend him a cent. Walter was about ready to throw in his cards and let Grampa take the pot, when Grampa said, 'How about your lucky piece?' "

"Lucky piece?" said Lewis.

"Yes. You see, Grampa had gotten into the game hoping that he would be able to relieve Walter of the lucky coin he carried. I know it sounds silly, but Grampa was convinced that Walter's lucky coin would get him through the battle without a scratch. Who knows why Grampa thought this? Pilots trust to baby booties and rabbits' feet. Grampa had heard Walter bragging about this coin, so he figured that maybe it would help him." Jonathan smiled sadly. "I think Grampa was so scared he would have trusted to anything to see him through the next day's battle."

"Was it magic?" asked Rose Rita. "The coin, I mean."

Jonathan chuckled. "No, I'm afraid not. But Grampa thought it was, and that's the important thing. To go on with the story, he told Walter to throw the coin in, and Walter refused. Walter was a bullheaded and rather stupid sort, and he didn't want to part with the coin. Finally, though, his friends persuaded him to throw it in. Then Walter and Grampa both showed their hands, and Grampa won. Walter was furious. He screamed and yelled and stomped and swore, and in the end, when Grampa started to rake in the money, he grabbed a pistol out of somebody's holster and shot Grampa in the leg."

"That's awful!" said Rose Rita. "Did Grampa Barnavelt die?"

"No, but the wound put him out of commission for a

long while. Walter, of course, was put under arrest immediately, and later on he got a dishonorable discharge from the Army. He might have gotten worse, but Grampa pleaded for clemency for him. You see, Grampa Barnavelt was really a rather soft-hearted and gentle man. He had no business trying to fight in a war."

Jonathan settled back in his chair and lighted his pipe. Mrs. Zimmermann and Lewis went out to the kitchen, and came back with chocolate-chip cookies and ice cream. Suddenly, as everyone was eating, Lewis looked up and said, "Did Grampa keep the coin? Is it still around?"

Jonathan laughed. "He sure did keep it! He put it on his watch chain and told everybody he met how he got it. I got so tired of hearing that story when I was a kid."

"Could we see it?" Lewis asked.

Jonathan looked startled. "See it? Well, I guess so, if I can find it. I imagine it's rattling around in this old trunk somewhere. Wouldn't you think so, Florence?"

"How would I know? It's your trunk. Let's have a look."

Jonathan, Mrs. Zimmermann, Lewis, and Rose Rita gathered around the old chest and started lifting out parcels and unwrapping them. There was a top hat and a black frock coat shiny at the elbows, and some books and three or four albums full of old photos, and one genuine cannon ball. Finally everything was out of the chest but the dust and the dead insects at the bottom. Everything, that is, except one small battered wooden box.

"I'll bet it's in there," said Lewis.

"I wouldn't count on it," said Jonathan. "But let's have a peek anyway."

He reached in and lifted the box out. There was no lock on it, and after a little tugging the lid came off, hinges and all. Inside were an old pair of rimless spectacles, a blackened tobacco pipe, and a heavy braided watch chain. A tiny silver coin was attached to the chain.

"Hey, it's really there!" Lewis reached into the box and carefully lifted the watch chain out. He handled it as if it were a string of diamonds. Now he and Rose Rita were examining the coin. It was a strange-looking thing, smaller and thinner than a dime. On one side was a Roman numeral III. On the other was a six-pointed star with a striped shield inside it. "United States of America" was printed around the outside of the star, and under the bottom point of the star was a date: 1859.

"What is it?" asked Lewis. He had never seen a coin like it in his life.

"It's a United States three-cent piece," said Mrs. Zimmermann. "Anyone ought to be able to see that."

Rose Rita laughed. "Oh, come on, Mrs. Zimmermann!

You're always kidding. You mean this coin was worth three cents way back then?"

"It certainly was. It's worth a little bit more now, because it's old, but it's not very rare as coins go."

"Why did they have three-cent coins?" asked Lewis. "Wouldn't it have been easier to just use three pennies?"

"You'll have to ask the United States Mint why they had three-cent pieces," said Jonathan. "At one time they had half cents and two-cent pieces and half dimes and all sorts of weird denominations. So, as Mrs. Zimmermann says, this coin is not so strange—except for the fact that it's part of the story I just told you."

Lewis looked at the coin and imagined it lying on a heap of money and swords and pistols in the red light of a campfire. He imagined Walter Finzer pulling a gun and shooting Grampa Barnavelt. Blood had been shed because of that coin. Lewis had read a lot, and he knew stories about kings who had fought and killed each other over small objects. Small objects like crowns and jewels and pieces of gold. The coin seemed to Lewis like something straight out of those old tales.

Lewis looked up at his Uncle Jonathan. "Uncle Jonathan, are you *sure* this coin isn't magic?"

"Sure as sure can be, Lewis. But just to set your mind at ease, why don't you give to to Mrs. Zimmermann for a minute? She knows all about magic amulets and talismans and things of that kind, and I think she could probably tell just by the feel of the thing. Couldn't you, Florence?"

"Yes, I could. At my final exam at the University of Göttingen, when I was getting my doctor's degree in Magic, I had to tell if certain objects were enchanted or not just by feeling them with my fingers. Here, let me see it."

Lewis handed the coin to Mrs. Zimmermann. She rubbed it back and forth between her fingers and stared at it thoughtfully for a few minutes. Then she handed it back to Lewis.

"Sorry, Lewis," she said, shaking her head. "It just feels like a hunk of metal. If it was magic, it would . . . well, it would kind of *tingle* in my hand. But there's nothing there. It's just an old coin."

Lewis held the coin up and looked at it sadly. Then he turned to Jonathan and said, "Can I keep it?"

Jonathan blinked absent-mindedly. "Hm?"

"I said, can I keep it?"

"Can you . . . ? Oh. Oh, sure. Go ahead. It's yours. Keep it as a souvenir of the Civil War." Jonathan patted Lewis on the shoulder and smiled.

Late that night, when Rose Rita and Mrs. Zimmermann had gone home and Jonathan had gone to bed, Lewis sat on the edge of his bed looking at the coin. It was too bad it wasn't magic. If it had been, it might've turned out to be one of those amulets that made you brave and strong and protected you from your enemies. Like the pin that an ancient king of Ireland wore in his shirt when he went into battle. As long as he kept the pin on, he couldn't be wounded. Lewis liked that story. He had never gone into battle with sword and shield, but he had gotten into a few fist fights, and he had always lost them. Maybe if he had had an amulet, he would have won those fights. Maybe if he had had an amulet, Woody Mingo would not have been able to steal his hat.

Oh well, thought Lewis, that's the way it goes. He put the coin in the drawer of his bedside table, turned out the light, and went to bed.

Lewis went to bed, but he didn't go to sleep. He lay there tossing and turning and thinking about Woody and the Sherlock Holmes hat and Grampa Barnavelt and Walter Finzer and the three-cent piece. After that he just lay there and listened to the sounds of the house: the clock ticking, the bathtub faucet dripping, the various cracks and creaks and snaps that a big old house makes when it is settling itself for the night.

Flip-flop. Lewis sat up straight in his bed. He knew that sound. He knew it very well—but it was not a nighttime sound. It was the sound of the mail slot.

The front door of Lewis's house had a slot in it for mail. The slot had a hinged metal cover over it, and when the mailman lifted the cover to slide letters in, the cover went flip-flop. Lewis and his uncle both loved to get mail, and no matter where they were in the house, when they heard the flip-flop sound, they came running. The mailman on their route was very talkative, and so he seldom got to their house before two-thirty in the afternoon. But as far as Lewis knew, the mail had never arrived at midnight.

Lewis sat there wondering for a few minutes. Then he got out of bed, put on his slippers and bathrobe, and padded downstairs to the front hall. There on the floor, just below the mail slot, lay a postcard.

Lewis picked the card up and carried it over to the hall window. The gray light of a full moon was streaming in. It was bright enough to read by—but there was nothing to read. The card was blank.

Lewis began to feel creepy. What kind of a message was this? He turned the card over, and was relieved to find that the card was stamped and addressed. But the stamp looked very old-fashioned, and the postmark was so blurred that Lewis couldn't tell where the card had been mailed from. The card was addressed in a neat, curlicued hand.

Master Lewis Barnavelt
100 High Street
New Zebedee, Michigan

/ 29 /

There was no return address.

Lewis stood there in the moonlight with the card in his hand. Maybe Rose Rita had gotten up in the middle of the night to play him a practical joke. Maybe—but it didn't seem likely. Lewis turned the card over and looked at the blank side again. His eyes opened wide. Now there was writing on the card.

Venio

Lewis's hand began to tremble. He had read about writing in invisible ink, but he had always heard that you had to dust the message with special powders or hold it over the fire to make the letters appear. This message had appeared all by itself.

And Lewis knew what the message said. He could read a little Latin, because he had been an altar boy once, and he knew what *Venio* meant: I come. Suddenly Lewis felt very afraid. He was afraid of being alone in the dark hallway. But as he stepped quickly across the hall to snap on the light, the card slipped out of his hand. It actually felt as if someone had grabbed it and pulled it away. Lewis panicked and flung himself at the wall switch. Warm yellow light flooded the hallway of the old house. There was no one there. But the card was gone.

CHAPTER THREE

The next morning, as soon as he got up, Lewis went downstairs to look for the mysterious postcard. He looked under the hall rug, and into the cracks between the floorboards. He looked into the blue Willoware vase where Jonathan kept his canes. He looked everywhere. The card had vanished. None of the cracks in the floor was wide enough for it to have slipped through, and the card couldn't very well have floated back out through the covered mail slot. *Where did it go?*

Lewis didn't feel like talking to Uncle Jonathan about the card, but as he ate his Cheerios that morning, a comfortable explanation occurred to him. The card was probably just part of Uncle Jonathan's magic.

Lewis had lived in the home of a practicing wizard for over a year now, and during that time he had come to expect strange sights and sounds. The mirror on the coat rack showed you your face when you looked in it—sometimes. But more often than not, it would show you Roman ruins in the desert or Mayan pyramids or Melrose Abbey in Scotland. There was an organ in the front parlor that sang radio commercials. And the stained-glass windows in the enormous old house changed their pictures from time to time, all by themselves. Maybe the ghostly card was one of Jonathan's little jokes. Lewis could have found out if his answer was right by asking Jonathan, since Jonathan controlled all the magic in the house. But he was afraid to ask. If his answer was wrong, he didn't want to know about it.

One afternoon in the middle of October, Lewis decided to go back to school early. Most of the time he waited out the noon hour at home, because he was afraid of getting beat up. But today he was going back early because Rose Rita had talked him into it.

Lewis and Rose Rita had had a long talk about his fears. She had tried to persuade him that the only way to conquer his fears was to meet them head-on. He had to force himself to go back to the playground right after lunch. After the first time, the second time would be easier, and so on. This was the way Rose Rita argued. Lewis had been stubborn at first, but he had finally agreed to try it her way. To make things easier for him,

Rose Rita had agreed to meet him in the alley next to the school. He wouldn't have to get into a football game or anything. The two of them would just stand around and talk. They could talk about the model Roman galley they were building out of balsa wood. It would be a lot of fun.

When Lewis got to the school, he peered down the long narrow alley. No Rose Rita. At the far end he could hear kids shouting and playing. Cautiously, he began to edge his way down the alley toward the playground. He always expected to get jumped, and sometimes it really happened.

Lewis had gotten about halfway down the alley when he heard something off to his left. It sounded like grunting and scuffling. Lewis turned and saw two kids fighting in the dark shadowy space between the buttresses of the Episcopal church. The kids were Rose Rita and Woody Mingo.

Lewis stood watching, paralyzed with fear. Woody had one hand around Rose Rita's waist, and with his other hand he was pulling her hair. Hard, so that it must really have hurt. But Rose Rita said nothing. Her eyes were closed, and her teeth were set in a rigid grimace.

"Come on," Woody snarled. "Take it back!"

"No."

"Take it *back*!"

"I said no, and—ow!—I meant—*no*!"

Woody grinned his nastiest grin. "Okay then—" He gave Rose Rita's hair a short vicious yank. Her grimace got tighter, and her teeth ground together. But she still refused to scream.

Lewis didn't know what to do. Should he run and get the principal, or go for the police? Or should he try to take on Woody all by himself? He thought about Woody's knife, and he was afraid.

Now Woody saw Lewis. He laughed, just the way he had when he stole Lewis's hat.

"Hey, fat guts! Arncha gonna rescue yer girl friend?" Woody gave Rose Rita's hair another yank, and she winced.

Rose Rita opened her eyes and glanced at Lewis. "Go away, Lewis!" she hissed. "Just go away!"

Lewis stood there, clenching and unclenching his fists. He looked toward the street, where cars were slowly rolling past. He looked toward the playground, where he could hear kids laughing and shouting and playing.

"C'mon, lard ass! You wanna try'n take me? Let's see ya try!"

Lewis turned and ran. Down the alley, out onto the sidewalk, across the intersection, up Green Street toward home. His feet slapped the pavement under him, and he could hear himself crying as he ran. He stopped halfway down Green Street because he couldn't run any more. His side hurt and his head ached and he wished that he were dead. When he had finally gotten his breath back, he wiped his eyes, blew his nose, and trotted the rest of the way home.

Uncle Jonathan was raking leaves in the front yard when Lewis came stomping moodily up the sidewalk.

"Hi, Lewis!" he called, waving cheerfully with his pipe. "Did they let school out early, or . . ."

Clang went the front gate. Slam went the front door a few seconds after. Jonathan dropped his rake and went in to see what was wrong.

He found Lewis crying with his head on the dining room table.

"God-dam dirty rotten no-good god-dam dirty . . ." was all Lewis would say, over and over.

Jonathan sat down in the chair next to him and put his arm around him. "Come on, Lewis," he said gently. "It's okay. What's wrong? Do you want to tell me what happened?"

Lewis wiped his eyes and blew his nose several times. Then, slowly and brokenly, he told his uncle the whole story. ". . . and I ran away and she'll never want to have anything to do with me ever again," he sobbed. "I wish I was *dead*!"

"Oh, I doubt if Rosie is going to scratch you off her social list," said Jonathan, smiling and patting him on the shoulder. "She just wanted to take care of herself, that's all. She's a real tomboy, and if she got into a fight with Woody, I guess she figured she could handle herself."

Lewis turned and looked at Jonathan through his tears. "You mean she won't hate me on account of I'm a coward and a weakling?"

"You're not either one of those," said Jonathan. "And anyway, if Rosie had wanted a lug for a best friend, she'd have found a lug. She's a very stubborn girl, and she does what she wants to do. And I think she likes you a lot."

"You do?"

"Mm-hmm. Now, I'm going to go finish raking the leaves, so we can have a bonfire in the driveway tonight. I'll write you a note Monday so you won't be in trouble with Miss Haggerty, and—well, why don't you go work on that ship model?"

Lewis smiled gratefully at his uncle. He hiccupped a few times, as he often did after he had been crying. "Okay, Uncle Jonathan. Thanks a lot."

Lewis went up to his room, and for the rest of the afternoon he was all wrapped up in the world of Greek and Roman triremes, and the great sea battles of Salamis and Actium. Just before dinner the phone rang. Lewis took the stairs two at a time, and almost fell on his face.

"Hi!" he panted as he picked up the receiver. "Is that you, Rose Rita?"

He heard a giggle at the other end. "If it hadn't of been, what would you have done?"

Lewis felt relieved. "Are you mad at me?" he asked.

"Unh-uh. I just called to find out what happened to you."

Lewis felt his face getting red. "I felt kinda sick so I went home. Did Woody beat you up?"

"Nope. A couple of the teachers came by and made us stop fighting. I would've fixed him if it hadn't've been for my darned hair. I think I'll get a crew cut."

"How come you were fighting?"

"Oh, I told him he was a dirty little sneak thief for stealing your hat, and he wanted me to take it back and I wouldn't."

Lewis was silent. He felt the way he had when Rose Rita had said that she wished she had been there to keep Woody from stealing the hat. It was a confusing feeling. He was grateful to her for sticking up for him, but it felt awful not to be able to fight and win your own battles. Boys were supposed to be able to do that.

"Are you okay?" Rose Rita asked. Lewis had been silent for a whole minute.

"Uh . . . yeah, sure. I was . . . I was just thinking," Lewis stammered. "Woody didn't hurt you, did he?"

Rose Rita snorted disdainfully. "Oh, he wouldn't do anything to me but pull my hair because I'm a *gurr-rul*. Hey, Lewis?"

"Yeah?"

"Let's get to work on that ship again. You want to bring it over to my house tonight?"

"Okay."

"See you after dinner. Bye."

"Bye."

Lewis was relieved to know that Rose Rita didn't hate him for running away. But he kept thinking about the fight between her and Woody, and that night he had a dream about it. In the dream, Woody had knocked Rose Rita down, and her head was bleeding. Lewis grabbed him and socked him and then Woody pulled his knife and held it up in front of Lewis's nose. Then Woody said, "I'm gonna cut your tongue out!" and Lewis awoke suddenly. He was sitting up in bed and his pajamas were drenched with sweat. It was a long time before he could get back to sleep again.

The next morning when Lewis got up, he decided that he was going to get thin and tough like Woody. He got down on the floor and tried to do ten pushups, but he could only do three before he collapsed. Then he tried sit-ups, but when he lay down flat on his back, he couldn't struggle up to a sitting position unless he thrashed around and used his elbows. He stood up and tried to touch his toes without bending his knees, but he couldn't do it. Trying made his head ache. Finally he tried jumping jacks. They were fun because you could clap your hands over your head when you did them. But the flab on Lewis's thighs clapped too, when his legs came together, and this sound depressed him. Also, he was afraid of bringing down the plaster in the room below. So he gave up and went downstairs to have breakfast.

It was Saturday morning, and Mrs. Zimmermann had come over to make breakfast. Although she lived next door, she usually cooked for the Barnavelts, and on Saturdays she always made something very special for breakfast. It might be doughnuts or pancakes and sausages or strawberry shortcake, or french toast with comb honey and peach preserves. This morning, Mrs. Zimmermann was making waffles. Lewis watched her as she poured some of the rich yellow batter onto the black iron grid. Then he remembered his resolution.

"Uh . . . Mrs. Zimmermann?" he said.

"Yes, Lewis?"

"I, uh, don't think I'll have any waffles this morning. Could I just have a bowl of corn flakes?"

Mrs. Zimmermann turned and looked at him strangely. She was about to go over and feel his forehead when she remembered what Jonathan had told her about the fight between Woody and Rose Rita. Mrs. Zimmermann was a very shrewd woman, and it didn't take her long to guess what Lewis had up his sleeve. So she shrugged her shoulders and said, "Okay. That'll just be a little more for me and your uncle."

Lewis managed to hold to his resolve all the way through breakfast. It was pure torture to see all those nice golden waffles and that thick maple syrup being passed back and forth in front of his nose. But he swallowed hard and ate his soggy, tasteless cornflakes.

After breakfast, Lewis went down to the junior high gym to work out. He punched the punching bag until his fists were sore. Then he rolled up his sleeve and flexed the muscle in his right arm. He couldn't tell if anything was happening, so he walked across the basketball court to find Mr. Hartwig. Mr. Hartwig was the gym instructor. He was a big cheerful man who was always throwing medicine balls at you and telling you to hit that line and suck in your gut and hup-two-three-four and stuff like that. When Lewis found him, Mr. Hartwig was organizing some informal boxing matches among boys who just seemed to be standing around doing nothing.

"Hi, Mr. Hartwig!" Lewis yelled. "Hey, can I see you for a minute?"

Mr. Hartwig smiled. "Sure thing, Lewis. What can I do for you?"

Lewis rolled up his sleeve again and held out his arm. He flexed the muscle, or what was supposed to be the muscle. "Do you see anything, Mr. Hartwig?" asked Lewis, hopefully.

Mr. Hartwig tried hard to keep from smiling. He knew Lewis, and he knew something about his problems. "Well, I see your arm," he said slowly. "Have you been working out today?"

"Yeah. Kinda. Doesn't it show?" Lewis flexed his arm again. He was getting embarrassed with all those kids standing around watching. Normally he wouldn't have done anything like this in front of them, but he really had to know. Mr. Hartwig was an expert. He could tell if Lewis's muscles were getting bigger.

Mr. Hartwig put his arm around Lewis and took him aside. "Listen, Lewis," he said quietly, "it takes more than five minutes with a punching bag to build up your muscles. You have to work at it for weeks and months and even years. So don't be discouraged if nothing happens right away. Okay? Now go back and hit that bag!" Mr. Hartwig smiled kindly and gave Lewis a light playful jab in the stomach, which was what he did when he liked you. Lewis winced. He thanked Mr. Hartwig and went back to the punching bag.

But his heart really wasn't in it now. If it was going to take years for him to build up a manly physique, he might as well knock it off and have lunch. It was almost one o'clock, and he was getting hungry.

Later, Lewis was sitting at the counter in Heemsoth's Drug Store. He had just had two hot dogs and two large cherry Cokes for lunch. Now he was leafing through a Captain Marvel comic book. Captain Marvel was slugging it out with the usual collection of crooks and villains. His uppercuts landed with sounds like ZOK! and POW! Lewis had tried a few uppercuts, but they had never landed on anybody's chin. The kids he had tried to use them on had just stepped away and laughed.

Lewis read all the stories in the comic book and then

flipped to the back. There were ads there for things like a Vacutex, an evil-looking gadget that resembled a hypodermic. It was supposed to suck out unsightly blackheads. That was more of a teenager's problem. Lewis had other things to worry about.

He turned to the last page, and there was the Charles Atlas ad. It was always there, and it was always the same. There was a little cartoon story about a 97-pound weakling who got strong so he could get even with the guy who kicked sand in his face at the beach. And there at the bottom of the ad was Charles Atlas himself, in a white bathing suit that always made Lewis think of a baby's diaper. Mr. Atlas looked as if he were covered with grease, and he was bulging and rippling all over with muscles. He was shaking his fist at Lewis and daring him to try his Dynamic Tension Exercises. Under the picture of Mr. Atlas was the little coupon that you were supposed to cut out. Lewis had been on the point of cutting it out many times, but he had always stopped for some reason or other. Now, he ripped out the page, folded it neatly, and slipped it into his pocket. That afternoon when he got home, he put the coupon in an envelope with a quarter and mailed it off to Charles Atlas.

Lewis kept at his diet and his pushups for three or four days, but by the end of that time it was getting pretty boring. He kept feeling his arms, but it didn't seem to him that any new muscles were arriving. And dieting meant that he felt crabby a good deal of the time. He began to realize that Mr. Hartwig was right. Getting thin and tough like Woody took work. You had to deny yourself things that you really wanted, and you had to slave away at things that were really very dull, like exercises. And even then, you couldn't be absolutely positively sure that you would get what you wanted after all your hard work.

Lewis began to weaken, and then he gave in completely. He decided that he would take a break and go back to his plan when he felt better. Before long he was munching Reese's Peanut Butter Cups and taking second helpings of strawberry shortcake with whipped cream. He stopped doing pushups and he never went near the punching bag again. Now and then he would check the mail to see if the Charles Atlas booklet had arrived, but it was never there.

If only there was an easy way of getting to be strong! Lewis thought about Grampa Barnavelt's lucky piece. Wouldn't it be great if it really was magic? Magic in a way that would let him mow down his enemies and protect Rose Rita from harm? That would sure be something! Then he could forget about dieting and pushups. Then . . .

But every time Lewis had this daydream, he remembered that Mrs. Zimmermann had examined the coin, and she had flatly stated that it was not magic. Mrs. Zimmermann was an expert on magic. She ought to know.

On the other hand, experts had been wrong before, like those people who claimed that men would never be able to fly. Lewis would argue with himself this way, back and forth, pro and con, until he was sick of the whole business. Then he would go up to his room and take the coin out of his drawer and press it between his thumb and index finger. Wasn't there a tingle there? No, there wasn't. Then he would get angry and shove the coin back in the drawer and slam the drawer shut. He did this over and over again, but nothing ever happened. Lewis fiddled with the coin so much, wishing over it and pressing it, that he began to think of it as his "magic coin." The phrase "magic coin" kept running through his mind like a broken record. He tried to think of other things, but the phrase kept coming back. Magic coin. Magic coin. Was it just wishful thinking, or was there something else at work?

CHAPTER FOUR

On a bright sunny Saturday afternoon in late October, Lewis and Rose Rita were poking around in Jonathan's library. Some people put a bookcase in a room and call the room a library, but that was not Jonathan's way. His library was crammed, floor to ceiling, with books. Lewis often went to this room to browse or just to sit and think. Today he was there with Rose Rita, looking for a Latin motto to put on the sail of the Roman galley they were building. The galley had turned into quite a project. Lewis and Rose Rita had sat up late many nights with strips of balsa wood and rubber cement and model airplane glue. They had the ship about half finished, but, as often happens, they had gotten hung up on an unimportant detail. Lewis had drawn a picture of Duilius, the great Roman admiral, on the sail, and he had found a motto to go with the picture: IN HOC SIGNO VINCES. The motto came from a carton of Pall Mall cigarettes; it wasn't appropriate, but it was the only one Lewis could find. Rose Rita had informed him that she thought the motto was stupid and senseless. Now the two of them were digging through the Latin books in Jonathan's collection, looking for a reasonable, appropriate, and suitably dignified motto. In other words, they were looking for a motto that Rose Rita liked.

"You know, Lewis, it would kind of help if your uncle would keep his books in better order," Rose Rita complained.

"It would, huh? Okay, what's wrong with the way my uncle keeps his books?" Lewis was getting tired of Rose Rita's crabbing, and he was beginning to fight back.

"What's wrong? Oh, not much. Just look at them! This section here is supposed to be Latin books, and there's adventure novels, and old phone books, and even a book by Mrs. Zimmermann."

Lewis was startled. He didn't know that Mrs. Zimmermann had written a book. "Gee, that's weird. What kind of a book is it?"

"I dunno. Let's see." Rose Rita took down from the bookshelf a dusty book in a black leather pebble-grained cover. A title was stamped on the spine in gold letters. It said:

AMULETS

by
F. H. Zimmermann
D. Mag.A.

Rose Rita and Lewis knelt down on the floor to examine the book. The first page was the title page. It said:

A FREE INQUIRY INTO
THE PROPERTIES OF MAGIC AMULETS

A dissertation submitted to
the Faculty of Magic Arts of the University of
Göttingen, in partial fulfillment of the
requirements for the Degree of
DOCTOR MAGICORUM ARTIUM
(*Doctor of Magic Arts*)

by
Florence Helene Zimmermann
June 13, 1922

English Language Copy

Lewis was amazed. Amazed, and fascinated. He knew that Mrs. Zimmermann had gone to college to learn how to be a witch, but he didn't know about this book.

"I bet your uncle would be mad if he knew we were looking at this," said Rose Rita, giggling.

Lewis glanced nervously toward the door. At one time Jonathan had kept his magic books out on the shelves with all the other books in his collection. But he had gotten concerned about Lewis's interest in magic, and so one day he had scooped up all the magic books he could find and carried them off to his bedroom closet. That was where they were now, locked up. All but this one, which Jonathan had forgotten about.

"Yeah, I'll bet he doesn't even know it's here," said Lewis.

"Well, serves him right for keeping such a messy library," said Rose Rita. "Come on, let's see what's in it."

Lewis and Rose Rita sat down on the floor and began leafing through Mrs. Zimmermann's book. They found out quite a bit about magic amulets. They read about the strange parchment found on the body of Bishop Anselm of Würzburg, and the lost amulet of Queen Catherine de Medici of France. Finally, at the end of the book, they came to a chapter with this title:

ON THE VARIOUS METHODS
OF TESTING AMULETS

Lewis thought about the coin in his drawer upstairs, and he began to get very interested. But what he read at first was disappointing. The book just said what Mrs. Zimmermann had said the night they found the coin: only a real wizard could test an amulet. Mrs. Zimmermann had tested the three-cent piece, using the method recommended by her own book. And the coin had turned out to be just a coin.

Rose Rita was getting pretty bored with amulets. "Come on, Lewis," she said impatiently. "We're wasting a lot of time. Let's go see if we can find something nice to put on our ship." She closed the book and started to get up.

"Wait a minute," said Lewis, opening the book again. "There's one more page. Let's see what's on it." Rose Rita heaved a deep sigh and sat down again.

They turned to the last page, and this is what they read:

> There are a few extremely powerful amulets that will not respond to the tests I have described. These amulets are very rare. I have never handled such an amulet, nor have I ever seen one, but it is said that one was owned by King Solomon, and that Simon Magus somehow contrived to steal one, so that for a time he seemed to be a very great magician indeed.
>
> These amulets of which I speak are so powerful that they do not appear to be magic at all. They do not respond to any of the standard tests. Yet, I am told that they will respond to this test:
>
> Place the amulet in your left hand, cross yourself three times, and say the following prayer:
>
> *Immo haud daemonorum, umquam et numquam, urbi et orbi, quamquam Azazel magnopere Thoth et Urim et Thummim in nomine Tetragrammaton. Fiat, fiat. Amen.*

Then, if the amulet is truly one of those I have described above, it will produce a tingling sensation in the hand. The tingling will last for only a few seconds, and after that the amulet will seem as dull and dead as any ordinary object. It will seem dead, but it will not be dead. I may add here . . .

Lewis looked up from the book. There was a strange light in his eyes.

"Hey!" he said. "Why don't we go up and get Grampa Barnavelt's coin and see if it's one of these?"

Rose Rita gave him an exasperated look. "Oh, come on, Lewis! She tested it for you the night we found it. Remember?"

"Yeah, but she didn't use this test. It says right here that the really strong amulets don't respond to the test she used."

"Unh-huh. And it also says that these strong amulets are very rare."

"Well, Grampa's coin *might* be one of them. You can never tell."

Rose Rita slammed the book shut and stood up. "Oh, all *right*! Go get your dumb coin and bring it down here and say dumb magic words over it and we'll see what happens. I'm so sick of this whole business that I'd like to drop your stupid coin down the sewer. Now, if you say all this junk here and nothing happens, will you shut up?"

"Yeah," said Lewis, grinning.

Lewis ran upstairs and yanked open the drawer of his bedside table. After a bit of fumbling and poking around, he found the coin. He could hear his heart beating and his face felt flushed. When he got back to the library, Rose Rita was sitting there in the leather armchair. She was leafing through a big book full of pictures of sailing ships.

"Well?" she said, without looking up. "Did you find it?"

Lewis gave her a dirty look. He wanted her to be interested in what he was doing. "Yeah, I found it. Now, come on and help me."

"Why do you need my help? You can read, can't you?"

"Yeah, I can read, but I don't have three hands. You have to hold the book for me so I can read it while I make the sign of the Cross with one hand and hold the coin with the other hand."

"Oh, all right."

There was a set of double doors in the middle of one wall of the library. They were glass doors, and they opened right out onto the side yard of the house. Lewis and Rose Rita took up their positions in front of these doors. Lewis stood with his back to the doors. The light fell over his shoulder onto the pages of the book that Rose Rita held up before him. In his left hand, Lewis held the coin. With his right hand, he slowly made the sign of the Cross on himself. He did it three times. Then he began to chant, the way he had heard Father Cahalen do during Mass:

"Immo haud daemonorum, umquam et numquam . . ."

As Lewis chanted, the room began to get darker. The light faded from the bright orange leaves of the maple tree outside, and now a strong wind was rattling the glass doors. Suddenly the doors flew open, and the wind got into the room. It riffled madly through the dictionary on the library table, scattered papers across the floor, and knocked all the lampshades galley-west. Lewis turned. He stood there silent, staring out into the strange twilight. His hand was still clenched tight around the coin.

Rose Rita closed the book and glanced nervously at Lewis. From where she stood she could not see his face. "Gee, that was weird," she said. "I mean, it was just like . . . like as if you had made it get dark outside."

"Yeah," said Lewis. "It was funny how it happened." He did not move an inch, but just stood there, looking out at the night.

"Did . . . did anything happen to the coin?" Rose Rita's voice was tense and frightened-sounding.

"Nope."

"You sure?"

"Yeah, I'm sure. It's just a dud. C'mon, let's get back to work."

Lewis moved quickly to the glass doors and shut them. Then he helped Rose Rita pick up the things that the little hurricane had strewn about the room. As he went back and forth, straightening and arranging things, he was careful to keep his face turned away from Rose Rita. The coin had jumped in his hand, and he did not want her to know.

CHAPTER FIVE

As soon as Rose Rita had gone home, Lewis clattered down the cellar stairs to his uncle's workshop. He dug around in the tool box until he found the wire clippers, and, after a little struggling, managed to cut the little metal loop that held the coin to the watch chain. Then he ran upstairs and rooted around in the drawer of his bedside table until he found his old St. Anthony medal. He had been given the medal after his first Holy Communion, and he had worn it for a while, but then he had gotten tired of it. After a lot of fussing with wire clippers and pliers, he managed to get the coin hooked onto the chain, where the St. Anthony medal had been before. He fastened the chain around his neck and went to the mirror to look at himself.

October turned into November, and the weather got colder. Lewis could see his breath in the morning when he opened the front door. He wore the magic coin all the time now: to church, to school, and even in bed at night. Jonathan, Mrs. Zimmermann, and Rose Rita had all at different times seen the chain around his neck, but they had assumed he was just wearing his St. Anthony medal again. Whenever he was undressing in his room, Lewis made sure that the door was shut and locked.

It would have been hard for Lewis to explain how the coin made him feel. The closest thing he could compare it to was the feeling he got when he went to the Bijou Theatre and saw a pirate movie. Lewis loved the cutlass duels and thundering broadsides and smoke and battles and blood. When he stepped out onto the street after seeing one, he could almost feel the sword hanging at his side and the long pirate pistol stuck in his belt. As he walked home, he imagined that he was wrapped in a heavy cloak and stalking toward the docks in some Spanish port, or pacing moodily on his quarter-deck as the planks under him shook to cannonade after cannonade. He felt grim and strong and brave and heartless and cruel. It was a good feeling, and it usually lasted about half of the way home. Then he was just plain old Lewis again.

The feeling that the magic coin gave Lewis was a bit like the pirate-movie feeling, except that the coin feeling lasted longer. The coin did other things for him too: for one thing, he found that his head was full of schemes and plots. He would walk along dreaming up ways to get even with Woody Mingo and the other kids who bothered him. Of course, he had dreamed of revenge before the magic coin came into his life, but his planning had never been so good. Sometimes Lewis had to shake his head to get rid of a plan that was too awful to think about.

And it seemed to Lewis that he was dreaming a lot more at night now. The dreams seemed to be in color, with music playing in the background—stirring military music. Lewis would dream that he was riding at the head of an army or leading his knights up over the walls of a castle. There were other dreams too, really frightening ones, but he could never remember them. He just woke up with the feeling that he had had them.

So Lewis wore the coin and waited for it to do something for him. And around about this time Woody Mingo began to make life really miserable for Lewis.

It was as if Woody sat up nights thinking of mean things to do: he managed to get a seat near Lewis in school, and when Miss Haggerty's back was turned, he would dart across the aisle and pinch Lewis in the neck. Hard, so that it hurt for a long time afterwards. Or he would goose Lewis when they were in the bathroom together, or he would put dead mice in Lewis's briefcase because he knew that Lewis was very much afraid of dead animals. Probably the most maddening thing that Woody did was to march Lewis down the stairs of the

school during fire drills. Lewis's school was a tall old brick building with shaky wooden staircases. The sixth-grade room was on the second floor, and when the fire bell rang and everyone lined up at the top of the staircase, Woody would slip in behind Lewis. Then he would put one hand in each of Lewis's hip pockets and march him down the stairs, saying, "Right butt, left butt, hup-two-three-four, *march!*" until Lewis got to the bottom, shaken and sick and almost in tears.

Lewis didn't understand why Woody had decided to pick on him. It was like those kids who jumped out at you when you were walking down the street, and wouldn't let you by till you had told them your name, and they had pounded you a couple of times on the arm. They were bullies, and so was Woody. Kids like that always seemed to be attracted to Lewis. He had hoped that his magic coin would help him to stand up to Woody but so far it hadn't. Lewis might be walking down the street with the coin around his neck, imagining that he was Blackbeard the pirate or Tom Corbett, Space Cadet. Then he would run into Woody and all his courage would evaporate, and he would find himself thinking about the red-handled jacknife that Woody carried in his pocket. But maybe the coin would help him yet. He hoped that it would.

One night Lewis went to bed thinking about how to get even with Woody Mingo. He fell asleep amid daydreams of exploding baseballs and poisoned peanut butter sandwiches, and trap doors that dropped people into cauldrons of boiling oil. So perhaps it is not very surprising that he had a wild and exciting dream that night.

In the dream Lewis had become a tall, big-boned Viking chieftain. He and his companions were fighting off an attack by some Indians. Lewis recognized the place where they were fighting. It was Wilder Creek Park, which was just outside the city limits. Lewis had been there on picnics a number of times. In the dream the wooden tables and the brick cook-stoves had vanished, and the park was weedy and overgrown. He and his men were drawn into a ring in the middle of the park, and Indians were attacking them from all sides.

The dream seemed to go on for hours. Knives whizzed past and arrows flew. Lewis was wielding a heavy battle ax, and each time he swung it, an enemy fell. He waded into the throng of painted savages, laying about him mightily and urging his companions on with deep-throated war cries. Lewis swung and swung, and Indians fell right and left, but still they kept on coming.

When he woke up the next morning, Lewis felt exhausted. Exhausted, but glowing and triumphant, as if he had just made an eighty-yard touchdown run on a football field. He sat there on the edge of his bed for a while, thinking about the dream. Suddenly he reached in under his pajama top and touched the coin. Darn! It felt perfectly ordinary, just as it always had, except for the time it had jumped and tingled during the saying of the magic spell from Mrs. Zimmermann's book. Lewis felt disappointed. He knew that very powerful amulets were supposed to seem dead, but just the same, he was disappointed. After a dream like that, the coin ought to have felt red-hot. At least, that's what Lewis thought.

He picked the coin up and eyed it skeptically. It hadn't really done anything for him yet. Nothing real, that is, except give him strange feelings and dreams. And maybe the coin hadn't even done that. Maybe the feelings and dreams had just come out of his own mind.

Lewis felt confused. He thought about the coin some more as he was getting dressed. It certainly was true that the coin had jumped in his hand that once—or had it? Lewis knew that you could get some very funny pinches and twinges in your body. Once on a hot summer day he had had the feeling that a worm was crawling across his back. But when he took off his shirt and looked, there was nothing there. What if . . . oh, the heck with it! Phooey on it! Lewis shook his head to get rid of all the conflicting thoughts that were banging around in his skull. By the time he had finished dressing, he felt better. In fact, he was beginning to get that pirate-movie feeling again. Lewis looked at himself in the mirror. He patted the coin. Maybe the coin had heard him. Maybe it knew that he was having doubts about its powers. Maybe it just wanted a chance to prove itself. Okay. He would give it a chance. Today would be the day the coin helped him take care of Woody Mingo.

CHAPTER SIX

That morning at breakfast, Lewis asked Mrs. Zimmermann to pack a lunch for him. He said that he was going to stay down at school during the noon hour. Jonathan and Mrs. Zimmermann both smiled happily. They were glad that Lewis was going to have fun with the other boys instead of skulking at home like a fugitive. And when Lewis went out the door, they saw that he was grinning from ear to ear.

"Rose Rita has been a good influence on him," said Jonathan, as he poured himself a second cup of coffee. "I hope she keeps it up."

Mrs. Zimmermann stood there staring at the front door. She scratched her chin thoughtfully. "Maybe it's good," she said, slowly, "but I can't help feeling that there's something funny about Lewis these days. I can't quite put my finger on it, but there's something wrong. Did you notice how tired he looked? Around the eyes, I mean. And yet he was raring to go. It's odd."

Jonathan shrugged. "It's always odd when a boy like Lewis does something different. But I wouldn't worry about him. I think he knows what he's doing."

Lewis hummed marching songs all the way to school. He really felt great. But when noontime came and he had eaten his lunch, he felt different. He began to get worried. By the time he had reached the edge of the playground, he could feel his courage ebbing away. Should he turn around and go home? Lewis paused. Then he pulled himself together, patted the amulet, and walked forward in quick nervous strides.

It was a gray November day on the playground. The football and baseball fields were covered with frozen footprints and bicycle ruts. Puddles of ice lay here and there. Lewis saw a group of boys getting ready to play football. They were lining up to be chosen, and the two captains were flipping a coin to see who got first choice. As Lewis drew near, he saw that one of the boys in the group was Woody. And once again Lewis's courage failed. He felt like going home. But he fought down his fear, and stayed.

Lewis slipped into the group of boys that were waiting to be chosen. He stood there with his hands in his pockets, hoping that no one would notice him. Near him, a boy who had been jumping up and down and slapping his sides stopped jumping and stared at Lewis as if he were a visitor from outer space. What was old lardo doing here?

One by one the boys got picked, until only two were left unchosen. They were Woody and Lewis. Woody glanced over at Lewis and grinned.

"Well, if it ain't lard ass. Djer uncle letcha out of yer cage today?"

Lewis stared hard at the ground.

The two captains were Tom Lutz and Dave Shellenberger. It was Tom's turn to choose, and he glanced from Woody to Lewis. Woody was good at sports, but the boys avoided choosing him because he was such a troublemaker.

"Oh, well. C'mon, Woody," Tom grumbled. Woody walked over to the group of boys on Tom's side.

For a minute it looked as if Dave Shellenberger would tell Lewis to go home. That was what usually happened on the rare occasions when Lewis showed up to play games with the other boys. But this time, for some reason, Dave chose Lewis. He motioned for him to come over to his side.

"C'mon, fatty," he said. "We'll make you our center. Need some beef in the line."

Lewis was in the game. He could hardly believe it.

After the kickoff, Lewis's side wound up with the ball. Lewis stood there, bent over, legs wide apart, rubbing the football back and forth over the frozen ground. The quarterback started a long count.

"Forty-three . . . twenty-four . . . three . . . zero . . . fourteen . . ."

Suddenly Lewis felt a sickening shock. He had been staring at the ground, and now he was on his back, looking up at the heavy gray sky.

"Ooops. Sorry. Guess I jumped the gun." It was Woody, of course.

"Hey, Woody, come on!" yelled Dave. "Cut out that kind of crap, will you?"

"I think lard ass here was off sides," said Woody, pointing down at Lewis.

"I was not, and stop callin' me lard ass!" Lewis was on his feet now, red-faced and angry.

"That's your name, lard ass," said Woody, carelessly. "Got any other names?"

Lewis hauled off and punched Woody in the stomach. Woody clutched at his middle. Pain and surprise were in his eyes. The punch had really hurt.

Several boys who were standing around gasped. Somebody yelled, "Fight! Fight!" and a circle formed around the two boys. Woody was angry now. He spat on the ground and swore. "Okay, you tub of guts," he snarled, moving in with his fists up. "Now you're gonna get it."

Lewis backed away. He felt like turning and running.

/67/

But now Woody was on him, swinging hard. The blows fell on Lewis's shoulders in a stinging rain. Lewis lunged and got his arms around Woody. Now the two of them were rolling over and over on the ground. Woody came out on top, and Lewis felt his head being pushed down into a frozen puddle. The thin ice cracked, and cold water bit into Lewis's scalp.

Lewis looked up at the ring of expectant faces hovering against the sky. Woody was astride him, sneering and triumphant.

"Go ahead, lard ass. Tell 'em what your name is." Woody put his hand on Lewis's face and shoved. Icy water stung Lewis's ears.

"No."

"Go *on*, I said! Tell 'em your *name!*" Woody dug his knees into Lewis's sides. It was like being caught in a nutcracker.

Suddenly Lewis lurched upward, and Woody fell over on his back. Now they were rolling over and over again, and this time Lewis came up on top. He was sitting with his full weight on Woody's chest. But Woody had a free arm. He reached up and punched Lewis on the ear. It stung, but Lewis didn't move. He grabbed Woody by the hair and banged his head on the ground.

"Come on, Woody. Say you give up!"

Woody glared defiantly up at Lewis. "No."

Lewis raised his fist, but then he hesitated. He had always been told that it was bad to hit someone who was down. Maybe he could just sit on Woody till Woody gave in. But as he was thinking this, some other power seized Lewis's hand and brought it down hard on Woody's nose. Blood gushed from Woody's nostrils. It ran down over his mouth and chin.

Lewis jerked his hand back and clutched it to his chest, as if he was afraid of what it might do if he let it loose again. When he looked down, he saw that Woody was staring up at him, his eyes wide with fear.

"I . . . I give up," Woody stammered.

Lewis got up and backed away. The boys who had been watching the fight looked from one to another in disbelief. No one knew what to say. They had all figured that Woody would wipe up the earth with Lewis.

Woody got up slowly. He was crying and wiping his bloody nose with his sleeve. One boy ran into the school to get a cold cloth to hold to Woody's nose, while others were advising him to hold his head back and press the bridge of his nose with two fingers. For the time being, Lewis was a hero. Dave Shellenberger slapped him on the back and said, "Way to go, baby!" Another boy asked him if he'd been doing exercises. Finally, when Woody's nose had been taken care of, the boys asked Lewis if he'd like to play football with them some more. Dave said that he could be fullback if he wanted to. But Lewis said, "Gee, no thanks, fellas. I just remembered something I was supposed to do. I'll see you all later." He waved and walked away.

Lewis didn't really have anything that he had to do. He just wanted to be alone with his thoughts. So he wandered off to a quiet part of the playground and started pacing. And as he paced, he thought.

He had figured that he would feel great after his victory, but he didn't. Strangely enough, he felt sorry for Woody, who had been showed up in front of all those kids. Woody had had a reputation as a tough guy. Now everybody would start picking on him. And something else was bothering Lewis. He hadn't intended to punch Woody in the nose. It was as if someone had grabbed his arm and brought it smashing down. Lewis knew that the amulet had done it, but all the same, he didn't like it. He didn't like the idea of being jerked around like a puppet on a string. He had wanted magic help, but he had wanted the help to stay under his control.

After he had paced a little more, Lewis pulled out his watch and looked at it. Lunch period was almost over. Maybe he would feel better if he told Rose Rita about what he had done—leaving out the part about the amulet, of course. Sure. That was a good idea. He would tell her all about his big fight with Woody, and she would be proud of him. And that would make him feel better about the whole business.

Lewis knew where he would find Rose Rita. She would be pitching in the girls' softball game. It was the wrong season for softball, but the girls weren't allowed to scrimmage around and get their skirts dirty in games like football, so they played softball all through the autumn until snow flew.

Lewis arrived at the girls' softball diamond just as Rose Rita was firing the ball up to the plate. The batter, a girl with yellow braids, swung like somebody chopping wood. She missed.

That was the end of the inning, and anyway the bell was ringing for the kids to come back to school. As Rose Rita walked off the field, Lewis noticed that she had a disgusted look on her face. But as soon as she saw him, she brightened up.

"Hi, Lewis!" she called, waving. She stopped in front of him, made a hideous face, and put her finger up to her forehead like a gun that was going to blow her brains out. "Yaah!" she said.

"What's wrong?" asked Lewis.

"Oh nothing. It's just that Lois Carver is such a rotten batter. I strike her out every time she comes up to bat. This last time I pitched to her with my eyes shut, just to see what would happen. But she struck out anyway."

"She did?" Lewis was only half listening to what Rose Rita was saying. He wanted to tell her all about the big fight.

"I got in a fight with Woody Mingo," he said.

Rose Rita looked surprised. "You did. Is that where you got that thick ear?"

"Yeah, but I gave him something worse. Pow! Right

in the kisser!" Lewis tried to imitate the punch he had used.

Rose Rita glanced at him skeptically. "Oh, come on, Lewis! Stop telling stories! You don't have to lie to *me*. I won't make fun of you because you got beat up."

Suddenly Lewis became very angry. He turned on Rose Rita and yelled at the top of his voice, "Okay, if *that's* the way you feel, I'll get somebody *else* to be my best friend!" He turned on his heel and stalked away, adding, over his shoulder, "See ya round!"

Lewis marched off toward the school building. He walked fast and didn't look back. By the time he got to the door, he found that he was crying.

CHAPTER SEVEN

As soon as Lewis got home from school that day, he called up Rose Rita, but her mother answered and said that she wasn't back yet. Later that evening, Lewis tried again, and got her. Both of them tried to apologize at once. Rose Rita had heard from several people about Lewis's fight with Woody, and she said that she was sorry for having doubted him. Lewis said he was sorry he had lost his temper. By the time the conversation was over with, everything seemed to be all right again. At least, for the time being.

A few days after his fight with Woody Mingo, Lewis began to get the feeling that company was coming. He didn't know why he had this feeling, but he did have it.

It started when he was setting the table. He dropped a knife, and then he remembered the old saying: If you drop a knife, then company is coming. Normally Lewis didn't believe in old sayings and superstitions. But the feeling he got was so strong that he began to wonder if there wasn't something in the old proverb after all.

That night, Lewis sat on his cushioned window seat and watched the snow come down. It was the first snowfall of the winter. Lewis was always very impatient for the first snow, and if it didn't stay on the ground, he got angry. But tonight's snow looked as if it was going to stay. It swirled past his window and drifted into dreamy shapes under the tall chestnut tree. It sparkled in the cold light of the street lamp across from Lewis's house. It piled up on window ledges and doorsteps.

Lewis sat there thinking about all the things he would do when there was a lot of snow on the ground. Like sledding down Murray's Hill with Rose Rita. Like walking home from church at night with Jonathan and Mrs. Zimmermann. Like wandering the snowy streets alone by moonlight and imagining that the snow-wall between the sidewalk and the street was the wall of a castle, and that he was pacing the ramparts, planning how to hurl back an enemy assault.

Lewis closed his eyes. He felt very happy. Then a picture appeared before his closed eyes. A very strange picture.

Lewis often saw pictures in the dark, just before he

went to sleep at night. Sometimes he would see, quite clearly, the streets of Constantinople or London. He had never been to these cities, so he really didn't know what they looked like, but he imagined that he was looking at Constantinople or London. He saw domes and minarets and steeples and streets and avenues. They appeared in the darkness behind his eyelids.

The picture that came to Lewis now was the picture of a man walking up the Homer Road toward New Zebedee. The Homer Road was a winding country road that ran between New Zebedee and the very small town of Homer. Lewis had been over the Homer Road quite a few times this last summer, going to and from Mrs. Zimmermann's cottage on Lyon Lake. As Lewis watched, the picture moved. The man was walking straight up the center of the road, leaving footprints in the snow behind him. Since the only light in the picture was moonlight, Lewis could not see too much of the man. In fact, he could not see enough to tell whether the figure was a man or a woman—but somehow he felt sure it was a man. The man had a long coat on—it flapped around his ankles as he walked. And he was walking fast.

Now the man was passing the gas station at Eldridge Corners. He paused to look at the old rusty signpost, and then he took the fork that led past the humming, brightly lit power house. Now he was crossing the railroad tracks just outside the city limits.

Lewis opened his eyes and looked out into the snowy yard. He shook his head. He wasn't at all sure he liked the picture that had come before his eyes. He couldn't say why the dark figure frightened him, but it did. He hoped that it was not the company that was supposed to be coming.

One afternoon, not long after Lewis had had this strange nighttime vision, something else happened. Lewis was on his way home from Rose Rita's house. He was just walking along, staring at his shadow, when he noticed a piece of paper lying on the sidewalk in front of him. For some reason, he stopped and picked it up.

It was just a sheet of blue-ruled notebook paper that some kid had been practicing his handwriting on. At the top of the page was one of these double rainbows you had to make when you were warming up during handwriting class. And below that was a neat row of small v's, and another row, this one of capital V's. The capital V's all looked just like the V in *Venio*, the word that had appeared on the postcard.

Lewis could feel his heart beating. He glanced quickly down the page and saw the word he dreaded. It was written on the bottom line of the sheet.

Venio

Lewis felt sick and shivery. The word on the paper squirmed before his eyes. As Lewis stood there trembling, a sudden gust of wind snatched the paper from his hand and blew it across the street. He started to go after it, but the wind was blowing so hard that by the time he had run across to get it, the paper was gone. Gone like the postcard.

Lewis felt that sick chill again. His heart continued to beat in thick heavy beats under his winter coat. "*Venio* means 'I come,'" Lewis repeated to himself. "*Venio* means 'I come.'" But who was coming? The man Lewis had seen in his daydream? The dark figure on the Homer Road? Whoever it was, Lewis didn't want to meet him.

As he walked home, Lewis began to argue with himself. He always did this when he was trying to fight his fears down. He dreamed up "logical explanations" for the things he was afraid of, and sometimes these explanations made the fears go away—for a while, at any rate. By the time he got to his house, Lewis had persuaded himself that the midnight postcard was just something he had dreamed about. You couldn't always tell when you were sleeping and when you were awake, after all. He had just dreamed that he had gone downstairs and found a postcard with *Venio* written on it. But what about the paper he had just found on the street? Well (Lewis argued) that was just some show-offy grade-school kid who had learned to write Latin. That was all it was. It was just a coincidence that the kid had used the same word that appeared on the postcard. Or maybe Lewis had just imagined that he saw the word *Venio* on the piece of paper. It could have been Veronica, or some name like that . . .

As he hung up his coat and went in to have supper, Lewis went on arguing inside his head. He wasn't really convinced by his clever explanations, but they made him feel better. They helped him to fight off the black shapeless fear that was forming in his mind.

That evening Lewis decided to do his homework down at the public library. The library was a pleasant place to work, with its old scarred tables and green-shaded lamps. Lewis went there a lot, to browse or to look things up. He packed his books into his briefcase and stomped off toward the library through the snow, whistling cheerfully.

Lewis worked at the library till closing time, which was nine. Then he packed up his books again and got ready to leave. Nine was a little late for him to be walking the streets of New Zebedee alone, but he wasn't worried. Nothing bad ever happened in New Zebedee. And besides, he had his amulet with him.

Lewis was about three blocks from the library when he saw someone standing under the street lamp on the corner. At first he was scared. The dark figure on the Homer Road flashed before his eyes. But then he laughed. Why was he so silly? It was probably just old Joe DiMaggio.

There was a bum in New Zebedee who called himself Joe DiMaggio. He wore a New York Yankees baseball cap and handed out pens shaped like baseball bats. The pens were all inscribed "Joe DiMaggio." Sometimes Joe helped the police check the doors of the shops on Main Street. And sometimes he waited under street lamps to jump out at kids and yell "Boo!" at them. That was probably who it was standing there under the light. Good old Joe.

"Hi, there, Joe!" Lewis called, waving at the still figure.

The figure walked forward out of the circle of lamplight. Now it was standing before Lewis. Lewis smelled something. He smelled cold ashes. Cold wet ashes.

The tall muffled figure stood there, silent, towering over Lewis. Lewis felt queasy inside. Joe was just a short little guy. It couldn't be him standing there. Frantically, Lewis fumbled with the zipper on his coat. His hand closed over the part of his shirt where the amulet was, bunching up the cloth so that the hard little object was inside his fist. And at that the figure took one sudden gliding step forward and spread its arms wide.

Lewis let go of the amulet with a shriek. He turned and ran, ran for his life, stumbling over snowbanks and in and out of slush puddles and over slippery smooth patches of ice till he reached the stone steps of the library. Then he scrambled up the steps and banged violently with his hands on the glass doors. He banged till the palms of his hands stung. Nobody came.

At last he saw a light come on in the foyer of the library. Miss Geer was still there. Thank God.

Lewis stood there with his face and hands pressed against the glass. He was half out of his mind with fear. At any second he expected to feel hands clawing at his back, to be spun around and pressed into the face of—he didn't dare think what.

Finally Miss Geer came. She was an old lady and had arthritis, so she walked slowly. Now she was fumbling with the lock. Now the door swung inward.

"My goodness, Lewis, if I was to tell your uncle that you were pounding away to beat the band like that—" Miss Geer stopped her scolding when Lewis threw his arms around her and shook her frail old body with his frightened sobs.

"There, there, Lewis. It's all right, it's all right, what in the world . . ." Miss Geer was not a mean old lady by any means. She liked children, and she especially liked Lewis.

"For heaven's sake, Lewis, whatever has happened to make you—"

"Please, Miss Geer, call my uncle," Lewis sobbed. "Call him and tell him to come down and get me. There's somebody out there, and I'm scared!"

Miss Geer looked at him, and then she smiled kindly. She knew about children and their wild imaginations. "There, there, Lewis. Everything's all right. Just sit down here on the step and I'll go call your uncle. It'll only take a minute."

"No, don't go away, Miss Geer. Please don't. I . . . I want to come with you."

So Lewis followed Miss Geer into her office and stood shifting nervously from one foot to the other as she asked the operator to give her the Barnavelt residence. It seemed to Lewis that Jonathan was taking forever to get to the phone, but finally he answered. Then he and Miss Geer talked for a little while. Lewis couldn't tell much from the noises Miss Geer made, but it seemed obvious that Jonathan was puzzled. As well he might be.

A few minutes later, Jonathan's big black car pulled up in front of the library. Lewis and Miss Geer were waiting on the front steps. As soon as Lewis was in the car, Jonathan turned to him and said, "What happened?"

"It was . . . it was something pretty awful, Uncle Jonathan. It was a ghost or a monster or something, and it . . . it tried to get me." Lewis put his face in his hands and started to cry.

Jonathan put his arm around Lewis and tried to comfort him. "There, there, Lewis . . . don't cry. Everything's all right. It was probably just somebody trying to scare you. Halloween is over with, but there's always someone who doesn't get the word. Don't worry. You're all right now."

That night Lewis lay wide awake in his bed, listening to his heart beat. His closet door was open, and he could see the clothes hanging in a shadowy row. Were they moving? Was something there, behind them?

Lewis thrashed up into a sitting position and frantically fumbled for the switch on his bedside lamp. He felt all over the lamp before he found it, but finally the light came on. There was nothing there. There were no dark shapes waiting to jump at him. None that he could see, at any rate. It was a long time before he could bring himself to get out of bed and look in the closet. Finally, though, he did. There was nothing behind the clothes. Nothing but plaster and wood and dust and his old shoes. Lewis went back to bed. He thought that maybe he would try to sleep with the light on, tonight.

Lewis tossed and turned. He rolled over to one side and then to the other. It was no good. He wasn't going to sleep. Well, if he wasn't going to sleep, he might as well think. He didn't have to think very hard. Lewis knew very well what was behind all the weird things that had been happening to him lately. The amulet. All his logical explanations had evaporated, and he was left with one thought: the amulet was haunted. It was haunted, and he had better get rid of it. So what if it had helped him beat up on Woody Mingo? So what if it did give him that wonderful pirate-movie feeling? Lewis thought about how he had felt when his hand closed around the amulet and the dark figure leaped at him. He shuddered. He just had to get rid of it.

Lewis raised his hands to his neck. But when they were a few inches away from the chain, they stopped. He grunted and pushed, but he couldn't force them to go any farther. His hands trembled. They shook like the hands of an old man who has the palsy. But they just would not close around the chain so that Lewis could take the amulet off.

Lewis sat up, panting. His pajama top was soaked with sweat. He looked at his hands. Didn't they belong to him any more? Lewis was scared. Thoroughly scared. And he felt helpless. What would he do if he couldn't take it off? He imagined the amulet and chain growing into his body as he got older and older until there was just a looped line and a bump on his skin to show where they were. Lewis's fear was close to panic now. He jumped out of bed and started pacing up and down the room. He would have to calm down before he could decide what to do.

He looked toward the fireplace, and he smiled. Every room in this enormous old mansion had a fireplace in it. Lewis's own personal fireplace was made of black marble, and there was a fire laid in it, though it was not lit. Little dry twigs underneath and bigger sticks above, on the andirons. There was a box of matches on the mantel. Lewis took them and knelt down to light the fire.

In a few minutes, he had a good blaze going. Lewis put up the screen and sat there on the rug, staring at the fire. Should he tell Uncle Jonathan about the amulet? Jonathan was a wizard. He would know what to do. Or Mrs. Zimmermann? She was a witch, and even more powerful than Jonathan. But Lewis was afraid of what they would think when they found out that he had been messing around with magic again. He should have turned Mrs. Zimmermann's book over to her the minute he found it. When she found out what he had done, she would probably be furious. And what would Jonathan do? Would he decide that one year was a long enough time to be Lewis's legal guardian? Would he send him off to live with Uncle Jimmy and Aunt Helen? Aunt Helen had a personality like a leaky inner tube. She sat in an easy chair and whined about her asthma all day. Lewis thought about what life with Aunt Helen would be like. No, he did not want to tell Jonathan and Mrs. Zimmermann about the amulet.

Then who could he tell? Rose Rita. Lewis grinned. Sure. He would call her up in the morning and they could get together to decide what to do. If he couldn't take the amulet off himself, then Rose Rita could do it for him.

The fire crackled cheerfully. Lewis felt better. He also felt very sleepy. After making sure that the fire screen was in place, Lewis stumbled off to the bed and threw himself down. If he had any dreams that night, he didn't remember them.

CHAPTER EIGHT

When he woke up the next morning, Lewis found his room filled with bright winter sunlight. The dark figure that had waited for him under the street lamp seemed like something he had read about or dreamed about. As he dressed, the pirate-movie feeling flowed back into him. He felt like a million dollars. Should he tell Rose Rita, after all? Lewis hesitated. Yes, maybe he ought to, just to get it off his chest. He could call her up before breakfast to catch her before she left the house. But when he got to the phone, Lewis's resolve melted. He stood there with the receiver in his hand while the operator said, "Number please? Number please?" and then he hung up. Oh well. He could talk to her at school.

Lewis saw Rose Rita several times that day at school. But each time, as he was working himself up to say something about the amulet, something tightened up inside him, and he wound up talking about the Notre Dame football team, or the galley they were building, or Miss Haggerty, or anything but the amulet. When he went home from school that day, Lewis still had not managed to tell Rose Rita what he wanted to tell her. But as he walked home in the winter dusk, Lewis saw that the street lights were on. He stopped. Beads of sweat were breaking out on his forehead. The horror of the figure under the lamp swept over him like an icy wave. Lewis pulled himself together. He clenched his teeth and doubled his fists. He was going to have to tell Rose Rita about the amulet, and he was going to tell her tonight.

That evening in the middle of dinner, Lewis laid down his fork, swallowed several times, and said in a dry husky voice, "Uncle Jonathan, can I invite Rose Rita over to stay tonight?"

Jonathan did a double take. "Hmph! Well, Lewis, this is rather short notice, but I'll see what I can do. I'll have to ask her mother's permission first."

After dinner, Jonathan phoned up Mrs. Pottinger, and got her permission for Rose Rita to spend the night over at the Barnavelts' house. Quite by accident, Jonathan discovered that Lewis had not yet asked Rose Rita if she wanted to come over. So he dragged Lewis to the phone and got him to make a formal invitation. Then everything was settled. Lewis and Jonathan went upstairs to one of the many spare bedrooms and made the bed, and laid out the guest towels. Lewis was excited. He was looking forward to a long evening of card games and stories and conversation. Maybe he could even get in a word about his amulet.

When Rose Rita got to Lewis's house, the dining room table was all laid out for poker. There were the blue and gold cards with CAPHARNAUM COUNTY MAGICIANS SOCIETY stamped on them; there were the foreign coins that Jonathan used as poker chips. On a plate with a bright purple border was a big pile of chocolate-chip cookies, and there was a pitcher of milk. Mrs. Zimmermann was there, and she promised not to pull any funny business with the cards. Everything was ready.

They played for a long time. Then, just as Jonathan was about to announce that it was bedtime, Lewis asked if he could have a few words with Rose Rita, alone in the library. As he asked this, Lewis felt that tightness in his chest again. And he felt a sharp pain right where the amulet was.

Jonathan chuckled and knocked his pipe out into the potted plant behind his chair. "Sure," he said. "Sure, go right ahead. State secrets, eh?"

"Yeah, kinda," said Lewis, blushing.

Lewis and Rose Rita went into the library and slid the heavy paneled doors shut. Now Lewis felt like somebody who is trying to breathe under water. But he dragged the words out, one by one.

"Rose Rita?"

"Yeah? What's wrong with you, Lewis? You look all pale."

"Rose Rita, remember when we said the . . . the magic words over the coin?" Lewis stopped and winced. He felt a sharp pain in his chest.

Rose Rita looked puzzled. "Yeah, I remember. What about it?"

Lewis felt as if someone was sticking red-hot needles into his chest. "Well, I . . . I kind of lied about it." Sweat was pouring down his face now, but he felt triumphant, because he was winning over whatever was trying to keep him from telling the truth.

Rose Rita's eyes opened wide. "You lied? You mean the coin was really . . ."

"Yeah." Lewis reached inside his shirt and brought the thing out for her to see. He expected it to be red-hot. But it felt cool to his touch, and it looked just the way it had always looked.

Now that he had gotten out the important part, Lewis found that he could talk more freely. He told Rose Rita about how he had punched Woody without meaning to; he told her about the postcard and the paper on the street, and the figure under the street lamp. Now it was like running downhill. He talked faster and faster until he had nothing more to say.

Rose Rita sat there, nodding and listening, through his

whole speech. When he was through, she said, "Gee, Lewis, don't you think we ought to tell your uncle and Mrs. Zimmermann? They know all about stuff like this."

Lewis looked terrified. "Please don't, Rose Rita! Please, please, don't! My uncle would get mad and bawl me out and . . . and I don't know what he and Mrs. Zimmermann would think! They told me never to mess around with magic again! Please don't say anything to them!"

Rose Rita had not known Lewis long, but she did know that he spent a great deal of time worrying about being bawled out. He worried about it even when he wasn't doing anything bad. And she didn't really know how Jonathan would react. Maybe he *would* lose his temper. So she shrugged and said, "Oh, okay! We won't tell them then. But I think you ought to give the darned thing to me so I can throw it down the sewer for you."

Lewis looked hesitant. He bit his lip. "Could we just maybe . . . kind of put it away for a while? You never know. When I grow up, it might be that I could do something with it."

Rose Rita looked at him over the tops of her glasses. "Like fly to the moon? Come on, Lewis! Stop kidding around. You just want to hang onto it. Give it here." She held out her hand.

Lewis's face suddenly grew hard. He stuffed the coin back in under his shirt. "No."

Rose Rita looked at him for a moment. Then she took off her glasses, folded them up, and put them in the holder in her shirt pocket. She jumped at him, and at the first lunge, got her hands around the chain that the coin was attached to.

Lewis got his hands on the chain too, and he struggled to keep it down around his neck. He fought hard, and Rose Rita was amazed at his strength. She had Indian-wrestled with him once, and she had won easily. But now it was different. They staggered back and forth across the floor of the library. Rose Rita's face got red; so did Lewis's. Neither of them said a word.

Finally Rose Rita gave one sharp yank and tore the chain through Lewis's sore fingers. And at that Lewis gave a wild yell and leaped at her. His hand raked down the side of her face. Blood flowed.

Rose Rita stood in the middle of the room, panting. In one hand she held the chain with the coin on it. With the other she gently touched the wetness on her cheek. Now that the coin was gone, Lewis felt as if he had just been shaken rudely out of a dream. He blinked and stared at Rose Rita and he felt ashamed. Tears came to his eyes.

"Gee, I'm sorry, I didn't mean to. I didn't mean to," was all he could say.

The study doors rolled back, and there was Jonathan. "Good lord, what's going on here? I heard this scream, and I thought someone was being killed!"

Rose Rita hastily stuffed the coin and chain into the pocket of her jeans. "Oh, it wasn't anything, Mr. Barnavelt. Lewis borrowed my Captain Midnight Secret De-coder Ring, and I said that he had kept it long enough, and we had a fight about it."

When she turned to face him, Jonathan saw Rose Rita's bloody cheek. "Wasn't anything? Wasn't any-thing? Did Lewis do that to you?" Jonathan turned to Lewis, and was on the point of giving him an angry lec-ture, when Rose Rita interrupted.

"It wasn't what you think, Mr. Barnavelt. I . . . I was scratching my face with the hook end of my glasses. You know, the part that fits down over your ear? Well, it must've gotten sharp somehow because it really gave me a scratch!" Rose Rita was very good at explanations on short notice. Lewis was grateful.

Jonathan looked from Lewis to Rose Rita. There was something fishy about all this, but he couldn't quite tell what. He thought about all the fights he had had with his best friend in grade school, and he smiled. "Oh well. As long as everything's all right."

Late that night, after everyone else was asleep, Rose Rita tiptoed downstairs and opened the front door. She was wearing only her slippers, pajamas, and bathrobe, but she went out anyway, down the shoveled walk and out the front gate. She walked to the corner and stopped by the iron grate of the storm sewer. Water from the melting snow was running down into it with a hollow chuckling sound. Rose Rita took the amulet out of her bathrobe pocket. She dangled it over the grate, swing-

ing it on its chain. All she had to do was let go, and it would be good-bye amulet.

But she didn't let go. A suggestion that seemed to come from outside told her that she shouldn't throw the thing away. Rose Rita stood there a minute, staring at the strange little object that had given Lewis so much trouble. She scooped the coin back into her hand and put it into her bathrobe pocket. As she turned back toward the house, she thought, "Maybe Lewis is right after all. We'll put it away for a while and see what happens. I'll tell him that I've thrown it away, so he won't be pestering me all the time about it. Maybe he can use it when he's older. He might be a great magician or something then. I'll guard it for him." She reached into her pocket to see if the coin was still there. Yes, it was still there. Halfway back to the house she stopped to check again. Then she laughed at herself for being such a fussbudget. She tromped up the creaky steps and went in to bed.

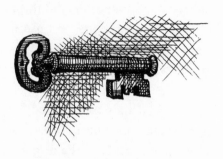

CHAPTER NINE

It was December now, and everyone in New Zebedee was getting ready for Christmas. Big tinsel-covered bells were strung across Main Street in several places, and the fountain at the traffic circle was turned into a Nativity scene. Jonathan lugged the Seagram's and Oxydol boxes down from the attic and began unsnarling the Christmas tree lights. They had been put away in neat little bundles, but they had somehow gotten all knotted up while lying quiet in their boxes. It happened that way every year. Jonathan and Mrs. Zimmermann began their usual argument about which was better, a tall skinny tree or a short squat one. Lewis unpacked the dirty cotton batting and arranged it around the circular mirror that was supposed to be the ice pond. He set up the little card-board village with the cellophane windows and put the celluloid deer out on the ice. Then, when the tree was all decorated and the lights were turned on, Lewis would sit on the couch and squint. He did this to make the tree lights into stars. Red and blue and green and white and orange stars, each with four long rays. Lewis liked the effect, and he would sit there squinting for long periods of time.

Every night as he undressed for bed, Lewis would look at the green streak on his neck. It had been left there by the tarnished chain that held the magic three-cent piece. The magic amulet that was gone forever. He knew it was gone; Rose Rita had told him so. She had told him that she had dropped it down the sewer, and he had be-lieved her. Now he was trying hard to feel good about not having the amulet. He was trying hard, but it was no use.

Lewis felt the way people feel when they give up something they like. Something that is bad for them, like Mounds bars or eating between meals. He felt a big empty space in his life, a hollow place cut out of his insides. Sometimes he woke up in the middle of the night scrabbling frantically for the amulet. And when he found it wasn't there, he burst into tears. But Lewis went about his everyday life as well as he could. He was distracted from his troubles by the Christmas preparations, and the fun he had playing with Rose Rita. He was happy a good deal of the time, and he might have eventually forgotten all about the amulet if something bad hadn't happened to him.

It was a dark December afternoon. Lewis and the other sixth-grade students were trying very hard to finish their math assignments, so they could be let out early. Miss Haggerty walked up and down the aisles, looking at papers and offering comments. When she was on the other side of the room, Woody Mingo started pinching Lewis.

"Ow!" Lewis hissed. "Cut it out, Woody!"

"Cut out what?"

"You know what I mean. Stop pinchin' me!"

"I ain't pinchin' you. It must be a sweat bee. Take a bath, and they won't sting you. Sweat Bee Barney-smell, Sweat Bee Barney-smell." Pinch, pinch.

Lewis felt deep despair. It was as if Woody had begun to realize that the amulet was gone. For a long time after their big fight, Woody had let Lewis alone. But in the last few days he had started in again. It was worse than before.

Lewis wanted to slug Woody, but he knew he'd get caught if he tried anything. Besides, he wasn't sure he could hurt Woody at all without his amulet. *Why did he ever agree to give it away?* It was one of the dumbest things he had ever done in his life.

Miss Haggerty walked to the front of the room and picked up her watch.

"Class," she said.

Everyone stopped working and looked up.

"Since you all seem to be doing quite well, I will keep my promise and let you out early. Some of you are not quite finished, but you may complete your work at home. Now, as soon as you have your desks all cleared off, and the room is quiet, you may go."

Desk tops slammed all over the room as the students began stuffing their pencils, paper, and books into their desks. Lewis put all his books away, and then he started stuffing his pens and pencils down the hole that the ink bottle sat in.

The students in Lewis's school didn't get to use ball-point pens. Not in school, at any rate. Ballpoint pens were supposed to be bad for your handwriting. So every-body had to write either with fountain pens, or with wooden pens, the kind that have metal points on the end. The ink the students used was kept in glass bottles which sat in round holes that had been cut in the upper-right-hand corner of each desk top. The holes went right through to the inside of the desk, so if you took the bottle out, you could put things into your desk through the hole. Of course, it would really have been easier just to lift the hinged wooden lid of the desk, but you couldn't have told Lewis that.

Lewis had about four pencils and a pen crammed into the hole. They were stuck against some books that were inside his desk, and they wouldn't go in. With his left hand he jiggled them around, trying to force them in. In his right hand he held the ink bottle. It dangled out over the aisle. Suddenly something hit Lewis's arm. Right on the funny bone. His arm went numb, his hand went limp, and the ink bottle shattered on the floor. Black ink spattered everywhere.

Lewis turned angrily in his seat. Woody was just pulling himself hastily back behind his raised desk top. And now Miss Haggerty was standing next to Lewis's desk.

"What seems to be the matter here?"

"Woody knocked the ink out of my hand," said Lewis, pointing.

Miss Haggerty did not seem to be interested in Woody. She kept on staring at Lewis. "And what, may I ask, was the ink bottle doing in your hand, Mr. Barnavelt?"

Lewis blushed. "I was just puttin' my pencils down into the hole," he mumbled.

The room was quiet. Dead quiet. Everyone, including Rose Rita, was looking at Lewis.

Miss Haggerty turned to the class and said, in a loud clear voice, "Class, do we *ever* take our ink bottles out of our desks?"

The class answered in long drawn-out unison. "NO-O, MISS HAG-GER-TY!"

Lewis's face burned. He felt angry and helpless. Now he heard Miss Haggerty telling him that he would have to stay after school and sand some of the ink off the floor. She didn't say how long it would take.

An hour after everyone else had gone, Miss Haggerty let Lewis go. His fingertips were sore from sandpapering, and he was so mad he could hardly see straight. As he stomped along the sidewalk toward home, he felt mad at everybody and everything, but especially at Rose Rita. It didn't matter that she had come over to his desk when the class was let out, just to say that she was sorry he had to stay after and to tell him that she hadn't chanted "No, Miss Haggerty" along with the rest of the class. That didn't matter. He was mad at her, and he felt that he had a very good reason.

If he had had the amulet with him in school that day, Lewis figured, it would have protected him. Woody would have been afraid to pick on him. The ink bottle would never have gotten broken, and he would never have been forced to stay after school. And who had told him to get rid of the amulet? Rose Rita. As Lewis saw it, everything that had happened to him that day was Rose Rita's fault.

The more Lewis walked, the madder he got. Why did Rose Rita have to butt in on everything, anyway? If only he could get the amulet back! But how could he? It was gone forever, down the storm sewer. By now it had been washed out into Wilder Creek and maybe even into Lake Michigan. It was no use . . .

Lewis stopped dead in the middle of the street. He happened to be crossing a busy intersection at the time, so cars honked at him and drivers put on their brakes in a hurry to avoid hitting him. Lewis heard the brakes screeching and the horns honking, and he broke out of his trance long enough to get safely across the street. But when he was on the other side, he went right on thinking the thought that had made him stop.

What if Rose Rita still had the amulet? What if she had been lying when she said she dropped it down the sewer?

The longer Lewis thought about it, the more certain he was that his wild guess was right. After all, he hadn't actually *seen* her drop the amulet down the drain. Maybe he had better try to get some information out of her.

On Friday of that week, a boiler burst in the basement of Lewis's school. Everybody got out early. Lewis and Rose Rita decided that they would spend the afternoon working on the Roman galley. It was nearly finished, but it needed a few final touches.

The galley stood in the middle of Rose Rita's desk up in her room. Around it were balsa wood shavings, bits of cardboard, and globs of dried model airplane glue. Lewis sat at Rose Rita's desk, hacking at a strip of balsa wood with his Boy Scout knife. He was trying to make a fancy battering ram to go on the prow of the ship.

"Gosh darn!" Lewis threw the jacknife down and glared at it.

Rose Rita looked up from the book she was leafing through. "What's wrong?"

"Oh, it's just this darned old knife. It wouldn't cut butter."

Rose Rita thought a minute. "Hey!" she said, "why don't we get out my Exacto knives? I forgot all about them. They're in my bureau drawer."

"Great! Which drawer are they in? I'll get them out." Lewis pushed his chair back and got up. He went to the dresser and started opening drawers and looking into them.

Rose Rita jumped up and ran to stop him. "Come on, Lewis! Hands off! That's my bureau, and my own private stuff is in there! And besides," she added, grinning, "you couldn't get into the right drawer anyway. It's locked, and I've got the only key to it, and I'm *not* going to tell you where it is. Now, go out and stand in the hall and close the door behind you. It'll only take a minute."

"Oh, okay!" Lewis grumbled. He stomped out into the hall and slammed the door behind him. As he stood there staring at the wallpaper, he thought, "Own private stuff, huh? I'll bet that's where you've got my amulet, right in there with your own private stuff. But don't worry, I'll get it back!"

A few minutes later, Rose Rita let Lewis come back into the room. The bureau drawers were all closed as before, but the Exacto knives were laid out on the desk. Lewis looked the tall black bureau up and down. Which drawer was it? It had to be one of the two up at the top,

because they were the only ones that had locks. But how was he going to get in without a key?

Rose Rita saw how Lewis was eyeing the bureau, and she began to get worried. "Come on, Lewis," she said, taking him by the arm. "There's nothing in there but my own stuff. Some of it I won't even let my mom look at, so don't feel too left out. Hey, let's get to work on the galley. Here, this is how the blades fit on the holders. . . ."

Late that night, Lewis lay awake, tossing and turning. He heard the grandfather clock in the study downstairs thud one o'clock, and then two, and then three. Lewis was trying to put together a plan for getting a look in the locked drawers of Rose Rita's bureau. But it was no use. Everything depended on his having the key, and he didn't have the faintest idea of where to look for it. He thought of ransacking her room some time when she was out, but he didn't see how he could do that without attracting her mother's attention. And he didn't want to make a mess. Everything would have to be done care-fully and secretly, so Rose Rita would not realize what was going on. Lewis was hoping that the amulet would be tucked away in some dark corner of one of those two drawers, some place that Rose Rita didn't look at very often. Lewis grimaced. Maybe Rose Rita checked the bureau every day, just to see if the amulet was there. Maybe he could have a fake one made . . . no, that sounded impossible. If he got the amulet away from her, and she found out about it, it would just be too darned bad.

But how was he going to get it? Lewis thought about skeleton keys and midnight break-ins with rope ladders and black masks and tool bags and the works. Then he thought, "Gee, what if it's not in her bureau at all? What if she really did throw it away?" In any case, he wasn't going to find out anything without the key to the drawer. And he didn't even know where to look for it.

Lewis got that hopeless feeling. As the clock struck four, he drifted off to sleep. That night, Lewis dreamed about keys. He was wandering through the many rooms of an old junk shop, and every room was full to the ceiling with keys. Keys of all sizes and shapes. Some of them were hooked together on rings, but most were just piled loose on the floor. He searched and searched, but he couldn't find the one he wanted.

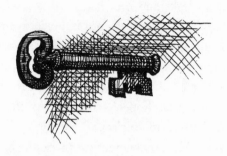

CHAPTER TEN

When Lewis woke up the next morning, he was still thinking about keys. But he wasn't any closer to finding the key to Rose Rita's bureau drawer. It was Saturday, and Rose Rita had an appointment to see her eye doctor. She was nearsighted, and her eyes were changing fast, so she had to get her glasses changed often. Lewis was going along with her today, to have his eyes examined. He didn't wear glasses, but Jonathan had noticed that Lewis was falling asleep over books a good deal, and he wondered if Lewis didn't need reading glasses. Lewis had protested, but finally he had agreed to go.

That afternoon Lewis and Rose Rita were sitting in Dr. Wessel's office, reading comic books. Lewis had just finished having his eyes examined. It was Rose Rita's turn now.

Dr. Wessel opened his office door and peered out into the waiting room. "Okay. Who's next?"

Rose Rita threw her comic book down and got up. "I guess I am," she said wearily. "See you later, Lewis."

As she got up to go in, Lewis noticed that she was still wearing her beanie. That darned beanie! She wore it everywhere. To church, in school, at dinner, and she probably even wore it in bed at night. It was weird.

Lewis went back to his comic book, but he was startled a few seconds later when he heard loud voices. Rose Rita and Dr. Wessel were having an argument behind the closed door. Suddenly Dr. Wessel jerked the door open and pointed at the hat rack by the mirror.

"There!" he said, firmly. "Put it there!"

"I don't want to! Who do you think you are? God?"

Dr. Wessel glowered at Rose Rita. "No, I'm not God. I'm just a crabby eye doctor, and I don't want you wearing that beanie while I'm testing your eyes. It bumps into my equipment, and it distracts me, and . . . well, I don't like it. Now hang it up out there, or go on home."

"Oh, all right!" Rose Rita stormed out into the waiting room and jammed her beanie onto one of the pegs of the hat rack. Then she marched back into Dr. Wessel's office. He closed the door quietly behind her.

Lewis glanced up at the beanie and grinned. Rose Rita sure was funny about it. He picked up his comic book and then, quite suddenly, he laid it down again.

What if the key was in the beanie?

Lewis got up and walked softly over to the hat rack. Carefully, he lifted the beanie down. He looked inside, and there, held to the cloth by a safety pin, was a small black key.

Lewis felt like cheering. It had to be the right key, it just had to be. He glanced nervously at the closed door of Dr. Wessel's office. How much time did he have? He had heard Rose Rita say that her sessions with Dr. Wessel took quite a while, because there were lots of things wrong with her eyes. Would she be in there for a whole hour? Lewis looked at the clock. He'd just have to chance it. He undid the safety pin, put the key in his pocket, put the pin back in the hat again, snapped it shut, and carefully put the beanie back. He hoped Rose Rita wouldn't hear the buttons on the beanie rattling. When he had done all this, Lewis stepped over to the office door and rapped on it.

"Rose Rita?"

"Yeah?"

"I . . . I just remembered that I have to go downtown and buy some tobacco for Uncle Jonathan. It'll only take a couple of minutes."

"Oh, take all the time you want! I'm likely to be in here for days."

"Uh . . . okay. I'll be right back."

Lewis struggled into his coat and hat and galoshes, and stumbled down the front steps of Dr. Wessel's office. Soon he was walking as fast as he could toward Rose Rita's house. His hand was closed around the cold key in his pocket, and as he walked, he planned. He had to think up something to say to Mrs. Pottinger.

When Lewis got to the front steps of the Pottinger house, he took a deep breath. Then he went up and rang the bell. After what seemed like a very long time, Mrs. Pottinger came to the door. She was surprised to see him.

"Why, Lewis! What are you doing here? I thought you were at Dr. Wessel's office with Rose Rita."

Lewis dug his hands into his pockets and stared at the doormat. "Well, yeah, I kinda was, but it's like this: Rose Rita and I were gonna go to Heemsoth's for a Coke afterwards, and I don't have enough money, and she said she left her wallet up on top of her dresser. Can I go get it?"

It seemed to Lewis as if thousands of years were passing between the time he finished this speech and the time Mrs. Pottinger gave her answer. He began to wonder if kids who were caught burgling other kids' bureaus got sent to the Detention Home.

Mrs. Pottinger did take a little while to answer him, because she was an absent-minded person. "Why, yes, I suppose it's all right," she said, at last. "If you had said it was *in* the bureau, I'd have said you were out of luck, because Rose Rita won't even let me poke around in there. Go ahead. If you can't find the wallet, I think I have some money."

"Gee, thanks a lot, Mrs. Pottinger. I'll just be a minute."

"Take your time." Mrs. Pottinger turned and walked back toward the kitchen. Lewis watched her go. She trusted him. And why shouldn't she? He was Rose Rita's best friend. He felt awful. He wanted to go hide in a cellar somewhere. But instead, he started up the stairs.

Lewis stood before the bureau with the key in his hand. He listened, expecting at any minute to hear Mrs. Pottinger's footstep on the stairs. But instead he heard the clatter and clink of the dishes she was washing. He turned and saw that he had left the bedroom door open. Quickly he walked over and closed it. Then he went back to the bureau. The two drawers at the top had locks. It had to be one of them. Probably the same key fitted both locks. At least, he hoped it did. Lewis decided to try the right-hand drawer first. He stuck the key in and turned it. But when he pulled, he found that the drawer wouldn't budge. Which meant that the drawer hadn't been locked in the first place. Lewis turned the key back the other way and slid the drawer out. It was stuffed full of Rose Rita's underwear. Lewis felt his face getting red. He slid the drawer back. The amulet might be in there, but he would check the other drawer first.

Lewis unlocked the left-hand drawer and slid it out. It was full of little boxes and junk. This had to be the right one. He took the drawer all the way out, set it on Rose Rita's desk, and started going through it. But just as he was opening the first box, Lewis heard a knock on the door.

"Everything all right in there?"

Lewis froze. Mr. Pottinger! He had forgotten all about him! Usually, Mr. Pottinger wasn't home during the day. But this was Saturday. He was out there in the hall, on the other side of the door, waiting for an answer. Lewis's mind was racing. What should he do? Answer? Or try to climb out the window?

Another knock. Sharper and more insistent than before. And then Lewis heard Mr. Pottinger's loud, resonant voice again. "I *said*, is everything all *right* in there?"

Lewis glanced wildy around. His glance fell on the doorknob. He was fascinated by it. It would start to turn at any minute, and then . . .

Lewis heard Mrs. Pottinger calling from the foot of the stairs. "For heaven's sake, calm down, George! It's just Lewis Barnavelt looking for Rose Rita's wallet."

"Well then why doesn't he answer me? I heard this noise in her room, and I knew she was out, so I wondered . . ."

"Well, stop wondering, and leave the poor boy alone. He didn't answer you because he's shy, and you scared him to death with all that bellowing. You were shy too once. I should think you'd remember that!"

Mr. Pottinger chuckled. "Yeah, I guess I was." He gave a light playful tap on the door and said, "Good hunting, Lewis!" Then he walked on down the hall, humming to himself. A door closed, and Lewis heard Mr. Pottinger running water in the bathroom.

Lewis was standing there by the desk with the lid of the Exacto blade box in his hands. He was shaking all over. When he finally got himself pulled back together, he went back to examining the contents of the drawer. A box of Exacto blades. A chestnut carved to look like a jack-o-lantern. A deck of miniature playing cards in a cardboard case. The case said "Little Duke Toy Cards." One by one Lewis took the things out and laid them on the green blotter. No amulet yet.

A box of little plastic chessmen with the label "Drueke" on the top. A pair of magnetic toys shaped like the Republican elephant and the Democratic donkey. And then a worn little blue case with "Marshall Field's, Chicago" stamped on it. A white address label had been pasted on under the Marshall Field's label. It said: "Miss Rose Rita Pottinger, 39 Mansion Street, New Zebedee, Michigan." Lewis opened the box and saw his amulet.

Lewis could hardly believe it. Tears came to his eyes. It was really there! With trembling fingers he picked up the chain and slipped it over his head. Then he buttoned the top button of his shirt. Lewis hated tight collars, and this button, which he had never done up before in his life, felt like it was choking him. But it didn't matter. He had to go back and face Rose Rita, and he didn't want her to see the chain around his neck.

Lewis stopped and listened. He couldn't tell very well with the door shut, but it sounded like Mrs. Pottinger was singing downstairs. She often sang while she did the dishes or the dusting. And the sound of running water continued. Mr. Pottinger was probably taking a bath. Good. Now he would have to get out as fast as he could.

Working quickly, Lewis began putting the various items back in Rose Rita's drawer. He hoped that she hadn't put them in some particular order, so that she could find out if somebody had been fooling around with her stuff. Well, if she had, it was just too bad. Some day she would look and find that the amulet was gone, but by then she would understand why he had had to take it. He would protect her with his strength and bravery. Lewis hoped that this was the way it would all turn out.

Lewis put the drawer back in place and turned the key in the lock. There! Now he could leave. He would just go back to Dr. Wessel's office and put the key back in the beanie and sit down to wait for Rose Rita as if nothing had happened.

Humming quietly to himself, Lewis walked down the hall and trotted down the stairs. He had just laid his hand on the knob of the front door when Mrs. Pottinger called from the kitchen. "Did you get what you wanted, Lewis?"

"Uh . . . yeah. Gee, thanks a lot. Bye." Lewis's voice was so high that it was practically a squeak. He was very nervous. Now the door had closed behind him. He was outside. He had gotten away with it. He could be strong now, without the aid of Charles Atlas or punching bags or anything.

But on the steps of the Pottingers' house, Lewis paused. He was thinking of the black figure. Would it come back, now that he had the amulet? This fear had been in the back of Lewis's mind ever since he began plotting to get the magic coin back. Lewis had kept the fear down with his usual "logical explanations." But it was still there.

"Oh heck," he said, out loud. "I'm just being a scaredy-cat. Nobody can hurt me now." For the fifteenth time, Lewis persuaded himself that the figure that had jumped at him outside the library was just some crazy guy. Every now and then they got loose from the Kalamazoo Mental Hospital, and they would do things like jump out naked from behind trees and scare people at night until the police caught them and put them back in the crazy house. That was who it had been under the street lamp. Some nut.

Lewis glanced up at the sky. It was getting dark. He decided that he'd better be getting back before Rose

Rita suspected that something was up. He buttoned his coat and started out.

As Lewis walked back along Mansion Street, it started to snow. Little white flakes whirled around him and stung his face. He felt funny, as if he didn't know where he was going. The familiar shapes of cars rolled by in the early winter dusk, but they seemed to Lewis like bug-eyed prehistoric monsters. Maybe there was a blizzard coming. Well, that was okay with Lewis. He would enjoy sitting by the fire in Jonathan's library, with a steaming cup of cocoa in his hand. He would watch the snow falling outside the window. It would be very cozy.

Lewis kicked his way through the snow that was piling up on the sidewalk. Little glittering spurts rose before him. Now he was passing the Masonic Temple, a tall four-story brick building. It rose over him like a black cliff. There was a dark archway in the front of the building. For some reason, Lewis stopped in front of it. He didn't know why. He just stopped and waited.

Now Lewis heard something. A rustling sound. An old newspaper blew out of the archway. It slithered toward him like a living thing. Lewis was frightened, but then he tried to laugh it away. What was there to be scared of in an old newspaper? It lay at his feet now. He bent over and picked it up. By the light of the lamp that was swinging in the wind at the corner, Lewis could

just barely read the masthead. It was the New Zebedee *Chronicle*, and the date was April 30, 1859. The date on the three-cent piece was 1859.

With a little cry of terror, Lewis let go of the paper. It refused to go, however. Like a friendly cat, the paper wrapped itself around his feet. Frantically, Lewis kicked at the thing. He wanted it to go away. But then he stopped kicking. He turned and looked toward the dark archway. A figure stepped forward from it.

Lewis opened and closed his mouth, but nothing came out. He wanted to say, "Oh, hi there, Joe!" to reassure himself, but he couldn't. Rooted to the spot, Lewis watched the figure come. A breath of cold ashes swept toward him.

Now the figure was standing before Lewis on the snowy walk. It raised a shadowy hand and motioned for him to come. And Lewis felt himself suddenly jolted forward. It was as if there was a dog collar around his neck and the figure was tugging at the leash. He couldn't resist. He had to go. Lewis stumbled forward, following the beckoning shape. The snow closed in and hid them both from sight.

CHAPTER ELEVEN

Rose Rita glanced up at the clock in the waiting room of Dr. Wessel's office. It was the third time she had looked at it in the last five minutes.

The clock said five-fifteen. Lewis had left the office at three-thirty or thereabouts. It was hard to believe that it had taken him nearly two hours to buy a can of tobacco, go home, and then come back. Except, of course, that he hadn't come back. No phone calls, no nothing. Rose Rita's session with Dr. Wessel hadn't taken too long. She had been sitting out in the waiting room stewing for more than an hour now, and she was just about fed up.

Rose Rita stormed out into the front hall and started

throwing on her outdoor clothes. Coat, scarf, boots, gloves. Boy, was she mad! She kept running through in her mind all the things she was going to say to Lewis when she saw him again. She reached up and snatched down her beanie. As she always did, she stuck her hand inside to see if the key was there. It was gone.

Rose Rita stood there staring at the safety pin that had held the little key. So *that* was what he was up to! Why, the dirty, sneaky, crooked, no-good . . . She felt more anger welling up inside her, making her even crabbier than she had been before. But then she stopped. Lewis had told her all about the amulet, about the figure waiting for him under the lamp and the ghostly messages that had come floating in out of nowhere. He had gone to get the amulet, and he had not come back.

Rose Rita opened the front door of Dr. Wessel's office and looked out. It was dark and it was snowing. She fought down her rising panic and said to herself, through clenched teeth, "I've got to get help. I've got to get help." Still saying this over and over, she hurried down the steps and started kicking her way through the snow.

Lewis's Uncle Jonathan was winding the mantel clock in the dining room when he heard a terrific hammering on the front door. When he got there, he found Rose Rita, red-faced, panting, and covered with snow.

"Mr. Barnavelt . . . Mr. Barnavelt . . . it's . . . we've got to . . . too late . . . took him . . . go find him . . ." Cold wet

bubbles were rising from Rose Rita's throat and bursting in her mouth. She couldn't talk any more.

Jonathan put his arm around her and tried to make her calm down. He told her that she'd better get out of that heavy wet coat. But when he tried to help her unbutton her parka, she shoved him away angrily. Rose Rita stood there trying to catch her breath. It took her some time. When she finally got her voice back, she stared straight at Jonathan and spoke as calmly as she could.

"Mr. Barnavelt . . . there's . . . there's something awful's happened to Lewis. You know that old coin you gave him . . . out of your grampa's trunk?"

Jonathan gave Rose Rita a strange look. "Yes, I remember. What about it?"

"Well, it's magic, and he took it away from me and now it's got him and we've got to . . ." Rose Rita broke down. She put her hands to her face and cried. Her whole body shook.

Several minutes later, Rose Rita and Jonathan and Mrs. Zimmermann were sitting around the kitchen table in Mrs. Zimmermann's house. Mrs. Zimmermann was holding Rose Rita's hand and comforting her. Rose Rita had just finished telling them both the whole story, as far as she knew it.

"Don't worry, Rose Rita," Mrs. Zimmermann said softly. "Everything'll be all right. We'll find him."

Rose Rita stopped crying and looked her straight in the eye. "Oh yeah? Well, how're we gonna do it?"

Mrs. Zimmermann stared at the table. "I don't know yet," she said in a low voice.

It was hard for Rose Rita to fight down despair. She wanted them all to jump into the car right away and zoom off in search of Lewis. But they didn't even know which way they ought to go. The kitchen clock fizzed, and Mrs. Zimmermann rapped the large purple stone of her ring on the white enamel of the tabletop. She was trying to think.

Suddenly Mrs. Zimmermann shoved her chair back and jumped up. "Of course! Come on, everybody. Get your things on. I know where we're going now."

Rose Rita and Jonathan were utterly mystified, but they followed Mrs. Zimmermann out to the front hall and started getting dressed. Jonathan put on his big fur coat and the hat that looked like a small black haystack. Mrs. Zimmermann put on her heavy purple cape and rooted in the hall closet until she found her umbrella. It was a small black umbrella with rust streaks running down it and a crystal knob for a handle. Rose Rita wondered why she wanted it.

As soon as everyone was ready, they went next door, and Jonathan got his car out of the garage. Now Rose Rita was squeezed into the front seat between Jonathan and Mrs. Zimmermann. As the car reached the corner of Mansion and High, Jonathan put on the brakes and turned to Rose Rita.

"Okay, Rosie," he said, "I think I'd better take you home now. It's getting late and your folks'll be wondering where you are. And I wouldn't think of taking you along on a dangerous journey like this one."

Rose Rita set her jaw and stared back at Jonathan defiantly. "Mr. Barnavelt, if you want to get rid of me you'll have to tie me up and dump me on my front porch."

Jonathan looked at Rose Rita for a second. Then he shrugged and drove on.

The big black car crawled down Main Street and rounded the traffic circle. The snow was coming down hard. It piled up on the figures of Mary and Joseph inside the columns of the fountain. Rose Rita saw that they were headed out of town now. The CITY LIMITS sign passed. So did the Athletic Field and the Bowl-Mor Bowling Alley. Jonathan had had a hurried consultation with Mrs. Zimmermann just before they left the house, and he seemed to know where they were going. Normally, Rose Rita would have been irritated about not being let in on their little secret. But she was so worried about Lewis that she didn't care where they went, as long as they were going somewhere to save him.

Now they were out in the country. The tire chains chinked steadily, and white dots came rushing out of the blackness. Rose Rita stared at them, hypnotized. She imagined that she was in a space ship plowing through the Asteroid Belt. The dots were meteorites. *Chink-chink* went the chains. *Swish-swish* went the windshield wipers as they slowly cleared the snow away. The white dots kept flying at the car. Rose Rita felt the warm breath of the heater on her legs. Although it was still early in the evening, she felt exhausted. Running through the snow from the doctor's office to Lewis's house had really tired her out. Her head began to fall forward . . .

"It's no use. We can't go any farther."

Rose Rita shook her head and wiped her eyes. "Huh?"

It was Jonathan who had spoken. He put the car into reverse and backed up a bit. Then he put it in first and pressed steadily down on the accelerator. The car rolled forward a little way, but then it stopped. The tires squealed and whined. Jonathan backed up and tried again. And again. And again. Finally, he turned the ignition off. He heaved a deep sigh, ground his teeth, and banged with his fists on the useless steering wheel. Before them on the road stretched a rippled desert of snow. It was too deep for them to drive through.

The car dripped and ticked into silence. White flakes began piling up on the windshield wipers. The three of them sat watching for what seemed like a long time, though it was really less than a minute. Then Mrs. Zimmermann cleared her throat. The sudden sound made

Jonathan and Rose Rita jump. They turned toward her, wondering what she was going to say. Now she thrust her arms through the armholes in her cape and picked her umbrella up off the floor of the car. "All right, everybody out. Buckle up your galoshes and button up your coats. We'll have to walk."

Jonathan stared at her. "*Walk?* Florence, are you crazy? It's still . . . well, how many miles would you say it was?"

"Not as many as you would claim, Weird Beard," said Mrs. Zimmermann, smiling grimly. "But in any case we're wasting time. We've *got* to walk. That's all there is to it." She opened the car door and slid out. Rose Rita followed her. Jonathan shut off the headlights and took the flashlight out of the glove compartment. Soon he was charging off after the other two.

Walking through deep snow is hard work. You have to keep lifting your feet up and down, up and down, out of one hole and into another, until your legs feel like they're going to fall off. It didn't take long for Jonathan, Mrs. Zimmermann, and Rose Rita to get tired out.

"Oh, this is useless!" Jonathan gasped. He tore off his hat and threw it down into the snow. "We'll never get there at this rate!"

"We have to," panted Mrs. Zimmermann. "Rest a minute and we'll go on. At least it's stopped snowing."

It was true. Rose Rita looked up, and she could see

stars. The moon was out too, a big full moon. By its light they could see their car in the distance, just around a bend of the road. They had not yet gotten out of sight of it.

"I have never seen such lazy people as the people in the Capharnaum County Highway Department," Jonathan grumbled. "They should be out here right now with their trucks!"

"Save your breath for walking," said Mrs. Zimmermann.

They started out again. Up and down, up and down, through the glimmering white stuff. Rose Rita began to cry. Her tears felt cold on her cheeks. "We'll never see Lewis again, will we? Will we?" she sobbed. "Not ever again!"

Mrs. Zimmermann didn't answer. Neither did Jonathan. They just kept slogging.

They had walked for what seemed like hours when Jonathan stopped and put his hand to his left side. "Can't . . . go . . . farther . . . hurts . . ." he gasped. "Shouldn't . . . eat . . . so much . . ."

Rose Rita looked at Mrs. Zimmermann. She seemed ready to collapse. Now Mrs. Zimmermann turned away and put her hands over her face. Rose Rita knew she must be crying.

"This is the end," Rose Rita thought. "This is the end of everything." But just then she heard a noise in the distance. A growling, scraping, grinding noise. She turned and looked back down the road. Yellow lights were flashing in the distance. A snow plow was coming.

Rose Rita could hardly believe her eyes. Tired as she was, she started jumping up and down and cheering. Mrs. Zimmermann took her hands away from her face and just stood watching. Jonathan picked up his hat, dusted it off, and jammed it back on his head. He blew his nose and wiped his eyes several times. "Well, it's about time!" he said in a hoarse voice.

Now the plow was getting closer. Rose Rita thought she had never seen anything so beautiful in her life. It was a festival of flashing lights and wonderful noises. Sparks flew from the big curved blade. The motor whined and rumbled. They could read the words on the door of the big yellow truck: CAPHARNAUM COUNTY PUBLIC WORKS DEPARTMENT.

Jonathan turned on the flashlight and yelled and waved. With a long grating roar the truck pulled to a stop next to the three travelers. Snow from the plow blade spattered them, but they didn't mind.

A window in the cab was rolled down. "Hey, are you the people that left your car in the middle of the road?"

"Yes we are, and what's it to you, Jute Feasel?" Jonathan roared. "I never was so glad to see anyone in my life! Can you give us a ride?"

"Where to?"

"Halfway up the Homer Road to the old Moss Farm."

"What the hell you want to go out there for?"

"Watch your language, Jute," Mrs. Zimmermann called. "We've got a young lady with us." Rose Rita giggled. It was well known in New Zebedee that Jute Feasel had the foulest mouth in town.

Jute agreed to drive the three of them where they wanted to go. He said he didn't understand it, and Jonathan said he didn't have to, and they left it at that. The cab of the truck was a bit crowded with four people in it, but somehow they all managed to squeeze in. Mrs. Zimmermann sat in the middle, and Rose Rita sat on Jonathan's lap. It was too hot in the cab, and the air was thick with the smell of the King Edward cigars that Jute always smoked. But they were on their way again.

The truck ground up and down hills and around curves, shooting snow in either direction. Jonathan sang "Drill Ye Tarriers" to keep everyone's spirits up. Jute sang the song about the three little fishies in the itty-bitty pool, which was the only song he knew that was fit for children to listen to. Snow-covered trees stared at them from the darkness on both sides of the road.

Finally, in the middle of nowhere, the truck stopped. There was a wire fence, and some trees, and the snow and the moonlight. And that was all.

"Well, here we are!" said Jute. "I don't know what the he . . . er, heck you want out here, but you're old friends, and I'm glad to oblige. You want me to send somebody out to get you?"

"Yes," said Jonathan. "Does that thing work?" He

pointed to a radio on the dashboard. There was a microphone attached to it.

"Sure it does."

"Well, then, I want you to phone up Oaklawn Hospital and tell them to send an ambulance out here as fast as they can. No, I'm not going to explain. Thanks, Jute, and we'll see you soon." He opened the door and jumped out of the truck. Mrs. Zimmermann and Rose Rita followed him. As they walked around the front of the truck, Rose Rita looked up and saw Jute's face. It looked green in the light from the dashboard, and it also looked puzzled. Jute was talking into the microphone, giving directions.

"Hey!" shouted Jonathan. "Look at this!" He waved his flashlight excitedly.

Mrs. Zimmermann and Rose Rita followed Jonathan over to the edge of the road. There were holes in the snow. Footprints.

"Wow!" said Rose Rita. "Do you think it's Lewis?" For the first time in hours, she was feeling hopeful.

"Can't tell," said Jonathan, shining the flashlight into the dark holes. "They're half full of snow, but they're about his size. Come on. Let's see where they go."

With Jonathan in the lead, the three of them walked along by the side of the road until they came to a place where the footprints turned toward the fence. It was a barbed-wire fence, about chest-high to a man. A yellow tin sign advertising DeKalb Corn hung from the top strand. It rattled in the freezing wind. Suddenly Jonathan gave a cry and stumbled forward. He flashed the light at the sign. "Look!"

Something was caught on the corner of the sign. Something that fluttered in the wind. A piece of brown corduroy. There was dried blood on it, and there were little dabs of blood on the sign.

"It's Lewis, all right!" said Mrs. Zimmermann. "I don't think he's worn anything but corduroy pants since I've known him. But the blood! He must have cut himself going over the fence."

"Come on," said Jonathan.

Over the fence they went, one at a time. Mrs. Zimmermann was the last one over, and she caught her cape on a barb, but she ripped it loose and hurried on. The footprints went off across a snowy field.

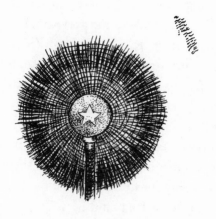

CHAPTER TWELVE

Jonathan, Rose Rita, and Mrs. Zimmermann stumbled across the snow-covered field. They were headed toward a little grove of pine trees. Jonathan was in the lead, and he played the flashlight beam over the footprints they were following, though they could be seen quite clearly by the light of the moon. The ground was uneven under the smooth layer of snow, and every now and then one of the three would stumble and fall. But in spite of this, they pressed on.

As they got closer to the dark grove of trees, each of them had the same feeling about it, though nobody spoke. They all felt that the trees were like a curtain hiding some scene from their eyes. They pushed on into the mass of fragrant boughs and shoved them aside. And there on the other side of the grove, they stopped.

Jonathan, Rose Rita, and Mrs. Zimmermann found that they were standing at the top of a low hill. At the bottom of the hill a wide space had been cleared in the snow. In the center of the patch of bare ground was a large well. Its top lay even with the ground, and nearby lay a heavy stone cover. Lewis stood a few feet away from the lip of the well. And a dark shape stood by the well, beckoning for Lewis to come.

Jonathan, Rose Rita, and Mrs. Zimmermann watched in horror. They could do nothing. Again the figure beckoned. Lewis stiffened. He did not move. Then the figure raised its hand and made a strange sign in the air. Lewis shuffled a few feet closer. Now he was almost at the edge of the well.

"Stop!" cried Mrs. Zimmermann. Her voice was loud and resonant, as if she were speaking under a dome.

Rose Rita turned and looked at her. Mrs. Zimmermann had changed. The folds of her ratty old purple cape were filled with orange light. A pale flickering light played over her homely wrinkled face. And in her hand, instead of an umbrella, she held a tall rod topped by a crystal sphere. Within the sphere a purple star burned. It threw a long violet slash, like a glowing sword, across the snow.

"I command you to stop!" Mrs. Zimmermann shouted again.

The dark shape hesitated. Lewis stood motionless, a few feet from the pit. Then a battle began.

It was like giant flashbulbs going off all over, all at once. It was like thunder, not only overhead but in the air all around and under the earth. Rose Rita fell to her knees in the snow and hid her face. When she raised her eyes again, the world lay in gray moonlight. Lewis had rushed back to the outer edge of the wide circle of snow. But the dark figure was still there by the well. And Mrs. Zimmermann lay crumpled in the snow. Near her lay the twisted wreckage of an old umbrella. The crystal knob had been shattered, as if by the blow of a hammer. Mrs. Zimmermann had lost.

Rose Rita sprang to her feet. She wanted to help Mrs. Zimmermann and help Lewis, to do everything all at once and save everybody. But she couldn't do anything. Jonathan was bending over Mrs. Zimmermann. It looked like he was trying to help her up. Rose Rita whirled frantically and looked down the hill. Lewis was shuffling toward the well once again. The dark figure kept motioning him forward, waving its arms in strange rhythmical gestures. Then Rose Rita heard Mrs. Zimmermann's voice. It was weak and raspy, like the voice of someone who has been sick for a long time.

"Rose Rita! Come over here! Come over here quick!"

Rose Rita thrashed through the snow till she was at Mrs. Zimmermann's side.

"Hold out your hand!" Mrs. Zimmermann barked.

Rose Rita held out her hand. Mrs. Zimmermann reached into her pocket and pulled out what looked like a piece of phosphorescent chalk. When she put it in Rose Rita's hand, it burned like an icicle.

"Take this and go to him! It's our only chance. Go on, run, before it's too late!"

Rose Rita took the thing in her fist and started down the hill. She expected it to be hard going, but it was strange. It seemed as if the snow was giving way in front of her. Before she knew it she was standing in the strange circular clearing. The shadow was still beckoning to Lewis. It took no notice of her.

And now Rose Rita was filled with anger at this horrible creature that was trying to kill Lewis. She wanted to rush at it and tear it to shreds. Was that what she was supposed to do, kill it? With the thing Mrs. Zimmermann had put in her hand? Or should she go straight to Lewis?

She didn't have long to make up her mind. Lewis's feet were touching the rock rim of the well. A slight push would send him plunging head first into darkness. With a loud screech Rose Rita ran forward. "Get away from him! Get away from him, don't you dare touch him, you filthy rotten thing!" she yelled.

The shadow turned and faced Rose Rita. And now it changed. Before, it had been a hooded, muffled shape. Now it was a ragged, spindly silhouette. A blackened,

shrunken corpse with living eyes. It moved toward her with outstretched, hungry arms. And Rose Rita heard what it was saying. She heard the words in her brain, although no sound was uttered. The thing was saying that it would wrap its arms around her and dive with her to the bottom of the dark, icy well. And there they would be, together, face to face, forever.

Rose Rita knew that if she thought, she would faint, or die. She clenched her teeth and rushed forward, saying over and over to herself the meaningless words of a commercial she had heard on the radio the other day. "Use Wildroot Cream Oil Charlie, use Wildroot Cream Oil Charlie, use . . ." The fearful shape rushed at her, and for a moment there was blackness all around her and the sickening, stifling smell of wet ashes. And then she was past it and standing by Lewis's side.

Lewis was actually teetering on the edge of the well. He had put one foot forward into nothingness, like somebody testing the water before he goes in. With a hard shove, Rose Rita pushed him sideways and back. Now her hands were around his neck, groping for the chain. Lewis did not resist. He acted like somebody who had been drugged. Still, it was hard for Rose Rita to get the chain off, because she had to hang onto the cold glowing object Mrs. Zimmermann had given her. She had a pretty good idea of what would happen to her if she let go of it.

With a jerk, Rose Rita pulled the chain up over Lewis's ears. She had it wadded in her hand now. When she turned toward the well, she saw the shape, muffled in darkness once again. It stood watching.

Rose Rita felt suddenly calm. Calm and triumphant.

"*You see this?*" she shouted, waving the amulet. "*Well, take a good look!*" And with that she flung the coin, chain and all, into the well.

There was a long second while the amulet fell. And then, from far below, came a tiny sound. *Plip*. And with that the dark hooded form vanished. It turned into a wisp of black smoke and was whipped away by the wind. Nothing was left, not even a smudge on the ground.

Rose Rita stood looking down into the well. It fascinated her. For a moment the well seemed like the only thing in the world. It was a great black whirlpool that would swallow her up. It was a dead eyesocket looking out of nothing into nothing. Rose Rita was caught in a sick convulsive shudder. She trembled from head to foot. But when she stopped trembling, her mind was clear. She stepped back from the edge of the well and turned to see if she could help Lewis.

Lewis was sitting on the ground crying. His face was red and raw from wind and snow and cold. His gloves were gone, his hat was gone, and there was a big piece torn out of his trouser leg. The first thing he said was, "Rose Rita, do you have a handkerchief? I have to blow my nose." Weeping with joy, Rose Rita threw her arms around Lewis and hugged him tight.

Now Jonathan and Mrs. Zimmermann were with them. They were crying too. But eventually Mrs. Zimmermann pulled herself together. She knelt down next to Lewis and started examining him like a doctor. She looked into his eyes, into his ears, and down his throat. She made him stick his tongue out and say "Aaah!" Jonathan and Rose Rita stood near, tense and nervous, waiting for Mrs. Zimmermann's verdict. Finally she stood up. She shook snow out of her cape and smoothed down her dress. "All that's wrong with *him*," she snorted, "is that he's been out in the weather too long. He's exhausted, and I think he has a cold. Rose Rita, would you hand me that thing I gave you?"

Suddenly Rose Rita remembered the object that had saved her. It was still in her hand, though it no longer glowed or felt cold. She opened her fist, and there was a glass tube about two inches long. Inside the tube was a perforated metal sleeve, and inside that were some pale violet crystals. On the end of the tube was a shiny gold-colored metal cap. There were words stamped into the top of the cap:

Rose Rita turned to Mrs. Zimmermann. She didn't know whether to laugh or cry. "You mean that's all it was? One of those things you stick in your nose when your head is all stuffed up?"

"Yes, of course," said Mrs. Zimmermann, impatiently. "Now give it here. Thank you." As she worked over Lewis with the inhalator, Mrs. Zimmermann added: "It's also a magic object, the first one I ever made. And up until a minute ago, I thought the thing was a total flop. You see, it was made so it would only work if it was in the hands of a child. It was supposed to protect the child who used it from evil creatures. And it was supposed to have certain healing powers. Well, after I made it I lent it to a niece of mine in Muskegon, and she kept it for years. She's a grown-up woman now, and a few months ago she sent the thing back in a box with a little note saying that it was very good for clearing out a stuffy head, but that she didn't see anything magic about it. So I put the silly thing in a pocket of my cloak and forgot about it—until just now." Mrs. Zimmermann chuckled grimly. "I guess my niece just led a dull life. She never ran into anything like that dark shadow by the well."

Mrs. Zimmermann stood up and shook snow out of her cloak. Rose Rita looked down at Lewis, and she felt like cheering. Lewis looked dazed, but remarkably healthy. Now Mrs. Zimmermann turned to Rose Rita. She handed her the tube. "Here. Take it. It's yours. For good."

Tears came to Rose Rita's eyes. "Thanks. I hope I never have to use it the way I did tonight."

"So do I," said Mrs. Zimmermann.

"And I," said Jonathan, helping Lewis to his feet.

After Jonathan had made an unsuccessful attempt to get the lid back on the well, the four of them set out for the road. When they got there, they found an ambulance with its motor running. And there was Jute Feasel with Jonathan's car.

"Hi everybody!" Jute called. "I thought maybe you'd need this. I left my truck back where your car was, so if you'd drop me off there, I'd be obliged to you."

"It's a deal," Jonathan called, over his shoulder. He was talking with the ambulance driver, telling him that he wanted Lewis to spend the night in the hospital because he was suffering from cold and exposure. After that, Jonathan did a good deal of conferring with Mrs. Zimmermann, and in the end it was decided that she would ride back in the ambulance with Lewis, and the others would go back in Jonathan's car.

On the way back to New Zebedee, everybody in the car was silent for a long time. Jonathan drove, Jute rode next to him, and Rose Rita sat all by herself in the back. As they passed the CITY LIMITS sign, Jute spoke up. "I don't mean to be nosy, but what the he . . . oh hell, you don't mind if I swear, do you, Rose Rita? What the hell was Lewis doing out at the old Moss Farm in the middle of the night?"

Jonathan had begun a very hemmy and hawy explanation, when Rose Rita butted in. "It's all very simple, Mr. Feasel. What really happened was, Lewis was out walking by the city limits when this man he'd never seen before stopped in his car and asked him if he'd like to drive out to Homer and back, just to look at the snow. Well, Lewis does dumb things some of the time, and he said sure, and jumped in. But when they were halfway to Homer, the guy turned out to be one of these crazy people you read about in the papers, so Lewis jumped out of the car and hid in the woods. That was where we found him."

Jute puffed on his cigar and nodded. "Lewis get a good look at this guy?"

"No. It was dark. And he didn't get his license number, either. It's too bad. They'll probably never catch him."

"Yeah." Jute rode the rest of the way in silence. He did wonder how Jonathan and the others happened to know where to go to find Lewis. There weren't any telephones in that grove of pine trees. But Jute had heard that Jonathan was a magician, and maybe magicians had ways of communicating with people in their families. With brain waves or stuff like that. At any rate, Jute didn't ask any more questions, and Rose Rita rode the rest of the way home with a self-satisfied smile on her face.

CHAPTER THIRTEEN

Lewis woke up the next morning in a whitewashed room full of light. New Zebedee's hospital was in an enormous mansion that had once been owned by a rich old lady. Lewis's room was in the attic. The ceiling at the foot of his bed sloped down almost to the floor, and next to his elbow was a white plaster tunnel running out to a curtained dormer window at the end. Icicles hung outside, but it was warm in the room.

There were other patients in the long room, and nurses came and went all morning. Near noon, Dr. Humphries came to look Lewis over. He was the Barnavelts' family doctor, and Lewis liked him a lot. He had a voice like a bass viol, and he cracked jokes a lot to put people at their ease. And he always carried a black leather bag full of rattling square pill bottles. Dr. Humphries put a wooden stick in Lewis's mouth and flashed a light down his throat. He looked in his ears and eyes. Then he patted Lewis on the shoulder, snapped up his bag, and told him that a couple of days rest at home was all he needed. They shook hands, and Dr. Humphries left.

A few minutes later, Jonathan came to get Lewis, and they went home. Lewis was ordered to bed by Mrs. Zimmermann, and that evening, when she brought his supper up to him, she told him that she had a surprise: she and Jonathan and Rose Rita had arranged a special pre-Christmas Christmas party for him. He could put on his slippers and bathrobe and come down to the study as soon as he liked.

At first Lewis was frightened, because he had seen pictures in the paper of children who were dying of some incurable disease, like leukemia. They were always given early Christmas parties. But after Mrs. Zimmermann had reassured him several times that he wasn't on the brink of death, he felt better. In fact, he could hardly wait for the party to begin.

Lewis was sitting by the Christmas tree. He was looking at the red plaid Sherlock Holmes hat that Jonathan had bought to replace the one Woody had stolen. In one hand Lewis held a glass of Jonathan's special Christmas punch. In the other he held a chocolate-chip cookie.

This time he didn't have to squint to make the Christmas tree lights turn into stars. He was blinded by tears of happiness.

Rose Rita was sitting crosslegged on the floor near Lewis's armchair. She was playing with another of his presents, an electric pinball machine. "Mrs. Zimmermann?" she said.

"Yes, Rose Rita? What is it?" Mrs. Zimmermann was over by the library table, adding more Benedictine to her punch. Every year she claimed Jonathan went light on the Benedictine, and every year she doctored her drinks to suit herself. "Yes, my dear? What do you want?"

"When are you going to tell us how you figured out where to go? I mean, how you knew where Lewis was?"

Mrs. Zimmermann turned and smiled. She dipped her index finger in the punch, stirred, and put her finger in her mouth. "Mmm! Good! How did I know? Well, that's a good question. I thought over what you had told me about Lewis's experiences with the magic coin, and one detail kept ringing a bell in my mind. It was a detail that you probably didn't think was very important."

"Which one was that?" asked Lewis.

"The way the ghost smelled. Rose Rita said that you had told her the ghost smelled of wet ashes. It smelled like a fire that has just been put out. Well now, I put this fact together with a couple of others that I knew." Mrs.

Zimmermann held up a finger. "One: on the night of April 30, 1859, a farmer named Eliphaz Moss was burned to death in his farmhouse out near the Homer Road. My grandfather had a farm near there, and he was part of the bucket brigade that tried to put out the fire. When I was a child, I remember him telling me how awful it was to suddenly see old Eliphaz come tearing out of that house. He was all on fire. Then with a hideous screech (so my grandfather said) he threw himself into—"

"The well?" Lewis asked. His face had turned very pale.

"The well," said Mrs. Zimmermann, nodding grimly. "The well put the poor man's fire out, and it drowned him too. It's a very deep well, and they never recovered the body. Later, after the fire, somebody made a big, granite cover for the well, and the cover became Eliphaz's tombstone. That, by the way, is what your uncle is out doing now—helping Jute get the lid back on the well."

The front door slammed. It was Jonathan. When he came into the library, he was red-faced from the cold, but rather gloomy-acting. As soon as he had poured himself a cup of punch, he seemed more cheerful, so Mrs. Zimmermann went on with her story.

"Of course, that's only part of the tale," she said, pouring herself another cup of punch. "The second part concerns Walter Finzer, the man Grampa Barnavelt won the three-cent piece from. He was Eliphaz Moss's hired man, and everyone always believed that he had set the fire that killed old Eliphaz Moss."

"Why did they think that?" asked Rose Rita.

"Because Walter was a foul-tempered, nasty, cruel, lazy lout, that's why!" growled Jonathan. "Of course, you may have gathered that from the way he behaved when Grampa won his lucky piece."

"Do *you* think Walter Finzer set the fire, Mrs. Zimmermann?" It was Lewis this time asking the question.

"Yes," said Mrs. Zimmermann, nodding. "I didn't used to think so, but I do now. It's hard to piece things together from such little scraps and bits of evidence, but I'd say that Walter killed Eliphaz by knocking him unconscious and then setting fire to the house. By the time Eliphaz woke up, the house was on fire and he was, too."

"Why did Walter want to kill old Elly . . . whosis?" asked Rose Rita.

"To keep Eliphaz from getting back at him. You see, I think Walter stumbled into the house while Eliphaz was performing a magic ritual. Do you remember the date of the fire? April 30, 1859. Anybody remember anything special about April 30? You keep quiet, Jonathan. I know you know the answer."

Lewis thought a bit. "Hey!" he said. "That was the date on the newspaper that I saw just before the ghost came to get me. And 1859 was the date on the coin, too."

"That just makes me more certain than ever that my

theory is right," said Mrs. Zimmermann, smiling. "You see, April 30 is Walpurgis Night. It's sort of like Halloween—a night that is dear to the hearts of those who dabble in the black arts. Eliphaz dabbled in witchcraft, or at least, most of the farmers in the area thought he did. My grandfather thought so, for one." Mrs. Zimmermann stopped and stared into her glass. "You know," she said slowly, "it must have been awfully lonely on farms in those days. No TV, no radio, no car to take you into town for a movie. No movies at all. Farmers just kind of holed up for the winter. Some of them read the Bible, and some of them read—other books."

"You read those other books, too, don't you, Mrs. Zimmermann?" said Rose Rita in a small frightened voice.

Mrs. Zimmermann gave her a sour look. "Yes, I do, but I read them so I'll know what to do when something awful happens. And as you saw out there, sometimes it isn't enough to know about all these terrible books. Not when the other side's got more muscle."

"You're getting off the subject, Florence," said Jonathan. "So old Eliphaz was a wizard. Do you mean he was making the magic amulet when Walter burst in on him?"

"Yes. Walter probably came in for a plug of chewing tobacco or a drink of whiskey after a hard day's work. And there was Eliphaz doing some strange mumbo-jumbo over a little tiny silver coin. A three-cent piece. Well, everybody dreams about having a magic doohickey that will solve all their problems. The two men were alone out there, and Walter was probably by far the stronger. So Walter hit Eliphaz on the head, set fire to the house, and lit out—with the amulet. Then Walter must have decided that it would not be good for him to hang around New Zebedee. So he enlisted in the Army. Then the Civil War came along, Walter ran into Grampa Barnavelt—and you know the rest."

Lewis looked puzzled. "How come the ghost of old Eli . . . whatever-his-name-is was after me? Did he think I stole his amulet?"

"Not exactly," said Mrs. Zimmermann. "You see, the amulet was supposed to have the power to summon up a spirit from the depths. A spirit that would do Eliphaz Moss's bidding. But when you're fooling around with evil spirits, you've got to be careful, and the way I figure it, Eliphaz was interrupted before he had finished enchanting the coin. So things came out kind of screwy, as they would if you put the wrong ingredients in a cake you were making. And Eliphaz's spirit—his ghost, his soul, call it what you like—his spirit was the one called up when Lewis said the prayer from my book over the coin."

Lewis shuddered. "You mean I called him up? The ghost that smelled like ashes?"

Mrs. Zimmermann nodded. "You most certainly did. The prayer you said is what we professional wizards call a prayer of waking and possession. First, you woke up the spirit that had been asleep, the spirit that haunted the amulet—Eliphaz's spirit. The amulet couldn't do a thing to anybody until you recited that prayer. That is why Walter could never do anything with it, and was finally willing—albeit grudgingly—to toss it into the pot in a poker game. And that is also why Grampa Barnavelt could wear the coin on his belly for forty years and not be affected at all."

"But wait a minute," said Rose Rita. "I handled the coin after Lewis woke it up. How come nothing happened to me?"

"If you'll let me finish, I'll tell you why," said Mrs. Zimmermann patiently. "I said the prayer was a prayer of waking and *possession*. Lewis not only woke the amulet up, he made it his. His, and his alone. No one else could wield it. Of course, the amulet could be taken from him by force—as it was—but no one else could do anything with it. It was his until it was destroyed. I don't know whether you realize it, Rose Rita, but you wiped out the enchantment that had been laid on the coin when you dropped it into the well. Water is the cleansing element, the element of rebirth. It wipes out all curses. Running water is best, but good old stagnant well water is okay, too. That's why the dark shape vanished when it did. The enchantment was over."

"I still don't see why old what-sis-name was after me," said Lewis.

Mrs. Zimmermann sighed. "Well, there again, we can

only guess. Eliphaz was trying to make an amulet of power. Amulets of power can be used to call up spirits —usually evil ones—and they can give the owner of the amulet wonderful powers. Simon Magus owned an amulet of power, and it is said that he could fly through the air and make himself invisible."

"Do they help you win fights?" asked Lewis in a weak little voice.

Mrs. Zimmermann chuckled. "Yes, they do. Eliphaz's ghost helped you win that fight with Woody. Eliphaz had been trapped into being the spirit of his own amulet— sort of like a genie in a jug, if you see what I mean. Well, he had to obey the rules. You summoned him, and he gave you power. But then, as time passed, Eliphaz's spirit began to take shape in this world. At first he only sent you messages to let you know he was coming— postcards and the like. Finally, he took on the form you saw under the street lamp, and in the shadows under the arch of the Masonic Temple. Well now, Lewis, if you had been a wizard, there would have been no problem. You would have tamed the spirit. You would have made Eliphaz carry out your commands. But you were just a little boy who didn't know what he was doing, so Eliphaz decided to turn the tables and carry you off to his . . . his home." Mrs. Zimmermann shuddered and stopped talking. She stared hard at the fire. She was thinking about the well and what was in it.

Everyone sat silent, and for a few minutes it looked as if it was going to be a very gloomy Christmas party. But then Jonathan cleared his throat loudly and announced that, seeing as how it was Christmas for Lewis, it might as well be Christmas for everybody.

"You mean we all get to open our presents?" said Rose Rita. She sounded very excited.

Jonathan nodded. "That is exactly what I mean. Come on, everybody. Dive in!"

Before long the floor of the study was awash in a sea of colored paper. Mrs. Zimmermann got a new umbrella to replace the one that had been destroyed in her duel with Eliphaz Moss's ghost. This new umbrella was not magic, but she said she would get to work on it soon. Jonathan got his usual seven or eight pounds of tobacco, and a meerschaum pipe carved in the shape of a dragon. The smoke was supposed to come out through the dragon's nose and mouth. Rose Rita got a fielder's mitt and a season ticket for four to the Detroit Tigers' home games in the coming season. Jonathan and Mrs. Zimmermann were both baseball fans, and they were always arguing, since Jonathan liked the Tigers and Mrs. Zimmermann liked the White Sox. Jonathan grinned with delight when he thought of how many times the four people in this room would be going to baseball games in the coming year. And Rose Rita would get to take them all, since it was her ticket.

The party went on for hours until finally everyone was so tired they could hardly keep their eyes open. Rose Rita and Mrs. Zimmermann went home, and the other two dragged themselves off to bed.

Several days later, Lewis was in the front hall tugging at a boot that just would not go on. Suddenly the mail slot flapped, and a smooth white packet fell onto the doormat. At first, Lewis was terrified. But then, after he had calmed down, he hobbled over to the door and picked the envelope up. Lewis started to laugh. It was the Charles Atlas booklet.

About the Author

John Bellairs's first book for young readers, *The House with a Clock in Its Walls*, was described by *The New York Times* as "a spell-binding chiller," and was chosen by them as one of the Outstanding Books of the Year, 1973.

Mr. Bellairs has also written several adult books, among them *The Pedant and the Shuffly* and *The Face in the Frost*. He grew up in Marshall, Michigan, and now lives in Haverhill, Massachusetts, with his wife Priscilla and their son Frank.

About the Artist

Mercer Mayer is the author-illustrator of the five wordless *A Boy, A Dog and A Frog* books, as well as *There's a Nightmare in My Closet*, *Terrible Troll*, and many others. He has also illustrated *The Crack in the Wall & Other Terribly Weird Tales* and all of John D. Fitzgerald's *The Great Brain* books.

Mr. Mayer was born in Little Rock, Arkansas, grew up in Hawaii, and now lives in Roxbury, Connecticut.

THE LETTER,
THE WITCH,
AND THE RING

JOHN BELLAIRS
drawings by Richard Egielski

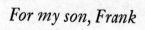

For my son, Frank

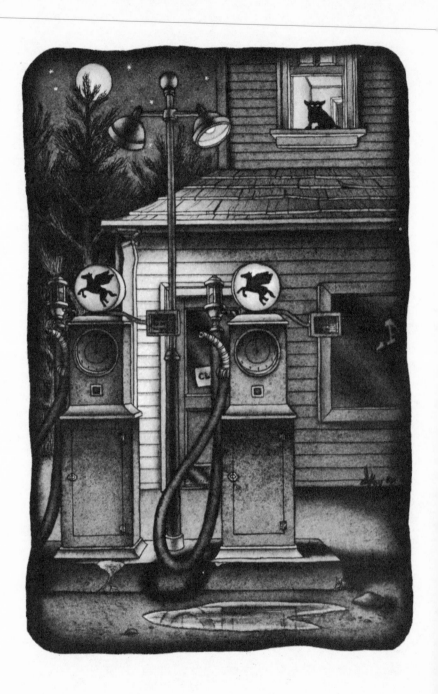

The Letter, the Witch,
and the Ring

CHAPTER ONE

"No, no, no, NO! I will not wear that silly uniform!" Rose Rita Pottinger stood in the middle of her bedroom floor. She was in her underwear, and she was glaring angrily at her mother, who held in her arms a freshly ironed girl scout uniform.

"Well, then, what am I going to do with it?" Mrs. Pottinger asked wearily.

"Throw it out!" Rose Rita screamed. She grabbed the uniform from her mother and flung it to the floor. Tears were in Rose Rita's eyes now. Her face felt hot and flushed. "Take it out and put it on a scarecrow or something! I tell you once and for all, Mother, I am *not* going to be a girl scout or a campfire girl, I am *not* going to Camp Kitch-itti-Kippi this summer and roast marsh-mallows and sing happy songs, I am going to spend this whole rotten summer batting a tennis ball against the side of the house until I'm so sick and . . . so sick and . . ." Rose Rita broke down. She put her hands over her face and cried.

Mrs. Pottinger put her arm around Rose Rita and helped her sit down on the bed. "There, there," she said, patting Rose Rita's shoulder. "It's not so bad as all that . . ."

Rose Rita flung her hands away from her face. She tore off her glasses and sat staring blearily at her mother. "Oh yes it is, Mom. It's every bit as bad as all that. It's awful! I wanted to spend the summer with Lewis and have a good time, and now he's going to that dumb boy scout camp. He'll be out there till school starts again, and I'm stuck here in this dumb town with nothing to do and nobody to have fun with."

Mrs. Pottinger sighed. "Well, maybe you can find another boy friend."

Rose Rita put her glasses back on and gave her mother a dirty look. "Mom, how many times do I have to tell you? Lewis isn't my boy friend, he's my *best* friend, just like Marie Gallagher used to be. I don't see why it should have to be any different just because he's a boy and I'm a girl."

Mrs. Pottinger smiled patiently at her daughter. "Well, my dear, it is different, and that's something you've got to understand. Lewis is twelve now, and you're thirteen. You and I are going to have to have a little talk on this subject."

Rose Rita turned away and watched a fly that was buzzing around on the window screen. "Oh, Mom, I don't want to have a little talk. Not now, anyway. I just want you to leave me alone."

Mrs. Pottinger shrugged her shoulders and got up. "Very well, Rose Rita. Whatever you want. By the way, what are you giving Lewis as a going-away present?"

"I bought him a genuine official Boy Scout Fire-Starting Kit," said Rose Rita sullenly. "And you know what? I hope he sets fire to himself with it and gets third-degree burns."

"Now, Rose Rita," said her mother soothingly. "You know very well that you don't want anything like that."

"I don't, huh? Well, let me tell you something, Mom . . ."

"I'll see you later, Rose Rita," said her mother, cutting her off. Mrs. Pottinger didn't want to listen to another of her daughter's ill-tempered outbursts. She was afraid that if she did, she might lose her temper herself.

Mrs. Pottinger got up and left the room, closing the door softly behind her. Rose Rita was alone. She threw herself down on the bed and cried. She cried for quite a while, but instead of feeling better after her cry, she felt worse. Rose Rita got up and glanced wildly around the room, searching for something that might cheer her up.

Maybe she could get out her bat and ball and go down to the athletic field and hit some flies. That usually made her feel good. She opened the door of her closet and immediately another wave of sadness swept over her. There, hanging forlornly on a nail, was her black beanie. She had worn it for years, but now it seemed silly to her. For half a year the black beanie had been hanging in the closet, gathering dust. Now, for some reason, the sight of it made Rose Rita burst into tears again.

What was wrong with her? Rose Rita would have given a lot to know. Maybe it had something to do with being thirteen. She was a teenager now, and not a kid. Next fall she would be in the seventh grade. Seventh and eighth grades were in Junior High. The junior high kids went to school in a big black stone building next to the high school. They had lockers in the halls like the high school kids, and they even had their own gym where they had Saturday night dances. But Rose Rita didn't want to go to dances. She didn't want to go on dates, with Lewis or anybody else. All she wanted was to keep on being a kid. She wanted to play baseball, and climb trees, and build ship models with Lewis. She looked forward to Junior High about as much as she looked forward to a visit to the dentist.

Rose Rita closed the closet door and turned away. As she turned, she happened to catch sight of herself in the mirror. She saw a tall skinny homely girl with black stringy hair and eyeglasses. I should have been a boy, Rose Rita thought. Homely boys didn't have as many problems as homely girls did. Also, boys could go to boy scout camp, and girls couldn't. Boys could get together for a game of flies and grounders and nobody thought there was anything strange about it. Boys didn't have to wear nylons and pleated skirts and starched blouses to church on Sunday. As fas as Rose Rita was concerned, boys really had the life. But she had been born a girl, and there didn't seem to be much she could do about it.

Rose Rita went over to the goldfish tank and fed her fish. She started to whistle and did a little dance around the room. Outside it was a beautiful day. The sun was shining. People were watering their lawns and kids were riding their bikes. Maybe if she didn't think about her problems, they would go away. It might turn out to be a nice summer after all.

That night Rose Rita went to Lewis's going-away-to-camp party. She didn't really want to go, but she figured she had to. Lewis was still her best friend, even though he was leaving her in the lurch by going away to camp, and she didn't want to hurt his feelings. Lewis lived in a big old house up on High Street. He lived with his uncle Jonathan, who was a wizard. And the lady next door, Mrs. Zimmermann, was a witch. Jonathan and Mrs. Zimmermann didn't run around in black robes waving wands, but they did know how to do magic.

Rose Rita figured that Mrs. Zimmermann knew more magic than Jonathan did, but she didn't show off so much.

The party that night turned out to be so much fun that Rose Rita forgot all about her troubles. She even forgot that she was supposed to be mad at Lewis. Mrs. Zimmermann taught Lewis and Rose Rita a couple of new card games (klaberjass and six-pack bezique, Winston Churchill's favorite card game), and Jonathan did one of his magic illusions, where he made everyone think that they were stumping across the floor of the Atlantic in diving suits. They visited some sunken galleons and the wreck of the *Titanic*, and even watched an octopus fight. Then the show was over, and it was time for lemonade and chocolate chip cookies. Everyone went out on the front porch and ate and drank and swung on the glider and laughed and talked until it was very late.

After the party was over, around midnight, Rose Rita was sitting in Mrs. Zimmermann's kitchen. She was staying over at Mrs. Zimmermann's house tonight, something that she always liked to do. Mrs. Zimmermann was really like a second mother to Rose Rita. Rose Rita felt that she could talk to her about practically anything. Now she was sitting there at the kitchen table, crumbling up the last chocolate chip cookie and watching Mrs. Zimmermann as she stood at the stove in her purple

summer nightgown. She was heating up some milk in a little pan. Mrs. Zimmermann always had to drink hot milk to calm down after parties. She hated the taste of the stuff, but it was the only way she could get to sleep.

"Some party, eh, Rosie?" she said, stirring the milk.

"Yeah. It sure was."

"You know," said Mrs. Zimmermann slowly, "I didn't even want there to be a party."

Rose Rita was startled. "You didn't?"

"Nope. I was afraid your feelings would be hurt. Even more than they already were, I mean—by Lewis's running out on you."

Rose Rita had not told Mrs. Zimmermann how she felt about Lewis's going away. She was amazed at how much Mrs. Zimmermann understood about her. Maybe it all went with being a witch.

Mrs. Zimmermann tested the milk with her finger. Then she poured it into a mug that was decorated with little purple flowers. She sat down across from Rose Rita and took a sip.

"Ugh!" said Mrs. Zimmermann, making a face. "I think the next time I'll slip myself a mickey. But back to what we were talking about. You're pretty mad at Lewis, aren't you?"

Rose Rita stared at the table. "Yeah, I sure am. If I hadn't liked you and Uncle Jonathan so much, I don't think I'd've showed up at all."

Mrs. Zimmermann chuckled. "It didn't look as if you

and he were on the best of terms tonight. Do you have any idea of why he's going to camp?"

Rose Rita crumbled up her cookie and thought. "Well," she said at last, "I guess he's tired of palling around with me and so he wants to be a big eagle scout or something."

"You're about half right," said Mrs. Zimmermann. "That is, he does want to be a boy scout. But he isn't tired of being your friend. I think Lewis wishes very much that you could be going to camp with him."

Rose Rita blinked back her tears. "He does?"

Mrs. Zimmermann nodded. "Yes, and I'll tell you something else. He can't wait to get back and tell you about all the great new things he's learned to do."

Rose Rita looked confused. "I don't understand. It sounds all mixed up. He likes me so he's going away so he can tell me how much fun it was not to have me around."

Mrs. Zimmermann laughed. "Well, when you put it that way, my dear, it does sound mixed up. And I will admit that it's all mixed up in Lewis's head. He wants to learn how to tie knots and paddle canoes and hike through the wilderness, and he wants to come back and tell you so you'll think he's a real boy and like him even more than you do now."

"I like him just the way he is. What's all this dumb stuff about being a real boy?"

Mrs. Zimmermann sat back and sighed. There was a

long silver case lying on the table. She picked it up and opened it. Inside was a row of dark brown cigars.

"Do you mind if I smoke?"

"Nope." Rose Rita had seen Mrs. Zimmermann smoking cigars before. It had surprised her at first, but she had gotten used to it. As she watched, Mrs. Zimmermann bit the end off the cigar and spat it into a nearby wastebasket. Then she snapped her fingers and a match appeared out of thin air. When the cigar was lit, Mrs. Zimmermann offered the match back to the air, and it disappeared.

"Saves on ashtrays," she said, grinning. Mrs. Zimmermann took a few puffs. The smoke trailed off toward the open window in long graceful swirls. There was a silence. Finally Mrs. Zimmermann spoke again. "I know it's hard for you to understand, Rose Rita. It's always hard to understand why someone is doing something that hurts us. But think of what Lewis is like; he's a pudgy shy boy who's always got his nose stuck in a book. He isn't good at sports, and he's scared of practically everything. Well. Then look at you. You're a regular tomboy. You can climb trees, you can run fast, and the other day when I was watching you, you struck out the side in that girls' softball game. You can do all the things that Lewis can't do. Now do you see why he's going to camp?"

Rose Rita couldn't believe what she was thinking. "To be like me?"

Mrs. Zimmermann nodded. "Exactly. To be like you,

so you'll like him better. Of course, there are other reasons. For instance, he'd like to be like other boys. He wants to be normal—most bright kids do." She smiled wryly and flicked cigar ashes into the sink.

Rose Rita looked sad. "If he'd've asked me, I would've taught him a lot of stuff."

"No good. He can't learn from a girl—it would hurt his pride. But look, all this talk is beside the point. Lewis is going off to camp tomorrow, and you're stuck here in New Zebedee with nothing to do. Well now, it just so happens that the other day I received a most surprising letter. It was from my late cousin Oley. Have I ever mentioned him to you?"

Rose Rita thought a second. "Gee, no, I don't think so."

"I didn't think I had. Well, Oley was a strange old duck, but . . ."

Rose Rita cut in. "Mrs. Zimmermann, you said 'late.' Is he . . ."

Mrs. Zimmermann nodded sadly. "Yes, I'm afraid Oley has gone to glory. He wrote me a letter while he was dying, and . . . well, see here now, why don't I just go get it and show it to you? It'll give you some idea of the kind of person he was."

Mrs. Zimmermann got up and went upstairs. For a while Rose Rita heard her banging around and shuffling papers in her large untidy study. When she came downstairs, she handed Rose Rita a wrinkled piece of paper

/ 13 /

with several little holes punched in it. There was writing on the paper, but it was very sloppy and shaky. Ink had been spilled in several places.

"This letter came with a bunch of legal documents for me to sign," said Mrs. Zimmermann. "It's all a very odd business and I'm not sure I know what to think of it. Anyhow, there's the letter. It's a mess, but you can read it. Oh, by the way, Oley always wrote with a quill pen when he felt he had something important to say. That's what made all those holes in the paper. Go ahead. Read it."

Rose Rita picked up the letter. It said:

May 21, 1950

Dear Florence,

This may well be the last letter I ever write. I fell ill suddenly last week, and do not understand it, since I have never had a sick day in my life until now. I don't believe in doctors, as you know, and have been trying to cure myself. I bought some medicine at the store down the road, but it hasn't helped a bit. So, as they say, it looks as if I am on my way out. In fact, when you get this letter, I will be dead, since I have left instructions for it to be sent to you with my will in case I kick off, as they say.

Now then, on to business. I am leaving you my farm. You are my only living relative, and I've always liked you, though I know you haven't cared

/ 14 /

that much for me. Anyway, let's let bygones be by-
gones. The farm is yours, and I hope you enjoy it.
And here is one final very important note. You
remember the Battle Meadow? Well, I was digging
there the other day, and I came across a magic
ring. I know you will think I'm kidding, but when
you handle the thing and try it on, you will know
I was right. I haven't told anyone about the ring,
except for a neighbor down the road. Maybe I am
a little funny in the head, but I know what I know,
and I think the ring is magic. I have locked the
ring in the lower left-hand drawer of my desk, and
I am going to have my lawyer send the key to you,
along with the key to the front door of the house.
So I guess that is all I have to say for now. With
luck I'll see you again some day, and if not, well,
I'll see you in the funny papers as they say, ha, ha.

Your cousin,
Oley Gunderson

"Wow!" said Rose Rita, as she handed the letter back
to Mrs. Zimmermann. "What a weird letter!"

"Yes," said Mrs. Zimmermann, shaking her head sadly,
"it's a weird letter from a rather weird person. Poor
Oley! He lived all his life up there on that farm. Completely alone. No family, no friends, no neighbors, no
nothing. I think it must have affected his mind."

Rose Rita's face fell. "You mean . . ."

Mrs. Zimmermann sighed. "Yes, my dear. I'm sorry to

disappoint you about that magic ring, but Oley was right when he said he was a little funny in the head. I think he made things up to make his life more interesting. That part about the Battle Meadow is right out of his childhood. A little bit of make-believe that he saved up. The trouble is, he saved it so long that he got to believing it was true."

"I don't get what you mean," said Rose Rita.

"It's all very simple. You see, when I was a girl, I used to go up to Oley's farm a lot. His dad Sven was alive then. He was a very generous sort, and was always inviting cousins and aunts up to stay for long periods of time. Oley and I used to play together, and one summer we found some Indian arrowheads in a meadow by a stream that runs out behind this farmhouse. Well, you know how kids are. On the basis of this little discovery we made up a story about how this had been a place where a battle had been fought between some settlers and a band of Indians. We even gave names to some of the Indians and pioneers who were involved in the battle, and we named the little field where we played the Battle Meadow. I had forgotten all about the Battle Meadow until Oley sent me this letter."

Rose Rita felt very disappointed. "Are you sure the part about the ring isn't true? I mean, sometimes even crazy people tell the truth. They really do, you know."

Mrs. Zimmermann smiled sympathetically at Rose Rita. "I'm sorry, my dear, but I'm afraid I know more about Oley Gunderson than you do. He was completely batty. Batty as a bedbug. But, batty or not, he left me his farm, and there are no other relatives around to contest the will on the grounds of insanity. So I'm going up there to have a look at the farm and sign a few papers. The farm is near Petoskey, right up at the tip of the Lower Peninsula, so after I've taken care of the legal folderol, I'm going to take the ferry across to the Upper Peninsula and drive all over the place. I haven't been on a really long car trip since gas rationing ended, and I've just bought a new car. I'm itching to go. Would you like to go with me?"

Rose Rita was overjoyed. She felt like jumping across the table and hugging Mrs. Zimmermann. But then a disturbing thought came to her. "Do you think my folks'd let me go?"

Mrs. Zimmermann smiled her most businesslike and competent smile. "It's all arranged. I called up your mother a couple of days ago to see if it would be all right with her. She said it sounded like a fine idea. We decided to save the news for you as a surprise."

There were tears in Rose Rita's eyes now. "Gee, Mrs. Zimmermann, thanks a lot. Thanks a whole lot."

"Don't mention it, my dear." Mrs. Zimmermann glanced at the kitchen clock. "I think we'd better be getting off to bed if we're going to be in any shape for tomorrow. Jonathan and Lewis will be coming over here for breakfast. Then off goes Lewis to camp, and off goes we to the wilds of Michigan." Mrs. Zimmermann got up and stubbed out her cigar in the kitchen sink. She went into the front room and started turning out lights. When she returned to the kitchen, she found Rose Rita still sitting at the table with her head in her hands. There was a dreamy look on her face.

"Still mooning about magic rings, eh?" said Mrs. Zimmermann. She laughed softly and patted Rose Rita on the back. "Rose Rita, Rose Rita," she said, shaking her head, "the trouble with you is, you've been hanging around with a witch, and you think magic is going to sprout up out of the cracks in the sidewalk, like dandelions. By the way, did I tell you? I don't have a magic umbrella anymore."

Rose Rita turned and stared at Mrs. Zimmermann in disbelief. "You *don't?*"

"Nope. As you recall, my old one got smashed in a battle with an evil spirit. It's totally done for. As for the new one, the one Jonathan bought me for Christmas, I haven't been able to do anything with it. I'm still a witch, of course. I can still snap matches out of the air. But as for the more serious, more powerful kinds of magic . . . well, I'm afraid I'm back in the bush leagues. I can't do anything."

Rose Rita felt awful. She had seen Mrs. Zimmermann's magic umbrella in action. Most of the time it just looked like a ratty old black umbrella, but when Mrs. Zimmermann said certain words to it, it turned into a tall rod topped by a crystal sphere, a sphere with a purple star burning inside it. It was the source of all Mrs. Zimmermann's greater powers. And now it was gone. Gone for good.

"Isn't . . . isn't there anything you can do, Mrs. Zimmermann?" Rose Rita asked.

" 'Fraid not, my dear. I'm just a parlor magician like Jonathan now, and I'll have to make the best of it. Sorry. Now, run up to bed. We've got a long day of traveling ahead of us."

Sleepily Rose Rita climbed the stairs. She was staying in the guest room. It was a very pleasant room, and, like most of the rooms in Mrs. Zimmermann's house, it was full of purple things. The wallpaper was covered with little bouquets of violets, and the chamber pot in the corner was made of purple Crown Derby china. Over the bureau hung a painting of a room in which almost everything was purple. The painting was signed "H. Matisse." It had been given to Mrs. Zimmermann by the famous French painter during her visit to Paris just before the First World War.

Rose Rita lay back on her pillow. The moon hung over Jonathan's house and cast a silver light on turrets and gables and steep slanted roofs. Rose Rita felt dreamy and strange. Magic umbrellas and magic rings were chasing each other around in her head. She thought about Oley's letter. What if there really was a magic ring up there, locked in his desk? That would sure be exciting. Rose Rita sighed and turned over on her side. Mrs. Zimmermann was a smart person. She usually knew what she was talking about, and she was probably right about that old ring. The whole story was just a lot of baloney. But as she drifted off to sleep, Rose Rita couldn't help thinking how nice it would be if Oley's letter were telling the truth.

CHAPTER TWO

Next morning Mrs. Zimmermann made popovers for breakfast. Just as she was pulling the pan out of the oven, the back door opened, and in walked Jonathan and Lewis. Lewis was pudgy and round-faced. He was wearing his brand-new boy scout uniform and a bright red neckerchief with BSA on the back. His hair was neatly parted and plastered down with Wildroot Cream Oil. Behind him came Jonathan. Jonathan always looked the same, summer or winter: red beard, pipe in mouth, tan wash pants, blue work shirt, red vest.

"Hi, Pruny!" said Jonathan, cheerfully. "Are those popovers ready yet?"

"The first batch is, Weird Beard," snapped Mrs. Zimmermann, as she dumped the heavy iron pan on the table. "I'm only making two pans. Think you can hold yourself down to four?"

"I'll be lucky if I get one, the way you grab them, Haggy. Watch out for her fork, Lewis. She stabbed me right here in the back of the hand last week."

Jonathan and Mrs. Zimmermann went on trading insults until breakfast was ready. Then, together with Lewis and Rose Rita, they sat down to the silent business of eating. At first Lewis didn't dare meet Rose Rita's eyes—he still felt bad about leaving her in the lurch. But then he noticed that she had a very smug look on her face. Jonathan noticed it too.

"Oh, all right!" said Jonathan, when he felt that he couldn't stand the suspense any longer. "What's the big secret? Rose Rita's got canary feathers all over her face."

"Oh, nothing much," said Rose Rita, grinning. "I'm just going up to explore around an old abandoned farm with Mrs. Zimmermann. The farm is supposed to be haunted, and there's a magic ring hidden somewhere in the house. It was put there by a madman who hanged himself later in the barn."

Lewis and Jonathan gaped. Rose Rita was embroidering a bit on the truth. It was one of her faults. Usually she was quite truthful, but when the occasion seemed to call for it, she could come out with the most amazing stuff.

Mrs. Zimmermann gave Rose Rita a sour look. "You ought to write books," she said dryly. Then she turned to Lewis and Jonathan. "Despite what my friend here claims, I am not running a Halloween Tourist Agency. My cousin Oley—you remember him, Jonathan—he died, and he left me his farm. I'm going up to see the place and drive around a bit, and I've asked Rose Rita to come with me. I'm sorry I didn't tell you about this before, Jonathan, but I was afraid you'd slip and spill the beans to Lewis. You know how good you are at keeping secrets."

Jonathan made a face at Mrs. Zimmermann, but she ignored him. "Well!" she said, sitting back and smiling broadly at Rose Rita and Lewis. "Now you both have something to do this summer, and that's how it should be!"

"Yeah," said Lewis sullenly. He was beginning to wonder if maybe Rose Rita wasn't getting the better deal after all.

After breakfast Lewis and Rose Rita volunteered to do the dishes. Mrs. Zimmermann went up to her study and brought down Oley's letter for Jonathan to see. He read it pensively while Rose Rita washed and Lewis wiped. Mrs. Zimmermann sat at the kitchen table, humming and smoking a cigar. When he had finished the letter, Jonathan handed it back to Mrs. Zimmermann without saying anything. He seemed thoughtful, though.

A few minutes later Jonathan got up and went next door to his house. He backed his big black car out of the driveway and pulled it up next to the curb. The back seat was full of Lewis's boy scout stuff: bed roll, pack, scout manual, hiking shoes, and a Quaker Oats box full of Mrs. Zimmermann's specialty—chocolate chip cookies.

Rose Rita and Mrs. Zimmermann stood at the curb. Jonathan was behind the wheel, and Lewis sat next to him.

"Well, good-by and *bon voyage,* and all that," said Mrs. Zimmermann. "Have a good time at camp, Lewis."

"Thanks, Mrs. Zimmermann," said Lewis, waving back.

"You two have a good time too, up there in the wilds of Michigan," said Jonathan. "Oh, by the way, Florence."

"Yes? What is it?"

"Just this: I think you ought to check out Oley's desk to see if there really is anything hidden away there. You never can tell."

Mrs. Zimmermann laughed. "If I find a magic ring, I'll send it to you by parcel post. But if I were you, I wouldn't hold my breath till it arrived. You've met Oley, Jonathan. You know how screwy he was."

Jonathan took his pipe out of his mouth and stared straight at Mrs. Zimmermann. "Yes, I know all about Oley, but just the same, I think you ought to watch out."

"Oh, sure, I'll watch out," said Mrs. Zimmermann carelessly. She really didn't feel that there was anything to worry about.

There were more good-bys and waves, and then Jonathan drove off. Mrs. Zimmermann told Rose Rita to run home and pack while she went inside to get her own things together.

Rose Rita ran off down the hill to her house. She was really excited by now, and impatient to get started. But just as she was opening the front door of her house, she heard her father say, "Well, I wish next time you'd consult me before you let our daughter go gallivanting off with the town screwball. For God's sake, Louise, don't you have any—"

Mrs. Pottinger cut him off. "Mrs. Zimmermann is not the town screwball," she said firmly. "She's a responsible person who's been a good friend to Rose Rita."

"Responsible, ha! She smokes cigars and she hobnobs around with old what's-his-name, the bearded character with all the money. The one who does magic tricks, you know his name . . ."

"Yes, I certainly do. And I would think that after your daughter had been the best friend of old what's-his-name's nephew for a solid year, the least you could do would be to learn his name. But I still can't see why . . ."

And on it went. Mr. and Mrs. Pottinger were arguing out in the kitchen, behind a closed door. But Mr. Pottinger had a loud voice, even when he was talking normally, and Mrs. Pottinger had raised her voice to match his. Rose Rita stood there a moment, listening. She knew from past experience that it would not be good to butt in on the argument. So she tiptoed quietly upstairs and started to pack.

Into the worn black valise that she used as a traveling bag Rose Rita threw underwear, shirts, jeans, toothbrush, toothpaste, and anything else she thought she would need. It felt great not to have to pack dresses and blouses and skirts. Mrs. Zimmermann never made Rose Rita get all dressed up—she let her wear what she liked. Rose Rita felt a sudden sense of hopelessness when she remembered that she wouldn't be able to be a tomboy forever. Skirts and nylons, lipsticks and powder puffs, dating and dancing were all waiting for her in Junior High. Wouldn't it be nice if she were really a boy? Then she could . . .

Rose Rita heard a horn beeping outside. That had to be Mrs. Zimmermann. She zipped up the valise and dashed downstairs with it. When she stepped out the front door, she found her mother standing there smiling. Her father was gone, so apparently the storm had blown over. Out at the curb was Mrs. Zimmermann. She was at the wheel of a brand-new 1950 Plymouth. It was high and boxy, and had a humpy sort of trunk. A strip of chrome divided the windshield in two, and the little square letters on the side of the car said CRANBROOK—

that was the name of that particular model. The car was bright green. Mrs. Zimmermann was angry about that, because she had ordered maroon, but she had been too lazy to send the car back.

"Hi, Rose Rita! Hi, Louise!" Mrs. Zimmermann called, waving to both of them. "Good day for traveling, eh?"

"I should say," said Mrs. Pottinger, smiling. She was genuinely happy that Rose Rita could be going on a trip with Mrs. Zimmermann. Mr. Pottinger's job kept the family in New Zebedee all through the summer, and Mrs. Pottinger had some idea of how lonely her daughter was going to be without Lewis. Fortunately Mrs. Pottinger did not know anything about Mrs. Zimmermann's magical abilities, and she distrusted the rumors she heard.

Rose Rita kissed her mother on the cheek. " 'Bye, Mom," she said. "See you in a couple of weeks."

"Okay. Have a good time," said Mrs. Pottinger. "Drop me a card when you get to Petoskey."

"I will."

Rose Rita ran down the steps, threw her valise in the back seat, and ran around to climb into the front seat beside Mrs. Zimmermann. Mrs. Zimmermann put the car in gear and they rolled off down Mansion Street. The trip had started.

Mrs. Zimmermann and Rose Rita took U.S. 12 over to U.S. 131, which runs straight north through Grand

Rapids. It was a beautiful sunny day. Telephone poles and trees and Burma-Shave signs whipped past. In the fields farm machines were working, machines with names like John Deere and Minneapolis-Moline and International Harvester. They were painted bright colors, blue and green and red and yellow. Every now and then Mrs. Zimmermann had to pull off onto the shoulder to let a tractor with a long cutting bar go by.

When they got to Big Rapids, Mrs. Zimmermann and Rose Rita had lunch in a diner. There was a pinball machine in the corner, and Mrs. Zimmermann insisted on playing it. Mrs. Zimmermann was a first-rate pinball player. She knew how to work the flippers, and—after she had been playing a particular machine for a while—she knew how much she could bang on the sides and the top without making the TILT sign light up. By the time she was through she had won thirty-five free games. She left them to be played off by the patrons of the diner, who were watching, open-mouthed. They had never seen a lady play a pinball machine before.

After lunch Mrs. Zimmermann went to the A&P and a bakery. She was planning to have a picnic supper at the farmhouse when they got there. Into the big metal cooler in the trunk she put salami, bologna, cans of deviled ham, a quart of vanilla ice cream, a bottle of milk, three bottles of pop, and a jar of pickles. Into a wooden picnic hamper she put two fresh loaves of salt-rising bread and a chocolate cake. She bought some crushed ice at a gas station and put it in the cooler to keep the food from spoiling. It was a hot day. The thermometer on the billboard that they passed on the way out of town said ninety.

Mrs. Zimmermann told Rose Rita that they were going to drive straight up to the farm now, without stopping. As they got farther and farther north, the hills began to grow steeper. Some of them looked as if the car would never be able to get up them, but it was funny how the hills seemed to flatten out under you as the car climbed. Now, all around her, Rose Rita saw pine trees. The wonderful fresh smell of them drifted in through the car windows as they sped along. They were approaching the vast forests of northern Michigan.

Late that afternoon Rose Rita and Mrs. Zimmermann were cruising slowly along a gravel road, listening to the weather report on the car radio. Without warning, the car began to slow down. It rolled to a halt. Mrs. Zimmermann turned the key and pumped the accelerator. All she got was the *rr-rr* sound of the starting motor trying to get the engine to turn over. But it wouldn't catch. After about the fifteenth try, Mrs. Zimmermann sat back and swore softly under her breath. Then she happened to glance at the gas gauge.

"Oh, don't *tell* me!" groaned Mrs. Zimmermann. She leaned forward and began hitting her forehead against the steering wheel.

"What's wrong?" asked Rose Rita.

Mrs. Zimmermann sat there with a disgusted expression on her face. "Oh, not much. We're just out of gas, that's all. I meant to fill up at that place where we bought the ice in Big Rapids, but I forgot."

Rose Rita put her hand to her mouth. "Oh no!"

"Oh yes. However, I know where we are. We're only a few miles from the farm. If you're feeling energetic, we could ditch the car and walk, but we don't even have to do that. There's a gas station a little ways up the road. At least, there used to be one."

Mrs. Zimmermann and Rose Rita got out of the car and started to walk. It was almost sunset. Clouds of midges hovered in the air, and the long shadows of trees lay across the road. Little patches of red light could be seen here and there among the roadside trees. Up and down hills the two travelers plodded, kicking up white dust as they went. Mrs. Zimmermann was a good walker, and so was Rose Rita. They reached the station just as the sun was going down.

Bigger's Grocery Store was surrounded on three sides by a dark forest of pines. The store was just a white frame house with a wide plate glass window in the front. Through the window you could see rows of stacked groceries and a cash register and counter in the rear. Some green letters on the window had once spelled SALADA, but now they just said ADA. Like many rural grocery stores, Bigger's was also a gas station. Out in front stood two red gas pumps, and near them was a white sign with a flying red horse on it. The horse was on the circular ornament on top of each pump too. In a weedy field next to the store stood a chicken coop. The coop stood in a fenced enclosure, but there were no chickens to be seen in the chicken yard. The tarpaper roof of the coop was caved in at one place, and the water pan in the yard had a thick green scum on it.

"Well, here we are," said Mrs. Zimmermann, wiping her forehead. "Now, if we can get Gert to come out and wait on us, we're all set."

Rose Rita was surprised. "Do you know the lady that runs this store?"

Mrs. Zimmermann sighed. "Yes, I'm afraid I do. I haven't been up this way for some time now, but Gert Bigger was running this store when I last came up to visit Oley. That was about five years ago. Maybe she's still there, and maybe not. We'll see."

As Rose Rita and Mrs. Zimmermann got closer to the store, they noticed a small black dog that was lying on the steps out in front. As soon as it saw them, it jumped to its feet and started to bark. Rose Rita was afraid it might try to bite them, but Mrs. Zimmermann was calm. She strode up to the steps, put her hands on her hips, and yelled, "Git!" The dog stood its ground and barked louder. Finally, just as Mrs. Zimmermann was getting ready to aim a good hard kick at the dog, it jumped sideways off the steps and ran off into the shrubbery at the end of the driveway.

"Dumb mutt," grumbled Mrs. Zimmermann. She walked up the steps and opened the door of the shop.

Ting-a-ling went the little bell. The lights in the shop were on, but there was no one behind the counter. Minutes passed as Mrs. Zimmermann and Rose Rita stood there waiting. Finally they began to hear some clumping and bumping around in the back of the shop. A door rattled open, and in walked Gert Bigger. She was a big rawboned woman in a shapeless sack of a dress, and she had an angry face. When she saw Mrs. Zimmermann, she looked startled.

"Oh, it's *you!* You haven't been up this way in quite a while. Well, what do you want?"

Gert Bigger sounded so nasty that Rose Rita wondered if maybe she had a grudge against Mrs. Zimmermann.

Mrs. Zimmermann answered in a quiet voice. "I'd just like some gas, if it won't trouble you too much. We ran out down the road a bit."

"Just a minute," snapped Gert.

She marched down the main aisle of the store and out the door, slamming it as she went.

"Gee, what an old crab!" said Rose Rita.

Mrs. Zimmermann shook her head sadly. "Yes, she gets worse every time I see her. Come on, let's get our gas and get out of here."

After a good deal of fussing around and cursing, Gert Bigger found a five-gallon gasoline can and filled it. Rose

Rita liked the smell of gasoline, and she liked to watch the numbers on the pump whirl. When the numbers stopped, Gert shut off the pump and announced the price. It was exactly twice what it said on the pump.

Mrs. Zimmermann looked hard at the woman. She was trying to figure out if Gert was kidding. "Are you having a little joke, Gertie? Look at those numbers there."

"It's no joke, dearie. Pay up, or you walk to the farm." She added, in a sneering voice, "It's my special price for friends."

Mrs. Zimmermann paused a minute, wondering what to do. Rose Rita was hoping she would wave her hand and turn Gert Bigger into a toad or something. Finally Mrs. Zimmermann heaved a deep sigh and opened her pocketbook. "There! Much good may it do you. Now come on, Rose Rita, let's get back to the car."

"Okay."

Mrs. Zimmermann picked up the gas can, and they started back down the road. After they had rounded the first bend, Rose Rita said, "What's the matter with that old lady, anyway? How come she's mad at you?"

"She's mad at everybody, Rosie. Mad at the world. I knew her when I was younger, back when I used to come up here and spend summers at the old farm. In fact one summer, when I was eighteen, she and I fought over the same boy friend, a guy named Mordecai Hunks.

I won the fight, but he and I didn't go together very long. We broke up at the end of the summer. I don't know who he married."

"Was Gertie mad at you for taking away her boy friend?"

Mrs. Zimmermann chuckled and shook her head. "You bet she was! And you know what? She's *still* mad! That woman is an expert grudge carrier. She remembers things people said years and years ago, and she's always planning to get even with somebody. I must say, though, that I've never seen her act quite the way she did tonight. I wonder what got into her?" Mrs. Zimmermann stopped in the middle of the road and turned. She looked back in the direction of Gert Bigger's store, and she rubbed her chin. She seemed to be thinking. Then, with a shrug, she turned and walked on toward the car.

It was dark now. Crickets chirped in the roadside weeds, and once a rabbit darted across their path and disappeared into the bushes on the other side. When Mrs. Zimmermann and Rose Rita finally got back to the car, it was sitting there in the moonlight, patiently waiting for them. Rose Rita had gotten to thinking of the car as a real person. For one thing, it had a face. The eyes were starey, like the eyes of cows, but the mouth was fishlike— mournful and heavy-lipped. The expression was sad, but dignified.

"The Plymouth is a nice car, isn't it?" said Rose Rita.

"Yes, I guess I'll have to admit that it is," said Mrs. Zimmermann, scratching her chin thoughtfully. "For a green car, it's not half bad."

"Can we give it a name?" said Rose Rita suddenly.

Mrs. Zimmermann looked startled. "Name? Well, yes, I suppose so. What kind of name would you like to give it?"

"Bessie." Rose Rita had once known a cow named Bessie. She thought Bessie would be a good name for this patient starey-eyed car.

Mrs. Zimmermann emptied the five-gallon can of gasoline into Bessie. When she turned the key in the ignition, the car started immediately. Rose Rita cheered. They were on their way again.

When they got to Mrs. Bigger's store, Mrs. Zimmermann stopped just long enough to stand the empty gas can next to the pumps. As the car chugged along toward the farm, Rose Rita noticed that the forest that ran behind Gert Bigger's store continued on down the road.

"That's a pretty big woods, isn't it, Mrs. Zimmermann?" she said, pointing off to the right.

"Uh-huh. It's a state forest, and as you say, a pretty big one. It runs all the way out to Oley's farm and then up north for quite a ways. It's a nice place, but I'd hate to get lost in it. You could wander around for days, and nobody'd find you."

They drove on. Rose Rita began to wonder what Oley's farm would be like. She had been daydreaming about the farm on the ride up, and she already had in her mind a very clear idea of what the place ought to look like. Would it really be that way? She'd see in a minute. Up a few hills, down a few hills, around a few curves, then down a long narrow rutty road overhung with trees. And then, suddenly, there was old Oley's farm.

It didn't look like Rose Rita's daydream, but it was nice. The barn was long and painted white. Like Bessie, it had a face: two windows for the eyes, and a tall door for a mouth. Near the barn stood the house. It was plain and square, with a square little cupola on top. The place looked totally deserted. Tall grass grew in the front yard, and the mailbox was beginning to get rusty. One of the windows in the barn was broken. As Rose Rita watched, a bird flew in through the hole. Off in the distance the forest could be seen.

Mrs. Zimmermann drove right up to the barn door and stopped. She got out and then, with Rose Rita's help, she rolled back the heavy door. A faint smell of manure and hay drifted out into the chilly air. There were two long rows of cattle stalls (both of them empty) and overhead Rose Rita could see hay. Some old license plates were nailed to the beams that supported the hay mow. When Rose Rita looked at them, she saw that they had dates like 1917 and 1923. Up among the rafters the shadowy form of a bird flew back and forth. Rose Rita and Mrs. Zimmermann stood there silent under the high roof. It was almost like being in church.

It was Mrs. Zimmermann who finally broke the spell. "Well, come on," she said. "Let's get the picnic hamper and the cooler and unlock the house. I'm starved."

"So am I," said Rose Rita. But when Mrs. Zimmermann opened the front door of the farmhouse and turned on the lights, she got a shock. The house looked as if a whirlwind had passed through it. Things were scattered everywhere. Drawers had been pulled out of dressers and cabinets, and the contents had been dumped out on the floor. Pictures had been taken down off the walls, and every book had been pulled out of a small narrow bookcase that stood in the front hall.

"Good Lord!" said Mrs. Zimmermann. "What on earth do you suppose . . ." She turned and looked at Rose Rita. They were both thinking the same thing.

Rose Rita followed Mrs. Zimmermann to the room that Oley Gunderson had used as his study. Against one wall of the room stood a massive roll-top desk. The top was rolled up, and all the cubbyholes at the back of the desk were empty. There were finger marks in the dust on the surface of the desk, and the pencils had been dumped out of the pencil jar. All the drawers of the desk had been pulled out and lay scattered around on the floor. The wood around the place where the bottom left-hand drawer had been was scarred and splintered— apparently it was the only drawer that had been locked. Near the desk lay a drawer with a badly chipped front, and in the drawer lay a Benrus watchcase covered with black leather.

Mrs. Zimmermann knelt down and picked up the watchcase. When she opened it, she found inside a small square ring box covered with blue velvet. Without a word, Mrs. Zimmermann opened the little blue box and looked inside. Rose Rita leaned over her shoulder to see.

The bottom half of the box held a black plush cushion with a slit in it. The slit appeared to have been widened, as if something too big for it had been crammed into the box. But whatever the something was, it was gone.

CHAPTER THREE

Mrs. Zimmermann knelt there on the littered floor, staring at the empty ring box. Suddenly she laughed.

"Ha! That's a good joke on whoever our burglar was!"

Rose Rita was dumbfounded. "I don't get what you mean, Mrs. Zimmermann."

Mrs. Zimmermann got up and brushed dust off her dress. She pitched the ring box contemptuously into the empty drawer. "It's all very simple, my dear. Don't you see? Oley must have blabbed around that ridiculous story about a magic ring. Someone must have believed him and figured that there was something valuable hidden here in the house. After all, you wouldn't have to think a ring was magic to want to steal it. Rings are usually made of precious metals, like gold and silver, and some of them are set with diamonds and rubies and suchlike. After Oley died, someone must have broken in. I can imagine what he found! Probably an old faucet washer. Well, it could be worse. They might have set fire to the place. The house is a mess though, and you and I will have to do some tidying up. Now then . . ."

Mrs. Zimmermann went on chattering as she straightened up Oley's desk, putting the pencils in the pencil jar and erasers into cubbyholes. Who the heck does she think she's fooling? Rose Rita thought. She could tell from the way Mrs. Zimmermann was acting that this was all just a cover-up. She had seen Mrs. Zimmermann's hand tremble as she opened the little box. She had seen how pale she looked. So there really is a magic ring, Rose Rita said to herself. I wonder what it looks like. She also wondered who had taken it, and what they were going to do with it. She had walked into a real live mystery, and she was so excited about the whole business that she really wasn't scared at all.

It was nearly midnight when Rose Rita and Mrs. Zimmermann finally sat down to have their picnic supper. They laid out their meal on the kitchen table and fetched some dusty plates and tarnished silverware from the cupboard over the sink. After that it was time to turn in. There were two adjoining bedrooms at the top of the stairs, each with its own small dark oak bedstead. Rose

Rita and Mrs. Zimmermann rummaged in a linen closet at the end of the hall, and they found some sheets. The sheets smelled musty, but they were clean. They made up their beds and said good night to each other.

Rose Rita had trouble getting to sleep. It was a hot still night, and not a breath of air was stirring. The curtains on the open window hung still. She tossed and turned, but it was no use. Finally Rose Rita sat up and turned on the lamp on the bedside table. She dug into her valise for the copy of *Treasure Island* that she had brought along to read, and she propped her pillow up against the head of the bed. Now then, where had she left off? Oh, sure. Here it was. Long John Silver had captured Jim, and they and the pirates were searching for Captain Flint's treasure. It was an exciting part of the book. Jim had a rope around his middle and was being dragged along over the sand by Silver, who swung along jauntily on his crutch . . .

Tap, tap, tap. As she read, Rose Rita began to be aware of a sound. At first she thought it was in her head. She often imagined sights and sounds and smells when she was reading, and now maybe she was imagining the sound of Long John Silver's crutch. *Tap, tap, tap, tap* . . . it didn't sound like that, though . . . more like a coin being rapped on a desk top . . . and anyway, a crutch wouldn't make any noise on the sand. It would just . . .

Rose Rita's head drooped forward. The book fell

from her hand. When she realized what was happening, she shook herself violently. What a dope I am for falling asleep, she thought at first, but then she remembered that she was trying to read herself to sleep. I guess it worked, Rose Rita thought, with a grin. *Tap, tap, tap.* There was that sound again. Where was it coming from? It certainly wasn't in her head. It was coming from Mrs. Zimmermann's room. And then Rose Rita knew what the sound was. It was Mrs. Zimmermann rapping her ring on something.

Mrs. Zimmermann had a ring with a large stone set in it. The stone was purple, because Mrs. Zimmermann loved purple things. It wasn't a magic ring, it was just a trinket that Mrs. Zimmermann liked. She had gotten it at Coney Island. She wore it all the time, and whenever she was thinking about something, thinking really hard, she rapped the ring on whatever happened to be around, chairs or tabletops or bookshelves. The door was closed between the two rooms, but Rose Rita could see, in her mind's eye, a clear picture of Mrs. Zimmermann lying awake, staring at the ceiling and rapping her ring against the sideboard of the bed. What was she thinking about? The ring, probably—the other ring, the stolen one. Rose Rita really wanted to go in and talk the whole matter over with Mrs. Zimmermann, but she knew that was not the thing to do. Mrs. Zimmermann would shut up like a clam if Rose Rita tried to talk to her about Oley Gunderson's magic ring.

Rose Rita shrugged her shoulders and sighed. There was nothing she could do, and anyway she was nearly asleep. She fluffed her pillow up, turned out the light, and stretched out. In no time at all, she was snoring peacefully.

The next morning, bright and early, Rose Rita and Mrs. Zimmermann got their things together, locked up the house, and drove off toward Petoskey. They had breakfast in a café there and went to see Oley's lawyer. Then they drove on toward the Straits. That afternoon they crossed the Straits of Mackinac in a car ferry called *The City of Escanaba*. The sky was gray, and it was raining. The ferryboat heaved ponderously in the choppy waters of the Straits. Off on their right Mrs. Zimmermann and Rose Rita could just barely see Mackinac Island, a gray blurry smudge. The sun was coming out when *The City of Escanaba* reached St. Ignace. They were in the Upper Peninsula of Michigan now, and they were going to have two whole weeks to explore it.

The trip started off well. They saw Tahquamenon Falls and drove along the shore of Lake Superior. They saw the Pictured Rocks and snapped photos of each other. They drove through rolling oceans of pine trees and stopped to look at streams that ran red because there was so much iron in the water. They visited towns with strange names, like Ishpeming and Germfask and Ontonagon. At night they stayed in tourist homes. Mrs. Zimmermann hated the new motels that were springing up all over the place, but she loved tourist homes. Old white houses on shady back streets, houses with screened porches and green shutters and sagging trellises with morning glories or hollyhocks on them. Mrs. Zimmermann and Rose Rita would settle down for the night in a tourist home and sit out on the porch playing chess or cards and drinking iced tea while the crickets chirped outside. Sometimes there was a radio in Rose Rita's room. If there was, she would listen to the Detroit Tigers' night games until she got sleepy. And then in the morning breakfast in a diner or café, and then back on the road again.

On the fourth day of their trip something odd happened.

It was evening. Rose Rita and Mrs. Zimmermann were walking down the main street of a little town. The sun was setting at the end of the street, and a hot orange light lay on everything. They had had their dinner and were just stretching their legs after a long day of driving. Rose Rita was ready to go back to the tourist home, but Mrs. Zimmermann had stopped to look in the window of a junk shop. She loved to browse in junk shops. She could spend hours sifting through all sorts of trash, and sometimes she had to be dragged away by force.

As she stood by the window, Mrs. Zimmermann

noticed that the store was open. It was nine o'clock at night, but the owners of junk shops often keep odd hours. She went in, and Rose Rita followed her. There were old chairs with ratty velvet upholstery, and bookcases with a few books in them, and old dining room tables with an incredible assortment of junk laid out on them. Mrs. Zimmermann stopped in front of one of these tables. She picked up a salt and pepper set shaped like a fielder's mitt and a ball. The ball was the salt.

"How'd you like this for your room, Rose Rita?" she said, chuckling.

Rose Rita said she would love it. She liked anything that had to do with baseball. "Gee, could I have it for my desk, Mrs. Zimmermann? I think it's kind of cute."

"Okay," said Mrs. Zimmermann, still laughing. She paid the owner twenty-five cents for the set and went on browsing. Next to a dusty bowl full of mother-of-pearl buttons was a stack of old photographs. They were all printed on heavy cardboard, and, from the clothes that people in the pictures were wearing, they must have been pretty old. Humming, Mrs. Zimmermann shuffled through the stack. Suddenly she gasped.

Rose Rita, who had been standing nearby, turned and looked at Mrs. Zimmermann. Her face was pale, and the hand that held the photograph was trembling.

"What's wrong, Mrs. Zimmermann?"

"Come . . . come over here, Rose Rita, and look at this."

Rose Rita went to Mrs. Zimmermann's side and looked at the picture she was holding. It showed a woman in an old-fashioned floor-length dress. She was standing by the bank of a river, and she had a canoe paddle in her hand. Behind her a canoe was pulled up on the bank. A man in a striped jacket was sitting cross-legged next to the canoe. He had a handlebar mustache, and he was playing a banjo. The man looked handsome, but it was impossible to tell what the lady looked like. Someone had scraped the face of the lady away with a knife or a razor blade.

Rose Rita still didn't see what was bothering Mrs. Zimmermann. But as she stood there wondering, Mrs. Zimmermann turned the picture over. On the back these words were written: *Florence and Mordecai. Summer, 1905.*

"My gosh!" exclaimed Rose Rita. "Is that a picture of you?"

Mrs. Zimmermann nodded. "It is. Or rather, was, until someone . . . did that to it." She swallowed hard.

"How the heck did a picture of you get way up here, Mrs. Zimmermann? Did you used to live up here?"

"No, I did not. I've never seen this town in my life before. It's all . . . well, it's all very strange."

Mrs. Zimmermann's voice shook as she spoke. Rose Rita could see very clearly that she was upset. Mrs. Zimmermann was the sort of person who usually gave you the feeling that she had everything under control. She was a calm sensible sort. So when she got upset, you knew there was a reason.

Mrs. Zimmermann bought the photograph from the old man in the shop and took it back to the tourist home with her. On the way she explained to Rose Rita that witches and warlocks hacked up pictures that way when they wanted to get rid of somebody. Sometimes they let water drip on the photo until the face was worn away; or they might scrape the face off with a knife. Either way, it was like making a wax doll of somebody and sticking pins in it. It was a way of murdering somebody by magic.

Rose Rita's eyes opened wide. "You mean somebody's trying to do something to you?"

Mrs. Zimmermann laughed nervously. "No, no. I don't mean that at all. This whole thing, finding the picture of myself up here and finding it . . . damaged, well it's all just a funny coincidence. But when you fool around with magic the way I do, well, you get some strange ideas into your head. I mean, sometimes you have to be careful."

Rose Rita blinked. "I don't get what you mean."

"I mean I'm going to burn the picture," Mrs. Zimmermann snapped. "Now, I'd rather not talk about it any more, if you don't mind."

Late that night Rose Rita lay in bed, trying to sleep. Mrs. Zimmermann was downstairs in the guest parlor, reading—at least that's what she was supposed to be doing. On a hunch Rose Rita got up and went to the window. She remembered that she had seen an incinerator in the back yard. Sure enough, there was Mrs. Zimmermann, standing over the wire incinerator. Something was burning with a soft red glow at the bottom of the cage. Mrs. Zimmermann stood hunched over, watching it. The reddish light flickered over her face. Rose Rita felt afraid. She went back to bed and tried to sleep, but the picture of Mrs. Zimmermann standing there over her fire, like a witch in an old story, kept coming back to her. What was going on?

CHAPTER FOUR

The next morning at breakfast Rose Rita tried to get Mrs. Zimmermann to talk about the photograph, but Mrs. Zimmermann rather curtly told her to mind her own business. This of course made Rose Rita more curious than ever, but her curiosity wasn't getting her anywhere. The mystery would have to remain a mystery, at least for the time being.

A few days later Rose Rita and Mrs. Zimmermann were in a town over near the Wisconsin border. Once again they had settled down in a tourist home for the night. Rose Rita went out to mail a couple of postcards, and on her way back she happened to pass a high school gym where a Saturday night dance was in full swing. It was a hot night, and the doors of the gym were open. Rose Rita stopped a minute in the doorway and looked in at the kids who were moving slowly around on the dance floor. A big ball covered with little mirrors revolved overhead, scattering coins of light on the dancers below. The room was softly lit with blue and red light. Rose Rita stood and stared. It was really a beautiful scene, and she found herself thinking that maybe going to dances would be fun. But then she glanced along the wall and noticed some girls standing by the sidelines. No one was dancing with them. They were just standing there, watching. It didn't look like they were having a very good time.

A wave of sadness swept over Rose Rita. She felt tears stinging her eyes. Would she be in that wallflower line next year? It would be better to climb on a train and ride out to California and be a hobo. Did they let girls be hoboes? Come to think of it, she had never heard of a girl hobo. What a lousy deal girls had, anyway! They couldn't even be bums if they wanted to.

Rose Rita felt angry all the rest of the way home. She stomped up the steps of the tourist home and slammed the screen door behind her. There on the porch sat Mrs. Zimmermann. She was playing solitaire. As soon as she saw Rose Rita, she knew something was wrong.

"What's the matter, my dear? Is the world getting to be too much for you?"

"Yeah," said Rose Rita sullenly. "Can I sit down and talk to you?"

"Sure thing," said Mrs. Zimmermann as she gathered the cards into a heap. "This was getting to be a pretty dull game, anyway. What's on your mind?"

Rose Rita sat down on the glider, swung back and forth a bit, and then said abruptly, "If I keep on being friends with Lewis, am I gonna have to go out on dates with him and go to dances and all that stuff?"

Mrs. Zimmermann looked a bit startled. She stared off into space for a minute and thought. "No," she said slowly, as she rocked to and fro on the glider. "No, I don't see that you have to do that. Not if you don't want to. You like Lewis as a friend and not because he shows up at your door with a bunch of flowers in his hand. I think it should probably stay that way."

"Gee, you're great, Mrs. Zimmermann!" said Rose Rita, grinning. "I wish you'd talk to my mom. She thinks Lewis and I are gonna get married next year or something."

Mrs. Zimmermann made a sour face. "If I talked to your mother, it would make things worse, not better," she said, as she started laying out another hand of solitaire. "Your mother wouldn't like it much if I started butting in on her family's business. Besides, she may be right. In ninety-eight percent of the cases, a friendship like yours and Lewis's either breaks up or turns into a dating friendship. You may discover next year that you and Lewis are going different ways."

"But I don't want that to happen," said Rose Rita

stubbornly. "I like Lewis. I like him a whole lot. I just want things to stay the way they are."

"Ah, but that's just the trouble!" said Mrs. Zimmermann. "Things *don't* stay the same. They keep changing. You're changing, and so is Lewis. Who knows what you and he will think six months from now, or a year from now?"

Rose Rita thought a bit. "Yeah," she said at last, "but what if Lewis and me just decided to be friends the rest of our lives? What if I never got married, not ever? Would people think I was an old maid?"

Mrs. Zimmermann picked up the deck of cards and began to shuffle it slowly. "Well," she said thoughtfully, "some people would say that I've been leading the life of an old maid for some years now. Since my husband died, I mean. Most women would've remarried, quick as anything, but when Honus died, I decided to try single life—widowhood, call it what you like—for a while. And you know, it's not so bad. Of course, it helps to have friends like Jonathan. But the point I'm trying to make is, there isn't any one way of doing things that's the best. I was happy as a wife, and I'm happy as a widow. So try different things. See what you like best. There are people, of course, who can only do one thing, who can only function in one kind of situation. But I think they're pretty sad people, and I'd hate to think you were one of them."

Mrs. Zimmermann stopped talking and stared off into

space. Rose Rita sat there, with her mouth open, waiting for her to say more. But she said nothing. And when she turned and saw the anxious way Rose Rita was looking at her, she laughed.

"I'm through with my sermon," she chuckled. "And if you think I'm going to give you a handy-dandy recipe for how to live your life, you're crazy. Come on. How about a quick game or two of cribbage before bedtime? Okay?"

"You're on," said Rose Rita, grinning.

Mrs. Zimmermann got out her cribbage board, and she and Rose Rita played cribbage till it was time to go to bed. Then they went upstairs. As always there were two adjoining rooms, one for Rose Rita and one for Mrs. Zimmermann. Rose Rita washed her face and brushed her teeth. She threw herself down on the bed, and she was asleep almost before her head hit the pillow.

Later that night, around two in the morning, Rose Rita woke up. She woke up with the feeling that something was wrong. Very wrong. But when she sat up and looked around, the room looked absolutely peaceful. The reflection of the moon floated in the mirror over the bureau, and the streetlamp outside cast a puzzly black-and-white map on the closet door. Rose Rita's clothes lay neatly piled on the chair next to her bed. What was wrong then?

Well, something was. Rose Rita could feel it. She felt tense and prickly, and she could hear her heart beating

fast. Slowly she peeled back the sheet and got out of bed. It took her several minutes, but she finally got up the courage to go to the closet and yank the door open. There was a wild jangling of hangers. Rose Rita gave a nervous little yelp and jumped back. There was no one in the closet.

Rose Rita heaved a sigh of relief. Now she was beginning to feel silly. She was behaving like one of those little old ladies who peek under their beds every night before they turn out the lights. But as she was about to get back into bed, Rose Rita heard a noise. It came from the next room, and when she heard it, all her fear came rushing back. Oh come on, Rose Rita whispered to herself. Don't be such a scaredy-cat! But she couldn't just go back to bed. She had to go look.

The door between Mrs. Zimmermann's room and Rose Rita's room was ajar. Rose Rita crept slowly toward it and laid her hand on the knob. She pushed, and the door moved softly inward. Rose Rita froze. There was somebody standing by Mrs. Zimmermann's bed. For a long second, Rose Rita stared wide-eyed and rigid with terror. Suddenly she gave a wild yell and leaped into the room. The door crashed against the wall, and somehow Rose Rita's hand found the light switch. The bulb in the ceiling flashed on, and Mrs. Zimmermann sat up, disheveled and blinking. But there was no one standing by the bed. No one at all.

CHAPTER FIVE

Mrs. Zimmermann rubbed her eyes. Around her lay the rumpled bedclothes, and at the foot of the bed stood Rose Rita, who looked stunned.

"Good heavens, Rose Rita!" exclaimed Mrs. Zimmermann. "Is this some kind of new game? What on earth are you doing in here?"

Rose Rita's head was in a whirl. She began to wonder whether she might be losing her mind. She had been sure, absolutely sure, that she had seen someone moving about near the head of Mrs. Zimmermann's bed. "Gee, I'm sorry, Mrs. Zimmermann," she said. "I'm really awfully sorry, really I am! I thought I saw somebody in here."

Mrs. Zimmermann cocked her head to one side and

curled up the corner of her mouth. "My dear," she said dryly, "you have been reading too many Nancy Drew novels. What you probably saw was my dress on this chair. The window is open, and it must have been fluttering in the breeze. Now go back to bed, for heaven's sake! We both need some more shut-eye if we're to go gallivanting all over the Upper Peninsula tomorrow."

Rose Rita stared at the chair that stood next to Mrs. Zimmermann's bed. A purple dress hung limply from the chair's back. It was a hot still night. Not a breath of air was stirring. Rose Rita did not see how she could possibly have mistaken the dress on the chair for somebody moving around in the room. But then what had she seen? She didn't know. Bewildered and ashamed, Rose Rita backed toward the door. "G-good night, Mrs. Zimmermann," she stammered. "I . . . I'm really sorry I woke you up."

Mrs. Zimmermann smiled kindly at Rose Rita. She shrugged her shoulders. "It's okay, Rosie. No harm done. I've had some pretty wild nightmares in my time. Why, I remember one where . . . but never mind. I'll tell you some other time. Good night now, and sleep tight."

"I will." Rose Rita turned out the light and went back to her own room. She lay down on the bed, but she didn't go to sleep. She put her hands up behind her head and stared at the ceiling. She was worried. First there had been that photograph, and now this. Something was happening. Something was going on, but she couldn't for the life of her figure out what. And then there was that business of the break-in at Oley's farm, and the empty ring box. Did that have anything to do with what had happened tonight? Rose Rita thought and thought, but she didn't come up with any answers. It was like having two or three pieces of a large and complicated jigsaw puzzle. The pieces didn't make any sense all by themselves. Rose Rita figured that Mrs. Zimmermann must be as worried as she was. In fact, she was probably more worried, since the strange things were happening to her. Of course, Mrs. Zimmermann would never let on that she was upset. She was always ready to help other people, but she kept her own problems to herself. That was her way. Rose Rita bit her lip. She felt helpless. And she had a strong feeling that something really bad was going to happen soon. What would it be? That was another thing she didn't know.

Next day, toward evening, Mrs. Zimmermann and Rose Rita were bumping along a rutty back road about twenty miles from the town of Ironwood. They had been driving for about an hour on this road, and now they were about ready to turn back. Mrs. Zimmerman had wanted Rose Rita to see an abandoned copper mine that had once belonged to a friend of her family. At every turn in the road she had expected to see it. But the mine never appeared, and now Mrs. Zimmermann was getting discouraged.

The road was just plain awful. Bessie jounced and

jiggled so much that Rose Rita felt as if she were inside a Mixmaster. Every now and then the car would go banging down into a pothole, or a rock would fly up and hit the underside of the car with a sound like a muffled bell. And it was another hot day. Sweat was pouring down Rose Rita's face, and her glasses kept getting fogged up. Sandflies buzzed in and out of the open windows of the car. They kept trying to bite Rose Rita on the arms, and she slapped at them till her arms stung.

Finally Mrs. Zimmermann put on the brakes. She turned off the motor and said, "Darn it all anyway! I did want to show you that mine, but it must have been on another road. We'd better turn back if we're going to . . . oh, Oh Lord!"

Mrs. Zimmermann clutched the steering wheel and doubled over. Her knuckles showed white under her skin, and her face was twisted with pain. She clutched at her stomach. "My . . . God!" she gasped. "I've . . . never . . ." She winced and closed her eyes. When she was able to speak again, her voice was barely a whisper. "Rose Rita?"

Rose Rita was terrified. She sat on the edge of her seat and watched Mrs. Zimmermann. "Yeah, Mrs. Zimmermann? What . . . what's the matter? What happened? Are you okay?"

Mrs. Zimmermann managed a feeble smile. "No, I'm not okay," she croaked. "I think I have appendicitis."

"Oh my gosh!" When Rose Rita was in the fourth

grade, a kid in her class had died of appendicitis. His folks had just thought that he had a bad stomachache until it was too late. Then his appendix broke open, and he died. Rose Rita felt panicky. "Oh my gosh!" she said, again. "Mrs. Zimmermann, what are we gonna do?"

"We . . . we have to get me to a hospital quick," Mrs. Zimmermann said. "The only catch is . . . oh. Oh no, please no!" Mrs. Zimmermann bent over again, writhing with pain. Tears streamed down her face, and she bit her lip so hard that it bled. "The only catch . . ." Mrs. Zimmermann gasped, when she could talk again, ". . . the only catch is that I don't think I can drive."

Rose Rita sat perfectly still and stared at the dashboard. When she spoke, her lips barely moved. "I . . . I think I can, Mrs. Zimmermann."

Mrs. Zimmermann closed her eyes as another wave of pain swept over her. "What . . . what did you say?"

"I said, I think maybe I could drive. I learned to, once."

Rose Rita was not exactly telling the truth. About a year ago she had gone out to visit a cousin of hers who lived on a farm near New Zebedee. He was fourteen, and he knew how to drive a tractor. Rose Rita had pestered him until he finally agreed to teach her how to shift gears and let the clutch in and out. He taught her on an old wrecked car that sat in a field near the farmhouse, and after he had showed her the ropes, Rose Rita practiced by herself until she had all the gear positions

straight in her head. But she had never actually been behind the wheel of a moving car, or even a car that just
had the motor running.

Mrs. Zimmermann said nothing. But she motioned for
Rose Rita to get out of the car. When she did, Mrs.
Zimmermann dragged herself over into the seat where
Rose Rita had been and slumped there against the door
with her hand on her stomach. Rose Rita walked around
and got in on the driver's side. She shut the door and sat
there staring at the wheel. She was afraid, but a voice
inside of her said, Come on. You've got to do it. She
can't, she's too sick. Come on, Rose Rita.

Rose Rita slid forward until she was sitting on the
edge of the seat. She would have moved the seat up, but
she was afraid it would hurt Mrs. Zimmermann. Fortunately Rose Rita was tall for thirteen, and she had grown
a lot in the past year. Her legs were long enough for her
to reach the pedals. Rose Rita tapped the accelerator
cautiously. Could she really do it? Well, she'd have to
try.

Mrs. Zimmermann had left the car in first gear. But
you couldn't start a car when it was in first gear, it had
to be in neutral. At least that was what Rose Rita had
heard from her cousin. Cautiously she pushed the clutch
pedal in and eased the lever up into neutral. She turned
the ignition key, and the car started instantly. Now,
with her right foot on the gas and her left on the clutch,
she pulled the gear shift lever forward and down. Slowly

she began to let the clutch out the way she had been taught to do it. The car shuddered, and the engine killed.

"You've . . . got to . . . give it the . . . gas," Mrs. Zimmermann gasped. "When you . . . let the clutch out. . . give 'er the gun."

"Okay." Rose Rita was tense and trembling all over. She put the car back in neutral and started it up again. This time when she let the clutch out, she really floored the gas pedal. The car took a little jump forward and stopped again. Apparently too much gas was just as bad as too little. Rose Rita turned to ask Mrs. Zimmermann what to do now, but Mrs. Zimmermann had passed out. She was on her own.

Rose Rita gritted her teeth. She was getting mad now. "Okay, we're gonna try again," she said in a quiet firm voice. She tried and again the motor killed. It killed the next time, too. But the time after that she managed, somehow, to let the clutch out and press the gas pedal at just the right rate. The car moved slowly forward.

"*Yay, Bessie!*" Rose Rita yelled. She yelled so loud that Mrs. Zimmermann opened her eyes. She blinked and smiled feebly when she saw that the car was moving. "Atta girl, Rosie!" she whispered. Then she slumped over sideways and lost consciousness again.

Somehow Rose Rita managed to get the car turned around and headed back toward Ironwood. It was dark now, and she had to turn the lights on. The road was totally deserted. No farms, no homes. Rose Rita remembered one ruined shanty that they had passed, but it didn't seem likely that there was anyone living in it. No. Unless a car just happened to come along, there would be no help until they reached the two-lane blacktop that led back to Ironwood. Rose Rita swallowed hard. If she could just keep the car going, maybe everything would turn out all right. She glanced quickly at Mrs. Zimmermann. She lay slumped against the door. Her eyes were closed, and every now and then she would moan faintly. Rose Rita clenched her teeth and drove.

On Bessie crawled, up and down hills, over bumps and rocks, and in and out of potholes. Her pale headlight beams reached out before her into the night. Moths and other night insects fluttered past. Rose Rita felt as if she were driving along in a dark tunnel. Dark pine trees lined the road on either side. They seemed to press forward until Rose Rita felt hemmed in. An owl was hooting in the woods somewhere. Rose Rita felt lonely and frightened. She wanted to drive fast to get out of this awful place, but she was scared to. The road was so bumpy that she was afraid to speed up. It was frightening to have a big heavy car under her control. Every time the car hit a pothole, the wheel lurched violently to the right or the left. Somehow, though, each time Rose Rita managed to get straightened out. Oh, please, she prayed, get us there, Bessie. Please get us there before Mrs. Zimmermann dies. Please . . .

Rose Rita was not sure when, but after she had driven

along the dark winding road for some time, she began to have the feeling that there was someone else in the car with them. Rose Rita didn't know why she had this feeling, but it was there, and it was very persistent. She kept glancing up toward the rear-view mirror, but she never saw anything. After a while the feeling got to be so maddening that Rose Rita stopped the car. She put it in neutral, pulled on the emergency brake, and, as the car throbbed, she turned on the overhead light and glanced nervously into the back seat. It was empty. Rose Rita flipped off the light, put the car back in gear, and drove on. But the feeling kept coming back, and she found that it took a strong effort of the will to keep her eyes from wandering toward the rear-view mirror. The car was rounding a sharp curve when Rose Rita happened to glance up, and she saw, reflected in the mirror, the shadow of a head and two glittering eyes.

Rose Rita screamed and jerked the wheel violently to the left. With a screech of tires, Bessie swerved off the road and plunged down a steep bank. The car bounced and jounced wildly, and Mrs. Zimmermann's inert body slammed first against the door and then slid over across the seat to bump against Rose Rita. Rose Rita, panic-stricken, clutched the wheel and kept trying to find the brake with her foot, but she kept missing it. Down into darkness they went. Now there was a loud swishing, crackling sound outside the car, and a funny smell. In the fevered whirling of her brain Rose Rita found her-

self wondering, What is that smell? The crackling and swishing got louder, and finally Rose Rita got her foot on the brake. Her body lurched forward, and her head hit the windshield. She blacked out.

CHAPTER SIX

Rose Rita dreamed that she was clinging to a piece of wood that was floating in the sea. Someone was saying to her, "Are you all right? Are you all right?" That's a dumb thing to be saying, thought Rose Rita. Then she opened her eyes and found that she was sitting at the wheel of Bessie. A policeman was standing next to the car. He reached in the open window and touched her gently.

"Are you okay, miss?"

Rose Rita shook her head groggily. She touched her forehead and felt a swelling lump. "Yeah, I guess so, except for this bump on my head. I . . . my gosh! What happened?" She looked around, and saw that the car was embedded in a large clump of juniper bushes. Juniper! That was the smell! Daylight was streaming in through the dusty windows of the car. And there, on the seat beside her, lay Mrs. Zimmermann. She was asleep. Or was she . . . ?

Rose Rita reached over and started shaking Mrs. Zimmermann's shoulder. "Wake up, Mrs. Zimmermann!" she sobbed. "Oh, please! Wake up, wake—"

Rose Rita felt the policeman's firm hand on her arm. "Better not do that, miss. You don't know if she's got any broken bones or not. We've got an ambulance coming, and they'll check her over before they try to move her. What happened? Fall asleep at the wheel?"

Rose Rita shook her head. "I was trying to drive Mrs. Zimmermann back to the hospital after she got sick all of a sudden. I got scared and I drove off the road. I'm only thirteen, and I don't have any license. Are you gonna put me in jail?"

The policeman smiled sadly at Rose Rita. "No, ma'am. Not this time, anyway. But I think it wasn't very bright of you to try to drive, even if it was an emergency and all. You might of gotten yourself killed. As a matter of fact, if these bushes hadn't of been here, you *would've* been killed. And so would your friend there. But she's breathin' okay. I looked at her a minute ago. All we have to do is sit tight till the ambulance gets here."

A little while later a big white ambulance with a red cross on the side pulled up on the road next to the police car. Two men in white uniforms got out and edged their way down the embankment. They had a stretcher with them. By the time they got to the car, Mrs. Zimmermann was just coming to. The two men checked her over, and when they were sure she could be moved, they gently eased her out of the car and made her lie down on the stretcher. Up the hill they went with her, slowly. When they had her safe in the ambulance, they went back for Rose Rita. It turned out that she was a little bruised and shaken up, but otherwise okay. She climbed the hill on her own and got in the back of the ambulance with Mrs. Zimmermann. Off they went, siren screaming, toward Ironwood.

Mrs. Zimmermann spent the next three days in the hospital at Ironwood. The mysterious pains never returned, and the doctors informed her that they had been in the wrong part of the body for appendicitis. Mrs. Zimmermann was puzzled and frightened. Somehow it was worse not to know what had caused the pains, and the thought that they might return at any time was enough to make her very nervous. It was like living with a time bomb that might or might not go off.

So Mrs. Zimmermann, much as she disliked the idea, stayed in bed while the doctors at the hospital ran a series of tests. Nurses stuck needles into her and drew blood. They gave her vile-tasting potions to drink and made marks on charts. She was x-rayed and put in front of, and inside of, all sorts of strange science-fiction machines. Doctors stopped by every now and then to talk with Mrs. Zimmermann, but they never told her anything that she wanted to know.

Meanwhile, Rose Rita became a lodger at the hospital. Mrs. Zimmermann explained the situation to the doctors, and she showed them her insurance policy (which she always carried around with her in her purse, just in case), and it clearly stated that she was entitled to a private room. The private room had two beds, and Rose Rita slept in one of them. She played cards and chess with Mrs. Zimmermann and listened to night games with her on the radio. It so happened that the White Sox were playing at Detroit, and Mrs. Zimmermann was a White Sox fan because she had once lived in Chicago. So Rose Rita and she had fun rooting for opposite sides, and they even argued a bit, though not very seriously.

Some of the time, when sitting around in the hospital room got to be dull, Rose Rita went out and wandered around the town of Ironwood. She went to the public library and a Saturday afternoon movie. Some of the time she just explored. She got lost once or twice, but people were very nice to her, and she always managed to find her way back to the hospital.

On the afternoon of Mrs. Zimmermann's third day in the hospital, Rose Rita happened to be passing a vacant lot where some boys were playing move-up. They were getting tired of move-up, but they didn't have enough for teams. When they saw Rose Rita, they asked her if she wanted to play.

"I sure do!" Rose Rita yelled. "But whatever side gets me, they have to let me pitch."

The boys looked at each other for a minute, but after a hurried consultation, they decided that Rose Rita could pitch if she wanted to. Rose Rita loved to play baseball, and she really loved to pitch. She was the only girl in her school who could throw a curve with a softball. She had hesitation pitches, and blooper pitches, and she even had a knuckle ball, though it didn't work very well, because it's hard to hold a softball with your knuckles. Her underhand fast ball was famous—so famous, in fact, that she usually had to be persuaded just to lob it up there to weak hitters so they wouldn't strike out all the time.

So Rose Rita wound up playing softball with a bunch of boys she had never seen before. She got a lot of hits, and she grabbed off some hard line drives with her bare hands. She pitched, and she pitched pretty well until she happened to strike out a big husky kid with a crew cut. He thought he was a pretty good ball player, and he didn't like getting struck out by a girl. So he started getting on Rose Rita. He did all sorts of things: he kept calling her Four Eyes, and whenever her team took the field, he went out of his way to run past her just so he could give her a good hard shove and say "Oops, parm me, lady!" in a nasty sneering tone of voice. Finally, near the end of the game, Rose Rita hit a long drive that looked like it would be good for three bases. But as she dived into third, headfirst, there was the lug with the crew cut, and he had the ball in his hand. He could have tagged her on the shoulder or the arm or the back, but he shoved the ball right square into her mouth. It really hurt. The game stopped while Rose Rita pulled herself together. She checked her front teeth to make sure they weren't loose and cautiously rubbed her swollen upper lip. She felt like crying, but she fought down the urge. After a few minutes, Rose Rita went on playing.

In the ninth inning, when the crew-cut lug was pitching for the other side, Rose Rita hit a bases-loaded home run and won the game for her team. When she crossed home plate, all the boys on her side gathered around her and yelled "Yay, Rose Rita!" three times. It really made her feel great. But then she noticed that the guy who had been calling her names was standing there on the pitcher's mound and glaring straight at her.

"Hey, Four Eyes!" he yelled. "You think you're really somethin', doncha?"

"Yeah, I do," Rose Rita yelled back. "What's it to you?"

"Nothin' much. Hey, Four Eyes. How much do you know about baseball? Huh?"

"A heck of a lot more than you do," Rose Rita snapped.

"Oh yeah? Prove it."

"Whattaya mean, prove it?"

"I mean, let's have a contest to see who knows more about baseball, huh? How about it? You chicken? Chick-chick-chick, chick-chick-chick!" The boy flapped his arms like wings and did a rather poor imitation of a chicken.

Rose Rita grinned. This was too big a chance to miss. It so happened that Rose Rita was a real baseball nut. She knew all sorts of facts about baseball, like Ty Cobb's lifetime average and the number of unassisted triple plays that there were on record. She even knew about Smead Jolley's great record, four errors on a single played ball. So she figured that she would give this wiseacre kid a beating at the baseball fact game and get even with him for the fat lip he had given her.

Everybody gathered around to watch the contest. One of the other boys, a watery-eyed blond kid who talked through his nose, was chosen to think up questions. At first it was a pretty tough battle. The lug turned out to be pretty good at baseball facts. He knew the strikeout kings, and who the last thirty-game winner had been, and a lot of other stuff. But Rose Rita knew the stuff that the lug knew, so it turned into a tense nasty grudge fight that went on for some time, with neither one able to gain an inch on the other. In the end Rose Rita won, because she knew that Bill Wambsganss of the Cleveland Indians had pulled the only unassisted triple play ever to be pulled during a World Series game. The lug had a chance at the question first, but he didn't know the answer. Then it was Rose Rita's turn, and she knew it right away. Several of the boys yelled "Yay, Rose Rita!" and one even ran up to shake her hand.

The lug just got red in the face. He glowered at Rose Rita. If he had been mad before, he was furious now. "You think you're pretty damn smart, doncha?" he snarled.

"Yeah," said Rose Rita happily.

The lug put his hands on his hips and looked her straight in the eye. "Well, you wanna know what I think? I think you're a pretty funny kind of girl, that's what I think. A pret-ty damn funny kind of a girl."

It was a stupid remark, but it stung Rose Rita. It stung like a slap in the face. To the amazement of everyone, she burst into tears and ran off the field. *You're a pretty funny kind of a girl.* Rose Rita had heard people say this about her before, and what was worse, she had thought it about herself. She had often wondered if there was really something wrong with her. She acted like a boy, but she was a girl. Her best friend was a boy, but most of the girls she knew had girls for best friends. She didn't want to go on dates, even though some of the girls she knew had already started to date and had told her how much fun it was. A funny kind of a girl—Rose Rita couldn't get the phrase out of her head.

Rose Rita stopped on a street corner. She took out her hanky and dabbed at her eyes, and then she blew her nose. From the way people were looking at her as they passed by, she figured she must really be a mess. Her face felt hot and flushed. Now she was mad at herself, mad because she had let that dumb guy get her goat that way. As she walked along, she told herself that she had a lot to feel good about: she had practically won the game single-handed for her team, and she had won the base-ball facts contest, in spite of what happened later. She started to whistle, and after two or three blocks of whistling, she felt better. She decided to go back to the hospital, just to see what was going on.

When Rose Rita walked into Mrs. Zimmermann's room, she walked in on an argument. Mrs. Zimmermann was sitting up in bed, and she was having it out with a worried-looking young doctor.

"But Mrs. Zimmermann," the doctor pleaded, "you're taking an *awful* chance with your health! If we had another day or so, we might be able to figure out—"

Mrs. Zimmermann cut him off contemptuously. "Oh, sure! If I were to stay here for a year, and if I were to lie very, very still, I'd get bedsores, and you'd know what to do about them, wouldn't you? Well, I'm sorry. I've wasted too much time as it is. Tomorrow morning, Rose Rita and I are hitting the road. You're just a bunch of quacks here, like most doctors."

"Now, Mrs. Zimmermann, I resent that. We've tried very hard to be nice to you, and we've also tried to find out about your pains. Just because all our tests have come out negative is no reason to . . ."

/ 77 /

The doctor went on, and then Mrs. Zimmermann started in again. Rose Rita sat down in an armchair and hid behind a copy of *Ladies Home Journal*. She hoped that they wouldn't notice her. The argument went on for some time, and the doctor pleaded, and Mrs. Zimmermann was about as nasty and insulting as Rose Rita had ever seen her be. In the end Mrs. Zimmermann won. The doctor agreed that she could leave tomorrow morning if she wanted to.

Mrs. Zimmermann watched as the doctor gathered up his clip board, his stethoscope, and his medicine bag. When the door had closed behind him, she raised her hand and motioned for Rose Rita to come over to the bed.

"Rose Rita," she said. "We're in trouble."

"Huh?"

"I said, we're in trouble. I sent my dress out to be dry-cleaned. You know the one—the dress I was wearing when those pains hit me. The same dress that was draped over the chair by my bed, the night you thought you saw someone in my room. Remember?"

Rose Rita nodded.

"Well, the dress came back today, and look what came with it." Mrs. Zimmermann opened a drawer in the table that stood by the side of her bed. She took out a small brown Manila envelope and shook the contents out into Rose Rita's hand. Rose Rita looked down and saw a small golden safety pin and a little strip of paper.

There was writing in red ink on the paper, but she couldn't read it.

"What's this?"

"It's a charm. The cleaners found it pinned to the inside of my dress. Don't worry—it can't hurt you. Those things can only be rigged up to work on one person at a time."

"You . . . you mean . . ."

"Yes, my dear. That little strip of paper caused the pains I had the other night." Mrs. Zimmermann laughed grimly. "I wonder what Doc Smartypants there would say if I told him about *that!* I'm sorry, by the way, that I was so mean to him, but I had to be, so he'd let us go."

Rose Rita was frightened. She put the strip of paper and the pin on the table and backed away. "Mrs. Zimmermann," she said, "what are we gonna do?"

"I don't know, Rose Rita, I just don't know. Somebody is after me—that much is clear. But who it is or why they're doing it, I just don't know. I have some ideas, but I'd rather not share them with you right now, if you don't mind. I've told you all this because I don't want you to feel guilty about driving off the road that night. You had every right to be scared. The thing you saw in the back seat, it . . . well, it wasn't in your head. It was real."

Rose Rita shuddered. "What . . . what was it?"

"I'd rather not say anything more right now," said Mrs. Zimmermann. "But I will tell you this. We've got to get home, and we've got to get home fast. I've got to get hold of my copy of the *Malleus Maleficarum*."

"The what?"

"The *Malleus Maleficarum*. It's a book that was written a long time ago by a monk. The title means The Hammer of Witches. That is, the book is a weapon to use in fighting off the attacks of those who fool around with black magic. It has a number of spells in it that will be of use to me. I should have memorized them long ago, but I didn't. So I need the book, and it's not the sort of thing you'd find at your friendly public library. We're going home the first thing in the morning, and I thought I ought to tell you why. I don't want to frighten you, but I figured you'd be frightened more if I went on being mysterious."

Rose Rita pointed at the strip of paper. "What're you gonna do with that?"

"Watch." Mrs. Zimmermann took a book of matches out of the drawer in the bedside table. She put the paper in an ashtray and lit it. While it burned, she made the sign of the cross over the ashtray and muttered a strange-sounding prayer. Rose Rita watched, fascinated. She felt scared, but she felt excited too, as if she had been suddenly swept out of her normal life and into an adventure.

That evening Rose Rita helped Mrs. Zimmermann pack. She got her own things together too. Mrs. Zimmermann informed her that Bessie was in the parking lot behind the hospital. A tow truck had pulled her up out of the juniper bushes, and the mechanics at a local garage had gone over her. She was all gassed and oiled and greased up, and ready to roll. A nurse came in with some papers for Mrs. Zimmermann to sign. The doctor paid one more visit, and said (rather coldly) that he hoped Mrs. Zimmermann had a good trip back. Everything was ready. Rose Rita and Mrs. Zimmermann crawled into bed and tried to get some sleep.

At first Rose Rita was too excited to sleep, but around midnight, she drifted off. Then, before she knew what was happening, she was awake again. Mrs. Zimmermann was standing by her bed. She was shaking her and shining a flashlight in her eyes.

"Come on, Rose Rita! Wake up!" Mrs. Zimmermann hissed. "We've got to go! Now!"

Rose Rita shook her head and rubbed her eyes. She fumbled for her glasses and put them on. "Wha . . . wha's the matter?"

"Wake up, I said! We're going to the farm. Now. We've got to!"

Rose Rita felt totally confused. "The *farm?* But thought you said . . ."

"Never mind what I said. Get dressed and follow me We're going back to the farm to . . . to get something I left there. Come on, you! Get a move on!" She shook Rose Rita again roughly, and flashed the light in her eyes. Rose Rita had never seen Mrs. Zimmermann act

this way before. Her voice was harsh, and her actions were rough and almost brutal. It was almost as if someone else had gotten inside of Mrs. Zimmermann's skin. And this business about going to the farm, instead of going straight home the way they had planned. What did it mean?

As Rose Rita dressed, Mrs. Zimmermann stood there, stiff and still, behind the white glaring halo of the flashlight. Rose Rita couldn't see her face, and she wasn't sure that she wanted to. When she was dressed, Rose Rita grabbed her valise and followed Mrs. Zimmermann. They tiptoed to the door, opened it a crack, and peered down the long dark hall. At the far end a nurse sat dozing behind a desk. An electric clock buzzed on the wall over her head. The whole hospital seemed to be asleep.

"Good!" said Mrs. Zimmermann, and she led the way down the hall to a set of stairs. The stairs led to the parking lot behind the hospital. There in the moonlight sat Bessie, the green Plymouth, staring patiently ahead as always. Rose Rita put the luggage in the trunk. Mrs. Zimmermann started the car, and they drove off.

It was a long hot dusty ride, all day, across the length of the Upper Peninsula. For Rose Rita, it was like a nightmare. Usually Mrs. Zimmermann was fun to travel with. She laughed and joked and sang songs, and talked a blue streak. When pestered, she even did little magic tricks, like snatching matches out of thin air, or throwing her voice into the weeds at the side of the road. But now, as they rode along, she was silent. She seemed to be brooding about something, but she wouldn't tell Rose Rita what it was. And Mrs. Zimmermann was nervous—very nervous. She glanced wildly from side to side, and sometimes got so jittery that she almost drove off the road. Rose Rita sat there rigid in her corner by the door, her sweaty hands at her sides. She didn't know what to do, or what to say.

The sun was going down over the Straits of Mackinac as Bessie chugged into the parking lot of the ferryboat landing at St. Ignace. A boat had just left, and Mrs. Zimmermann and Rose Rita had to wait a solid hour for the next one. They waited in silence, neither of them saying a word the whole time. Rose Rita went out and bought some sandwiches. It was her own idea—Mrs. Zimmermann had not stopped for lunch. Finally, though, the boat came in. It was called the *Grand Traverse Bay*. The sky was dark, and the moon was rising over the Straits, when Mrs. Zimmermann drove Bessie up the rattling gangplank and down into the black echoing hold of the ship.

When the car was parked, and the chocks had been placed under the wheels, Rose Rita started to get out, but then she discovered that Mrs. Zimmermann was just sitting there motionless behind the wheel.

"Mrs. Zimmermann?" Rose Rita called nervously. "Aren't you coming up?"

Mrs. Zimmermann gave a little start and shook her

head. She stared at Rose Rita as if she had never seen her before. "Come up? Oh . . . yes. Yes, of course. Be right with you." She got out of the car and, like a sleepwalker, clumped up the steps to the deck.

It ought to have been a very beautiful crossing. The moon shone down, silvering the decks and the ripply water of the Straits. Rose Rita tried to get Mrs. Zimmermann to walk around with her on the deck, but she wouldn't do it. She sat rigid on a bench and stared at her shoes. Rose Rita was frightened. This wasn't an adventure anymore. She wished, wished with all her heart, that they had never come on this trip. She wished they were back home in New Zebedee. Maybe if they were home, Uncle Jonathan, or Doc Humphries, or somebody, could figure out what was wrong with Mrs. Zimmermann and make her act like her old self again. Rose Rita didn't feel as if she could do anything for Mrs. Zimmermann. She felt utterly helpless. All she could do was tag along. Tag along, and wait.

An hour or so later Mrs. Zimmermann and Rose Rita were driving down the gravel road that led to Oley Gunderson's farm. They passed Gert Bigger's store and saw that it was closed. A tiny night light burned on the porch.

Rose Rita couldn't stand it any longer. "Mrs. Zimmermann," she burst out. "Why are we going to the farm? What's this all about?"

At first Mrs. Zimmermann was silent. Then she said,

in a slow dull voice, "I don't know why. There's something I have to do there, but I can't remember what it is."

They drove on. Gravel crackled and popped under the car's tires, and sometimes long leafy branches whipped across the doors or the roof. Now it began to rain. Big drops started to splat on the windshield, and Rose Rita heard the dull rolling of thunder. Flashes of lightning leaped out in front of the car. Now they were at the farm. As they drove into the yard, a bright flash lit up the front of the barn, showing the two staring window-eyes, and the yawning mouth of the door. It was like a monster mouth, opening to swallow them up.

Because it was raining outside, Rose Rita and Mrs. Zimmermann went into the house by way of the long covered walkway that ran from the house to the barn. But when they unlocked the door and tried to turn the lights on, nothing happened. Mrs. Zimmermann had forgotten to pay Oley's overdue electric bill, and the current had been shut off since their first visit. After digging around in a cupboard, Mrs. Zimmermann found a kerosene lamp. She lit it and put it on the kitchen table. Rose Rita opened up the picnic hamper, and they sat down to eat the sandwiches Rose Rita had bought. They ate in silence. In the smoky yellow light Mrs. Zimmermann's face looked haggard and worn. She also looked tense, very tense, as if she was waiting for something to happen. Rose Rita looked nervously over her shoulder. Beyond the circle of friendly lamplight the house lay in shadow. The staircase was a well of darkness. Rose Rita realized, with a sudden sick feeling, that she would have to go up those stairs to bed. She didn't want to go to bed. She didn't want to stay in Oley's house for another minute. She wanted to bundle Mrs. Zimmermann into the car and make her drive them back to New Zebedee, even if they had to drive all night. But Rose Rita didn't say anything. She made no move. Whatever the spell was that lay over Mrs. Zimmermann, it lay over Rose Rita too. She felt utterly totally powerless.

Outside it was pouring. There was a tin roof on the front porch, and the sound of the rain hitting it was a steady drumming roar. Finally, with an effort, Rose Rita pushed back her chair. She stood up.

"I think we . . . we oughta go to bed, Mrs. Zimmermann," she said hoarsely. Her voice was faint and seemed to be coming from deep down inside her.

"You go on, Rose Rita. I want to sit here and . . . and think a bit." Mrs. Zimmermann's voice was wooden and mechanical, and unbelievably weary. It almost sounded as if she were talking in her sleep.

Rose Rita backed away fearfully. She picked up her valise, took out her flashlight, and turned toward the stairs. As Rose Rita went up the steps, flashlight in hand, her shadow and the shadow of the railing danced weirdly on the wall next to her. Halfway up Rose Rita stopped and looked down. There sat Mrs. Zimmermann in the circle of yellow lamplight. Her hands were folded on the table, and she was staring straight ahead of her. Rose Rita had the feeling that, if she called to her, she wouldn't get any answer. She swallowed hard and went on up the stairs.

The bedroom with the black walnut bed was just as Rose Rita had left it. She began to peel back the spread, but halfway she stopped. She stopped because she had heard a noise from downstairs. A single small noise. Tap. The sound of Mrs. Zimmermann's ring. Now the sound was repeated, three times over. Tap . . . tap . . . tap. The sound was slow and mechanical, like the ticking of a big clock. Rose Rita stood there, flashlight in hand. She listened to the sound and wondered what it meant.

Suddenly a door slammed.

Rose Rita gave a little yelp and spun around. She dashed out of the room and down the stairs. On the landing she froze. There was the table, with the lamp burning on it. There was Mrs. Zimmermann's purse, and her cigar case. The front door was open. It banged gently in the wind. Mrs. Zimmermann was gone.

CHAPTER SEVEN

Rose Rita stood on the front porch of the farmhouse. Her flashlight dangled from one hand and made a pool of light at her feet. Slashes of rain cut across her shoes, and lightning lit up the wildly thrashing trees across the road. Thunder rolled. Rose Rita felt stunned. She felt as if she were walking in her sleep. Mrs. Zimmermann was gone. But where had she gone, and why? What had happened to her?

Cupping her hands to her mouth, Rose Rita called, "Mrs. Zimmermann! Mrs. Zimmermann!" but she got no answer. Slowly she picked her way down the steps, waving the flashlight in front of her. At the bottom of the steps she stopped and looked around. If Mrs. Zimmermann had run out the front door and down the front steps, it ought to have been easy to tell which way she went after that. The front yard was full of long grass, and Rose Rita and Mrs. Zimmermann had not touched it on the night before, because they had come into the house by using the covered walkway. Now, as Rose Rita moved her flashlight around, she saw a little patch of grass trampled down at the bottom of the steps. But no path led away, in any direction. The grass grew all around, tall and shiny and untouched. It was as if Mrs. Zimmermann had evaporated.

Panic seized Rose Rita. Yelling "Mrs. Zimmermann!" at the top of her voice, she thrashed through the wet grass till she came to the road. She looked to the right. She looked to the left. Nothing but darkness and rain. Rose Rita fell to her knees in a puddle and started to cry. She covered her face with her hands and sobbed bitterly. The cold rain poured down on her and soaked her to the skin.

At long last she got up. Staggering like a drunken person, half blinded by tears, she made her way back to the farmhouse. But on the front porch she stopped. She did not want to go back into that house. Not now, in the dark. With a shudder Rose Rita turned away. But where could she go?

Bessie. She thought of Bessie sitting in the barn. The barn was a dark spooky place, like the house, but Bessie was a friendly creature. Rose Rita really thought of the car as a living breathing person now. She could go and sleep in the car. It wouldn't hurt her—it would protect her. Rose Rita took a deep shuddering breath, clenched her fists, and started walking toward the barn. Rain slashed across her as she went.

The sound of the big white door rolling back echoed in the high raftered ceiling of the barn. There was Bessie, waiting. Rose Rita patted her hood and climbed into the back seat. She locked all the doors. Then she lay down and tried to sleep, but it was no use. She was too tense. All night Rose Rita lay there, wet and frightened and tired and alone. Once or twice she sat up suddenly when she thought she saw a face at the window of the car. But it was all her imagination—there was no one there.

As she lay staring at the ceiling of the car and listening to the storm, Rose Rita thought. Mrs. Zimmermann had disappeared. Disappeared as if by magic. In fact, there was no "as if" about it. Mrs. Zimmermann's disappearance had been caused by magic.

Rose Rita went over the sequence of events in her mind: first there had been Oley's weird letter about a magic ring, and then the empty ring box. Then came the mutilated photograph, and the shadow Rose Rita had seen moving around in Mrs. Zimmermann's bedroom that night. Then those horrible pains, and the slip of paper, and the strange way Mrs. Zimmermann had behaved on the trip back to the farm. But what was the key to the whole thing? Was the ring the key? Did somebody have it, and had they used it to do things to Mrs. Zimmermann? That seemed like a reasonable explanation to Rose Rita. But a heck of a lot of good reasonable explanations were going to do her. Mrs. Zimmermann was gone, and Rose Rita didn't know where to go to find her. Maybe she was dead. And as for the magic ring, if there was such a thing . . . well, Rose Rita didn't know who had it, and she hadn't the faintest idea of what she would do if she *did* know. So there she was.

Rose Rita thought like this, in endless circles, all the night long, while thunder rolled overhead and lightning lit up, now and then, the high dusty windows of the barn. Finally morning came. Rose Rita stumbled out into the sunlight to find everything looking sparkling and fresh and green. Blackbirds were gorging themselves on the mulberries in a crooked old tree in the front yard. Rose Rita felt a sudden burst of cheerfulness, but then she remembered Mrs. Zimmermann, and she burst into tears again. No, she said firmly to herself, blinking back her tears and brushing hair out of her eyes. You're not going to cry. That's not any good, you dumb dope. You've got to *do* something!

But what was she going to do? Here she was, alone, three hundred miles from home. For one wild instant she thought that she might drive Bessie all the way back to New Zebedee. After all she had driven the car for a little way, on that back road near Ironwood. But Rose Rita was scared. Scared of getting picked up by a policeman, scared of having an accident. Besides, driving home wouldn't help find Mrs. Zimmermann. She had to think of something else.

Rose Rita sat down on the front steps, put her head in her hands, and thought some more. Should she call up her folks and have them come and get her? She could hear what her father would say: "You see, Louise, that's what happens when you let Rose Rita run around with screwballs! The old bat flew off on a broom and left Rose Rita there to rot. Well, maybe the next time you think of letting our daughter go tooting off with a screwball you'll . . ." Rose Rita winced. She didn't want to face her father, not without Mrs. Zimmermann. Rose Rita thought some more.

Rose Rita racked her brains. She crossed and recrossed her legs and bit her lip and fumed. She was a real fighter, and she wasn't going to abandon Mrs. Zimmermann. Not if there was something she could do.

Rose Rita jumped up and snapped her fingers. Of course! What a dope she had been! Why hadn't she thought of this before? There was that book, that Mallet of Something, or whatever it was called. The book that Mrs. Zimmermann had been going home to get when she changed her mind—or somebody changed it for her. But Rose Rita didn't have the book. She didn't even know where she could get a copy. She sat down again.

Rose Rita thought about magic books for a while.

Rows of them, standing on shelves, books with spotted vellum covers and curly writing on their spines. *That was it!* Jonathan had magic books. He had a whole big collection of them. And what was more, he had the key to Mrs. Zimmermann's house. If he couldn't find that old Mallet Whatchmacallit, he could just go next door and dig it out of Mrs. Zimmermann's bookcase. Also, Jonathan knew about magic, because he was a wizard himself. Rose Rita could tell him what had happened, and he wouldn't think she had gone off her rocker. Good old Jonathan! He would know what to do.

Rose Rita got up and went into the house. There was an old-fashioned crank phone on the wall in the kitchen. Rose Rita took the receiver off the hook and gave the crank a few twirls. The bell inside the box rang, but the line was dead. Mrs. Zimmermann had forgotten to pay Oley's electric bill, and she had also forgotten to pay the phone bill.

Rose Rita hung up the receiver and stood there, feeling depressed. But then she remembered Gert Bigger's store. There was probably a phone there she could use. Rose Rita didn't want to have anything more to do with the crabby old woman who had cheated Mrs. Zimmermann that night they ran out of gas, but she didn't see any way around it. Gert Bigger's store was only a couple of miles down the road. Rose Rita sighed. She would just have to walk there and get help.

Rose Rita started out. It was already a hot day, even

though it was early in the morning, and the road was dusty. Steam rose from Rose Rita's clothing, which was still wet from the night before. She wondered if she would catch cold, but she didn't wonder very hard. Catching cold was the least of her worries right now.

It was farther to Gert Bigger's store than Rose Rita had thought it would be. Flies were buzzing around when Rose Rita rounded a bend and saw the store shimmering there in the heat. It looked pretty much the way it had when she saw it the first time. But as she got closer to the store, Rose Rita noticed one difference. There was a chicken in the chicken yard. Just one. A bedraggled-looking white hen. As soon as the chicken saw Rose Rita, it began to cluck excitedly and run back and forth. Rose Rita smiled. She had had a white hen for a pet once. It was called Henny Penny. This poor lonely chicken reminded her of it. Rose Rita wondered why the chicken was so excited, and then she noticed a stump in one corner of the yard. There was an ax leaning against it. It looked as if old Henry Penny was going into the pot before long. Poor thing, Rose Rita thought. It probably thinks I'm coming to chop off its head.

Rose Rita turned away and started up the steps to the store, but as she did so, she almost stepped on a small black dog. It was the same dog that had barked at her and Mrs. Zimmermann that other time. It must have been hunched down on the steps in the shadow, because Rose Rita could have sworn that the steps were empty when she glanced at them a second before. Imitating Mrs. Zimmermann, Rose Rita pulled back her foot as if she were going to kick the dog, and, as before, the dog ran off into the shubbery and disappeared.

Rose Rita walked up the steps. She opened the door and looked in. There was Gert Bigger, kneeling in the middle of the floor. She was unpacking cereal boxes and stacking them on a shelf.

"Well," she said, glaring at Rose Rita. "What do *you* want?"

"I . . . I have to make a phone call," said Rose Rita. Her voice was trembling as she spoke, and she was afraid she was going to burst into tears.

"You do, huh? Well, you better have some money handy. There's a pay phone over there on that wall." Gert Bigger pointed towards a scarred black phone at the end of the counter.

Rose Rita dug into her pocket and came up with a dime and a couple of pennies. She would have to make it a collect call.

As she walked down the aisle toward the phone, Rose Rita was aware that Gert Bigger was watching her. She wondered why. Oh, well, thought Rose Rita, she's just nosy. She dumped her coins on a little shelf in front of the phone and read the yellow sheet of instructions. For a collect call, she would have to dial O for the operator. Rose Rita put her finger in the O-hole and was just starting to dial, when she saw, out of the corner of her eye, that Gert Bigger was still staring at her. She had let her work go and was just kneeling there in the middle of the aisle, watching.

Rose Rita stopped in mid-dial. She took her finger out and let the little wheel click back into place. She had just had a very strange thought: What if Gert Bigger had done something to Mrs. Zimmermann? She had a grudge against Mrs. Zimmermann—Rose Rita knew that. And she lived close to Oley's farm. She might've broken in to steal that magic ring after he died. It was a crazy notion, and Rose Rita knew it was crazy. But she still wondered if she might be onto something.

She turned, and her gaze met Gert Bigger's.

"What's the matter now?" Gert Bigger growled. "You forget the number you were supposed to call?"

"Uh . . . yeah, I mean, no ma'am, er . . . never mind," Rose Rita stammered. She turned to the phone. This is dumb, she told herself. That crabby old lady isn't any witch. She doesn't have any magic ring. Just stop playing detective and make your crummy phone call and get it over with!

Rose Rita dialed O and got the operator. She told her that she wanted to make a collect call to New Zebedee, Michigan, to Mr. Jonathan Barnavelt. His number was 865. Rose Rita waited. She heard vague scratchy and fumbly sounds, and then she heard the buzzing sound that meant that the operator was ringing Jonathan's phone. *Bzz. Bzz. Bzz.*

"I beg your pardon," said the operator, "but the party does not answer. Would you—"

"Please try a little longer," said Rose Rita. "Please, ma'am. It's an emergency."

"Very well." The ringing went on.

As she waited, Rose Rita's eyes began to wander. On the wall next to the phone she saw an old photograph in a black frame. It was a picture of a man in an old-fashioned suit. He had a handlebar mustache . . .

Rose Rita froze. She knew who the man was. He was the man in the picture Mrs. Zimmermann had found in the junk shop. And now she remembered his name: Mordecai. Mordecai Hunks. He was the man Mrs. Zimmermann and Gert Bigger had fought over, a long time ago. He was the reason for Gert Bigger's hatred of Mrs. Zimmermann, her long-standing grudge. It was all beginning to fall together now . . .

Rose Rita turned her head slightly and glanced toward Mrs. Bigger. But at that moment a horn beeped outside. Somebody wanted gas. Gert Bigger heaved a discontented sigh, got up heavily, and stumped to the door.

"I'm sorry, Miss," said the operator, "but I cannot continue to ring the party's number. Would you care to call back at another time?"

Rose Rita was startled. She had forgotten about the phone call she was making. "Uh . . . okay," she mumbled. "I'll . . . uh, try later. Thanks."

Rose Rita hung up the phone and glanced quickly

around. Now was her chance. Behind the counter was a doorway covered by a heavy brown curtain. Rose Rita looked again toward the front of the store. Through the wide plate glass window, she could see Gert Bigger pumping gas. And now she saw another car pulling up on the other side of the pumps. The old bat would probably be out there for a while. Rose Rita took a deep breath, pulled the curtain aside, and ducked in through the doorway.

She found herself in an ugly little room with pale green walls. There was a coal company calendar on the wall and a bare bulb dangling from the ceiling. A small iron safe stood in one corner, and against the long wall was a high narrow shelflike desk. On the desk was a faded green blotter with columns of figures added up all over it. Arranged neatly next to the blotter were a bottle of Parker's Quink, a pile of wooden pens with rusty metal nibs, a brown gum eraser, and several well-sharpened pencils. On the other side of the blotter was an account book with a green cardboard cover. The date 1950 was printed on the cover. There was nothing here that looked in any way magical.

Rose Rita's heart sank. She felt foolish for doing what she was doing. But wait a minute. What were these? Rose Rita knelt down. Under the desk was a shelf, and on it were piled more green-covered account books. They looked just like the one on the desk, except that they were very dusty and had different dates. 1949,

1948, and so on back. Rose Rita opened one up. Just dull columns of figures. Debits, credits, receipts, and stuff like that. She was about to put the book back when she noticed something sticking out of the middle. She pulled it out and found that it was a folded piece of paper. When she opened the paper, she found a drawing done in pencil. It looked like this:

Rose Rita held the paper with trembling hands. She could feel her heart beating faster. She was no wizard, but she knew what this was, because she had once been allowed a closely supervised look into one of Uncle Jonathan's magic books. The drawing was a magic pentacle, one of those charms that witches and wizards use when they want good things or bad things to happen. Rose Rita stared at the drawing. She stared at it so long and so hard that she did not hear the soft tinkle of the bell as the front door of the store was quietly opened and carefully closed. A board creaked behind her. Suddenly the curtain was whipped aside, and Rose Rita turned to find Gert Bigger standing over her.

"Well now! What do you think you're doin'? Eh?"

CHAPTER EIGHT

Rose Rita knelt there on the floor and looked up at Gert Bigger's angry face. In her trembling hands she still held the piece of paper with the strange drawing on it.

Gert Bigger stepped into the little room and pulled the curtain shut behind her. "I asked you, Miss, what you think you're doing? There's a law against trespassing, you know, and there are reform schools for girls who steal things. Would you like your parents to know what you've been up to? Eh? Would you?"

Rose Rita opened her mouth to speak, but all that came out was "I . . . I . . . please . . . I didn't mean . . ."

Gert Bigger took a step forward. She reached down and snatched the paper from Rose Rita's numb fingers.

Silence fell while Gert Bigger stood there looking from the paper to Rose Rita and back to the paper again. She seemed to be trying to make up her mind.

At that moment the bell on the front door of the store jangled, and a voice yelled "Yoo-hoo, Gertie! Are you home?"

Gert Bigger turned and swore under her breath. Rose Rita jumped up and ducked out through the narrow curtained opening. She sprinted down the main aisle of the store, right past the surprised face of a middle-aged woman with a shopping bag in her hand. Slam went the door behind her. Rose Rita clattered down the steps and dashed across the road. She ran blindly, and she could hear herself crying as she ran. She cut across the corner of a cornfield, trampling the wrinkly green plants underfoot. Her feet found a pathway of green grass that ran along the edge of the cornfield and up over the top of a low hill. Rose Rita ran up it, ran as hard as she could, until she collapsed under a droopy elm tree that grew near a flat-topped boulder. She threw herself down on the grass, tore off her glasses, and cried.

Rose Rita lay there crying for a long time. She was tired and hungry and frightened and alone. She hadn't had any food at all since last night, and she had gotten almost no sleep. At first she was afraid that Gert Bigger would come after her. At any moment her hand would be on Rose Rita's shoulder. But Gert Bigger never came. Rose Rita went on crying, but she could feel her body

starting to relax. She didn't care about anything now . . . anything at all. It was a delicious feeling. Slowly her mind started to drift off. It was so nice lying here in the shade . . . so very, very nice . . . but it would be even nicer to be home. Home . . . in . . .

Rose Rita's eyes closed. A soft breeze rustled through the corn, and in the distance a fly was lazily buzzing. Rose Rita shook her head, fighting weakly against the drowsiness that was falling over her. She was trying to think of something. What was it? She never found out, because in a very few minutes she was fast asleep.

"Hey you, wake up! You better wake up! Don't you know it's bad to sleep on the wet ground? You might catch cold. Come on, wake up."

Rose Rita awoke to hear this worried insistent voice speaking to her. She shook her head and looked up. All she saw was a blur. Then she remembered her glasses. After fumbling a bit in the grass near her, she located them and put them on. When she looked up, Rose Rita saw a girl about her own age. She was wearing a short-sleeved plaid shirt and jeans, and muddy army boots. The girl had straight dishwater-blonde hair, and it was combed down on both sides of her head. Her face was longish, and it had a sad worried expression. The dark eyebrows curved up into worry lines. Rose Rita thought that she had seen this face somewhere before. But where?

When she remembered, she almost laughed. The girl looked just like the Jack of Clubs.

"Hi there," said the girl. "Gee, I'm glad you woke up! Didn't anybody ever tell you it was bad to sleep on the ground when it's wet? It rained last night, you know."

"Yeah, I know," said Rose Rita. She got up and put out her hand. "I'm Rose Rita Pottinger. What's your name?"

"Agatha Sipes. They call me Aggie for short. I live up that way, over that hill. This's my father's farm. By the way, are you the one that stomped all over those corn plants back there?"

Rose Rita nodded sadly. "Yeah, that was me. I'm sorry, but I was crying so hard that I didn't look where I was going."

The girl looked worried. "You oughtn't to do that kind of thing. Farmers work hard for their living." She added, in a less severe tone, "Why were you crying?"

Rose Rita opened her mouth, but then she hesitated. She wanted to tell her troubles to someone, but she wanted to be believed. "My friend Mrs. Zimmermann is lost, and I don't know where to find her. We were staying at a farm down the road last night, and she ran out the front door and just disappeared."

The girl rubbed her chin and looked wise. "Oh, I'll bet I know what happened. She probably went walkin' in the woods and got lost. It happens to lots of people up here in the summertime. Let's go up to my place, and we'll call up the sheriff's department, and they'll send out some people to look for her. They'll find her all right."

Rose Rita thought of the circle of trampled grass in front of the farmhouse. The circle with no path leading away. It was no use. She'd just have to tell the truth and risk the consequences. "Do . . . do you believe in magic?" she said suddenly.

The girl looked startled. "Huh?"

"I said, do you believe in magic?"

"You mean ghosts and witches and magic spells and stuff like that?"

"Yeah."

Agatha grinned shyly. "Yeah, I do. I know you're not supposed to, but I can't help it." She added, in a worried voice, "Sometimes I think there's a ghost in the cellar in our house, but Mom says it's just the wind at night. You don't think there's a ghost in our cellar, do you?"

"How would I know?" said Rose Rita, in an irritated voice. "Hey, do you want to hear about what happened to Mrs. Zimmermann or don't you?"

"Sure I want to hear. I really do. Tell me all about it."

Rose Rita and Agatha Sipes sat down on the grass under the elm tree. Rose Rita's stomach growled, and she remembered that she hadn't eaten since last night. She was terribly hungry. But she wanted to tell her story, and Agatha seemed eager to listen. Rose Rita began.

She told the whole story, as far as she knew it, from Oley's mysterious letter and the empty ring box, on through the very strange things that had been happening to her and Mrs. Zimmermann lately. When she got to the part about Mrs. Zimmermann's disappearance, Agatha's eyes grew wide. And when she described her run-in with Mrs. Bigger, Agatha's eyes got even wider, and her mouth dropped open. She glanced nervously in the direction of Gert Bigger's store.

"My gosh!" she said. "It's a wonder she didn't kill you! And you know what? I bet she's the one who made your friend disappear."

Rose Rita looked strangely at Agatha. "Do . . . do you know anything about her? Mrs. Bigger, I mean?"

"I sure do. She's a witch."

Now it was Rose Rita's turn to be flabbergasted. "Huh? How do you know?"

"How do I know? Because last year I worked in the Ellis Corners library, and she came in and took out every last book about magic that we had, that's how I know. Some of 'em were in the Reference Room, and she couldn't take 'em out, so she just sat there for hours and read. I asked Mrs. Bryer the librarian about her, and she said Mrs. Bigger had been doing that for years. Said she had library cards for all the libraries around here, and took out all the magic books she could find. Mrs. Bryer says she reads the covers off of 'em and never takes 'em back till the library starts houndin' her. Isn't that weird?"

"Yeah, it sure is." Rose Rita felt strange. She was wildly elated, because her hunch had been proved right —at least, she felt that it had been proved right. But at the same time she felt helpless and scared. If Mrs. Bigger really was a witch, what could she and Aggie do about it?

Rose Rita got up and paced around. Then she sat down on the flat-topped boulder and lapsed into deep thought. Aggie stood near her, looking uncomfortable. She shifted nervously from one foot to the other, and puckered up her eyebrows into the most worried frown she had produced yet. "Did I say something wrong, Rose Rita?" she asked, after several silent minutes had passed. "If I did, I'm sorry, I really am."

Rose Rita shook herself out of her trance and looked up. "No, Aggie, you didn't say anything wrong. Honest you didn't. But I just don't know what to do. If you're right, and old Mrs. Bigger is a witch, and she has done something to Mrs. Zimmermann, then . . . well, what can we do? Just the two of us, I mean."

"I don't know."

"Neither do I."

More silence. Silence for a good five minutes. Then Aggie spoke up again.

"Hey, I know what let's do. Let's go home to my house and have some lunch. My mom always fixes a lot of food, because we have a really big family, and I'm sure there'd be enough for you. Come on. After lunch

/ *109* /

maybe we can figure out what to do. You can't think good on an empty stomach. That's what my dad says, anyway."

Rose Rita looked reluctant, but she really didn't have any better ideas. On the way to the farmhouse Aggie talked a blue streak. She talked about things that she was worried about, like rabies and tetanus and electrical shock and mayonnaise that has been left out of the icebox too long. Rose Rita, however, was only half listening. She was still thinking, trying to make up her mind what to do. Should she give up playing Nancy Drew, girl detective, and call her folks and have them come and get her? No. Rose Rita was a stubborn girl, and she still thought she might be able to find Mrs. Zimmermann without the aid of her parents. What Aggie had told her about Mrs. Bigger and the magic books had made her more certain than ever that Mrs. Zimmermann had been carried off by witchcraft of some kind. So Rose Rita went back to her idea of calling Jonathan. She would do that as soon as she got to Aggie's house. With her mind racing along in high gear, Rose Rita tried to figure out what her next move would be. What should she say to Mrs. Sipes about what had happened?

They were within sight of the farmhouse when Rose Rita reached out and grabbed Aggie's arm. "Wait a minute, Aggie."

"Why? What's the matter?"

"We have to think up a story to tell your mother. I

can't tell her what I told you. She'll think I'm crazy. I can't even tell her my real name, because then she'd want to call up my folks, and I don't want her to call them up."

Aggie frowned. "I don't think you ought to lie to my mother. It's not nice to lie, and anyway I think you'll get caught. My mom is pretty smart. She'd see through it in a minute."

When people disagreed with Rose Rita, it usually made her mad. But in this case she was doubly mad, because she was proud of her ability to make up alibis and excuses. Making up excuses is hard, and it is not quite the same thing as telling tall stories. You have to be able to come up with a story that people will believe. And Rose Rita could really do that—most of the time.

Rose Rita threw an irritated glance at Aggie. "Your mom isn't the smartest person in the world, I bet. And anyway, I'm good at making things up. All we have to do is sit down and figure out a story. Then we both memorize it, so there won't be any slip-ups."

Now it was Aggie's turn to be crabby. "Oh yeah? What're we gonna tell her? Here's my new friend, Rose Rita, who just fell out of a flying saucer?"

"No, dope. We don't tell her something like that. We tell her something she'll think is true. And then we call Uncle Jonathan and get him to tell us what kind of spell to say to make Mrs. Bigger tell us what she did with Mrs. Zimmermann. Okay?"

Aggie bit her lip and wrinkled up her forehead. She took a deep breath and let it out. "Oh all right. But if we get caught, I'm gonna say it's all your fault. I'm not gonna get bawled out just because you think it's nice to lie to people."

Rose Rita gritted her teeth. "I don't think it's nice to lie. But we have to, that's all. Now come on. This is what we'll say . . ."

A bell began to ring. A little sharp clangy handbell was calling people in for lunch at the Sipes farmhouse. Aggie started forward, but Rose Rita grabbed her arm and dragged her over behind a forsythia bush. She put her lips to Aggie's ear and started to whisper.

CHAPTER NINE

The Sipes farmhouse was big and white, with a wide
screened-in porch. Spirea bushes grew next to the porch,
and there were peony bushes in the front yard. A large
apple tree grew on one side of the house, and from one
of its saggy limbs hung a tractor tire on a rope. There
were kids' things scattered all over the yard. Baseball
bats, bicycles, tricycles, puzzles, dolls, toy trucks, and
plastic machine guns. Things like that. But when Aggie
opened the front door, Rose Rita was struck by how neat
and clean the house was inside. All the woodwork shone
with polish, and there were doilies or embroidered runners on all the tables, chests, and shelves. There was a
flowered carpet on the staircase, and a shelf clock ticking

in the front hall. A pleasant smell of cooking was in the air.

Aggie took Rose Rita straight out to the kitchen and introduced her to her mother. Mrs. Sipes had the same long face and worry eyebrows that her daughter had, but she seemed friendly enough. She wiped her floury hands on her apron and greeted Rose Rita warmly.

"Hi! Glad to meet you! I wondered what was keeping Aggie. I rang the bell for lunch about five times, and I had just about given up on her. What did you say your name was?"

Rose Rita hesitated, just a second. "Uh, Rosemary. Rosemary Potts."

"What a nice name! Hi, Rosemary! How're you? Are you visiting in the neighborhood? I don't think I've seen you around before."

Rose Rita squirmed uncomfortably. "Uh, no, you haven't on . . . on account of I was just up here on vacation with . . . with Mrs. Zimmermann." Rose Rita paused. "She's a friend of my family, a real good friend," she added quickly.

"Yeah," Aggie added. "Mrs. Whatsername and Rose . . . uh, Rosemary's family are real good friends, they really are. Only Mrs. . . . Mrs. . . ."

"Zimmermann," said Rose Rita, giving Aggie a dirty look.

"Oh, yeah. Mrs. Zimmermann. Well, old Oley—you

know him, Ma—he left Mrs. Zimmermann his farm, and she and Rosemary came up to look at it, and last night Mrs. Zimmermann wandered off into the woods out behind the farm, and she disappeared."

"Yeah," said Rose Rita. "I think she must've gotten lost. Anyway, I can't find her anywhere, and I'm getting scared."

Rose Rita held her breath. Would Mrs. Sipes believe this tale?

"Oh, Rosemary!" exclaimed Mrs. Sipes, putting her arm around her. "What an awful thing to happen! Look, I tell you what I'll do. I'll get on the phone and call up the sheriff's office and they'll get some of their men out there, right away quick, to search for her. There was someone who got lost in the woods up here only last year, and they found him before he got hurt. So don't worry. Your friend'll be all right."

Inwardly Rose Rita breathed a sigh of relief. She hated to lie about Mrs. Zimmermann's disappearance, and she was (in reality) worried sick about her. But she just didn't know what Mrs. Sipes would say if she were to tell her that Mrs. Zimmermann had disappeared right into thin air.

Later, after the call to the sheriff's department had been made, Rose Rita was sitting at a long dining room table with Aggie and seven other children and Mrs. Sipes. Rose Rita was sitting at the head of the table, in the place where Mr. Sipes usually sat. Mr. Sipes was away overnight in Petoskey, on business.

Rose Rita looked around the table. It was a worried-looking family. They all had those long faces and upturned eyebrows. There were tall kids and short kids, five boys and two girls (counting Aggie) and a baby in a highchair. On the table was a big platter of corned beef, potatoes, onions, and carrots, and there were more vegetables and some dumplings in the two smoking dishes that stood nearby. There was a cutting board with freshly baked bread on it, and there were two big pitchers of milk. Mrs. Sipes said grace, and then everybody dug in.

"Let Rosemary have some first," said Mrs. Sipes. "She's our guest, you know."

It took Rose Rita a second to recognize her new name. In fact she was startled when someone shoved a tureen of mashed carrots at her. "Oh . . . uh, thanks," she mumbled, and she helped herself to some.

Later on, when everyone had been served, Mrs. Sipes said in a loud clear voice, "Children, I think you should know that Rosemary here has had an accident. The friend she was traveling with got lost in the forest, and we're trying to find her. We've sent the sheriff's patrol out to look for her."

"I think anybody who gets lost in the woods over here must really be dumb," said a tall boy with black curly hair.

"Leonard!" said Mrs. Sipes in a shocked voice. "That will be *quite* enough out of you!" She turned to Rose Rita and smiled sympathetically. "I must apologize for my rude son. Tell us, Rosemary, where do you come from?"

"New Zebedee, ma'am. It's a little town way down near the bottom of the state. Probably you never heard of it."

"I think I know where it is," said Mrs. Sipes. "Now then. I really think we'd better notify your parents. They'll want to know what's happened. What is your father's name?"

Rose Rita stared at the tablecloth. She stuck out her lower lip and looked as sad as she could. "My folks are dead. Both of them. I live with my uncle Jonathan. He's my legal guardian, and his name is Jonathan Barnavelt, and he lives at 100 High Street."

Mrs. Sipes looked surprised and saddened. "My lord, you poor girl! What a string of misfortunes! First your parents dead, and now this to happen to you! Tell me, my dear. How did it happen?"

Rose Rita blinked. "How did what happen?"

"How did your parents happen to die? Excuse me for going into something so sad right at this present moment, but I couldn't help wondering what had happened to them."

Rose Rita paused. There was a mischievous gleam in her eye. She was beginning to enjoy her own lying. At first she had been afraid of being found out, but now that Mrs. Sipes had swallowed both the lost-in-the-forest story and the orphan story—not to mention Rose Rita's fake name—Rose Rita began to think that she would swallow anything. And inwardly she was chortling at her own cleverness in having made up the part about Jonathan being her guardian. There was a good one, since it would allow her to call up Jonathan and find out what she wanted to know, without any more fooling around. Rose Rita had intended to just say that her folks had been killed in a car accident, but now she decided to try for something fancy. It wouldn't do any harm.

"My folks got killed in a funny kind of way," she began. "You see, my dad used to be a forest ranger. He used to walk around in the woods a lot and make sure there weren't any forest fires, and that kind of thing. Well, one day he came across this beaver dam, and it was a really weird-looking kind of dam—all messy and screwed up. My dad had never seen a beaver dam that looked like it, not ever, and he wondered how come it looked the way it did. You see, what he didn't know was, the dam had been built by a beaver that had rabies. And then my dad brought my mom out to look at the dam, and the beaver bit 'em both, and they died."

Silence. Dead silence. Then Aggie's sister tittered, and one of the boys laughed.

"Gee," said Leonard in a loud sarcastic voice, "I

would've thought that if a beaver had the rabies, he would just run off into the woods and die. Wouldn't you think so, Ted?"

"Yeah," said the boy who was sitting next to Leonard. "I never heard of anyone gettin' bit by a beaver that had rabies. And anyway, if that's what really happened, how'd you ever find out? If your folks got bit and died, they wouldn't of told you nothin', would they?"

Rose Rita could feel her face getting red. Everyone was looking at her, and she felt as if she were sitting there without any clothes on. She stared hard at her plate and mumbled, "It was a real rare kind of rabies."

More silence. More staring. Finally Mrs. Sipes cleared her throat and said, "Uh, Rosemary, I think you'd better come into the other room with me for a minute, if you don't mind. And Aggie, you'd better come too."

Aggie got up and followed Rose Rita out of the room. With Mrs. Sipes leading the way, the glum little procession wound its way up the stairs and into a bedroom at the front of the house. Rose Rita and Aggie sat down side by side on the bed, and Mrs. Sipes closed the door softly behind her.

"Now then," she said, folding her arms and staring hard at Rose Rita. "I have heard incredible stories in my time, but this one just about takes the cake. I thought there was something odd about that orphan tale, but— Rosemary . . . by the way, is that your real name?"

Rose Rita shook her head. "No, ma'am," she said, in a tearful voice. "It's Rose Rita."

Mrs. Sipes smiled a faint little smile. "Well, at least it's fairly similar. Now listen, Rose Rita," she said, staring straight into her eyes, "if you're in some kind of trouble, I'd like to help you. I don't know what moved you to concoct that ridiculous story about the beaver, but you'll have to lie better than that if you want to grow up to be a con man, or a con girl, or whatever it is you want to be. Now do you suppose you could tell me, honestly and truly, what happened and why you're here?"

Rose Rita glared balefully at Mrs. Sipes. She wondered what Mrs. Sipes would say if she told her about the patch of trampled grass with no path leading away from it. "I told you, Mrs. Sipes," said Rose Rita stubbornly, "I told you that my friend Mrs. Zimmermann is lost, and I don't know where she is. Honest to God."

Mrs. Sipes sighed. "Well, my dear, I suppose *that* part of your story may be true. But I have never heard such an atrocious lie as that beaver story, really I haven't! Bit by a rabid beaver, indeed! And now you tell me that your real name is Rose Rita. All right, let's have some more of the truth. Are your parents dead, or alive?"

"My folks are alive," said Rose Rita, in a dull hopeless voice. "And their names are George and Louise Pottinger, and they live at 39 Mansion Street in New Zebedee, Michigan. And I'm their daughter. I really am. Honest. Cross my heart and hope to die."

Mrs. Sipes smiled sympathetically at Rose Rita. "There now. Isn't it easier to tell the truth?"

Not much, thought Rose Rita, but she said nothing.

Mrs. Sipes sighed again and shook her head. "I don't understand you, Rose Rita. I honestly don't. If it's true that you were traveling with a friend of your family's named Mrs. Zimmermann—"

"It's true, all right," said Rose Rita, interrupting. "Her handbag is still on the kitchen table in that crummy old farmhouse, and it's probably got her driver's license and a lot of other stuff in it with her name on it. So there." She folded her arms and glared fiercely at Mrs. Sipes.

"Very well," said Mrs. Sipes calmly. "As I was saying, if that part of your story is true, why on earth did you try to hide your parents' identity?"

An answer sprang into Rose Rita's head, an answer that was partly true. "On account of my dad doesn't like Mrs. Zimmermann. He thinks she's a screwball, and if she turns up alive, my dad'll never let me go anywhere with Mrs. Zimmermann ever again."

"Oh, now, I think you're being rather hard on your father," said Mrs. Sipes. "I don't know him, of course, but it's hard to believe that he'd think Mrs. Zimmermann was a screwball just because she got lost in the woods. Lots of people get lost, every day."

Yeah, thought Rose Rita, but if he ever found out

Mrs. Zimmermann was a witch, he'd sure go through the roof. Besides he can't help us. Uncle Jonathan is the only one that can. Rose Rita wriggled impatiently and dug her heel into the rug. She felt like a prisoner. If only Mrs. Sipes would just go away so she could call up Uncle Jonathan and find out what to do about Mrs. Bigger! He could give her a magic formula to use, and then everything would be all right. It was all very frustrating. It was like almost having your hands on something and having someone slap your hands away every time you made a grab. She needed that book, the magic book with the funny name. But she couldn't do a thing until Mrs. Sipes left her alone.

While Rose Rita sat there stewing, Mrs. Sipes rattled on about responsibility and honesty, and how your parents were really your best friends if you gave them half a chance. When Rose Rita tuned back in on her, she was saying ". . . And so I think that what we have to do now is call your folks up and tell them what happened. They'll want to know that you're okay. Then I'll drive over to the Gunderson farm and see if everything is all right. You probably left everything wide open, and there are people who just walk in and take things, you know. After that all we can do is wait." Mrs. Sipes walked over and sat down next to Rose Rita on the bed. She put her arm around her. "I'm sorry to have been so hard on you, Rose Rita," she said softly. "I know you must be very upset because of what happened to your friend. But the police are out there now, combing the woods. I'm sure they'll find her."

Fat chance, thought Rose Rita, but again she said nothing. Now if only Mrs. Sipes would get in her car and go over to the farm and leave her here alone! *Go away, Mrs. Sipes! Go away.*

First, though, Rose Rita had to call her folks up. There was no getting around that. The three of them went downstairs, and Rose Rita called up her parents, long distance. Mrs. Pottinger answered the phone, and Rose Rita once again recited her story about how Mrs. Zimmermann had disappeared from the Gunderson farm in the middle of the night and had probably gotten lost in the woods. Mrs. Pottinger was the sort of person who got flustered easily, and when she heard of Mrs. Zimmermann's disappearance, she really got rattled. But she told Rose Rita not to worry, that she and Mr. Pottinger would be up there to get her as soon as they could, and she insisted on being called the moment there was any news about Mrs. Zimmermann. Then Mrs. Sipes took the phone, and she gave Mrs. Pottinger directions for getting to the Sipes farm. After that Mrs. Pottinger talked to Rose Rita a few minutes more, and then she hung up. And then, after a bit of fussing, Mrs. Sipes got into her car and drove off in the direction of the Gunderson farm.

Rose Rita stood by the front window watching Mrs.

Sipes's car as it disappeared over a hill. Aggie stood by her, watching, with her habitual worried expression.

"What're you gonna do now?" she asked.

"I'm gonna call up Lewis's Uncle Jonathan, right away quick. If he doesn't know what to do about old Mrs. Bigger, then nobody does!" Rose Rita felt excited. She already imagined herself armed with a spell and confronting Mrs. Bigger.

Rose Rita went back to the front hall and picked up the telephone. She glanced nervously around to make sure none of the other Sipes kids was in earshot. None of them was. Aggie stood by Rose Rita, anxiously waiting, as she asked for the long distance operator. "I want New Zebedee, Michigan, number 865, please, operator. The residence of Mr. Jonathan Barnavelt. This is a collect call."

Rose Rita and Aggie waited. They could hear the operator ringing Jonathan's phone. *Bzz. Bzz. Bzz.* Eight times she let it ring, and then she said, in that singsongy voice that Rose Rita knew so well, "I am sorry, but the party does not seem to answer. Would you care to call later?"

"Yeah," said Rose Rita, in a dull hopeless voice. "I'll call later. Thanks." She hung up the phone and sat down on the hassock next to the phone table. "Gosh darn!" she said angrily. "Gosh darn it all anyway! *Now* what are we gonna do?"

"Maybe they'll find Mrs. Zimmermann in the forest," said Aggie hopefully. She was having trouble keeping Rose Rita's lies separate from the true story in her head. Rose Rita just looked at her. "We'll try again," she muttered. "He's got to be home sometime."

Rose Rita tried three more times in ten minutes, but each time the result was the same. After a little while Mrs. Sipes came back. She was beaming, because she had found Mrs. Zimmermann's handbag on the kitchen table in Oley's house, and in the handbag she had found Mrs. Zimmermann's driver's license, her car keys, and a lot of other identification. So now she was convinced that Rose Rita was telling her the whole truth. Rose Rita was glad she was convinced. Now if only Mrs. Sipes would go off to some far corner of her farm, so she could try Jonathan's number again!

But Mrs. Sipes stayed right at home the rest of the day. Rose Rita swung on the front porch swing, and played stickball with Aggie, and helped her feed the cows and slop the hogs. When she wasn't doing anything else, Rose Rita chewed her nails. *Why wouldn't Mrs. Sipes leave?* There was only one phone in the house, and since it was on a table in the front hall, it was hardly private. Mrs. Sipes was not the sort who would stand over Rose Rita while she called, but she might be in the other room, and what would she do if she heard Rose Rita asking Jonathan for a spell that would free Mrs. Zimmermann from Gert Bigger's enchantments? No, she would have to be alone to make a call like that, and Rose Rita knew it. She waited for her chance, but her chance never came.

That evening, as Rose Rita and Aggie helped Mrs. Sipes get dinner ready, the phone rang. It was Mrs. Pottinger. It seemed that their car had broken down on the road. Something had gone wrong with it—the differential, she thought it was. Whatever it was, they wouldn't be in until tomorrow morning. Was there any news about Mrs. Zimmermann? No, there wasn't. Mrs. Pottinger said they were sorry about the delay, but there was no help for it. They'd be there when they got the car running again.

Rose Rita felt like a prisoner who has gotten a stay of execution. Now she would have more time to try to get Uncle Jonathan! "Oh come on, Uncle Jonathan!" she prayed under her breath. "Next time, be home! Please be home! Please!"

Rose Rita spent the evening playing parcheesi and Michigan rummy with Aggie and some of the other Sipes kids. Before she knew it, it was time for bed. She took a bath, which she badly needed, and put on a clean pair of pajamas from her valise, which Mrs. Sipes had brought back from the farmhouse. When Rose Rita was all cleaned up, Mrs. Sipes told her that she was sleeping in the extra bed in Aggie's room. Aggie's room was all flouncy and frilly and pink, a regular girl's room. There was a big teddy bear in the rocking chair in the corner, and there was a vanity table with a round mirror and some perfume bottles on it. Even though she was a farm girl and wore jeans a good deal of the time, Aggie seemed happy to be a girl. She said she looked forward to going to Junior High, and dates and dances and proms and stuff like that. She said that it was a relief sometimes to get out of her jeans and the boots that smelled of manure and go to a square dance at the Four-H Building. Rose Rita wondered if she would think that way herself in the fall. Meanwhile, she had other things on her mind.

That night Rose Rita lay wide awake, listening to the sounds of the house. Her heart was beating fast, and she felt very nervous. The Sipes family went to bed at ten, because they had to be up at six in the morning to do chores. No exceptions were allowed. And considering the fact that there were eight children in the family, the house quieted down pretty fast. By ten-thirty you could have heard a pin drop in the hall.

"Are you awake, Rose Rita?" Aggie hissed.

"Of course I'm awake, you dope. I'm gonna go down in a few minutes and try Uncle Jonathan's number again."

"Do you want me to go with you?"

"No. It'd make too much noise if both of us go. Just sit tight, and wait."

"Okay."

Minutes passed. When Rose Rita was finally sure that the house was asleep, she got out of bed and tiptoed downstairs to the telephone. There was a hall closet near the phone, and fortunately the cord was long. Rose Rita took the phone into the closet, shut the door, and squatted there under the coats. Whispering as loudly as she dared, she asked for Jonathan's number again. Again the operator tried. Ten times, fifteen, twenty times. It was no use. He was away—probably gone for the night.

Rose Rita hung up the phone and put it back on the table. She tiptoed back up the stairs to Aggie's room.

"How'd it go?"

"No soap," Rose Rita whispered. "Maybe he's gone to visit his sister in Osee Five Hills. He does that every now and then, and I don't know her number. I don't even know what her name is. Oh gosh, what are we gonna do?"

"I dunno."

Rose Rita gripped her head with her hands and tried to think. If she could have shaken some thoughts out of her head, she would have done it. There had to be some way, there had to be . . .

"Aggie?"

"Shhh. Not so loud. My ma'll hear us."

Rose Rita tried whispering more softly. "Okay. I'm sorry. Hey, Aggie, listen. Does Mrs. Bigger live in her store? I mean, in back of it, or upstairs?"

"Nope. She lives about two miles down the road in a little house that sets way back from the road. How come you want to know that?"

"Aggie," said Rose Rita in a loud excited whisper, "how'd you like to help me break into Mrs. Bigger's store? Tonight!"

CHAPTER TEN

As soon as Aggie saw what Rose Rita's plan was, she tried to back out. She thought up a thousand reasons for not going to Mrs. Bigger's place, that night or any other night. They might get caught and put in reform school. Aggie's mom would catch them, and bawl them out, and tell Rose Rita's folks. Mrs. Bigger might be there, hiding in a closet and waiting for them. The store would be all locked up, and they wouldn't be able to get in. They might get bitten by Mrs. Bigger's dog. And so on and so forth. But Rose Rita was not impressed by Aggie's arguments. She had only known Aggie for a short while, but she knew by now that Aggie was a worrywart. Worrywarts always imagine that terrible things are going to happen. They imagine dangers where dangers don't exist. Lewis was a worrywart, and he was always fussing and fretting about something. Right now Aggie was acting just like Lewis.

To Rose Rita everything seemed clear. Mrs. Bigger was a witch, and she was always reading magic books. She probably had a copy of the Mallet of Whatever-it-was, the book that Rose Rita had to have if she was going to save Mrs. Zimmermann. It might be in her home, or it might be in her store somewhere. It was very likely to be in her store, since she spent a lot of time there and probably read while she worked. After all, Rose Rita argued, she had found that magic charm tucked away in one of Gert Bigger's account books. Well, if she had found that, she might find other things. Rose Rita ignored the holes in her argument. She didn't want to see them. Already she was beginning to be carried away by the idea of bearding Gert Bigger in her den. She imagined herself armed with a great book from which she read strange grim-sounding incantations, magic words that would bring Gert Bigger to her knees and make her bring Mrs. Zimmermann back from . . . from wherever Gert Bigger had sent her. It occurred to Rose Rita, of course, that maybe Mrs. Bigger had used her magic to kill Mrs. Zimmermann. Well, thought Rose Rita grimly, if she's done that, I'll make her bring Mrs. Zimmermann back—back from the dead. And if I can't do that, I'll make her pay for what she did. A tremendous anger was building in Rose Rita's mind. Righteous anger. She hated that big rawboned woman with the nasty sneering manner and the insults and lies and dirty rotten cheating ways. She was going to fix her, and fix her good. In the meantime, however, she had to persuade Aggie to go along with her plan. It wasn't easy. Rose Rita argued and wheedled, but Aggie was a stubborn girl—about as stubborn as Rose Rita. And Aggie was especially stubborn when she was scared.

"All right, Aggie," said Rose Rita, folding her arms and glaring. "If *that's* the way you're gonna be, I'll just go by myself!"

Aggie looked hurt. "You mean it? Really?"

Rose Rita nodded grimly. "Uh-huh. Try and stop me."

Actually, Aggie could have stopped Rose Rita easily, and Rose Rita knew it. All she had to do was shout, and Mrs. Sipes, who was a very light sleeper, would be down in the room asking them what all the racket was about. But Aggie didn't shout. She really did want to be in on the adventure. On the other hand, she was afraid.

"Come on, Aggie," Rose Rita pleaded. "We won't get caught, I promise you. And if we get our hands on a copy of that book I told you about, we can really fix old Mrs. Bigger's wagon. You'd like that, wouldn't you?"

Aggie's forehead wrinkled up. Her eyebrows got so worried that they almost met. "Gee, I still don't know, Rose Rita. Are you sure that whatchamacallit book'll be there?"

"Of course I'm not sure, dopey. But we'll never find out if we sit here all night. Come on, Aggie. Please!"

Aggie looked uncertain. "Well, how're we gonna get in? The doors and windows'll all be locked."

"We can figure that out when we get there. Maybe we'll have to break a window or something."

"It'd make a lot of noise," said Aggie. "And you might cut yourself on the glass."

"We'll pick the lock then. People do it all the time in the movies."

"This isn't the movies, this is real life. Do you know how to pick locks? Huh? Do you? I bet you don't."

Rose Rita felt totally exasperated. "Look, Aggie," she said, "if we get there and we can't find any way to get in, we can give up and come back. Okay? And if there is a way to get in, you won't even have to come inside with me. You can stay outside and be the lookout. Come on, Aggie. I really need you. How about it? Huh?"

Aggie scratched her head and looked uncertain. "You promise I won't have to come in with you? And if we can't get in, we'll come straight back here?"

Rose Rita drew a cross on her stomach with her finger. "I promise. Cross my heart and hope to die."

"Okay," said Aggie. "Wait'll I get my flashlight. We'll need it."

Working as quietly as they could, Rose Rita and Aggie got into their clothes and put on their sneakers. Aggie dug a long-barreled flashlight out of her closet and poked around in her dresser drawer till she found an old boy scout knife. It had a black wrinkly plastic handle, and inside a little glass bubble at one end of the handle was a compass. Aggie really couldn't say why she was taking along this particular piece of equipment, but she thought it might come in handy.

When they were all ready, the two girls tiptoed to the door of the bedroom. Aggie led the way. Carefully she opened the door, just a crack, and looked out.

"Okay!" she whispered. "Just follow me."

The two girls tiptoed down the hall and down the stairs. They walked softly through rooms that lay gleaming in moonlight till they reached the back door. The back door was propped open because it was a hot night, and the screen door was unhooked. They went out, closing the door softly behind them.

"Wow!" breathed Rose Rita. "That part was easy!"

Aggie smiled shyly. "Yeah. I've done it before. I used to go frog-spearin' with my brother down to the crick there, but my mom caught us and gave us heck. I haven't been out in the middle of the night since then. Come on."

Aggie and Rose Rita started walking down a rutty wagon road that ran between two plowed fields. They climbed a little fence and trotted along a grassy track that ran parallel to the main road. Rose Rita saw at once that they were going back by the way they had come on the previous day when Aggie found Rose Rita sleeping next to the cornfield. Now the field was on their left, rustling softly in the night breeze. Stars were clustered thick overhead, and crickets chirped in the tall grass.

Before long the girls passed the place where they had met. There was the droopy elm tree and the flat-topped boulder. They had been chattering excitedly, but now they grew quiet. They were not far from Mrs. Bigger's store.

At the edge of the gravel road the two girls paused. There was Gert Bigger's grocery store, shut up for the night. A yellow insect lamp lit up the front door, and through the wide plate glass window the girls could see a night light burning in the rear of the store. The sign with the flying red horse creaked gently in the wind, and the two gas pumps looked like soldiers on guard.

"Here we are," whispered Aggie.

"Yeah," said Rose Rita. She felt something tighten up in her stomach. Maybe this was a dumb plan after all. She was about to ask Aggie if she really felt like going ahead with their plan, but she swallowed her fears and crossed the road. Aggie followed, glancing about her nervously.

"It looks okay," said Aggie, when they were both on the other side of the road. "Her car's always parked over there when she's here, and it's gone."

"Good! Do you think we ought to try the front door?"

"Well, you can if you want to. But I'm sure it'll be locked."

Rose Rita trotted up the steps and rattled the door. It was locked. Locked tight. She shrugged and ran back down the steps.

"Come on, Aggie. That's one down, and a lot to go. It's such a hot night that she might have left one window open. Let's check the windows." Rose Rita could feel her courage and her habitual optimism coming back. Everything would work out all right. They'd find a way in.

Apparently Rose Rita's optimism was catching. Aggie brightened up and became—for her—confident. "Hey, that's an idea! Okay, we'll check."

As they passed around the side of the building, the girls heard a loud clucking sound. There behind the fence was that poor bedraggled white chicken. It looked even more beat-up and scrawny than it had when Rose Rita saw it the day before. Old Gertie oughta feed it, Rose Rita thought. As before, the hen was very excited. It ran back and forth behind the fence, clucking and flapping its wings.

"Oh be quiet!" Rose Rita hissed. "We're not gonna chop off your head! Just cool down, for heaven's sake!"

The two girls started to inspect the windows on the side of the house. The ones on the first floor were shut tight, and it was likely they were locked as well. Just to make sure Rose Rita got up on an orange crate and tried to move one of them. It wouldn't budge an inch.

"Darn it all anyway!" she grumbled as she got down off the crate.

"Oh, don't give up yet!" said Aggie. "We haven't tried the . . . oops. Watch out!"

Rose Rita whirled around in time to see a car pass by. Its headlights swept across the side of the store and were gone. If the driver had been paying attention, he would have seen the two figures standing next to the store. But, apparently, he had not noticed. Rose Rita felt exposed, as if she were in a fishbowl. She felt the danger of what she was doing.

"C'mon," she said, tugging nervously at Aggie's arm. "Let's go around to the back."

The two girls walked around to the rear of the store. The little white hen, which had never stopped squawking since the time they arrived, kept it up until they disappeared around the corner of the building. Rose Rita was glad when it finally shut up. It was beginning to make her nervous.

The two girls tried the back door. It was locked. Then they stepped back and surveyed the rear wall of the building. The first floor windows had heavy iron grills over them—probably they were the windows of the storeroom, where the groceries were kept. There was one window on the second floor, and—Rose Rita stepped back to make sure—yes, it was open! Not wide open, but open a crack.

"Wow!" said Rose Rita, pointing. "Do you see that?"

Aggie looked doubtful. "Yeah, I do, but I don't see how you could wiggle in through a crack like that."

"I'm not gonna wiggle in through the crack, dumbo! That crack means that the window isn't fastened. So if I climb up there, I can open it up."

"How you gonna do that?"

Rose Rita looked around. "I dunno yet. Let's see if there's anything to climb up on."

Rose Rita and Aggie poked around in the back yard of Gert Bigger's store for a while, but they didn't find any ladders. There was a toolshed, but it had a padlock on it. Rose Rita went back to the window and peered up at it owlishly. She rubbed her chin.

There was an apple tree growing near the store, and one of its branches nearly touched the sill of the window she wanted. But Rose Rita was an experienced tree climber, and she knew that the branch would start to bend as soon as she tried to climb out on it. By the time she got near the end of the branch, it would be bent way down. So that was no good. On the other hand there was a trellis nailed to the side of the house. It ran right up next to the window. If she could climb up on it, she might be able to get hold of the sill and swing herself over. It was worth a try.

Rose Rita took a deep breath and flexed her hands. She walked up to the trellis. It was covered with thick thorny vines, but there were places, here and there, where you could put your hands. Rose Rita put a foot on one slat and a hand on another. She swung herself up so her weight was on the trellis, and hung there, waiting to see what would happen. Nails skreeked as the trellis started to pull out from the wall.

"It doesn't look too good," said Aggie, screwing up her mouth into a very worried scowl. "If you climb any farther, you're gonna break your neck."

Rose Rita said nothing. The trellis was still attached to the wall, so she put another foot up. Then another foot, and another hand. With a loud splintering, crackling, rustling, and squeaking noise, the trellis leaned lazily sideways. Nails and broken pieces of wood dropped to the ground. Rose Rita leaped free of the wreckage and landed on her feet. Aggie, with a little cry, dropped the knife in the grass and ran to Rose Rita's side. She found her standing there, sucking a cut thumb and glaring hatefully at the ruined trellis.

"Darned thorns anyway!" Rose Rita grumbled.

"Gee, is she ever gonna be ticked off!" said Aggie. "Mrs. Bigger, I mean."

Rose Rita wasn't listening. She was wondering if maybe she could scale the side of the building. It wasn't very far up to the second story, and the white clapboard strips looked as though they might give her a handhold. She tried, but she slid down. She tried again, with the same result. She stood there, panting and redfaced. For the first time, she doubted the wisdom of her plan.

"Let's go home," said Rose Rita bitterly. She felt the tears stinging her eyes.

"Are you giving up already?" said Aggie. "Gee, I don't think that's a very good idea. We haven't looked at the other side of the store."

Rose Rita gave a start and looked at Aggie. She was right! Rose Rita had been so wrapped up in the problem of the upstairs window that she had forgotten all about the far side of the building, the one side that they hadn't checked out yet. Hope and optimism came flowing back.

"Okay. Let's go look," said Rose Rita, grinning.

On the far side of the store thick bushes grew up close to the windows, but there was a little tunnel in the shrubbery where you could sidle in if you hunkered down a bit. Rose Rita and Aggie bent over and edged their way in under the bushes. They looked up and saw that the windows on this side had grates and padlocks like the ones on the back of the store. But down at ground level was a cellar entrance. The old-fashioned kind, with two slanting wooden doors. Aggie shone her flashlight over the door. There was a pair of metal fixtures where the two doors met. Obviously they were meant to hold a padlock, but there was no padlock in the holes. The door was unlocked.

Cautiously Rose Rita gripped the handle of one of the heavy wooden doors. She lifted it, and a smell of earth and mold rose to her nostrils. It was like a breath from the grave. Rose Rita shuddered and stepped back. She

dropped the door. It fell with a loud clatter.

Aggie gave Rose Rita a frightened look. "What's wrong, Rose Rita? Did you see something?"

Rose Rita passed a hand over her forehead. She felt dizzy. "I . . . no, I didn't, Aggie, only . . . only I got scared. I d'no why, but I did. I guess I'm just a scaredy-cat, that's all."

"It's funny, isn't it?" Aggie mused, as she stared down at the door. "All those bars and locks on everything else, and she leaves this open. It's weird."

"Yeah. Maybe she didn't think anyone'd go pokin' around under these bushes." Rose Rita realized that this was a pretty weak explanation, but it was the only one she could come up with. There was something very strange about this open door. She just couldn't figure it out.

Suddenly Rose Rita thought of something. She picked up the cellar door again and opened it all the way. She opened the other door panel too. Then she took the flashlight from Aggie and stepped down into the dark opening. At the bottom of a short flight of stone steps Rose Rita found a black door with a dirty cobwebbed window. She put her hand on the porcelain knob and found that it felt surprisingly cold. Rose Rita turned the knob and pushed cautiously. At first she thought the door was locked, but when she pushed harder, it opened with a loud dismal rattle.

Inside the cellar it was pitch-dark. Rose Rita played the beam of her flashlight around and saw vague shapes hunched in the gloom.

"Are you okay?" called Aggie nervously.

"Yeah, I . . . I think so. Look, Aggie. You stay up here and keep watch. I'm goin' in and have a look around."

"Don't stay too long."

"Don't worry, I won't. See you later."

"Okay."

Rose Rita turned and flashed her light up. There stood Aggie with her worried frown. She was waving feebly. Rose Rita swallowed hard and thought about Mrs. Zimmermann. She turned and went in.

As she crossed the cold stone floor, Rose Rita glanced nervously from side to side. In one corner a furnace squatted. With its upraised metal arms, it looked like some kind of monster. Near it was a freezer. It reminded Rose Rita of a tomb. She laughed nervously. Why did everything seem so scary? This was a perfectly ordinary basement. There weren't any ghosts or monsters in it. Rose Rita walked on.

In a far corner of the basement she found a flight of wooden steps leading up. Slowly she climbed. The steps creaked loudly under her feet. At the top of the steps was a door. Rose Rita opened it and looked out. She was in the store.

Groceries stood piled in shadowy ranks. Cans, bottles,

jars, and boxes, half lit by the weak little bulb that
burned over the cash register. Outside the wide front
window a car passed. Rose Rita could hear a clock ticking slowly, but she couldn't see it. She walked across the
room and opened a door. Here were steps leading up.
She started to climb.

Halfway up the steps Rose Rita noticed something
that made her stop: a picture hanging with its face
turned to the wall. Curious, she reached up and turned
it over. The picture showed a saint with a halo. He was
clutching a cross and staring up toward heaven with
wide unearthly eyes. Hurriedly Rose Rita turned the
picture back toward the wall. A violent shudder passed
through her body. Why had she been so frightened? She
didn't know. When she had calmed down, she went on
up the stairs.

At the top of the steps was an L-shaped hallway, and
halfway along it was a paneled door. There was a key
sticking out of the door. She turned it, and the door
swung open. Rose Rita waved her flashlight around, and
found that she was in a small bedroom.

There was a light switch just inside the door. Rose
Rita's hand moved toward it, but then she stopped.
Would it be a bad thing to turn the light on? She
glanced toward the window. It was the only one in the
room, the window she had tried to reach by climbing
the trellis. The window looked out on the dark mass of
trees behind the store. Gert Bigger was miles away. If I

turn on the light, Rose Rita thought, people will just figure it's old Gertie up here counting her money. She snapped the switch and started looking around.

It was a very ordinary room. The only thing odd about it was its lived-in look, but it occurred to Rose Rita that maybe Gert Bigger stayed here during the winter, on nights when the weather was so bad that it was impossible to drive home. In one corner stood a small iron bed. It was painted green, and the wrought iron posies on the bars of the headboard were touched up in pink. Nearby was a closet without any door. Ordinary ladies' dresses hung on the rack, and wadded nylons lay on the floor near a heavy-looking pair of black ladies' shoes. There was a shelf in the closet, and something like a blanket lay folded up on it. Nothing unusual here.

Rose Rita walked across the room and examined the dresser. There was a mirror on top of it, and in front of the mirror was a collection of bottles and jars. Jergen's lotion, Noxzema, Pond's lotion, and a big blue bottle of Evening in Paris perfume. On the white linen runner lay tweezers and combs and brushes, and bits of tissue paper, and little curls of dark brown hair. There was a box of Kleenex, too.

Rose Rita turned and gazed around the room. Was there anything else here? There was. On a low table next to the bed was a large book. A big heavy book with a tooled leather cover. The pages were edged with gilt, and there were fussy gilded decorations on the spine and on the cover. A soiled red marker was sticking out of the book.

Rose Rita could hear her heart beating. She swallowed hard. Could this be it? She went closer, and opened the heavy front cover. Her face fell. It wasn't the book she wanted. It was something called *A Cyclopaedia of Jewish Antiquities*, by the Reverend Merriwether Burchard, D.D., Litt.D. Well, at least it was a book of some sort. Rose Rita started leafing through it.

The book was printed in double columns of tiny black print, and it was full of dark mysterious engravings. According to the captions, the pictures showed The Temple of Solomon, the Ark of the Covenant, the Brazen Laver, the Seven-Branched Candlestick, and things like that. Rose Rita knew what some of the things in the pictures were. There were engravings like these in her grandmother's family Bible. Rose Rita yawned. It looked like a pretty boring book. She looked around and sighed. This certainly wasn't any witch's den. Maybe she was wrong about Gert Bigger being a witch. Rose Rita realized, with a sinking heart, that her witch theory was based on a lot of guesswork. Mrs. Bigger might have had a picture of Mordecai Hunks on her wall, but what did that prove? As for the photo Mrs. Zimmermann had found, it might all have been just a coincidence. As for the strange drawing and Mrs. Bigger's odd reading habits, well, she might just be one of those people who want to be a witch. Mrs. Zimmermann had told Rose Rita once that there were lots of people who would love to have magical powers, although there wasn't chance in a million that they would ever get them. People like that would read magic books in hopes of getting to be magicians, wouldn't they? Well, wouldn't they?

Rose Rita began to wonder if she hadn't made a terrible mistake. Some strange things had happened to her and Mrs. Zimmermann, but that didn't mean that old Mrs. Bigger had made them happen. She picked up her flashlight off the bed and was about to go downstairs when she heard a noise. A faint scratching at the door of the bedroom.

Terror gripped Rose Rita for an instant, and then she remembered something that made her laugh. Mrs. Bigger had a dog. A small black dog. Probably she had locked it in the store for the night.

With a sigh of relief, Rose Rita opened the door. It was the dog, all right. It trotted across the room and hopped up on the bed. Rose Rita smiled and turned toward the door. But she stopped again, because the dog had made a very odd sound. A sound very much like a human being coughing. Animals sometimes make human sounds. The cries of cats are, on certain occasions, just like a baby's wails. Rose Rita knew that, but still the sound made her stop. The hair on the back of her neck stood up on end. She turned slowly around. There on the bed sat Gert Bigger. Her hard brutal mouth was set in the evilest of smiles.

CHAPTER ELEVEN

Rose Rita lay in darkness. She felt a slight pressure on her eyes and knew that there was something covering them, but she didn't know what it was. She would have reached up to uncover her eyes, but she couldn't. Her hands were crossed on her breast, and though she could feel them, she couldn't move them. She couldn't move any part of her body, nor could she speak, but she could hear, and she could feel. As she lay there, a fly—it felt like a fly—landed on her forehead and walked the length of her nose before buzzing away.

Where was she? Probably in the bedroom above Gert Bigger's store. It felt as if she was lying on a bed, anyway. And there was a blanket, or something like a blanket, drawn up over her body. It felt heavy, and the room was hot and still. Tiny rivulets of sweat ran down Rose Rita's body. Why couldn't she move? Was she paralyzed, or what? There came back to her now, like a bad dream, the terror she had felt when she saw Gert Bigger sitting on the bed, leering at her. She must have fainted then, because she could not remember anything after that.

Rose Rita heard a lock click. A door creaked open. Heavy footfalls crossed the room and stopped next to her head. A chair creaked.

"Well, well, well. And how are you, Miss Nosy? Hmmm? Not speaking to me? That's not nice. You know, I'm the one who ought to be insulted, the way you broke in here and rummaged around. Were you tryin' to find out if I was a witch? Well, you can relax. I am."

Gert Bigger laughed, and it was not at all the kind of laugh that you would expect to come out of a big husky woman like her. It was a high-pitched tinny giggle. Rose Rita thought it sounded like the laughter of a crazy person.

"Yes, sirree," Gert Bigger went on, "it all started when that old fool of a Gunderson dropped in here one night. He was half-crocked, and he started talkin' about this magic ring he had found on his farm. Well, at first I thought he was just foolin', but I got to thinkin' later— what if it's the truth? You see, I've always wanted to be able to work magic. I've studied up on it a lot. Well, after old Oley kicked off, I broke into his place and hunted around till I found the darned thing. It's on my finger right now. Did you read in that book what that fella Burchard said about it? It's all true, you know, every word. Here, let me read it to you."

Rose Rita heard the sound of fingers riffling through the pages of a book. "Here it is, where I stuck the marker. You must've seen it when you were pokin' around, though sometimes you nosy types don't see what's right under your nose." She giggled again. "Ready? Here it is. '. . . No account of Jewish antiquities would be complete without mention of the legendary ring of King Solomon. According to the great historian Flavius Josephus, King Solomon possessed a magic ring that enabled him to do many wonderful things. The ring gave him the power of teleportation, that is, the ability to be whisked from place to place, unseen. It conferred upon him the powers of sorcery and divination, and enabled him to humiliate his enemies by changing them into lowly beasts. In this manner, it is said, King Solomon brought low the king of the Hittites, when he turned him into an ox. The ring also enabled Solomon to change his own shape at will—his most favored form is said to have been that of a small black dog, in which shape he prowled about, spying on his enemies and finding out many secrets. But the greatest power of the ring was one which Solomon, wisest of men, never chose to use. The ring could, if the wearer desired it, give long life and great beauty. To obtain this gift, however, the wearer was obliged to call upon the demon Asmodai. It may be for this reason that Solomon refused to exercise this power of the ring. For, we are told, he who sups with the Devil . . .' "

The book slammed shut. "That's enough of you, Reverend," muttered Gert Bigger. "Well, there you are, Miss Nosy. Isn't that interestin'? But I'll tell you what is most interestin' of all. You came here at just the right time, you really did. I was goin' to do somethin' to you when I caught you pokin' around in my back room, but later, I says to myself, I says, 'She'll be back!' And you did come back, you did, you did!" Gert Bigger let out a peal of shrill laughter. "I left the padlock off of my cellar door, and you went right in, like the little fool that you are. Well, you're gonna find out what it's like to monkey around with witches. Florence found out, and I'm not through with her yet, not by a long shot." She paused and made an unpleasant spitting sound. "Phah! Oh, didn't I know, didn't I know what she was up to when she showed up here, pretendin' she was out of gas! I knew about her and all that magic monkey-do of hers, that college degree and all, and I says to myself, 'She's after the ring!' I was real worried then, because I didn't know how to handle the ring proper, cept'n for the black-dog trick. Well, after you folks went up north, I learned. I sent that photograft up there, and that

/ 152 /

was me you saw in Florence's room. I showed up in the back seat o' your car for a coupla seconds too. Scared the dickens out o'you, didn't I?" She laughed shrilly. Then, after another pause, she continued, in a grimmer tone, "Well, fun's fun, but I'm through playin' around. I've got Florence, and I'm gonna fix her good, so she'll never be able to get my ring from me, not ever!

"A course," she added, "I've got a special grudge against her for makin' my life miserable. If me'n Mordy had got married, my life would've been better. The old fool that I was married to used to beat me up. You don't know what it was like. You don't know at all." Gert Bigger's voice cracked. Was she crying? Rose Rita couldn't tell.

Gert Bigger rambled on, in her hard angry voice. She explained to Rose Rita that she had put her under a death spell. When dawn came, she would die. They would find her body here surrounded by the paraphernalia of Gert Bigger's magic. But Gert Bigger would be gone. In fact there would be no Gert Bigger, because she would be a young beautiful woman. She had it all figured out: she would go away to another place and change her name. She had drawn all her money out of the bank—it was in the safe downstairs. With a new name and a new life she could start making up for all the rotten things that had happened to her. And before she left, she would settle accounts with Florence Zimmermann, for good and for all.

After she had finished talking, Gert Bigger left the room and locked the door. Rose Rita stared hopelessly into the darkness that lay around her. She thought about Aggie. Aggie was her only hope. Rose Rita had no idea how much time had gone by since she left Aggie standing outside the cellar door. She hoped that Gert Bigger hadn't captured Aggie too. Rose Rita prayed, though her mouth stayed shut and no sound came out. Please, God, help Aggie to find me. Make her get help before it's too late. Please God please . . .

A long time passed. At least it seemed like a long time, though Rose Rita had no way of telling how long it was. Her wristwatch was still on her wrist, ticking, but it did her no good. How would she know when it was dawn? She would know when she was dead. Tick-tick-tick-tick. Rose Rita could feel her body growing numb. She couldn't feel her hands on her breast any more. She had a horrible vision of herself as a severed head lying on a pillow. It was such an awful thought that she tried to get rid of it, but it kept coming back. Please, God, send Aggie, send somebody. Tick-tick-tick-tick . . .

Brr-rrr-rrring. A doorbell was ringing. It rang several times, and then Rose Rita heard the muffled tinkling of the little bell above the door of the store. She heard nothing after that—if people were talking, she couldn't hear them. Silence. More time passed. Then Rose Rita heard the lock on the bedroom door click. Footsteps, and the creak of a chair as somebody heavy sat down.

"My lord, it takes all kinds to make a world!" said Gert Bigger. "Who do you suppose I've just been talkin' to? Guess. Give up? Mrs. Sipes, who lives down the road. Her and her daughter . . . Aggie I think is her name. They were all wrought up because Aggie said I kidnaped you. Imagine that!" Gert Bigger giggled. "They had even brought a cop along with 'em to search the place. Well, I know my rights. He didn't have no search warrant, and I told him so. I says to him, I know my rights and you can't come in, and no, I don't know nothin' about no little girl! So there! Imagine the nerve of 'em, comin' here like that!" Gert Bigger laughed again. The chair creaked as she rocked back and forth, laughing. The tiny flame of hope in Rose Rita's mind flickered out. She was going to die, and there was nothing that anyone could do about it.

Gert Bigger left the room, and there was another long dark silence. Rose Rita kept hearing little sounds, but she couldn't figure out what they were. Finally the door creaked open again, and she heard Gert Bigger walking around the room. She was humming to herself, and there was a sound of drawers opening and shutting. She was packing up, getting ready to leave. After what seemed like a long time, Rose Rita heard the latches of a suitcase snap shut. Gert Bigger walked over to her chair by the head of the bed and sat down again.

"How're you doin'? Hmm? Feel anything yet? This spell comes over you gradual-like, or so I'm told. But it

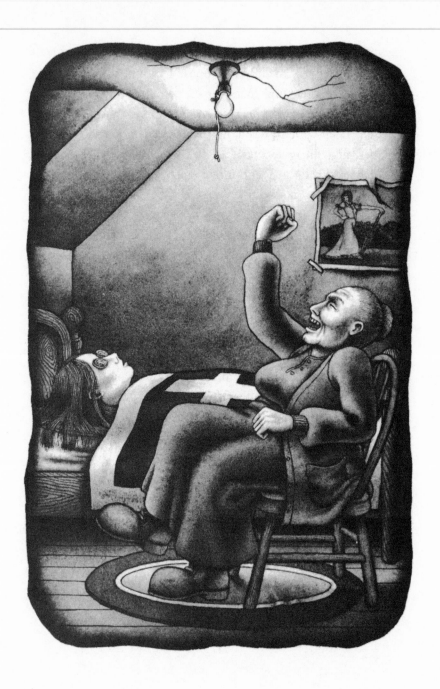

won't be over with till dawn, and that's still a ways off yet. Okay now. I'm all ready to go. I haven't taken care of Florence yet, but I think I'll do that on my way out. I want her to see what I'm like after I've been changed. And you know what? Seeing as how you've been so nice and quiet, I'm gonna let you watch me do my little quick-change act. Well, uh, of course I'm kiddin' in a way, because I really can't let you see me. I'd have to take those things off of your eyes, and that would break the spell, and we can't have that, can we? No sir-ree. But I tell you what I'll do. I'll sit right here in this chair and summon up old Asmodai, and you can hear his voice. How'll that be? Let me see now, what is it that I do? Oh yes . . ."

Gert Bigger clapped her hands three times and said in a loud commanding voice, "Send Asmodai to me! Now!"

At first nothing happened. Then, slowly, Rose Rita began to feel the presence of something evil. Feeling returned to her body. Her flesh was covered with goose bumps, and she felt cold. The air grew thick, and it was hard to breathe. Out of the darkness a harsh whispery voice spoke.

"Who calls upon Asmodai?"

"I do. I am wearing the ring of King Solomon, and I want to be changed. I want to be young and beautiful, and I want to live for a thousand years." Gert added quickly, "But I don't want to get old. I want to stay young, all the time."

"So be it," said the whispery voice.

As soon as the whispery voice had finished speaking, Rose Rita heard a small sound. It was a sound like somebody dropping a quarter on the floor. Then there was a sound like a strong wind roaring through the room. The room trembled, as if the ground underneath the building was quaking. Rose Rita heard all sorts of rattling clattering sounds. The bed shook, and whatever had been on her eyes slid off. She sat up and shook her head groggily. Rose Rita looked around. Where were her glasses? What had Gert Bigger done with them? She groped around on the nightstand and found them. She put them on and glanced around. Gert Bigger was gone. She had not heard her go out, and the key was sticking out of the inside of the door. On the bed next to her, Rose Rita saw two silver dollars. They must have been the things over her eyes. And she found that she was lying under a heavy black woolen blanket. It had a white border and a big white cross on it. Rose Rita knew what it was. She had been to a funeral at the Catholic church in New Zebedee, and she had seen a casket covered with a blanket just like this one. With a violent shudder she thrust the thing away from her and sat up.

Rose Rita felt sick. She felt like somebody who has been in bed with the flu for two weeks. When she tried to stand up, she sat down again suddenly. Sweat was pouring down her face. As she gazed woozily around the room, it occurred to her to wonder just what had happened to Mrs. Bigger. Probably she had had her wish granted, and she was out in Hollywood, living it up with Lana Turner and Esther Williams and all that crowd. Rose Rita didn't know, and she didn't care. She felt dizzy, and she couldn't stop shuddering. Her head was as light as a wicker basket. Finally, with an effort, she forced herself to stand up. Now she remembered something, something that had puzzled her. That sound, like a coin hitting the floor. What was it? Rose Rita got down on her hands and knees and looked under the bed. And at that moment she heard, from downstars, a terrific pounding and banging. The doorbell rang about eight times, and a muffled voice yelled, "Open up! Open up in the name of the law!" They were back! Aggie and her mom and the cops! Rose Rita glanced toward the door. What if Mrs. Bigger had left her ring behind? Wouldn't it be great to be able to run downstairs to meet Aggie with the ring of King Solomon in her fist? Rose Rita bent over and scrabbled in the dust under the bed. There it was! She reached out and hooked the ring with her finger. Now she drew the ring to her and closed her fist around it.

And with that something happened. A shudder ran through Rose Rita's body, and she felt . . . well, *strange*. She felt proud and bitter and angry, angry at the people who had come to drag her back to her old life.

"Okay, Mrs. Bigger," the voice boomed. "We're gonna give you a count of ten before we break the door down! One . . ."

Rose Rita got up and glared fiercely at the door. The expression on her face was so hateful that she hardly looked like herself at all. A wild light was in her eyes. So they were coming to get her! Well, they'd have to catch her first. She rushed to the door and unlocked it. With the ring still clutched tight in her fist, Rose Rita dashed out into the hall. At the far end of the hall was a half-opened door, and she could see stairs leading down. It wasn't the staircase she had come up by, it was another one, leading to the back of the building. Rose Rita ran toward it.

"Six . . . seven . . ."

Down the stairs she clattered. At the bottom was a door with a night lock and a chain. Working furiously, yet never letting the ring out of her hand for a second, Rose Rita undid the locks and chains and bolts.

"Ten!" There was a loud crash and a babble of voices shouting. In the middle of it all Rose Rita heard Aggie yelling "Rose Rita! Are you all right?" Rose Rita hesitated. She glanced waveringly toward the front of the store, where all the noise was coming from. Then her face hardened, and she gripped the ring tighter. Rose Rita turned and ran, out past the toolshed and the clothesline, toward the dark mass of trees that grew right up to the edge of Gert Bigger's back yard. The shadow of the pines seemed to reach out and swallow her up.

CHAPTER TWELVE

Rose Rita ran through the woods, her feet slapping the ground under her. Bits and pieces of scenery jolted past, branches and stumps, and fungi laddering tall dark trunks. She ran on a crooked path covered with brown pine needles, a path that wound deeper and deeper into the woods. Sometimes she fell or barked her shins on a stump, but each time she got up and kept on running. Faster and faster she ran. Branches whipped across her face and arms, leaving angry red marks, but the pain of the cuts just made her run faster. As she ran, her mind was filled with a wild jumble of thoughts. Images leaped before her, like flashes of lightning. Rose Rita saw them as clearly as if they had been printed on the air. She saw the boy with the crew cut who had yelled, "You're a pretty funny kind of a girl!" She saw the girls standing on the sidelines at the Saturday night dance. She saw the black prison-like junior high building where she had to go next fall. She saw girls in flouncy dresses, girls who wore nylons and lipstick and mascara, asking her, "What's the matter with you? Don't you want to go on dates? Dating is fun!"

As Rose Rita ran, she thought she could hear someone behind her, calling her name. The voice was faint and far-off, but she was sure she had heard it call to her once or twice. No, Rose Rita panted. You're not gonna get me. I've had about enough, I've had about enough, and I'm gonna get what I want . . .

On and on Rose Rita ran, pell-mell, through the dark pine forest. She left the path behind and half slid, half ran down a steep bank. The bank was covered with pine needles, and pine needles are slippery. She lost her footing and tumbled, head over heels. Over and over she rolled. When she got to the bottom, dazed and sick and shaken, the first thing she did was make sure that she had the ring with her. There it was, still clutched tight in her fist. Rose Rita opened her hand only long enough to make sure the ring was safe. Then she closed her fist tight, staggered to her feet, and started running again. There was something inside her head that kept driving her on, something relentless and mechanical, like a piston.

Go on, go on, it said. Keep going, keep going, keep going, keep going . . .

Rose Rita splashed across a shallow little stream and started to climb the bank on the other side. But the bank was steep, and it was hard climbing with one hand doubled up into a fist. Rose Rita paused, panting, halfway up. Why not put the ring on? She opened her hand and gaped stupidly at the small heavy object. It was too big—it would fall off her finger. How about putting it in her pocket? No, there might be a hole in the pocket. It might get lost. She had to know, all the time, that it was there. Rose Rita closed up her fist and climbed on, one-handed. She was a good climber, and there were roots here and there that could be used like the rungs of a ladder. Up she went. When she got to the top she paused to catch her breath.

"Rose Rita! Rose Rita! Stop!"

Rose Rita whirled. Who was that? It was a voice she knew. She was on the point of turning back when that driving piston in her head started up again. Go on, go on, go on, let's go, let's go, let's go. Rose Rita glared back across the stream. There was wild insane anger in her eyes now. "Come and get me!" she snarled through her teeth. Then she turned and ran on.

On into the forest Rose Rita plunged. But now her legs were starting to give out. They felt like rubber. Lying under that spell on Gert Bigger's bed had weakened her, the way a long illness would have. Her side hurt, and when she tried to catch her breath, watery bubbles kept bursting in her mouth. She was wringing wet with sweat, and her glasses were fogged up. Rose Rita wanted to stop, but the driving piston wouldn't let her. It forced her on until, finally, she reeled out into a little clearing. Rose Rita fell to her knees and looked around. Where was she? What was she doing? Oh, yes, she was going to . . . she was going . . . to . . . The world was starting to spin around her. Dark trees and starlit sky and gray grass whizzed past, like the things you see out of a car window when you're going very fast. Rose Rita fell down on her back and passed out.

The first thing that Rose Rita saw when she woke up, some time later, was a small cold pale moon shining down on her. She sat up and shook her head. All around her the dark trees stood, a ring of shadows cutting off escape. But she didn't want to escape, did she? No. She had come here to do something, but she couldn't for the life of her remember what it was. Rose Rita felt a pain in her left hand. She picked her fist up off the grass and stared at it as if it was something that belonged to somebody else. Slowly she opened her stiff cramped painful fingers. In her palm lay a large battered ring. She had been holding it so long, and so tight, that it had dug a deep red welt into her hand.

Wincing, Rose Rita turned the ring over with her fingers. It was made of gold—at least it seemed to be. And it was a signet ring. There was a design cut into the flat surface on the top. A face. A staring face with blank eyeballs and lips curled into a cold evil smile. Rose Rita was fascinated by the face. It seemed so lifelike. She half expected to see the lips part and to hear a voice speak.

And then she remembered why she was here.

Rose Rita stood up, swaying, in the gray moonlit clearing. She slid the ring onto the third finger of her left hand and held it there so it wouldn't fall off. Rose Rita gasped. The ring had shrunk to fit her hand! But she had no time to think of these things. A voice was in her head, telling her what to do. She clapped three times in weak imitation of Mrs. Bigger and said, in as loud a voice as she could manage, "I . . . I call upon As . . . Asmodai! Come to me! Now!"

A shadow fell across the gray starlit grass. And Rose Rita heard the harsh whispery voice that she had heard in Gert Bigger's room.

"I am called Asmodai. What do you want?"

Rose Rita shivered. She felt cold and frightened and alone. She wanted to rip the ring from her hand and throw it away. But she couldn't. An insistent angry voice, her own voice inside her head, went on talking. It told her what she had to do. It told her that she had to change, that she could solve all her problems now if only she had the courage. It also told her that she would only have this one chance, and that she'd never get another.

The whispery voice spoke again. It sounded faintly impatient. "I am called Asmodai. What do you want? You are the wielder of the ring of Solomon. What do you want?"

"I . . . I want . . . what I want to do is . . . what I want is . . ."

"Rose Rita, stop! Stop what you're doing and look at me!"

Rose Rita turned. There at the edge of the clearing stood Mrs. Zimmermann. The folds of her dress were filled with orange fire, and her homely wrinkled face was lit by the light of invisible footlights. A purple halo hovered about her, and its light fell upon the gray grass.

"Stop, Rose Rita! Stop what you're doing and listen to me!"

Rose Rita hesitated. She took the ring between her thumb and finger and started to take it off. It was on tight, but it could be moved. Now the voice in Rose Rita's head got louder. It told her not to listen to Mrs. Zimmermann. It told her that she had the right to be happy, to do what she wanted to do.

Rose Rita swallowed hard and licked her lips. She turned toward the shadow that waited, hovering, nearby. "I . . . I want to be a . . ."

Mrs. Zimmermann spoke again in a loud echoing com-

manding voice that seemed to fill the whole clearing. "I command you, Rose Rita, to give me that ring! Give it to me now!"

Rose Rita stood, hesitating. Her eyes were wide with fear. Then, like a sleepwalker, she turned and walked toward Mrs. Zimmermann. As she walked, she began working the ring loose from her finger. Up it slid, painfully, from one joint to the next. It was off now and lying in the palm of her right hand. Mrs. Zimmermann reached out and took it. She glanced at it scornfully and slipped it into the pocket of her dress. The halo faded and the footlights died. The folds of Mrs. Zimmermann's dress were just black creases now.

"Hi, Rose Rita," said Mrs. Zimmermann, smiling. "Long time no see."

Rose Rita looked nervously behind her, but the shadow was gone. Then she collapsed into Mrs. Zimmermann's arms and sobbed. Her whole body shook, and as she cried, she felt as if she were getting something poisonous and putrid out of her system. When she had cried herself out, Rose Rita stepped back and looked at Mrs. Zimmermann. Her face was pale and drawn, but her eyes were cheerful. She looked and talked like herself.

"What . . . what happened to you, Mrs. Zimmermann?" was all Rose Rita could think of to say.

Mrs. Zimmermann laughed softly. "I might ask you the same question, my dear. By the way, were you scared of me when I showed up just now?"

"I sure was. I was afraid you'd wave your wand and . . . hey!" Suddenly Rose Rita remembered. Mrs. Zimmermann's wand had been destroyed, and she had not made another. She was next-door to powerless as a witch. Then how . . . ?

Mrs. Zimmermann could tell what Rose Rita was thinking. She laughed again. It was a pleasant sound, and nothing like Gert Bigger's insane giggle. "Rose Rita," she said, chuckling, "you have been flimflammed. I bluffed you. You see, I can still make myself look pretty darned terrifying, with footlights and haloes and all, but if you had chosen to go on with what you were doing, I wouldn't have been able to do a thing to stop you. Not a blessed thing."

Rose Rita stared at the ground. "I'm glad you bluffed me, Mrs. Zimmermann. I almost did something awful. But . . . but what happened to you? The other night, I mean. Where did you come from just now?"

"From the chicken yard," said Mrs. Zimmermann, smiling wryly. "Haven't you guessed by now?"

Rose Rita's mouth dropped open. "You mean . . . you mean you were . . . ?"

Mrs. Zimmermann nodded. "Uh-huh. And I'll never be able to look a plate of chicken salad in the face again, as long as I live. Gertie did that to me with the ring. But in order for me to have been brought back to my proper shape, something must have happened to her. Do you know what it was?"

Rose Rita was utterly confused. "I . . . I thought maybe you had figured out some way to break the spell she put on you. Isn't that what you did?"

Mrs. Zimmermann shook her head. "No, my dear. Even in the days when I had my magic wand, I would not have been strong enough to defeat someone who had a ring like that one. No, Rose Rita. All I know is this: one minute I was behind that fence, leading my, uh . . ." (she coughed) ". . . my, uh, chickeny life, and the next minute, I was standing there like my old self. Something must have happened. Maybe you can tell me what."

Rose Rita scratched her head. "You got me, Mrs. Zimmermann. Mrs. Bigger was gonna kill me with a spell, but in the middle of it all, she disappeared. She was gonna use the ring to call on . . . to call on . . ." It was strange, but now that she didn't have the ring on her finger anymore, Rose Rita couldn't remember the name of the devil that Mrs. Bigger had called on.

"Asmodai?" said Mrs. Zimmermann.

"Gee. That's it. How'd you know?"

"I didn't get a doctorate in Magic Arts from the University of Göttingen for nothing. Go on."

"Well, she called on whatsisname, and she said she wanted to be young and beautiful and live for . . . for a thousand years, I think it was. Anyway, she disappeared, so I figure the magic must have worked. But I guess she didn't know there'd be an earthquake along with all the rest of the presto-chango. The coins slid off

/ *170* /

my eyes, and that's how I got loose."

"Lucky for you," said Mrs. Zimmermann. "I'm sure old Gertie didn't count on that happening. And there may have been some other things she wasn't counting on."

"Huh? What do you mean?"

"I'm not sure what I mean, just yet. Right now, however, I think we'd better be getting back to the store. When I ducked out of the chicken yard, there was an incredible ruckus going on inside the store. It sounded like they were turning the place inside out. But I figured you needed me more than they did. I just barely caught sight of you as you were hightailing it for the woods. I'm an old woman, and I can't run very fast, so you got ahead of me. But I didn't have any trouble following you. You left quite a trail in the underbrush. And anyway, I was a girl scout leader back in the old days. Come on."

As it was, Rose Rita and Mrs. Zimmermann didn't have much trouble finding their way back to the store. They followed the swath of trampled grass and broken branches and muddy footprints back to the little path, and from there on it was easy.

Later the two of them were trotting briskly along the needle-strewn path when all of a sudden Mrs. Zimmermann said, "Look!" She pointed off to the left, and there Rose Rita saw a young slender willow tree. It stood, all alone, amid tall pines.

"Look at what?" said Rose Rita, puzzled.

"That willow."

"Oh yeah. It's just a tree. What about it?"

"What about it? Well, for one thing, you don't usually see willows all by themselves in the middle of pine forests. You find them in willow groves, by the banks of rivers and lakes and streams. And there's something else wrong. Its leaves are trembling. Can you feel any wind?"

"Nope. Gee, that is weird. Do you think maybe it's blowing over there, but not here?"

Mrs. Zimmermann rubbed her chin. "Tell me, Rose Rita," she said suddenly. "Can you remember the exact words Mrs. Bigger used? When she got herself changed, I mean."

Rose Rita thought. "Gee, I don't think I can. Something about being young and beautiful and living a long time, like I said before."

"That tree is young, and it certainly is beautiful," said Mrs. Zimmermann quietly. "As for how long it will live, I really couldn't say."

Rose Rita looked at the tree, and then she looked at Mrs. Zimmermann. "You mean . . . you mean you think . . ."

"Like I said before, I don't know what I think. That is, I'm not sure. But something had to happen to return me to my present shape. If a witch is changed into something else—a tree, for instance—she isn't a witch any longer, and all her enchantments are broken. Come on, Rose Rita. Time's a-wasting. We'd better get back."

It was fully daylight when Rose Rita and Mrs. Zimmermann stepped out into the clearing behind Gert Bigger's store. They walked around to the front and found Aggie Sipes and her mother standing there. They were watching the two policemen, who, in turn, were staring at some things that lay piled on the front steps of the store. It was quite an odd collection. A funeral pall, a big wooden cross, some brown beeswax candles, a tarnished silver censer, a gilded incense boat, and an aspergillum—otherwise known as a holy water sprinkler. There was a big pile of books, too. Among them was the book that Rose Rita had found on Gert Bigger's bedside table.

As soon as Aggie caught sight of Rose Rita coming around the corner of the store, she gave a wild yell and ran toward her.

"Rose Rita, you're okay! Gee, I thought you were dead! Wow! Hooray! Whee!" Aggie hugged Rose Rita and jumped up and down. Mrs. Sipes came over too. There was a big smile on her face.

"Are you Mrs. Zimmermann?" she asked.

"I am," said Mrs. Zimmermann. The two women shook hands.

The two policemen walked over and joined the welcoming committee. They looked suspicious, as policemen often do. One of them had a note pad and a pencil in his hand.

"Okay," he said brusquely. "Are you the Mrs. Zigfield that got lost last night?"

"Yes. Zimmermann's the name, by the way. Please excuse my appearance, but I've been through quite a lot." Mrs. Zimmermann did indeed look as if she had spent the last two nights in the woods. Her dress was tattered and torn and had burrs all over it. Her shoes were wet and muddy, and her hair was a mess. There was pine pitch all over her hands and her face.

"Yeah," said Rose Rita. "We . . . we uh . . ." She realized with a sudden shock that she couldn't tell these people what had happened. Not and expect to be believed, that is.

"We, ah, had quite an experience, the two of us," Mrs. Zimmermann cut in quickly. "You see, I went walking out behind the Gunderson farm night before last, and I got lost in the woods. I know you'll think I was daffy for going out in the rain like that, but the fact is, I like walking in the rain. I love the sound of rain hitting the fabric of an umbrella—it's sort of a cozy sound, like rain on a tent roof. I hadn't intended to walk very far, but before I knew it, there I was, off the path and lost. Then, to make matters worse, the wind started blowing up a gale, and it blew my umbrella inside out, so I had to throw it away. Too bad too, because it was such a nice umbrella. But as I was saying, I got lost, and I've been wandering about for two days. Luckily I studied botany in college, and I know a little about what herbs and berries are safe to eat. So I'm a bit worn out, but otherwise okay, I think. Just by chance I ran into Rose Rita, and she guided me back to civilization. And from what she tells me, she's had quite a horrifying experience herself. It seems that the old lady who runs this store had her bound and gagged and locked in a closet. Then she gave her some drug and took her out into the woods and left her to starve. Fortunately Rose Rita knows a little wood-craft, and she was on her way back when she met me. Also," she added, reaching into her pocket, "we found this out in the woods, and when it got light, we were able to use it to help us find our way back."

It was Aggie's boy scout knife! The knife with the compass in the handle. Mrs. Zimmermann had found it where Aggie dropped it in Gert Bigger's back yard.

Rose Rita stared at Mrs. Zimmermann in pure admira-tion. She had told some good lies in the past, but never any quite as good as this one of Mrs. Zimmermann's. But then Rose Rita remembered Aggie. She knew the real story of how Mrs. Zimmermann had disappeared. And she knew about the knife, since she was the one who had dropped it. Would she spill the beans? Rose Rita glanced nervously at her and saw, to her surprise and irritation, that Aggie was trying hard to suppress a giggle. It was the first time Rose Rita had ever seen Aggie laugh.

But Aggie said nothing, and fortunately her mother did not notice the laughing fit that had come over her. The policeman with the note pad hadn't noticed either.

He had been busy jotting down every word Mrs. Zimmermann said. "Okay now," he said, looking up from his work. "Mrs. Zigfield, you got any idea what happened to the old lady that ran this store?"

Mrs. Zimmermann shook her head. "None whatsoever, officer. Can't you find her?"

"Nope. But we're gonna put out an all points bulletin for her arrest. Boy was she crazy! Did you see all this stuff?" He pointed toward the pile at the foot of the steps.

Mrs. Sipes looked at Mrs. Zimmermann with wide worried eyes. "Mrs. Zimmermann, what do you make of all this? Do you think Mrs. Bigger was a witch?"

Mrs. Zimmermann stared straight at her. "A *what?*"

"A witch. I mean, look at all these things. I can't imagine why else she would have . . ."

Mrs. Zimmermann put her tongue between her teeth and made a *tsk-tsk* sound. She shook her head slowly. "Mrs. Sipes," she said, in a shocked voice, "I don't know what you've been telling your daughter, but this is the twentieth century. There are no such things as witches."

CHAPTER THIRTEEN

When the Pottingers arrived at the Sipes farm later that morning, they found the Sipeses, their eight children, Mrs. Zimmermann, and Rose Rita, all huddled around a radio on the front porch of the farmhouse. They were listening to a radio report on what had come to be known as "the Petoskey witch case." The Pottingers were, of course, pretty tense to begin with, but when they found out that their daughter had, for a little while, been the prisoner of an elderly lunatic who imagined herself to be a witch—well, they really got the jitters. Mrs. Zimmermann did her best to calm them down. She pointed out that, after all, she and Rose Rita were safe, and the whole adventure—terrifying as it had been—was over. It seemed clear that if he could have found some way to do it, Mr. Pottinger would have blamed the whole affair on Mrs. Zimmermann's "screwballishness," but he didn't have time to do any blaming, what with all the fuss and flurry and tearful reunions going on around him. Mr. Sipes, who had come back from his business trip earlier that morning, took Mr. Pottinger out to show him the barn, and the Pottingers were invited to stay for lunch.

Around two that afternoon the Pottingers drove back to New Zebedee with Rose Rita. Rose Rita and Aggie had a tearful farewell at the car window, and they promised to write to each other a lot during the next year. The last thing that Aggie said as the Pottingers were about to drive away was, "I hope you don't get a flat tire. They're awful hard to fix." Mrs. Zimmermann stayed behind. She said, rather mysteriously, that she had some "business to attend to." Rose Rita figured that it had something to do with the magic ring, but she knew from past experience that Mrs. Zimmermann wouldn't tell her anything more until she was darned good and ready.

About a week after she got back to New Zebedee, Rose Rita received a purple-bordered letter in the mail. Inside was a piece of lavender-colored stationery, and on it this message was written:

My dear,

I'm back, and so is Lewis—for the time being. It seems that the pump that supplies the water to his camp broke down, and they're sending the kids home till they get it fixed. Sometime or other, Lewis will be going back for the rest of the camp session, but in the meantime, you are hereby invited to a coming-home-from-camp-for-now party for Lewis at my cottage on Lyon Lake next Saturday. Plan to stay overnight. If it's okay with your folks, I'll be around to get you in Bessie after lunch. It should be a lot of fun. Bring your swimming suit.

> *Yours,*
> *Florence Zimmermann*

PS: Don't bring any presents for Lewis. He's bringing home enough stuff from camp as it is.

Rose Rita had no trouble persuading her mother to let her spend the night at Mrs. Zimmermann's cottage. And so on Saturday off she went, valise in hand, to Lyon Lake. All the way out to the cottage Rose Rita tried to find out if Mrs. Zimmermann had discovered anything about the ring. But Mrs. Zimmermann said nothing. When they pulled into the driveway of the cottage, there was another car parked in front of them. Jonathan's car.

"Hi, Rose Rita! Gee, you look great!" There was Lewis. He was wearing his bathing suit.

"Hi, yourself," Rose Rita yelled, waving. "Where'd you get that sun tan? Out at the camp?"

Lewis grinned happily. He had been hoping she would notice. "Yeah. Hey, hurry up and get into your suit. Last one in is a wet hen!" Lewis reddened and covered his mouth with his hand. He had heard some of the story of Gert Bigger and the ring from Jonathan, and he knew what he had said.

Rose Rita glanced quickly at Mrs. Zimmermann, who was coughing rather loudly and trying to blow her nose at the same time.

As soon as Rose Rita had gotten her suit on, she ran down the long sloping lawn and dived into the water. Lewis was there ahead of her. He was swimming! Back and forth, up and down. It was only dog paddling, but for Lewis, that was something. For as long as Rose Rita had known him, Lewis had been scared of the water. Usually when he went in, he just stood around and splashed, or floated on an inner tube.

Rose Rita was overjoyed. She had always wanted for Lewis to know how to swim, so they could go swimming together. Of course, he was still scared of deep water, but he was getting more confident. Next year, he said, he'd get his Intermediate Swimmer's card for sure.

Later Rose Rita and Lewis were sitting on the lawn with towels wrapped around them. Nearby, on lawn chairs, were Jonathan and Mrs. Zimmermann. Jonathan was wearing his white linen suit, which he only wore on special occasions during the summer. The last special occasion had been V-J Day, so the suit was looking rather yellow, and it smelled of mothballs. Mrs. Zimmermann was wearing a new purple dress. She had thrown away the one she had been wearing on her vacation, because there were so many unpleasant memories associated with it. She looked rested and healthy. On a small table between her and Jonathan was a pitcher of lemonade and a plate heaped with chocolate chip cookies.

Lewis looked at Mrs. Zimmermann with awe. He was dying to ask her what it had felt like to be a chicken, but he couldn't think of any polite way of putting the question. Besides she was likely to be sensitive on the subject. So Lewis just ate his cookie and drank his lemonade and said nothing.

"All right, Florence," said Jonathan, puffing impatiently at his pipe. "We're all dying to know. What did you find out about the ring? Eh?"

Mrs. Zimmermann shrugged. "Almost nothing. I searched high and low in Oley's house, but all I found were these." She dug into a pocket of her dress and handed Jonathan three or four very rusty iron rings.

"What are these?" he said, turning them over. "Are they rejects from Oley's magic ring factory?"

Mrs. Zimmermann laughed. "No . . . at least, I don't think they are. I found them in a bowl in the back of the cupboard in Oley's kitchen. Do you really want to know what I think they are?"

"What?"

"Well, the Vikings used to wear leather breastplates with iron rings sewed to them. They called the breastplates byrnies, I think. Anyway, these rings look like some I saw once in a museum in Oslo. I think Oley must have dug these up, along with the arrowheads—and the ring."

"Now wait a minute, Florence. I know I've got a beard, but it's not long and white, and I've still got most of my marbles. Are you trying to tell us that the Vikings brought that ring over to America with them?"

"I'm not trying to tell you anything, Weird Beard. I'm just showing you what I found. You can think what you like. I'm just saying that these rings *look* like Viking artifacts. The Vikings roamed all over the world. They even went to Constantinople. And a lot of the treasure of the ancient world found its way there. There are a thousand other ways they might have found the ring, of course. I don't know. As I say, you can think what you darned please."

Mrs. Zimmermann and Jonathan got into a long pointless argument over whether or not the Vikings ever came to America. In the middle of all this, Lewis interrupted.

"Excuse me, Mrs. Zimmermann, but . . ."

Mrs. Zimmermann smiled at Lewis. "Yes, Lewis? What is it?"

"Well, I was just wondering . . . are you sure it really was King Solomon's ring?"

"No, I'm not sure," said Mrs. Zimmermann. "Let's just say that I think it's likely. After all, the ring behaved the way Solomon's ring was supposed to behave. So it probably was that very same ring. On the other hand, there are lots of stories about magic rings that are supposed to have really existed. Some of the stories are true, and some of them are false. It might have been one of the other rings, like the ring of the Nibelungs. Who knows? I am, however, fairly sure that it was magic."

"What did you do with the darned ring?" asked Jonathan.

"Hah! I've been waiting for you to ask that! All righty. If you must know, I melted it down in Oley's cookstove. One of the properties of gold is that it will melt at a fairly low temperature. And from all I know about magic, once a magic ring loses its original shape, it loses its powers too. Just to be on the safe side, however, I put the ring (or what was left of it) in a baby food jar along with some lead sinkers. Then I rented a rowboat and rowed out on Little Traverse Bay, and dropped the jar into the drink. Good riddance to bad rubbish, as my father used to say."

Lewis could not contain himself any longer. He had heard from Rose Rita the story of how Mrs. Zimmermann had failed to remake her magic umbrella, and he felt bad about it. He wanted Mrs. Zimmermann to be the greatest magician in the world. "Mrs. Zimmermann!" he burst out. "How come you wrecked the ring? You could've used it, couldn't you? I mean, it wasn't really evil, was it? You could've done something really good with it, I'll bet!"

Mrs. Zimmermann gave Lewis a sour look. "You know who you sound like, Lewis? You sound like those people who keep telling us that the atomic bomb is a really wonderful thing, that it isn't really evil, though it has been put to evil purposes." Mrs. Zimmermann heaved a deep sigh. "I suppose," she said slowly, "I *suppose* that Solomon's ring—assuming that that's what it really was—could have been put to some good use. I thought about that before I melted the thing down. But I said to myself, 'Do you really think you're such an angelic creature that you could resist the urge to do nasty things with that ring?' Then I asked myself, 'Do you want to sit on the blamed thing for the rest of your life, always worrying and fidgeting for fear someone like Gert Bigger might grab it away from you?' The answer to both those questions was no, and that is why I decided to get rid of the ring. As you may know, Lewis, I don't have much magic power anymore. And you know what? It's a relief! I'm going to spend the rest of my days snapping matches out of the air and trying to beat Weird Beard over here at poker. Not," she added, with a sly glance at Jonathan, "that either of those things takes a great deal of talent to do."

Jonathan stuck out his tongue at Mrs. Zimmermann, and then both of them laughed. It was a happy relaxed sound, and Lewis and Rose Rita joined in.

There was more swimming, and more eating. After the sun went down, Jonathan built a bonfire down on the beach, and they all roasted marshmallows and sang songs. Lewis handed around presents. They were all things he had made at scout camp. He gave Jonathan a copper ashtray, and he gave Mrs. Zimmermann a necklace of purply-white seashells. To Rose Rita he gave a leather belt and a neckerchief slide that he had whittled. It was painted green with yellow spots, and the lump on the front was supposed to look like a toad. Well, at any rate, it had eyes.

Much later that evening, after Lewis and Jonathan had gone home, Rose Rita and Mrs. Zimmermann were sitting by the embers of the bonfire. Out across the darkened lake they could see the lights of other cottages. From somewhere came the sleepy drone of a motorboat.

"Mrs. Zimmermann?" said Rose Rita.

"Yes, my dear? What is it?"

"There's a couple of things I have to ask you. First of all, how come that ring didn't put the old whammy on you the way it did on me when I picked it up? When I gave it to you, you just looked at it as if you couldn't have cared less, and then you stuck it in your pocket. How come?"

Mrs. Zimmermann sighed. Rose Rita heard her snap

her fingers, and she saw the brief tiny flare of a match, and she smelled cigar smoke. "Why wasn't I affected?" said Mrs. Zimmermann, as she puffed. "You know, that's a good question. I guess it's because I'm really happy the way I am. You see, I think a ring like that can only exercise power over someone who isn't satisfied with himself. Or herself."

Rose Rita blushed. She still felt ashamed of what she had tried to do with the ring. "Did . . . did you ever tell Uncle Jonathan what . . . what I was gonna do when you stopped me?"

"No," said Mrs. Zimmermann softly. "I did not. As far as he knows, the ring dragged you off to some mysterious meeting with the devil. Remember, you never actually said what you wanted to do, though it wasn't hard for me to guess. And by the way, don't feel so bad. Lots of people would have wished for worse things than you wished for. Far worse things."

Rose Rita was silent for a while. Finally she said, "Mrs. Zimmermann, do you think I'll have a lousy time in school this fall? And what about when I'm a grownup? Will things be different then?"

"My dear," said Mrs. Zimmermann slowly and deliberately, "I may be a witch, but I'm not a prophet. Seeing into the future was never my line, even when I had my magic umbrella. But I will tell you this: You have a lot of wonderful qualities. When you tried to drive Bessie, for example. Lots of girls your age would've been too chicken even to try. That took guts. It also took guts to break into Mrs. Bigger's store in the hope that you might be able to rescue me. And another thing: The women who are remembered in history, women like Joan of Arc and Molly Pitcher, are not remembered because they spent all their time powdering their noses. As for the rest, you'll just have to wait and see how your life turns out. That's all I can say."

Rose Rita said nothing. She poked in the ashes with a stick while Mrs. Zimmermann smoked. After a while, the two of them got up, kicked some sand over the fire, and went to bed.

About the Author

Many of the events in John Bellairs's books are drawn from things that happened or that he wished *would* happen when he was growing up in Marshall, Michigan.

The Letter, the Witch, and the Ring is the third and final book in the *House with a Clock in Its Walls* trilogy. The two earlier books, *The House with a Clock in Its Walls* and *The Figure in the Shadows*, were both chosen by *The New York Times* as Outstanding Books of the Year.

John Bellairs is the author of several adult books, including *The Face in the Frost*. He lives in Haverhill, Massachusetts, with his wife Priscilla and their son, Frank.

About the Artist

Richard Egielski was born in New York City, where he still makes his home. He studied at Pratt Institute and Parsons School of Design, and is interested in both magazine and book illustration.

The Letter, the Witch, and the Ring is his first book for The Dial Press.